IAN HAMILTON MYSTERIES

EDINBURGH
MIDNIGHT

ALSO BY CAROLE LAWRENCE

Ian Hamilton Mysteries

Edinburgh Twilight

Edinburgh Dusk

IAN HAMILTON MYSTERIES

EDINBURGH MIDNIGHT

· CAROLE LAWRENCE ·

THOMAS & MERCER

Text copyright © 2020 by Carole Bugge

Published by Thomas & Mercer, Seattle

www.apub.com

Amazon, the Amazon logo, and Thomas & Mercer are trademarks of Amazon.com, Inc., or its affiliates.

ISBN-13: 9781542008655
ISBN-10: 1542008654

Cover design by Kirk DouPonce, Dog Eared Design

Printed in the United States of America

For Kegan Isaack,
most excellent and awesome nephew
and truly kind soul

Coming back to Edinburgh is to
me like coming home.

—Charles Dickens

CHAPTER ONE

EDINBURGH, 1880

December settled over Edinburgh in the winter of 1880 with the persistence of an unwelcome houseguest. The sky turned a pervasive, troubled gray, sporadically spitting snow over the city's jumble of stone buildings, stolid and stoic as her inhabitants, who hardly knew what to expect from one day to the next. Occasionally a proper storm blew in from the west, blanketing the city in a layer of cottony snow, soft as sugar. But even that rarely lasted—no sooner would a hastily erected snowman spring up in St. Andrew Square than the mercury would rise overnight. The next day would find him a sad, dripping remnant with lopsided coal eyes, a tartan scarf dangling from his rapidly melting form.

Even the festivities of the Christmas season provided little relief from the bleak weather, the holiday having been effectively banned in Scotland in 1640 as a "popish festival." The citizens of Edinburgh continued to decorate their homes with evergreens, holly, and candles in the windows, but it was not an official holiday, and did not feature the gift giving, caroling, and feasting enjoyed by the English. The Scots were forced to wait for Hogmanay, or New Year, which they often started celebrating a week beforehand to make up for the lack of a proper Christmas.

And so on a particularly dreary December morning Detective Inspector Ian Hamilton slogged his way through the remnants of a half-hearted snowfall already melting underfoot, making the cobblestones slick and treacherous, dripping from eaves in slow, steady droplets, like the inexorable ticking of a clock, as the old year wound down to its inevitable end.

His destination was the High Street police station, along a route he had trudged more times than he could count in the past seven years. Passing an omnibus full of sleepy office workers on George IV Bridge, he turned right onto the High Street, past St. Giles and the Mercat Cross, the royal unicorn looking cold perched high atop the pedestal. The traditional site of proclamations and official announcements, the cross was also the historical venue for hangings, burnings, and other gruesome forms of public punishment.

The sky was threatening more punishment of its own as Ian reached police chambers at 192 High Street. Mounting the solid stone steps, he swung open the heavy wooden door and entered the building that had become as familiar as his comfortable flat on Victoria Terrace. The desk sergeant gave him a drowsy nod—the weather seemed to have put a damper on everyone's mood.

The door to Detective Chief Inspector Crawford's office was closed, which meant he was not to be disturbed. But no sooner had Ian settled at his desk with a cup of tea than the door opened, and his boss emerged. DCI Crawford did not look sleepy—he looked troubled. His thinning ginger hair sprouted in unruly wisps, and his blue eyes were narrowed.

"Ah, there you are, Hamilton," he said, plucking at his generous thicket of muttonchops. "Can you spare a minute?"

"Certainly, sir."

"Bring your tea," said Crawford, heading back toward his office. The chief inspector was a large, ungainly man, and as he lumbered away, Ian was reminded of a red-haired walrus.

"Close the door behind you, and have a seat," the chief said, lowering his bulk into his desk chair, which creaked in protest. "You are aware that our most recent attempts to apprehend well-known criminals in the act were dismal failures."

"There was the Happy Land raid last week, and before that the Leith Dock gang—"

"And we have the headlines to go with it," Crawford growled, tossing a stack of newspapers at him.

Ian glanced at the already familiar prose.

LEITH GANG STRIKES AGAIN!

Midnight Raid Gone Wrong

Edinburgh City Police Fail Again—Is Anyone Safe?

Crawford sighed heavily. "The public is losing faith in us, Hamilton."

"Yes, sir."

"And the criminals are growing bolder. The question is," Crawford said, with a wave of his fleshy hand, "*why* they were such a disaster."

"I've been wondering that myself, sir."

The chief tugged at his ginger muttonchops. "It seems to me our usual sources have suddenly become unreliable."

"But why now?"

"Precisely my question. Have any of your sources changed recently?"

"No."

"Still working with that little street urchin?"

"I am, and he has proven quite reliable."

"No doubt you reward him well enough," Crawford said, frowning.

3

"I do indeed."

"Hmph," Crawford grunted. Rummaging through his desk drawer, he pulled out a piece of paper. "Here's a list of our known informants. I'd like you to check out each one of them for reliability."

"That's quite an assignment, sir."

"Which is why I picked you, Hamilton. You should be flattered."

"'He that loves to be flattered is worthy o' the flatterer,'" Ian replied. "Sorry, sir—just slipped out," he added, seeing Crawford's face darken. The chief hated it when he quoted Shakespeare.

"See here, I don't expect you to do it overnight. Take what time you need."

"Can I have Dickerson?"

"Can you trust his discretion?"

"Absolutely."

"Very well—but keep it to yourselves, at least for now."

"Will do, sir," Ian said, rising from his chair. "How is your wife doing?"

"Better," Crawford said, beaming. "Her appetite is much improved. That Dr. Bell really is quite the genius—sees things other people don't. Please thank your brother for intervening on my behalf."

"I will, sir," Ian said, and left the office.

As he headed toward his desk, he caught the eye of John Turnbull, a sallow, narrow-shouldered constable who attempted to hide his premature baldness with an unconvincing, ill-fitting toupee. He had tried to sabotage Ian's last case because he thought Ian had humiliated him in public. The expression on Turnbull's pockmarked face was pure contempt, which his sickly smile did nothing to conceal. Ian had never liked the constable, and had always suspected the feeling was mutual, but now there was no doubt the two were enemies. As he returned to his desk, he wondered if perhaps he should begin his investigation with Turnbull.

"Morning, sir."

He turned to see the smiling face of Sergeant William Dickerson. Like DCI Crawford, Dickerson was fair of skin with ginger hair, but nearly a foot shorter, like a miniature version of the chief, minus the whiskers. As usual, he carried a bag from Daily Bread, the bakery on Cockburn Street.

"Morning, Sergeant," said Ian. "What have you got today?"

"Selkirk bannock," Dickerson replied in his rolling Lancashire accent. "Fresh outta oven, couldn't resist." A buttery raisin loaf, Selkirk bannock was originally made of barley meal, but was now commonly made with risen bread flour. It was Dickerson's favorite, probably accounting for half a stone or so of the excess weight around his middle. "Would ye like some, sir?"

"No, thank you. Do you have a minute?"

"Certainly, sir," Dickerson said, wiping his mouth.

"This way," Ian said, heading toward the front entrance.

"Shall I get my coat?"

"No. We're just going out to the hall."

Dickerson cocked his head to the side, like a confused spaniel. "Sir?"

"Come along."

The hall was empty, but just to be sure, Ian climbed half a flight up to the next landing. Dickerson trudged after him, brushing crumbs from his uniform.

"Wha' is it, sir?" he said when they reached the landing.

Ian explained what Crawford had said to him, as the sergeant listened closely, biting his lip. "Any questions?" Ian said when he was finished.

"Jus' one, sir."

"Yes?"

"How on earth are we t'know who's lyin', sir?"

"'Ay, there's the rub.'"

"Oh, that reminds me, sir—I've sommit I need t'mention."

"Don't tell me you're doing another Shakespeare play with the Greyfriars Dramatic Society."

"Not exactly."

"What, then?"

"It's, uh, Dickens this time."

"Dickens?"

"Yes, sir. The society is doin' *A Christmas Carol* and I'm t'play the Ghost of Christmas Present."

"Good on you, Sergeant."

Dickerson smiled nervously and fingered the shiny brass buttons on his uniform. "D'ye think—I mean, will DCI Crawford . . . will he—"

"Will he approve? I should think it depends on what frame of mind he's in when you tell him."

"Good point, sir," Dickerson said, an anxious expression on his ruddy face. The chief's moods were as unpredictable as the squalls rolling in from the Firth of Forth.

"Tell you what," Ian said. "I can tell him if you like—do what I can to make him cheery, and then drop it casually."

"Oh, *would* ye, sir?" the sergeant said, his eyes moist.

"It's the least I can do," Ian said, "considering that you started me on my own thespian career."

"An' you were bloody good as Old Hamlet's ghost, sir! D'ye wan' a part in this production? Because I can ask the director—"

"No, no," Ian replied hastily. "I'm quite happy to keep my theatrical exploits in the past."

"Whatever y'say, sir—but if ye change yer mind—"

"Much appreciated, but it's not likely."

There was the sound of a door opening on the landing below them. Ian peered down the stairs to see Constable Turnbull exit the police chambers, a searching look on his rutted face, lips compressed in determination. As the constable walked down the single flight to the main entrance, Ian wondered if Turnbull had seen him and Dickerson leave.

"Yon Turnbull has a lean and hungry look," he murmured.

"Beg pardon, sir?"

"We should get back inside."

"Aye, sir. Were that Constable Turnbull leavin' jes now?"

"It was."

"You don' like 'im much, do ye, sir?"

"I don't trust him," Ian remarked.

But the question now facing him was whom, if anyone, he could trust.

CHAPTER TWO

The day passed in a flurry of routine and paperwork, as was often the case on a Monday. The city's unluckier miscreants were in custody after being apprehended over the weekend. With the excesses of Saturday night behind them, the denizens of Scotland's capital settled down to the dull if familiar workday ritual, and before Ian knew it, the clock chimed five, signaling the end of his shift. He had spent the day pondering what Crawford had told him. The sergeant had thrown him meaningful glances all afternoon—apparently Dickerson's idea of discretion didn't include facial expressions. Ian resolved to speak to him about it, but before he could say anything, Dickerson slipped away to attend rehearsal.

Ian was already regretting his agreement to join his Aunt Lillian at a séance later that evening—he disapproved of her passion for the occult, but somehow had let her persuade him to join her at Madame Veselka's weekly meetings. Hastily donning his cape, he swept out the door before DCI Crawford could block his escape with another impossible request.

The sun had already long ago retired for the night, the air crisp and cold as he headed for his aunt's flat. His brother, Donald, had rolled his eyes at breakfast when he heard of Ian's plans for the evening, and in truth Ian couldn't blame him.

"So you're going to indulge Lillian's superstitions?" he had said, smiling in his superior, ironic way as he pierced another sausage with his fork. Donald was never a sylph, but his recent decision to forsake the bottle had only increased his already prodigious appetite. "What good could possibly come from that?"

To his dismay, Ian had no good answer. He had made the promise last week, in the heat of the moment, after Lillian delivered a passionate defense of spiritualism, a glass or two of his favorite single malt having loosened his resolve. He regretted it almost immediately, but the sight of her eager face had haunted him all week, and he had neither the heartlessness nor the courage to cancel on her.

And Donald had certainly enjoyed lording his foolishness over him. "Who knows?" he had proclaimed with mock sincerity, chewing on sausage as he poured more coffee. "Maybe you'll have a visitation of your own."

Now, crossing George IV Bridge as a cold wind picked up, swirling the remains of the last snowfall, he trudged onward as a tram passed by full of weary-looking passengers. He wondered if some were the same who had passed him that morning. Even the pair of sturdy bay geldings pulling the vehicle looked tired, though he could tell from the length of their stride that they were stable bound. Horses always knew the direction of their barn, and no matter how weary, quickened their pace when they were headed home. Ian wished he were in front of his own fire, toasting his feet in front of the flames.

Any regrets vanished when he saw his aunt's delighted expression as she answered the door.

"Right on time, you are," she said. "Come in out of the cold, won't ye?" Aunt Lillian had lived in Edinburgh for years, but when she got excited, her Glaswegian roots showed in her accent. "I thought we'd have a wee bite before we go," she said, leading him into her cozy parlor, where a fire blazed merrily in the grate. "Nothing fancy, mind you—just a bit of cock-a-leekie soup and a nice hunk of cheddar."

"Can I help?" he asked as she fussed about setting the small round oak table she used for informal suppers.

"Why don't you give the fire a poke? Won't be a minute," she said, bustling into the kitchen. "And you can open that bottle of Montrachet, if ye'd be so kind."

Aunt Lillian was tall and straight and thin, so much like her younger sister that sometimes when he saw her from the corner of his eye, Ian imagined for a moment his mother was still alive. It was an empty fantasy—it was long these seven years since his parents had been laid to rest in Greyfriars graveyard. Since their untimely death, he had grown even closer to his aunt. Though very different temperamentally, she shared her sister's build and facial structure, as well as mannerisms and vocal inflections. Being with her fed his hunger for his dead mother.

He had also come to love and respect his aunt for her own sake. Fiercer and more independent than her sister, Lillian was forceful and opinionated, and had become a strong guiding presence in Ian's life. So when she suggested that he accompany her to one of her precious séances, he had found it impossible to deny her.

"There we are," she said, placing two steaming bowls of soup on the table. "If you wouldn't mind fetching the bread and cheese we'll get started."

"Of course," Ian said as the aroma of leeks and barley filled the room, his stomach contracting with hunger. On the kitchen counter was a wooden tray containing a round loaf of brown bread, which Lillian preferred over the more expensive white bread, a large wedge of yellow cheese, and a slab of fresh butter. Ian recognized the tray as a present from his mother—he had helped her pick it out years ago. It was painted with a Highland scene of purple heather in full bloom and reminded him of his Inverness childhood.

"This meal was one of Alfie's favorites," Lillian said as they pulled their chairs up to the table in front of the fire, the crackling of the wood blending with the wind whistling through the eaves. "He had simple tastes—one of the many things I loved about him."

"The breeze is picking up," Ian said, avoiding the topic of her dead husband. Lillian believed that Madame Veselka communicated with dear Alfie, who had been dead for some years now. Ian had been very fond of Uncle Alfred, but did not believe in ghosts, the afterlife, or indeed anything supernatural. But he had resolved to keep his opinions to himself tonight and sit quietly while his aunt enjoyed herself.

"Madame Veselka has to go to Paris later this week, which is why she's holding her meeting on a Monday instead of Friday," Lillian remarked as Ian helped himself to a slice of cheese, sharp and tangy and creamy. "That's what my friend Elizabeth Staley tells me, at any rate."

"Elizabeth Staley?"

"You'll meet her tonight. She's a retired schoolteacher. We've become quite friendly over the past months."

"This is a wonderful cheddar," he said. "Where did you get it?"

"I know how you feel about Madame Veselka," she said with a knowing smile. "All I ask is that you keep an open mind."

"Consider your request granted. Now, how about some more of that Montrachet?" he said, pouring some into her glass as the wind heaved and sucked at the windowpanes. Ian shivered as the dry branches of the old yew tree outside rapped against the glass, as if beckoning them out into the night.

CHAPTER THREE

Madame Veselka's flat occupied the ground floor of a crumbling tenement on Blackfriars Street. They were greeted by a fresh-faced blond girl of about twenty who smiled when she saw Lillian.

"Good to see you again, madame," she said in a pronounced Prussian accent, curtsying. "I am Gretchen," she told Ian. "Please to come in. The others are in the parlor."

They were ushered into a plush, old-fashioned sitting room. Nearly every surface was draped in fabric, from the heavy burgundy drapes to the tasseled cloth covering the wide oval table in the center of the room. A fire burned in the grate, and the air was thick with sage incense. No gaslights were lit—other than the fire, a dozen candles provided the only source of illumination. A snowy Persian cat sat curled in one of the overstuffed armchairs, its blue eyes thin slits in a forest of white fur.

Besides Lillian's friend, retired schoolteacher Elizabeth Staley, the attendees included a tiny, pinch-faced woman dressed all in black, clutching an enormous cloth handbag; an army major; and his son, a sullen young man with thick blond hair in need of a trim. After being served sherry by Gretchen, they conversed in hushed voices, casting nervous glances in the direction of a beaded curtain at the far end of the room.

After learning that the major was here to speak with his dead wife, and that the tiny woman, who bore the very Welsh name of Bronwyn Davies, was in search of communication with a dead sister, Ian was becoming restless.

"When is she likely to appear?" he whispered to Lillian as he accepted a second glass of sherry from the comely Gretchen.

"She likes to make an entrance," his aunt replied. "It shouldn't be long now."

Her prediction was soon rewarded. The curtain at the other end of the room swayed, the beads clacking softly against each other as they parted to reveal a large woman elaborately dressed in layers of contrasting prints and colors. Her plump wrists were festooned with bracelets, each finger sporting a different ring. The paisley scarf wrapped around her head did not fully contain the mass of unruly black curls beneath it. Her skirts swayed and swished, and the odor of gardenias filled the room.

"Welcome to tonight's séance," she said in an accent that was clearly meant to evoke French origins, but Ian detected another flavor lurking within it. He wasn't certain, but he thought she was unsuccessfully concealing Romany roots. He glanced at Lillian, but his aunt appeared enraptured by the medium's presence.

"So good to see so many familiar faces," Madame Veselka said, casting her eyes around the room until her gaze fixed on Ian. "What brings you here tonight, young man?"

"I came with my aunt," Ian replied, a little curtly.

"You are most welcome," she replied graciously, which made him regret his tone of voice.

"Please, let us begin," she said, as Gretchen appeared with an empty tray to collect the sherry glasses. The guests followed the medium's lead to sit around the oval table. Ian chose a seat next to Lillian, across from the retired major, who sat, back straight as a rod, his bushy white mustache perfectly symmetrical. "Let us all join hands," said the madame, and Ian felt his aunt's thin, cool fingers close over his.

The yellow candlelight cast a warm glow on the deep-plum wallpaper. Ian smelled candle wax mixed with Madame Veselka's heavy gardenia perfume. How suitable she should choose the aroma of a flower associated with death, he thought, wondering if it was purposeful. He looked at the others, their shining faces expectant as children's. As the medium let her head fall back, speaking in a low, thrilling voice, his aunt's grip on his hand tightened.

"'Tis the dark of night, when phantoms stretch their ghostly limbs through the mists of time, their hoary heads draped in the veil of death. Come, O spirits! Come, departed ones! Give us your wisdom, show us your long-forgotten faces! Visit our world once more, you creatures of the shadows!"

"She's damned poetic, I'll give her that," Ian whispered to Lillian. His remark was rewarded with a swift poke in the ribs. "Ow!" he muttered. "That hurt."

"Shh!" Lillian hissed. "Unless ye want another."

Ian fell silent. His aunt's elbow was sharp, and he believed her threat.

Madame Veselka leaned forward in her chair. "Is there one here you wish to speak to?"

Silence. A yawn fought its way up Ian's throat, and as he attempted to stifle it, the medium spoke again—in an entirely different voice, throaty and rich.

"Bear, is that you?"

Icicles speared Ian's heart. Bear was his mother's nickname for him. As a child, he owned a dog who once cornered a beaver. Having recently immersed himself in a fairy tale involving bears, he mistook the animal for a bear, which had been extinct in Scotland for centuries. After that incident, his mother dubbed him Bear.

He felt his aunt's hand tighten around his own. And for a brief moment, the heaviness surrounding his heart evaporated like smoke. A happy vision of the past swam before his eyes. The house in Queens Gate still stood, his mother in the kitchen, her head wreathed in steam from the kettle, his father's hoe clanking as he tinkered in their small back garden. Ian's eyes swelled and burned, his throat constricted, and he longed to call out to his mother.

But that was followed by a cold, hard anger as reality pressed its way through his joyful vision. This was nothing but a ruse. The medium had somehow wrangled information from his aunt, and was using it in an attempt to trick him. He stood up abruptly, tipping his chair over. The tiny woman to his left gave a little yelp as it clattered to the floor, and everyone else looked up at him with alarmed expressions. The exception was Madame, who remained seated, her eyes closed.

"This is absurd," he declared. "I'm leaving."

As he strode from the room, the medium's voice floated after him, unperturbed and calm. "To some, much is given. To others, much is taken away. Of both, much is expected."

He snorted in disgust and stalked out, seizing his coat and hat from the front hall rack. The door banged with a hollow thud behind him. As he stood on the street in the cold winter wind, his fury gave way to regret. Once again, his rage and impatience had gotten the better of him; he had embarrassed his aunt and everyone else in the room. There was no excuse for it—his behavior was churlish and selfish, and he owed them all an apology. He glanced at the building behind him. There was no point in going back now—he would wait until another time, he reasoned, hoping it was common sense and not cowardice prevailing. A white plume of smoke curled up from the chimney, quickly dissipating in the chill air.

Pulling his hat low over his face, he hunched into the wind and headed toward Victoria Terrace. Donald was on call at the infirmary, so

Ian had the flat to himself, with only his black-and-white cat, Bacchus, for company.

Flinging himself into a chair by the fire, he attempted to read, but the volume of Robert Louis Stevenson stories that had so recently consumed him failed to draw his attention. Putting the book aside, he roamed the flat restlessly, Bacchus following him, meowing plaintively. Thinking the cat had probably not been fed, Ian found some leftover haddock in the icebox, and scooped a generous portion into the cat's dish. Bacchus sniffed at it, flicked his tail, then picked at it delicately.

"You've bamboozled me into a second supper, have you?" Ian said.

The cat gazed up at him with innocent round eyes, blinking slowly.

"Thought so. Still, I don't suppose it'll hurt you."

The doorbell rang. Glancing at the kitchen clock, Ian saw it was nearly ten. He went to the front door and peered through the peephole to see Aunt Lillian standing on the stoop, her thick shawl wrapped around her thin shoulders. A stab of guilt pierced his heart as he flung open the door.

"Where's Donald?" she said, stamping her feet to shake off the snow clinging to her boots.

"At the infirmary," Ian said, taking her wrap.

"At this hour?"

"Doctors must learn to keep all hours," he said, hanging the coat on the bentwood rack in the foyer. "Tea?"

"I thought you'd never ask."

She followed him into the parlor, settling in front of the fire while he busied himself in the kitchen. Bacchus followed, curling around his legs.

"Get on with you," Ian said. "You'll get no more food from me."

The cat ignored him, almost tripping him as he poured the boiling water into the pot.

"Now then," Lillian said as he laid the tea tray on the sideboard, "would you like to explain what on earth got into you?"

Ian frowned. "If you've come for an apology—"

"Why would I expect that from someone as bloody-minded as you?"

Ian picked up the poker and gave the logs in the fireplace a shove. "I was about to say I owe you one."

"Well," she said. "Let's have it, then."

"I'm sorry."

"That's it?"

"What else do you want me to say?"

"An explanation would be nice."

Ian leaned against the mantel, arms crossed. "You told her about my nickname, didn't you?"

"I don't know what you mean."

"She could not possibly have known what my mother called me unless someone told her."

"I told her nothing."

"You wouldn't lie to me."

"Is that a question?"

"No," he said, pouring her tea. "It's a statement of fact. You wouldn't lie to me, so clearly she got the information some other way."

"How, Ian? How on earth would she ferret out something like that?"

"I don't know, but I mean to find out."

"You're being childish. Why can't you accept there are things in heaven and earth—"

"Not dreamt of in my philosophy?"

"Yes. Exactly."

"Ghosts don't walk the earth, Auntie. Shakespeare may have been a great writer, but he lived in a time of superstition and ignorance."

"You say I'm no liar, yet you'll not believe me when I say I've spoken to my dear departed Alfred?"

"There's a difference between lying and self-delusion."

Lillian shook her head sadly. "You're a hard one, Ian."

"I believe in scientific evidence, Auntie, not the rantings of some third-rate trickster."

"Those facts you hold so dear won't keep you warm on cold Scottish nights."

He had no reply. He stared into the fire, the thirsty flames wrapping themselves around the logs, greedily consuming the wood even as they flickered dimly and died.

CHAPTER FOUR

The next morning Donald was already at breakfast when Ian shuffled in.

"You look terri—" Donald began, but a look from Ian silenced him. "Have some kippers," he said, pointing to a covered dish on the table.

"No, thank you."

"Eggs, then."

Ian sank into a chair, rubbing his forehead. "Is there coffee?"

"Help yourself," Donald said, waving a plump hand toward the coffee service on the sideboard.

"Thank you," Ian said, pouring himself a cup from the matching pitcher. Made of fine bone china, the entire set was a gift from Lillian, with a pattern of tiny bluebells, a reminder of spring in the Highlands.

"I take it things did not go well last night," Donald remarked.

"They did not." Ian considered whether to tell his brother what transpired, but thought better of it. He had not yet sorted it out in his own mind, still troubled and confused by both Madame Veselka's behavior and his own.

"Oh, by the way, that little street urchin stopped by for you," Donald said, slicing off the top of his soft-boiled egg and placing it on his plate.

"His name is Derek," Ian said, spooning sugar into his cup.

"He claims to have information for you."

"Did he say what it related to?"

"He did suggest it might be worth something to you."

"He's usually right."

Donald took a bite of egg, delicately wiping his mouth with his napkin. "Forgive me, but your relationship strikes me as peculiarly mercantile. If you don't mind my asking, what exactly—"

"I find him helpful," Ian said, reaching for the cream. Bacchus sat at his feet, tail swishing, eyes on the cream pitcher. Ian knew Donald fed the cat from the table when he wasn't around but didn't think it worth confronting him; his brother would simply lie.

"Still, he does seem to have a price tag attached," Donald said, scooping out another steaming mouthful of egg. A tiny, perfectly round drop of yolk fell on his lapel; frowning, he swiped at it with his napkin. Donald was not a tidy eater—when he came home in the evening, Ian could usually tell what he had dined on earlier.

"If you slept on the street every night, you might see things differently," Ian remarked.

"Perhaps," Donald said, batting away the black-and-white paw creeping over the lip of the table. Irritated, the cat skulked off, tail flicking impatiently. "But I don't trust him."

"Neither do I. Given half a chance, no doubt he'd rob me blind," Ian replied, biting into a piece of toast smeared with currant jam.

"Then why do you continue to—"

"Because I *need* him. I trade in information, and not every source is eligible for sainthood." Ian put down his toast and regarded his brother. "You must have come across some scoundrels in your travels."

Donald laughed. "How very diplomatic of you. You mean my years of debauched wandering?"

"Whatever you care to call it."

His brother leaned back in his chair and brushed the crumbs from his lap. "I not only knew them, for a while I was one of them—which is why I have a keen eye for the type."

"He's just a boy. And an orphan."

"Aren't we all?" Donald murmured, almost to himself.

"How are you managing to pay for medical school, by the way?"

"Believe it or not, I managed to accrue some savings in my years of wandering. Lillian is helping out a little. And next term I hope to get a post as teaching assistant. Which reminds me, I should like to pay for my share of the rent, starting this month."

"Absolutely not."

"But—"

"When you're a successful surgeon, you can pay all the rent, if you like. But for now it's out of the question."

Donald rose from the table and folded his napkin neatly before tucking it into the monogrammed silver napkin ring, another gift from Lillian. "You're a stubborn man, O Brother Mine, but I will defer to your will just this once. And now, I must attend rounds. Mustn't be late, or HRG will not be pleased."

"HRG?"

"His Royal Genius. It's what I call Dr. Bell—behind his back, of course."

"Mind you don't get caught. He doesn't strike me as someone with a well-developed sense of humor."

"Of course, I do think the man is extraordinary," Donald said, lumbering out to the kitchen with his plate. Ian thought he had gained a stone or so since giving up drink, but would never say anything to discourage his brother from his resolution.

"What are you up to today?" Donald said, returning, wiping his hands on a hand towel. Bacchus trailed after him, scanning the ground for discarded tidbits. "Mrs. McGinty's pig on the loose again? Or are you leaving the barnyard patrol to Sergeant Dickers?"

"You mean Dickerson?" His brother knew the sergeant's name perfectly well, but couldn't resist goading Ian whenever possible. The habit was a carryover from their childhood, and Ian was used to it, though he wondered why Donald seemed compelled to needle him. "That reminds me—DCI Crawford said to thank you again for setting up the consultation with Dr. Bell."

"My pleasure. I trust his wife is feeling better?"

"Much better, and he is indebted to you."

"Nonsense. Bell's the one who diagnosed intermittent inflammation of the bowel. And his treatment is positively ingenious. Instead of avoiding certain foods, he encouraged her to eat smaller meals at regular intervals. That and the occasional dose of laudanum seems to be effective in a majority of patients." Donald sighed. "What a keen intellect."

"To what do we owe such uncharacteristic modesty?"

"If there is one thing I cannot abide, it is predictability," Donald said, taking a final sip of coffee. "Life is dull enough as it is."

There was a knock at the door.

"Why, hello, Doyle," Donald said, opening it. "What brings you here at this ungodly hour?"

"I was just passing by." Arthur Conan Doyle stood on their doorstep, dressed in a handsome green tweed walking suit, belted at the waist.

Ian was gladdened at the unexpected appearance of his friend—the mere sound of Doyle's voice lifted his mood. He had no doubt the young medical student had this effect on many people, with his good humor and kind blue eyes.

"You'd better come in," said Donald. "It's beastly out there."

Doyle complied after stamping the snow from his shoes on the mat.

"You look quite the country squire," Donald remarked. "All you need is a bird dog and a brace of pheasants over your shoulder."

Doyle laughed in his open, sunny way. "I would sooner be out hunting than going to classes. I'm not a natural scholar like you."

"The only thing that comes naturally to Donald is eating," Ian said, coming through from the parlor, coffee in hand.

"I would sooner be a bit pudgy than a wraith like you," Donald retorted. "You see how he torments me?" he asked Doyle, who smiled.

"I know you well enough to imagine you give as good as you get."

"And so he does," Ian agreed. "It's good to see you."

"And you, my dear fellow," his friend said, giving his hand a hearty shake. "I expected you to be off chasing criminals." He turned to Donald. "And I thought you might be headed to the infirmary for morning rounds."

"And so I am," Donald replied, wrapping a blue-and-green scarf around his neck. A gift from Aunt Lillian, the scarf represented the Hamilton hunting tartan, though Lillian herself was a member of the Grey clan.

"I'm on my way out as well," said Ian.

"Splendid," said Doyle. "Shall we walk together, at least as far as police chambers?"

"By all means," Donald replied, though Ian thought he looked disappointed. Doyle was so agreeable that no doubt each brother would have preferred to monopolize his attention. "Come along, then," Donald said as Ian reached for his cloak.

"Mustn't keep HRG waiting, eh?" Ian said.

Doyle burst into his characteristic laugh, a sort of brisk bark; it reminded Ian of a well-fed seal. "Ha! I see your brother has shared his little nickname for Dr. Bell."

"Not to be revealed upon pain of death," Donald said, throwing open the door. "Come along, or we really shall be late."

"By the way, I have something to show you when you have time," Doyle told Ian as the three men stepped into the icy December air, leaving Bacchus alone in the empty flat, with only the steady ticking of the grandfather clock in the hall to keep him company.

CHAPTER FIVE

When Ian arrived at police chambers, he was startled to see Aunt Lillian pacing in front of his desk. She looked agitated. At first he thought she had come to continue their conversation from the night before, but one look at her face told him otherwise.

"What is it?" he said. "What's wrong?"

"You remember my friend Elizabeth Staley? From the séance?" she added, seeing his blank look.

"Of course—the schoolteacher. What's happened?"

"We were to breakfast together this morning, as we often do after a session with Madame, but when I turned up, she was—" Lillian turned away, her jaw working, like a fish gasping for air. "I found her in her flat . . ."

"Perhaps you should sit down."

Lillian shook him off, taking a deep breath. "She was at the bottom of the basement stairs, as if she had fallen. But," she said, looking him in the eye, "something's not right."

"What do you mean?"

"Come with me and I'll show you. It's not far from here."

"I just have to check with—" Ian began, but as he spoke, the door to DCI Crawford's office opened, and his massive head poked out.

"Go with your aunt," Crawford said. "If there's a murderer on the loose, best we find out earlier rather than later."

"Thank you, sir," said Ian. "Where does she live?" he asked Lillian.

"Albany Street, near the corner of Dublin Street."

They took a cab to a well-maintained building on Albany Street, whereupon Lillian produced a key from her handbag.

"You have her latchkey?" Ian said as they mounted the steps to the front door.

"Sometimes I feed her cat," she replied, unlocking the door.

She led him through the tidy ground-floor flat, with its slightly tattered armchairs and white crocheted antimacassars, past a table in the parlor set for tea, with a blue-flowered plate of raisin scones and cherry jam. The room was silent save for the ticking of a ship's clock on the mantel. Ian shivered at the eerie stillness so familiar to him from other crime scenes, the heavy emptiness where a violent death had occurred, the ineffable feeling of loss. There was a sense of absence, as if life had been sucked from the air itself; the atmosphere felt thinner and more fragile.

"This way," Lillian said, showing him to an open door leading down a sturdy set of basement stairs. At the bottom was the prostrate body of a woman.

"You touched nothing?"

"Of course not!" she scoffed, as if the question itself was an insult.

He crept gingerly down the stairs, taking note of everything he observed. Her body lay on the staircase, head on the last step, her torso and legs on the higher steps, as if she had tumbled forward while descending the stairs. The wall of the staircase was splattered with blood, and upon examining her body, Ian concluded it came from the sizable wound on the side of her head.

At the bottom of the stairs was an upturned laundry basket, the contents spilled out onto the hard-packed dirt floor. Lifting the basket carefully, he examined the ground beneath it. The cellar smelled damp, of earth and apples and aromatic plants. Looking around the low-ceilinged space, Ian spied a bushel basket of apples in the corner, a wooden washing tub with attached wringer, and bunches of herbs hanging upside down from an improvised clothesline. An empty coal scuttle sat waiting to be filled. The cellar was as neat and organized as the flat upstairs, everything in its place, no sign of a struggle. The only evidence of violence was the blood on the walls and the gash in Miss Staley's head. He took some time examining the railing and each step before climbing back up to where his aunt stood, watching anxiously.

"You are entirely correct," he told her. "This was no accident."

"How can you tell?"

"There are numerous clues. For one thing, she appears to have hit her head on something, yet there is no concentrated area of blood on the railing or any of the steps. The blood on the wall suggests a violent blow of some kind. It is spread out over a large area, and you can tell from the shape of the droplets that it hit at considerable velocity."

Lillian frowned. "The shape of the droplets?"

"Yes. Observe how they are long and narrow."

"So they are," she said, peering at them through her spectacles.

"I have been studying the properties of blood evidence. The shapes made upon impact vary according to velocity, distance, and angle."

"And how are you coming by all this blood for your . . . study?"

"Conan Doyle has been very helpful in that regard. At any rate, this blood was traveling quite fast, which accounts for the long, narrow droplets."

"I see."

"Furthermore, there is the matter of her skirts."

"I beg your pardon?"

"Did you not remark how they are modestly draped over her legs?"

"Yes."

"Does that not strike you as odd?"

"You mean if she had fallen down the stairs—"

"Gravity would likely have resulted in a less ladylike position."

"Possibly, but that's hardly conclusive."

"There is one more thing. Come," he said, beckoning her to follow him down the steps. "Mind how you tread."

They descended together, careful not to touch poor Miss Staley, into the cellar with its faint odor of mildew and dried aromatic herbs. "Do you see any blood on the laundry or the basket?" he asked.

Stooping to look, Lillian examined it carefully. "No."

"Yet look at this," he said, lifting the basket. On the floor beneath it was the same scattered pattern of blood as on the staircase.

"That's odd," she said. "What do you make of it?"

"She did not have the laundry basket when she was attacked. It was placed there by her killer."

"But why?"

"To make it look like she fell while going down to do the laundry."

"So she was actually attacked—"

"She was assaulted on the stairs, most certainly, but whoever killed her felt compelled to place the overturned laundry basket there to make the accident narrative more plausible, as if she dropped it when she fell. However, they neglected to realize that this little flourish would betray them in the end. Sometimes it is best to leave well enough alone."

"I knew it," Lillian said softly. "Elizabeth Staley is not the sort of woman to trip over herself doing housework."

"Can you think of anyone who might wish her harm?"

"I didn't know her that well, but I'm not aware of any enemies. She never mentioned anything of the kind."

"Is there a back entrance to the flat?"

"No, just the front. And the cellar doors."

"I examined them—bolted shut from the inside. And neither the front door nor the entry to her flat showed signs of damage. They were both closed when you arrived?"

"Yes, I had to use my key. Why?"

"There is a strong likelihood Miss Staley knew her assailant. Not only that, it was someone she trusted well enough to turn her back on—the location of the wound suggests the blow was struck from behind."

"Good heavens," said Lillian, her voice unsteady.

"Do you know any of her friends or family?"

"I believe she has a married sister in Aberdeen. Emily, I think. She never mentioned her last name." There was a pause, and Ian could hear the slow drip of a faucet in the kitchen. *Plunk, plunk, plunk* . . . Did the killer neglect to turn it off after washing the blood from his hands?

"What do we do now?" Lillian asked.

She looked shaken and frightened, and Ian had an impulse to envelop her in his arms, but members of the Hamilton and Grey clans did not do such things. Such an action might thoroughly mortify her.

"What I want you to do is go straight home, lock the doors, and don't open them to anyone except me."

"What about Donald?"

"Yes, of course. Can you do that?"

"I suppose so," she replied, but she looked rather cross. "I can't stay locked up forever, you know."

"Would you just humor me this once?"

"Very well," she said with a sigh. "What about poor Elizabeth?"

"I'll ask DCI Crawford if he wants an autopsy. I think the cause of death is rather evident, but I'll leave it up to him."

"Must you cut her open? It seems to me she's been through enough."

"There is always the chance that she was drugged before she was attacked, and that could provide another piece of evidence."

Lillian shook her head sadly. "Poor Elizabeth."

"I'm going to hail you a cab—mind you go home straightaway, lest it should be poor Lillian next."

She rolled her eyes at him, but he could tell that for once she was grateful he was taking charge.

"If you think of anything that might be useful, please write it down. I'll come by later to ask more questions, but first I want to see if I can glean anything from her neighbors. Do you happen to know any of them?"

"No. I've seen one or two coming and going, but I can't say I know anyone."

"You get along home now, and make yourself a nice cup of tea."

After seeing his aunt off, Ian had a thorough look around the rest of the flat. There was no sign of blood in the kitchen or anywhere other than the basement stairs. Surely the killer had some blood on his person—or did he come prepared with a second set of clothing? There was no discarded clothing in the trash bins, either in the flat or in the alley. An exhaustive search for the murder weapon yielded nothing—the killer must have taken it with him.

Ian went into the building stairwell and knocked on the doors of the four other flats in the building. The only response he got was from a tall, elegantly dressed young man in the flat one flight above, who claimed to be on his way out. He gave his name as James Milner and claimed to know Elizabeth Staley only by sight.

"I haven't lived here long, you see," he said, tying his cravat.

"Did you happen to see or hear anything unusual this morning?"

Mr. Milner furrowed his brow. His hair was pale as wheat, his eyes of the lightest blue, and his skin so smooth that Ian doubted he could grow a beard if he tried. "Let me see . . . as a matter of fact, I heard a sort of—thumping, if you will. Like the sound of something being dropped."

Ian's pulse quickened. "What time was this?"

"It was just around eight o'clock, you see, because I was having my morning coffee, and I heard the milkman shortly afterward."

"You said you heard a thumping. Could it have been the sound of someone falling down a flight of stairs?"

"I suppose it could, now that you mention it."

"And did you happen to see the milkman when he came?"

"No. I wasn't properly dressed, so I didn't collect the milk until later."

"And did you happen to notice if Miss Staley's milk had been collected?"

"I assume it had. Mine was the only bottle remaining on the stoop."

"Thank you, Mr. Milner. You have been very helpful," Ian said, handing him his card. "Please contact me if you think of anything else."

"Certainly."

"Oh, one more question. Can you think of anyone who might want to harm Miss Staley?"

The young man's face reddened. "As I said, I didn't really know her except in passing."

"So you did. Thank you again," said Ian, tipping his hat. Pulling his cloak around his body, he stepped lightly down the stairs, pausing in the street for a moment before heading back in the direction of police chambers. He pondered who might want to kill poor Miss Staley. She seemed such an inoffensive woman, bookish and shy, someone you wouldn't notice in a crowd, the kind who blended into the background easily. He wished he had spoken with her more at the séance, and cursed himself for being so impatient to leave.

He thought about the milk bottles. The other tenants either collected theirs, had no delivery that day, or did not use milk—an unusual occurrence in Edinburgh, where residents were great devourers of milk, cheese, and cream.

Turning south onto Dublin Street, he stepped aside to let a fine landau pass. It was drawn by a pair of shining black geldings, and the driver seemed to be in a hurry, urging on the high-stepping horses with a flick of his long whip. The carriage was royal blue, trimmed in gold, and bore the Scottish version of the royal coat of arms—a mirror image of the English one, with the unicorn on the left side of the shield, the lion on the right. The unicorn carried the familiar blue-and-white Scottish flag, St. Andrew's Cross, while the lion waved the English standard, the red-and-white Cross of St. George.

Ian concluded the carriage belonged not to the Queen but probably to a high-ranking Scottish official, perhaps on his way to his office on Melville Crescent. Passing by the private Queen Street Gardens, he pondered the privileged lives within elegant Georgian townhouses, a deep contrast to the misery embalmed in Old Town's squalid alleys. Gazing at the wide, clean expanse of Heriot Row with its tidy, geometrically pleasing three-story row houses, he realized he preferred the unpredictable turmoil of Old Town. It was dark and dangerous and depressing but somehow more *human*.

Now, approaching the dividing line between New Town and the sordid slums of Old Town, Ian pondered the dual nature of a killer who seemed harmless enough to gain entry to a helpless spinster's flat yet was ruthless enough to brutally murder her.

CHAPTER SIX

Before turning onto the High Street, Ian stopped to give money to a blind beggar perched on a three-legged stool near the entrance to Waverley Station.

"How's business?" he inquired, slipping a coin into the man's hand.

"Is 'at you, Detective Inspector?"

"Hello, Brian."

"There's no mistakin' yer voice."

"Have you anything to tell me?"

"That depends."

"On what?"

"On wha' it's worth to ye."

"That would depend on how useful the information is."

Brian licked his lips. "Half a crown."

"I just gave you that."

Brian smiled, his teeth as stained as the gray cobblestones beneath their feet. "So ye did. A shilling, then."

"It's a steep price."

"It's valuable information."

"Very well," Ian said, digging another coin from his pocket.

"Ta very much," Brian said, fingering the coin eagerly before tucking it into his jacket pocket.

"Well?" Ian said, leaning over him.

"Come closer. The walls have ears."

Ian bent down so his ear was near the man's mouth. The aroma of cheap tobacco, stale whisky, and undigested cheese and onion pie wafted into Ian's nostrils.

Brian lowered his voice to a whisper, nearly drowned out by the rumble of steam engines as a train pulled in and out of Waverley Station.

Ian made him repeat what he said until he was satisfied he had heard correctly.

"You're right," he said, straightening up. "That was worth another shilling."

"Always glad t'be o' service."

"I wonder if you would do me a small favor."

"Name it," Brian said, licking his lips.

Ian looked around, and spotted a sleek young man loitering near a lamppost, but when he glanced back a moment later, the man had disappeared.

"It concerns misinformation."

"How so?"

"We have reason to believe one or more of our sources has gone sour—"

"An' ye'd like my help findin' out who it might be."

eneccccdbrvgnggthvdguvngdejtncbiecnctcfulbcr

"Will do, chief, will do."

"Of course I will remunerate you for your time."

"A' course. I kin always count on you, Detective."

Ian pressed another coin into the beggar's hand, but as he walked away, he wondered whether he had made a mistake in trusting the man. Brian had never failed him, and yet . . . It was unlikely, but he had to entertain the possibility that his oldest informant was no longer what he seemed to be.

When Ian arrived at police chambers, the door to DCI Crawford's office swung open as soon as Ian entered the main room.

"Well," Crawford said, lumbering toward him, "was it murder most foul?"

"Most definitely," Ian replied, hanging his cloak on the rack near the front entrance.

"*Hamlet*, first act, I believe," Crawford couldn't resist adding, with a smug little smile.

"Well done, sir."

Crawford appeared to have been waiting for his return, because as soon as Ian disposed of his outerwear, the chief beckoned him into his office.

"Any suspects?" Crawford said, sinking heavily into his desk chair.

"None so far—I know little about the victim as yet," Ian replied, taking the chair opposite. His relationship with the chief had become relaxed enough that he no longer waited for an invitation to sit when summoned to Crawford's office.

"Yet she's a friend of your aunt's?"

"They attend the same weekly séance."

"Indeed?" Crawford stroked his whiskers. "My wife goes in for all that, but between us, I think it's bosh and bunkum. They have a medium, I suppose?"

"They do indeed—a Madame Veselka."

"Mysterious and exotic foreigner, claims to communicate with the dead?"

"Exactly."

Crawford sighed. "Well, I s'pose it's harmless enough, as long as she doesn't milk them dry."

"I have no idea how much Madame Veselka charges for her sessions."

"You'd best keep an eye on your aunt, see she doesn't succumb to a charlatan."

"My aunt has means. And a level head, I believe, even in regards to mediums."

"A very sensible woman," Crawford said. "And a damn fine photographer. Please tell her that we may again be requesting her services."

"I certainly will."

"Good," the chief said, twisting a piece of string between his fingers, a sign that he was anxious. "Now then, I'd like to discuss what we talked about yesterday." He rose and paced behind his desk, glancing out the window to the street below, where the sound of horses' hooves and wooden cart wheels on cobblestones competed with the sound of children's voices. Glancing at the clock above the filing cabinet, Ian remembered Sergeant Dickerson mentioning that his younger sister was to have a half day at school, though he had forgotten it until now.

As if reading his mind, DCI Crawford turned to him and frowned. "Where is Dickerson, by the way? Haven't seen him all day."

Ian's first instinct was to cover for the sergeant. "I sent him off to interview friends of the deceased," he lied.

That seemed to satisfy the chief. "I see," he said, plucking at a stray whisker. "I expect you'll want to be getting on with your investigation, but as to this other matter . . ."

"I have reason to believe there is to be a concentrated criminal action very soon."

Crawford sat down again and leaned forward over his desk. "Do you know—" he began, but was interrupted by a knock at the door. "Come in!" he bellowed.

The door opened to admit Sergeant Dickerson. His cheeks were ruddy; he was perspiring and out of breath.

"Beg pardon, sir," he began.

"How did your interviews fare?" said Crawford.

"Sir?"

Ian turned and glared at him. The detective's back was to Crawford, so the chief couldn't see his expression, but the bewilderment on Dickerson's face only deepened, as if someone had requested that he recite *The Iliad* in the original Greek.

"The *murder inquiry*, Sergeant," Ian said tightly. "Have you concluded all your interviews?"

Dickerson finally caught on, nodding his head vigorously. "Oh, yes, sir! I wen' straightaway, like—"

"Good man," Ian interrupted.

"Could you discuss that later?" said Crawford. "Detective Hamilton was just telling me something of interest on another matter."

"A' course, sir—whatever ye say." Dickerson loosened the collar of his uniform, wiping sweat from his still-damp forehead.

"Please, have a seat," said the chief. Dickerson complied, perching on the edge of the captain's chair nearest the door.

Ian repeated what Brian had told him.

"So there's t'be a big robbery?" Dickerson said eagerly.

"I presume that's what it is," said Ian, "though the details are still somewhat vague."

"Do ye know when?"

"Within a fortnight."

"And how is it that you came by this information?" asked Crawford.

"I'd rather not reveal my source at this time."

"Even to me?" the chief said, frowning.

"I don't want to compromise him in any way, lest he be found floating in the Water of Leith," he said, referring to the main river snaking through Edinburgh before emptying into the Firth of Forth.

Dickerson shuddered. "I shouldn't like that t'happen. Feel horrible guilty, I would."

"And yet you trust him?" Crawford asked. "Even in light of what we discussed?"

"I do," Ian replied, though in all truth he was beginning to wonder whom he could trust.

"Any more details?"

"The target is Murray and Weston."

Crawford's jaw dropped. "On Princes Street?"

"The same." Murray and Weston were the most respected jewelers in Edinburgh, and had received more than one commission from the Queen herself.

"Good Lord. That's outrageous." Sitting behind his desk, he tugged at his whiskers, chewing on his lip. "We need confirmation. The word of a snitch isn't enough to go on."

"I agree entirely," said Ian. "We'll do what we can, eh, Sergeant?"

"Yes, sir," Dickerson replied.

"Now, about this other matter. Have you any news for me?" Crawford asked Ian.

"I suggest that this upcoming robbery—"

"If that's what it is—"

"May be a chance to root out any source of false information."

"Like if we should get a conflictin' bit of information from another source?" said Dickerson.

"Exactly," said Ian. "We have to keep a careful watch on our informants."

"Hmm. Maybe you're right," Crawford said, drumming his fingers on the desk. "Get on it, will you?"

"Right away, sir. 'Better three hours too soon than a minute too late,'" said Ian. Raising his left eyebrow, Crawford scowled at him. "*The Merry Wives of Windsor*," Ian added quickly. "Not his best play, of course."

"Of course," Crawford echoed, though it was hard to tell if he was being sarcastic. "Off you go, then. Oh, and tell your aunt I'm very sorry about the death of her friend."

"I will, sir."

"If you need manpower on that case, just ask. Meanwhile, I'll put some undercover men on patrol at Murray and Weston."

"Yes, sir," Ian said, and left the office, Dickerson trailing behind him. "Where on earth were you this morning?" he asked when they were out of earshot.

"Sorry, sir—it were my sister, y'see. It won' happen again."

Sergeant William Dickerson looked after his younger sister like a brooding mother hen, with a devotion Ian found touching.

"Everything all right, is it?"

"It were a matter of bullying at school, an' she were gettin' into fights tryin' to protect the girls what were bein' picked on."

"That's quite admirable."

The sergeant sighed. "I wish the headmistress saw it that way, sir—she don' like fightin'."

"Then she should look to the girls who are causing the trouble in the first place."

"I'm afeard she's less devoted t'justice than to peace an' quiet."

Ian frowned. "Let me know if I can be of any help."

"I wish ye could, sir, but the headmistress don' take kindly t'interference."

Just then the front door to the station house opened, and in stepped Derek McNair—thief, pickpocket, ragamuffin, and Ian's most valuable source of information. Breezing past the desk sergeant, he sauntered over and planted his bony posterior on Ian's desk.

"So," he said, helping himself to a biscuit from a tin on the desk, "wha' do I haf t'do ta git yer attention, issue an engraved invitation?"

CHAPTER SEVEN

"Didn' yer brother tell you I were lookin' fer ya?" Derek asked, calmly chewing the biscuit. "Oiy, kin I get a cuppa 'round here?"

"Yes, he did, and no, you may not," said Ian. The boy wore an overcoat several sizes too large over a blue jumper and scuffed trousers tied around his narrow waist with a frayed bit of rope. His boots were in relatively good condition, if several sizes too large. His hands were encased in thick woolen gloves missing the tips of several fingers.

"Then why didn' ye meet me?" he said.

"I wasn't aware a meeting had been arranged."

Derek sighed and hopped off the desk. "Ye'd best have a word wi' yer brother 'bout not passin' on messages proper like. Well, let's go, then," he added, brushing biscuit crumbs from his clothes. "Oh, an' them biscuits are stale."

"I'm sorry the cuisine isn't up to your standards."

"Come along, then," the boy said, strolling past the desk sergeant as if daring him to throw him out. "I ain't got all day."

"If DCI Crawford inquires, I'll return later this afternoon," Ian told Sergeant Dickerson.

"Yes, sir," he said, frowning. Dickerson was not Derek McNair's biggest fan.

"Where are we going?" Ian said, fetching his cloak from the rack.

"Ye'll find out when we git there," said Derek as they left the station house.

Ian followed the boy past St. Giles, where a group of schoolboys were spitting energetically on the Heart of Midlothian mosaic built into the paving stones—ostensibly to express their disdain for the former location of the notorious Tolbooth prison, though Ian suspected it was merely young boys enjoying an opportunity to spit with impunity.

They passed another group of boys playing gird and cleek, known in England as hoop and stick. Derek glanced at them with contempt as they trotted alongside the rolling wooden hoops, tapping them with sticks to keep them moving forward without toppling over. The boys—about his age—collapsed to the cobblestones in laughter as one of the hoops tottered and fell, tripping them, as the other continued rolling until it collided with a rag picker's cart parked by the entrance to Parliament Square.

"Silly muckers," Derek muttered as they passed the giggling boys.

"Don't you ever play that game?"

Derek snorted. "It's fer children."

"What do you consider yourself, then?"

"I ain't no foolish child, that's fer sure."

"So no games for you?"

"Ain't got time, Guv—I got better things t'do."

"Such as fondling strange women?"

"There's nothin' strange 'bout the women I fondle," he replied with a sly smile.

"You're going to lose a hand one day if you keep it up, you know."

"I'd best get on wi'it, then," he replied, turning onto George IV Bridge.

They continued on through the Grassmarket, where Ian inhaled the aroma of pitch, tar, and linseed oil wafting down from the rows of wholesale shops on Bow Street. They turned onto King's Stables Road, where Grassmarket became West Port, and these odors were replaced by the earthy smell of horse manure. Here the cobblestones were rough from heavy use, chipped from decades of clops from hooves of horses, sheep, and cattle, and the unforgiving drumming of carriage wheels and wooden carts. High above them the castle perched on its rocky parapet, gray stones against a dull December sky.

"Where are you taking me?" said Ian as Derek darted past half a dozen smartly dressed soldiers on matching black stallions, their white belts gleaming on their scarlet uniforms, their high fur hats making them appear even taller upon their mounts.

Ignoring the question, the boy led him past a row of low stables being mucked out by sleepy-looking attendants in thick barn coats and knee-high green Wellies. The sweet, musty aroma of hay and horse sweat permeated the air as Ian followed the boy to the rear of a row of stalls. The horses regarded him with wide, mild eyes as he passed, snorting softly, their breath misting in the chill air. A small black mare nipped playfully at Ian's shoulder, shaking her head so that her long dark mane flopped over one eye. Ian liked horses, though he had not as much skill around them as Derek—another of the boy's unexpected abilities. Derek pointed to a small booth near the back of the stalls, evidently a place for grooms and stable hands to eat or play cards while on duty.

"How did you find this place?" said Ian.

"One a' the stable hands owes me a favor," the boy replied as they turned the corner to reveal the single occupant of the booth.

To Ian's surprise, sitting at the booth, dressed in a trim black waistcoat and matching cravat, was Terrance McNee, a.k.a. Rat Face—pickpocket, cardsharp, con man, and general miscreant. At their first meeting some six months ago, Ian had trounced his brawny companion, Jimmy Snead, in a bar fight, which unexpectedly caused the big man to become Ian's devoted ally. Both Snead and McNee had helped him greatly with the case he was working on at the time, but he had seen little of either of them in the months that followed.

McNee's sharp face broke into a smile when he saw Ian.

"Good to see you again, Detective. I trust you've been well."

"And I trust you've been keeping out of trouble."

"Please, have a seat. You look surprised to see me."

"I confess I am," Ian admitted, sliding into the bench opposite him. Derek perched himself upon a wooden chair next to them, chewing on a sprig of straw. Ian thought about cautioning him about his choice of refreshment, but figured the boy had ingested much worse in his life on the streets. He turned to Rat Face, who was idly shuffling a dog-eared pack of cards, sliding each one through his long fingers with mesmerizing dexterity.

"Why didn't you just come to me yourself?" said Ian. "Why all this cloak-and-dagger business?"

"If I were seen speaking with you, it might not go well for me," Rat Face replied, stroking his neatly trimmed mustache. The small goatee he had grown since Ian last saw him failed to hide his weak chin, which, along with his long, pointed nose, were plainly the reason for his nickname.

"If you're willing to risk it, there must be something in it for you," said Ian.

"That depends rather on your generosity," his companion replied, his small black eyes focused on the deck of cards.

Derek rose from his chair. "Why don' I jes keep an eye out t'make sure the coast is clear?"

"If necessary, there is a back entrance we can slip out of," said Rat Face.

"You seem prepared for any eventuality," Ian remarked as Derek sauntered toward the stable's front entrance.

"I find it advisable to always have an escape plan."

Ian leaned back in the wooden booth. "To what do I owe the pleasure of this meeting?"

His companion lowered his voice. "I understand you are making inquiries regarding the fire that killed your parents."

"How do you—"

Rat Face dismissed his question with a wave of his hand. "It is my business to know things."

"Do you have information?"

"The question is whether or not it is useful to you." Digging deep into his waistcoat pocket, he pulled out a small, crumpled black bag. It appeared to be made of black velvet, though in the dim light it was hard to tell. Reaching inside, he carefully extracted a pair of teardrop pearl earrings and placed them on the table.

"Do you recognize these?"

Ian stared at the earrings. A blackness threatened to engulf him, as his mind struggled to comprehend the meaning of this. His vision suddenly felt surrounded by darkness on all sides, as if he were inside a tunnel; his mouth dried up, and sweat beaded on his upper lip. Saliva suddenly spurted into his mouth, and he felt he was going to be sick.

"I see that you do," Rat Face said rather more gently.

"They belonged to my mother. Where did you get them?"

"I won them in a card game from a particularly unsavory specimen of humanity. A surly little petty thief by the name of Nate Crippen. Specializes in burglary, though he'll turn his hand to any nasty job—for the right price."

"And he got them—?"

Rat Face leaned into him, and Ian could smell the tobacco on his breath. His teeth were yellow and pointed, like those of the animal that had inspired his nickname. "The thrawn puggy was deep into his cups by that time—I didn't know whether or not to believe him when he told me."

"Told you what?"

"He's a meater, you see," he said, using the street term for coward. "So I wasn't sure—"

"What did he *tell* you?" Ian rasped, his voice hoarse with emotion.

"He was given them to do a job—nasty sort of work."

"Which was—?"

"He claimed he was paid to set a fire."

"When?"

"Some years ago. He wasn't very clear on the exact details."

"Who paid him?"

"He was either unwilling or too drunk to share that information. But he was babbling about it being a policeman's house."

Ian picked up one of the earrings and held it between his fingers. The pearl glistened with the mysterious beauty of the sea, pink and ivory with touches of aquamarine at the edges. So perfect, this by-product of the lowly oyster, a creature that had neither sight nor reason yet could produce such beauty that men would risk their lives for it.

"What do you want for these?"

Rat Face shrugged. "We can discuss the matter of my expenses later."

Ian placed the earrings back on the table and locked eyes with Terrance McNee.

"Take me to this person."

"I'll be in touch," said Rat Face, rising smoothly from his seat. In one graceful move, he slipped out of the booth, passed the last stall, and disappeared. Caught flat-footed, Ian snatched up the earrings and stumbled after him. Seeing a narrow door at the back of the building, he went through it, but when he entered the alley behind the building, there was no sight of the man. Ian stood, blinking in the glare of the overcast sky, but Rat Face had vanished.

CHAPTER EIGHT

He found Derek McNair leaning on the stall of a muscular gray gelding, running his fingers through the horse's coarse mane. The animal snorted softly as Ian approached, the breath from its nostrils misting in the cold air.

"What did you know of this?" Ian said.

The boy petted the horse's velvety muzzle and shrugged. "Not much, Guv. It weren't my place t'inquire wha' the meetin' were about. I reckoned it were related to one a' yer cases, right?"

Ian peered at him, unsure whether he was lying or not. He knew from experience the boy was a damned good liar, but couldn't see what he had to gain in this instance, so decided to believe him.

"In a manner of speaking," he said. "It relates to my parents' death."

"Blimey," Derek said, his eyes wide. "An' you're thinkin' they was murdered, right?"

"Yes. And this has confirmed my suspicion."

He began walking in the direction from whence they had come, and the boy fell into step beside him. Snow swirled around them as the dull December sky finally made good on its threat of pending precipitation.

"What'd he tell ye?"

"The less you know, the better. I'd rather not get you mixed up in this."

"But I'd like t'help."

"It's not safe. There are unsavory characters involved."

"I'm as unsavory as they come, Guv."

"Alas, if only that were true. There are dark players in this game, and I'd rather not put you at risk."

"Wha' about Rat Face?"

"He can take care of himself." But even as he said the words, they sounded hollow.

Snow continued to gather as they walked, so Ian flagged down a hansom cab.

"Come along," he said when Derek hesitated. "I'll drop you off."

"Ta very much, but—"

"What?"

"Don' really know where I'm goin' yet. My usual lodgings ain't so good when it's snowin'."

Ian imagined what his "usual lodgings" consisted of—the back lot of a deserted building, a church doorstep, a grate beneath the eaves of a pub.

"I'll drop you at my flat. Tell my brother you're staying the night."

The boy didn't have to be asked twice. In half a second he had climbed in next to Ian, rubbing his hands against the cold. They rode in silence for a few minutes, then Derek cleared his throat. "D'ye think . . ." he began with unaccustomed shyness.

"What?"

"Might I 'ave a bath?"

"Yes," Ian replied. "You may have a bath. And if you don't steal anything and are very, very well behaved, you may have a small sip of whisky."

"*Now* yer talkin'!" Derek crowed, his bravado restored.

After letting the boy into the empty flat—Donald being no doubt still at school—Ian instructed him to lock the door behind him and let no one in. He then returned to the waiting cab and continued on to the High Street police station.

He found Sergeant Dickerson scribbling away at his desk. DCI Crawford was not in his office.

"He went t'take 'is wife t'see Dr. Bell," said Dickerson when Ian asked. "He wants a report tomorrow on the murder of yer aunt's friend."

"Did he say anything about the autopsy?"

"He said Dr. Bell agreed t'do it."

"But that would be Dr. Littlejohn's province." Dr. Henry Littlejohn was Edinburgh's police surgeon, and as such was responsible for autopsies in cases of suspicious deaths.

"He said Bell wants t'do a demonstration lecture fer students."

Ian frowned. Public autopsies had been common in Edinburgh until the notorious Burke and Hare murdered victims whom they then sold to Dr. Joseph Knox for dissection. His public lectures drew large crowds, but after William Burke was hanged in front of twenty thousand people and publicly dissected the next day, the practice was banned, and autopsies were done in private.

Medical school students and doctors still regularly attended dissections, though Ian was not keen on the idea of Dr. Bell using Elizabeth for a demonstration. He did not like the man, though he admired his skill and deductive powers. He could still remember the icy, analytical look in Bell's eyes when he autopsied the poor prostitute murdered during Ian's last case. The physician possessed a coldness that repelled Ian—perhaps because he sensed the potential for the same trait within himself.

"What have you there?" Ian asked, glancing at Dickerson's papers.

"I'm jes writin' down questions t'ask when interviewin' witnesses."

"Well done, Sergeant. I've been considering ways to structure the investigative process."

51

"How so, sir?"

"I'm working on constructing a chart to keep track of information, and to make sure we don't leave anything out of the process."

"That sounds quite useful, sir."

"I'd like to begin tomorrow by making up a list of Miss Staley's acquaintances, friends, and relatives."

"There's the folks wha' attended the séances, for starters."

"Quite right—we should begin with them."

The front door opened and a half dozen uniformed constables shuffled in. The evening shift had arrived.

Dickerson glanced nervously at the wall clock. "Beg pardon, sir, but I've rehearsal tonight."

"Get on with you, then."

"Thank you, sir," he said, gathering up his things.

"Mind you come in bright and early tomorrow."

"I promise, sir," he said, scurrying out the door.

The new arrivals nodded to Ian as they gathered round the tea service, as was the custom when starting a shift. Very little business was done in Edinburgh without the accompaniment of a good strong cup of black tea sweetened with plenty of sugar and milk.

Ian recognized Constable John Turnbull among them, and saw him turn to snigger after Dickerson as he left.

"Have you heard we have a *thespian* in our midst?" he said, emphasizing the word to make it sound like something shameful. His mouth curled in a sneer, emphasizing the pockmarks on his cheeks.

"What's that?" asked Sergeant Bowers, a plain-faced, well-meaning young man with pale pink skin and white blond hair. A favorite of DCI Crawford, he had recently been promoted from constable to sergeant.

"It means an actor, don' it?" said Constable McKay. Tall and muscular, he was a little older than the other two and known for his physical prowess and utter fearlessness.

"Like a theater actor?" Bowers said, stirring a third lump of sugar into his tea.

"I wasn't aware there was another kind," Turnbull remarked drily. "Though why any self-respecting policeman would want to be seen prancing around wearing rouge and tights, I couldn't say."

Ian had an impulse to flatten him. He considered Turnbull the worst kind of scoundrel, one who would mock his colleagues behind their back, then flatter and fawn over his superiors. Ian longed to give him a good thrashing. Grabbing his cloak, he threw it over his shoulders and left the station house before he did something he might regret. A blast of arctic air hit him as he stepped onto the High Street, making him stagger backward. Tugging his cap low over his face, he headed in the direction of the Royal Infirmary, the wind whistling at his back like a pack of angry dogs.

CHAPTER NINE

It was just past six o'clock, and Fiona Stuart was only halfway through a double shift at the Royal Infirmary, but her feet already hurt, her lower back was sore, and she had a headache coming on. Sighing as she pulled a thermometer from the mouth of a drowsy tram driver, she wiped the sweat from her brow. The driver had come down with a case of influenza, which had swept through the city as the changeable winter weather shot a spasm of illness through Scotland's capital.

Colds, catarrh, influenza—the wildly swinging temperatures and damp chill even seemed to increase complaints of lumbago and rheumatism, with beds on all the wards filled to capacity. To top it off, the hospital was shorthanded, as nurses and doctors were felled by the same array of illnesses, so the remaining staff was forced to take on extra shifts.

"Wha's it say, then, luv?" inquired the tram driver, before being seized by an attack of coughing.

"You have a slight temperature," Fiona replied, thrusting a handkerchief at him. "Cover your mouth when you cough."

"Ta very much," he said, taking it. "Sorry, luv," he added sheepishly.

"I'll be back later," she said, casting a glance around the ward before leaving. No one seemed to be in dire need of her at the moment, so she headed for the linen closet. She breathed a sigh of relief as she sank into the chair in the corner of the small room. It was just a straight-backed wooden chair, but getting off her feet for a few minutes was inexpressibly delicious. There was a small lounge for the nurses, but Head Nurse Meadows didn't seem to believe in breaks of any kind, and Fiona had been the recipient of her disapproving glare on more than one occasion. It was much safer in the linen closet. She breathed in the quiet darkness, the sweet smell of cedar and freshly washed cotton sheets, borax and laundry soap.

She closed her eyes just for a moment . . .

"Nurse Stuart?"

Her body stiffened to attention as her eyes flew open. The voice brought her back to consciousness with a sickening thud. Harsh, dry, and stern, it could only belong to one person.

"Yes, Nurse Meadows?"

"What on earth are you doing in here?" Meadows stood silhouetted in the doorway, her long sinewy arms crossed, her square-jawed head cocked to one side. Fiona was glad she couldn't quite make out her facial expression. She had seen it often enough—steely gray eyes narrowed, thin lips pursed, as if she had just consumed a particularly sour lemon.

"I—I had a headache. I was just resting my eyes."

"I trust you are better now."

"Yes, thank you," Fiona lied.

"Then what are you waiting for? Chop, chop! There are patients waiting."

Fiona fought to keep from yawning as she followed Nurse Meadows out of the closet. She could feel Meadows' eyes on her as she walked away, down the long corridor toward the wards. Fiona didn't believe the woman ever slept. Or if she did sleep, it was with one eye open, like the hundred-eyed watchman Argus from Greek mythology. She was like a bat, or a spider, or some as yet undiscovered species of nocturnal lizard.

As she rounded the corner, turning right toward the accident and injury ward, she was surprised to see a familiar face.

"Hello, Miss Stuart," said Ian Hamilton.

Taken unawares, she was unable to suppress the look of delight that flashed across her features. "Good afternoon, Detective," she said, carefully composing her face into a neutral expression. "What brings you here today?"

"I've come to see Conan Doyle. Have you any idea where I might find him?"

"Of course," she replied, disappointment digging a little hole in her stomach. There was of course no reason he would be there to see her, considering how she had treated him in the past. "Follow me," she said, striding briskly down the polished corridors.

Fiona Stuart had determined at an early age that men would not rule her life. She had watched too many women succumb to marriages with men they did not like. While she understood the allure of comfort and security, she chafed against the notion that a woman's place was in the home, resenting the inequities that made it difficult for a woman to make her own way in the world. She had watched helplessly year after year as her mother struggled beneath her father's will, shrinking to a diminished version of herself, until finally taken by consumption, the ultimate wasting disease.

Fiona did not hate men, but she did not trust them, and had resolved never to put herself at their mercy if she could help it. Her mother's memory trailed her like a sad ghost, appearing whenever she felt the temptation of sexual attraction. Though she had felt the pull of Ian's personality from the first moment she saw him, she had no intention of falling for the handsome detective.

But she imagined his warm breath on her neck and heard his firm, light tread as he followed her down the hall. Warring emotions surged in her breast. She was grateful that so long as he was behind her, her face could not betray her feelings. She did not want to reach their destination, where she would have to leave him. She longed for the corridor to stretch on forever. But they reached Doyle's tiny office all too soon, and he came to the door in response to her knock.

"Hello," he said, smiling in his broad, open way.

Fiona liked Conan Doyle—most people did. He was kind and unaffected and had a way of making you feel as if you were important. She sometimes wished she were attracted to him—she sensed Doyle was a man who would never treat a woman badly. But she was much more drawn to Detective Hamilton's moody restlessness. He was like an opaque lake, and she was intrigued by his unexplored depths.

"I hope I'm not interrupting," Hamilton said. "You mentioned you had something to show me."

"Ah, yes!" Doyle said. "Indeed I do."

"If this is an inconvenient time—"

"Not at all—come in, please. Would you care to see as well, Nurse Stuart?"

"Thank you, but I must attend to my duties," she replied. How she would have loved to stay and observe whatever crime-solving techniques the two men were collaborating on, but she had patients waiting, and Nurse Meadows was not of a forgiving disposition. A second reprimand in one day would almost certainly end in unpleasant consequences.

She walked away from the two men reluctantly. In spite of Conan Doyle's generous offer, she was keenly aware of the gap between them— she was just a nurse, whereas he was no doubt on his way to an illustrious career as a doctor in one of the finest medical institutions in the world. As a woman, she had limited options, and the thought pierced her like a scalpel cutting into her flesh. While the two men discussed the latest exciting developments in medicine and crime solving, she would be taking temperatures, emptying bedpans, and cleaning up vomit.

After attending to patients in the accident and injury ward, she returned to the linen closet to get sheets for the tubercular ward. Since it had been discovered some years ago that the disease was contagious, some of the nurses were frightened to go near the patients. Fiona Stuart disdained such fear. She took precautions, of course, as she had while nursing her mother through her last illness, and would not be dissuaded from doing her duty now.

As she gathered fresh linens from the supply closet, she thought of the courage of her hero and mentor, Sophia Jex-Blake, who took on the Scottish medical establishment nearly single-handedly—and nearly won. *But not quite.* After an ugly fight, Jex-Blake was finally able to matriculate into the medical school at the University of Edinburgh, though she was not allowed to graduate. Forced to get her degree in Berlin, she returned to Edinburgh as Scotland's first female physician. Fiona worshipped her, and volunteered at her clinic for women whenever possible.

Carrying an armload of fresh sheets, Fiona walked to the end of the hall and turned right into the corridor that led to the tubercular ward. Seeing Detective Hamilton emerge from Doyle's office, she hastened her steps to catch up. As they neared the front door, she called to him.

"Detective?"

He turned and saw her. "Hello again," he said with a smile, which made her stomach do a little dip.

She took a deep breath. "May I have a word?"

"Certainly. What can I do for you?"

She looked down at her sagging black stockings, her shoes scuffed and in need of polish. Her feet hurt, and she was hungry. "The fact is," she said, "I owe you an apology."

"For what?"

"For being utterly beastly to you."

"Oh?"

"During your last case, I was rude and unmannerly."

"I hadn't noticed."

She glanced at his face for any hint of sarcasm, but his expression gave little away. Still, she had the unsettling feeling he was mocking her.

"The fact remains, my behavior was unwarranted and unbecoming."

"Unwarranted, perhaps, but unbecoming? I'm not so certain of that," he said with a smile, and she felt her forehead burn.

"I'm afraid I have a tendency to take on causes. I can be cantankerous when I think women aren't being taken seriously just because they're women."

"I'll admit your reactions did feel a bit harsh at times."

"All I can say is I'm sorry."

"And I am deeply sorry if I gave any indication I would fail to take a woman seriously—just because she's a woman." He cocked his head to one side and gazed at her, and she felt confused and excited. "I cannot imagine anyone failing to take you seriously, Miss Stuart."

She paused, unsure what to say next. He stood, arms crossed, a faint smile on his absurdly handsome face. A lock of curly black hair had fallen onto his forehead, and she longed to reach up and brush it back.

"Well," she said lamely, "I'd best get on with my duties."

"Yes, I suppose so."

She peered at him. *Was he mocking her?* "See here," she said abruptly. "I've a mind to make it up to you properly."

"Indeed?" he said, rocking back on his heels.

What was he smiling at? Did he find her ridiculous?

"I should like to buy you dinner," she said curtly, as if daring him to say no.

"When did you have in mind?"

"Is Th-Thursday night convenient?" she said, furious that she was stammering.

"Most agreeable."

"Shall we say eight o'clock, then, at Le Canard? You know the place?"

"I do indeed. I shall see you then," he said, and swept out the entrance with a few strides of his long legs.

As the door closed behind him, she realized she had been holding her breath. Exhaling, she turned around and retraced her steps back down the corridor. But the familiar landscape had changed in some subtle, indefinable way. The gaslight reflecting in the tall arched windows was more intense, the marble walls gleamed more brightly, and the muted sound of voices from nearby wards sounded like singing. Her hunger had vanished, and her feet no longer hurt. In fact, she felt like dancing. Turning right toward the nurses' station, she took a little skip before vanishing around the corner, leaving a faint trace of lavender in her wake.

CHAPTER TEN

Ian returned home to find Donald in Ian's dressing gown, sprawled out on the parlor sofa. The cat was perched precariously on his protruding belly, like a remora on a whale shark. When Ian entered the room, his brother looked up from the medical textbook he was reading and scowled.

"What on earth possessed you to deposit that imbecilic street urchin on me without so much as a by-your-leave?"

Ian sank into the wing chair closest to the fire. "Derek McNair is many things, but imbecilic is not one of them."

"Lawless, then. Rude, crude, vulgar."

"Words you used to describe yourself not so long ago."

"Touché, brother. A hit—a very palpable hit. Or should I leave the Shakespeare quotes to you?"

"I shall be glad to be relieved of the burden."

"Seriously, though, did you think I would be receptive to the idea?"

"I did not give it much consideration, to be honest."

"Why not?"

"Because it is my flat."

The moment Ian said the words, he knew it was a mistake. Donald's face darkened, and he sat up abruptly, dislodging Bacchus, who landed on the carpet, tail twitching irritably.

"See here," Donald began. "If you have any notion—"

"Please calm yourself. I didn't mean to suggest—"

"One may not *mean* a great many things, but nonetheless—"

"I beg you not to take offense."

"What you meant was that since you pay the rent, you may do as you like. Is that not true?"

Ian rubbed his forehead wearily. "I confess I did not expect you to object to him so vociferously."

Donald stood up and pulled the robe around his rotund middle. Since it was Ian's dressing gown, it did not quite reach. "It isn't that I dislike the boy so much, though I am not as enamored of him as you are. It's the principle of the thing."

"What's e-na-mored mean?"

They turned to see Derek McNair standing in the doorway. He was dressed in Ian's second-best nightshirt, which was so long it trailed behind him. His unkempt brown hair stood up on all sides, and his eyes were crusted with sleep. The brothers exchanged glances.

"So wha' do it mean?" he repeated.

"It means you like something," Ian said finally.

"Rather a lot," Donald added.

"Din' know ye liked me even a bit," Derek said. "That's good t'know."

At first Ian thought he might be serious, but Derek's left eyebrow was raised sardonically, and his mouth curled in a smile.

"What are you doing out of bed?" said Ian.

"It were kinda hard t'sleep wi' the two a you goin' on like that."

"How much of that did you hear?"

"Enough t'know y'like me—rather a lot," he added, imitating Donald's voice perfectly.

Donald reddened. "Here now, why don't you have a glass of warm milk or something and get back to bed?"

"I'd sooner 'ave a beer."

"You may not—" Donald began.

"Oiy," Derek interrupted. "Yer brother promised me whisky."

"Only a sip," Ian said in response to Donald's look.

"Well, I ha'nt had it yet."

"Very well," said Ian. "And then straight to bed."

"Kin I sleep wi' the cat?" he said, looking at Bacchus, who had returned to the recently vacated sofa, and was industriously cleaning himself.

"If he'll go with you."

The boy was placated with an ounce or two of cream sherry, which they kept around for Lillian. After licking his lips and carefully wiping his mouth with his sleeve, Derek picked up the cat and lugged him in the direction of Ian's bedroom. To Ian's surprise, Bacchus submitted, legs dangling as the boy held him around the middle. Derek was so small and Bacchus so large the boy had to wrap both arms around the cat.

"Hold on a minute," said Ian. "Just exactly where are you sleeping?"

"I let him use your bed," said Donald.

Ian frowned. "I never suggested—"

"You weren't usin' it, were ye?" said Derek. "An' don' worry—I took a bath."

"He can move to the couch when you turn in," Donald said.

"He most certainly will," Ian muttered as the boy trundled off to bed, the curiously passive Bacchus hanging limply in his arms.

Donald leaned over to put a log on the fire. "This wood is wet, but it's all I have at the moment."

Ian took the pearl earrings from the pocket of his waistcoat, where he had been carrying them all day, and laid them on the small mahogany table by the sofa.

When Donald saw them, he went pale. "How did you get these?" he asked quietly.

"So you recognize them."

"Of course I recognize them! How did they survive the fire?"

Ian lowered himself onto the sofa. Lacing his fingers together, he leaned forward and fixed his gaze upon his older brother. "If you know something you haven't told me, now would be the time to say so."

Donald took a seat across from him. "Do you really think I would hide anything from you?"

"You hid the fact that our mother had a lover."

"But I told you!"

"Not until two months ago. Why did you wait so long?"

"You were so young at the time—"

"Too young for the truth?"

"It would have just upset you."

"What else are you hiding from me?"

"Nothing—I swear."

Ian looked at his brother's face, shiny with sweat and sincerity. Ian had no idea what secrets might still be lurking in family closets, and perhaps Donald was as much in the dark as he was.

"So where did you get these?" his brother repeated.

Ian told him of his meeting with Rat Face. Donald listened closely, and when Ian had finished, was silent for some time. The only sounds in the room were the soft hissing of the damp wood in the grate and the faint ticking of the grandfather clock in the hall.

"Then the fire was set deliberately?" Donald said finally.

"It appears that way."

"By whom, and why?"

"The obvious answer would be some vengeful miscreant from Father's past."

"He did put away a fair number of criminals." Donald leaned back against the couch cushions and sighed. "You will never understand this, but I have never wanted a drink so much since I gave up alcohol."

"I do understand. I could do with one myself."

"Please don't abstain on my account."

"It won't make you—"

"I would be a sorry specimen if that were all it took to weaken my resolve."

"Are you quite sure?"

"Allow me some vicarious pleasure."

Ian went to the sideboard and poured himself a generous tumbler of whisky.

"I just want to smell it," Donald said, leaning over the glass and inhaling deeply. With a sigh, he pushed the medical textbooks to the side and sat back down on the sofa. "Now then, what are you going to do about this new information?"

"I'm going to track down this Nate Crippen and wring the truth out of him."

"Mind how you go, Ian. These are murky waters."

"I mean to get to the bottom of this," he said, taking a drink of whisky, feeling the welcome burn as it slid down his throat.

"There are evil forces in this godforsaken town. I should hate to lose my landlord in a violent way," Donald added with a sly smile.

"I have no intention of dying."

"I am glad to hear it, but if you delve deeper into this, there may be others who have a different notion."

At that moment the wind picked up outside, hurling a sheet of freezing rain at the window. It slapped against the panes before sliding to the ground.

"'Hell is empty, and all the devils are here,'" Donald murmured.

The quote from *The Tempest* seemed appropriate, given the onslaught of weather outside. Ian shivered, unable to shake the thought that perhaps his brother was right.

CHAPTER ELEVEN

Ian did not fall asleep immediately. The storm gathered in volume as it swept in from the sea, carrying more freezing rain and hail, shaking the window frames and rattling the panes. He lay awake listening to the howl of the wind, imagining the creatures out in the fields beyond town, huddled miserably against each other in wet masses, waiting out the storm. He was glad to have a warm bed and a fire to come home to, but could not escape thoughts of Edinburgh's unluckier citizens, with little more shelter than sheep or cattle out in cold, comfortless pastures.

When he finally fell asleep, he drifted in and out of disturbing dreams before finding himself in his parents' house before the fire. Somehow vaguely aware he was dreaming, Ian drifted from room to room, looking for other members of his family, when he heard raised voices coming from behind a closed door.

His parents were arguing, though he was unable to make out what they were saying. He put an ear to the keyhole but could not distinguish actual words, though it was clear they were both agitated. His mother rarely expressed anger, and it was startling to hear the edge in her voice. As he listened, his dog, Rex, pushed his wet nose into Ian's palm. Ian stroked his head absently, but the dog poked his muzzle more insistently into his hand, as if trying to get Ian's attention.

Turning away from the closed door, Ian smelled smoke, terror filling his being so completely he was unable to move. He tried to knock on the door, but his body would not obey his commands. His throat was equally unresponsive to his frantic attempts to call out, frozen, as if panic had drained the air from his body. The smoke thickened, filling the hallway, and he could hear the hiss and crackle of flames coming from behind him.

He finally managed to turn around, and through the gathering smoke, he saw a figure coming toward him. It was a human form but seemed to be made of fire. As it approached Ian, he saw that it was wearing a long, gleaming white robe. From its head sprouted a single flame, like the head of a candle. Neither the age nor the sex of the creature was evident, and as it came closer, it stretched its shimmering arms toward him.

He awoke with a gasp, the smell of smoke still in his nostrils. He tiptoed through the silent flat to see the fire smoldering feebly in the grate. His brother lay fast asleep on the sofa, a discarded medical textbook on the carpet next to him. Bacchus had reclaimed his spot on Donald's stomach, glancing sleepily at Ian through half-closed eyes. The ticking of the hall clock was the only sound apart from his brother's light snoring. The freezing rain had abated, leaving a moody, starless sky as a sliver of moon struggled to break through the clouds.

Since Donald was on the sofa, Ian wondered what had become of Derek. The last he remembered was his brother ushering the sleepy boy from his bedroom. Tiptoeing into Donald's room, he found Derek fast asleep in his brother's bed, nearly obscured beneath a mountain of quilts. Had the cold the boy endured day after day seeped into his bones, so that no amount of blankets could warm him? He wondered if Donald had given up his bedroom out of sentiment, or simply fallen asleep before reclaiming it. He knew Donald well enough to know that if questioned about it, his brother would claim he had merely surrendered to exhaustion while studying.

Ian padded back to his own room, feeling somehow less lonely, comforted by the presence of others in his flat. Climbing beneath the bedclothes, he stared out the window at the inky December night. A few months ago, sharing his living quarters with anyone else would have filled him with dread; a year ago it would have been unthinkable. Yet here he was, comforted by the presence of three other sentient beings in his home. (Donald had debated the issue of whether Bacchus was indeed sentient, though the cat seemed to prefer him to Ian, which Donald claimed only proved the contrary nature of felines.) Ian gazed at the emerging moon as it struggled bravely through the clouds, before he finally fell into a thankfully dreamless sleep.

He awoke to the aroma of bacon and coffee. Throwing on a spare dressing gown, he went through to the dining room to find Derek and his brother feasting on coddled eggs, black bread with jam, and thick slices of bacon.

"Good morning," Donald sang out. "I've just made a fresh pot of coffee."

"What makes you so blasted cheerful today?" Ian said, sitting across from Derek, who was stuffing his face as fast as he could.

"'E's jes foun' out classes are off t'day," the boy muttered through a mouthful of bread, a bit of jam dangling from his chin.

"Really? Why?" Ian said, pouring himself some coffee.

"Conan Doyle stopped by a while ago to say Dr. Bell is attending to the Queen and has canceled all his morning lectures."

"The Queen?"

"Yes, didn't you know? Dr. Bell is HRH Victoria's personal surgeon whenever she's in Scotland."

"Another reason for his arrogance, I suppose," Ian said, pouring cream in his coffee.

"He's not as bad as all that. Doyle gets on with him famously."

"Conan Doyle gets on with everyone."

Disappointed at hearing he had missed his friend, Ian looked at the hall clock. "Good Lord, it's after nine. I'm late! Why didn't you wake me?"

"You were sleeping so peacefully. And you didn't ask me to wake you."

"Blast," Ian muttered, gulping down the rest of his coffee.

"At least have some breakfast," Donald called after him as he hurried back to the bedroom to get dressed.

Ten minutes later he was more or less ready, though the stubble on his cheeks was evidence of his hasty ablutions. Grabbing a slice of bacon, he shoved it between two slices of bread before throwing on his cloak.

"You'll get indigestion!" Donald called after him as he rushed out the door.

It was not far to police chambers, but as he was late, Ian hailed a cab and was soon dashing up the stairs two at a time. He found Sergeant Dickerson already at his desk, engrossed in a pile of papers.

"Studying more investigative techniques, Sergeant?" Ian said, sitting at his own desk.

"Actually, sir, I were jes workin' on my lines fer the play," he said, slipping the papers into a drawer. "You weren't here yet, an' I had a few minutes t'spare. Sorry, sir."

"I'm the one who should apologize for being late."

"Everythin' all right, is it, sir?"

"The fact is, I overslept."

Dickerson shook his head. "You've been workin' too hard as usual."

"Not hard enough, I should think—I don't have any useful leads on who killed Miss Staley."

"It's only been a day, sir. Have you interviewed other people what attend séances?"

"That's precisely what we're doing today. We'll start with Madame herself."

"Yes, sir."

"Bring your notebook. Have you seen DCI Crawford?" Ian said, glancing in the direction of his office.

"I don' believe he's come in yet, sir."

That struck Ian as odd, but he said nothing. He hoped Crawford's wife had not taken a turn for the worse.

"Never mind," he said. "Come along."

It wasn't far to Blackfriars Street, just the other side of South Bridge. When they arrived at Madame Veselka's residence, the front rooms were dark and quiet, and Ian thought no one was at home. But when they knocked, a light went on in the back of the flat. Quick footsteps were followed by the sound of heavy bolts sliding in the front door, which opened to reveal the medium's young servant, Gretchen. She wore an apron over a plain gray frock, her blond braids wound around her head. Even in such unassuming attire, there was something attractive and fresh about her. Her skin glowed with the vitality of youth, her pink cheeks sprinkled with a light dusting of freckles and her cornflower-blue eyes bright and inquisitive.

"Can I help you?" Even her Prussian accent was charming, Ian thought, and it was evident Dickerson felt the same. The sergeant stared at her, his cheeks reddening, as he stammered to find words.

"We're—w-with th' Edinburgh City Police," he said finally.

"Yes," she replied, looking at Ian. "This gentleman is known to me." Though accented, her English was rather good.

Dickerson looked at him quizzically.

"I attended a séance here with my aunt earlier this week," he explained. "And I apologize for my rudeness," he told Gretchen. "My behavior was reprehensible."

"Yes, it was," she said, but he thought he saw a slight smile as she turned away. "Please, do come in."

They followed her into the opulently furnished sitting room, much the same as Ian remembered, minus the candles. In the dim winter light filtering through the lace curtains, it didn't have the same aura of mystery. There was no sign of the Persian cat, though the chair he formerly occupied had a thin layer of long white hairs.

"Madame is in a private consultation at the moment," said Gretchen. "Please, may I bring you some tea?"

"Thank you, no," said Ian, though he could sense Dickerson's disappointment.

She cocked her head to one side. "You Scottish do like your tea, I believe?"

"We do, but—"

Just then the beaded curtain in the back of the room parted, and Madame Veselka stepped through it. Dressed in a simple blue frock, without the kohl eyeliner and rouge, she looked younger than she had the other night. Her wrists and hands were bejeweled as before, but her manner was less affected than he remembered. If she was surprised to see him, she gave no hint of it.

"Good morning, gentlemen." Her accent seemed less pronounced than he remembered.

"Please forgive me, Madame," Gretchen said hastily. "I did not care to interrupt your session."

"It's quite all right, my dear," she replied as a timid-looking young woman carrying an enormous carpet bag emerged from behind the curtain. She wore a dark-blue travel suit and boots that had seen some wear. "Good day, Miss McGundy," Madame said. "Remember what I told you—at the next full moon."

"Yes, Madame," the young lady said shyly, darting past the men toward the front door. Gretchen reached out to open it for her.

"At the full moon," Madame repeated as Miss McGundy slipped through the door. "Now then," she said, turning her attention to the policemen, "please have a seat. Gretchen, some tea, please." When the girl hesitated, Madame turned to Ian. "You will of course join me in a pot of tea? You Scottish enjoy your tea, no?"

Ian was struck by the fact that Gretchen had used nearly the exact same phrase, including the odd grammar. "Yes, thank you," he said, noting the look of relief on Dickerson's face.

"I assume you are not here to apologize," Madame Veselka said, settling into a white painted wicker chair with plush burgundy cushions.

"I do indeed owe you an apology," Ian said. "My behavior—"

She dismissed him with a wave of her jeweled hand. "I should have realized you were not ready for such a revelation. But when the spirits come, there is little I can do to control what they say."

Aware that Dickerson was staring at him, Ian pressed onward. "In any case, I was rude, and I am sorry. But as to the real reason for our visit—" he began, as Gretchen appeared with a tea tray. Dickerson brightened visibly at the sight of a plate piled high with golden flaky pastries.

"Gretchen is an excellent cook," Madame said. "What have we today?"

"Kuchen mit Schlagsahne," Gretchen replied, setting the tray down on the sideboard.

"Pastries with whipped cream," Madame Veselka translated.

"Shall I be the mother?" Gretchen asked. Ian made note of her slightly erroneous use of the common phrase. "How do you like your tea, Detective?"

"Milk and one sugar, please," said Ian.

Once they were served, Madame leaned back in her chair and sipped delicately at her tea. "Now then, Inspector, as to the real reason for your visit. What is it, pray?"

Ian looked at Dickerson, who was biting into a pastry, a look of bliss on his face. "We're here 'bout a murder," he mumbled through flakes of *Kuchen mit Schlagsahne.*

Madame Veselka exchanged a glance with Gretchen. It was hard to tell for certain in the dim light, but Ian thought the girl's face went a shade paler, and she bit her lip.

The medium turned to Ian. "What has that to do with us?"

"I'm sorry to tell you the victim was one of your clients."

Madame's grip tightened on the arm of her chair, but when she spoke, he thought she deliberately tried to sound casual.

"We call them guests, not clients."

"One of your guests, then."

"Indeed? Who is the unfortunate person?"

"Elizabeth Staley."

There was a clattering sound as the teaspoon slipped from Gretchen's fingers and fell to the floor. "Oh, dear, I am most sorry, Madame!" she said, stooping to pick it up.

"No harm done, my dear," the medium replied kindly. "Gretchen was rather fond of Miss Staley, and this is quite a shock, as you can imagine."

"I am sorry to bring you this news."

"How was she—"

"The results are not yet official, but it appears she was bludgeoned."

Gretchen gave a little squeak and clapped her hand over her mouth.

"Oh, dear," said Madame Veselka. "This is most distressing."

Ian looked at Sergeant Dickerson, who was digging into his second pastry. "Your notebook, Sergeant?"

"Right—sorry, sir!" he said, hastily extracting it from his pocket.

"How long has Miss Staley been coming here?"

"*Sechs*—six months," Gretchen blurted out.

"Surely not that long," Madame Veselka corrected her. "Isn't it more like four months?"

"Perhaps you are right, Madame. Yes, of course," the girl replied, looking away. "Not more than four months. But she has not missed a week, I think."

"Can you think of anyone who might wish her harm?"

The medium shook her head. "I know very little of her, apart from the fact that she has a dead sister—she came to me desperate to contact her."

"Did she have any success?"

"She did, I am glad to say."

"Which explains her continuing presence month after month."

Madame Veselka frowned. "There is no guarantee that those on the other side will cooperate, Inspector. I explain that to all my guests."

"And yet you seem to have an impressive success rate."

She fixed him with a critical stare, and he noticed for the first time how large her dark eyes were, the irises almost as black as the pupils. "You have made your position clear, Mr. Hamilton," she said icily. "However," she continued, leaning into him, "you cannot hide forever. What happened the other night was no fluke, I can assure you."

Sergeant Dickerson frowned and bit the tip of his pencil. "Wha' is she on about, sir?"

"Nothing of import, Sergeant," Ian replied.

"Is there a record book of your—guests?" Dickerson asked.

"I'm afraid not."

"Could you make us one?" said Ian.

"I suppose so. I have a good memory for people."

"I would like a list of your current and recent guests as soon as you can manage."

"Certainly. I'll have Gretchen bring it to you."

"How long have you been in Edinburgh?" said Ian.

"Let me think . . . it's going on seven years, now, isn't it, Gretchen?"

The girl nodded vigorously as she refilled Madame's teacup. *"Ja, sieben Jahre."*

"And Gretchen has been with you the whole time?" the sergeant said, writing in his notebook.

"I don't know what I'd do without her," she replied with a sigh. "More milk, please, dear," she added, and Gretchen scurried over with the cream pitcher.

"She came over with you from . . . ?" said Ian.

"Europe," Madame Veselka answered with a smug little smile.

The cat that ate the canary, Ian thought. "Could you be more specific?" he said, knowing it was a lost cause.

"Here and there. We both moved around a lot."

Dickerson was undeterred. "But you were born where?"

"I am Russian, and Gretchen is from a Prussian family."

"May I ask what is your surname?" Ian said to Gretchen.

"Mueller," she replied softly. "It is German for—"

"Miller," said Ian. "I have a little German."

"A common enough name," Madame said, sniffing.

"Did Miss Staley socialize with any of your other guests—outside of your séances, I mean?" said Ian.

"I know very little of what goes on outside of here, I'm afraid. I wish I could be more helpful," she said, rising, "but I have a private consultation arriving any minute, and I must prepare myself."

"Thank you for your time," Ian said, handing Gretchen his teacup.

Sergeant Dickerson stood up, a cascade of pastry crumbs tumbling to the floor like sailors deserting a sinking ship. "Here's my card if y'think of anythin' else." Gretchen stepped forward and took it, handing it to the madame. "Ta very much fer tea an' cakes."

"She really was anxious to speak with you, you know," Madame Veselka told Ian, laying a heavily jeweled hand on his arm.

He recoiled from her touch and mumbled something about being late for another interview.

"You should not be afraid," she murmured softly as they headed toward the door. Ian tried to cover his discomfort with a cough, which fooled no one. He could sense Dickerson's curiosity as they put on their coats.

The ever-helpful Gretchen saw them out, and as they turned to leave, she stepped onto the stoop.

"I saw Miss Staley speaking with the major after the session. I could not make out what they were saying, but I had the feeling they knew each other."

"Thank you, Miss Mueller," Ian said, wondering why she was reluctant to tell them in front of her employer. "If you think of anything else, please contact me—anytime," he added, handing her his card.

"Danke schön." She slipped it into her apron pocket. "I must go," she said, and slipped back inside, closing the door behind her.

"What do you think of Madame Veselka?" Ian asked as they walked north on Blackfriars Street.

"She's a close one, she is," Dickerson replied as they passed the United Presbyterian Church. It was built in 1871, but its sharply steep gables and tall, narrow windows evoked the city's medieval past. Though not a believer, Ian loved churches, and it was one of his favorites.

"Did you note her response when we mentioned the murder?"

"No, sir."

"She asked what that had to do 'with us'—not 'with me,' but *us.*"

"An' what would be the significance of that, sir?"

"It implies a closer relationship with Gretchen than simply mistress and servant."

"Wha' d'ye think that would be?"

"That is a very good question, Sergeant," Ian said as they turned the corner onto the High Street.

"What were all that 'bout someone wantin' to speak wi' you, sir?"

"Just a fanciful notion she has about a dead person trying to contact me."

"Did it happen at séance, sir?"

"As DCI Crawford would say, it's all bosh and bunkum."

"Is it, sir?"

"It is indeed," Ian said as they sidestepped a wagon full of potatoes and turnips wobbling unsteadily up the High Street, pulled by a sleepy-looking chestnut mare. But a tiny seed of doubt began to sprout in his mind, making him wonder how much longer he could trust his own beliefs about anything.

CHAPTER TWELVE

They passed Bell's Wynd, where a thinly dressed girl in a dingy frock and tattered shawl was selling watercress from a weather-beaten basket. Ian fished a half crown from his pocket and gave it to her. Her eyes widened as she looked up at him.

"Ye've made a mistake, sir—"

"It's no mistake."

"I haen't got enough change fer—"

"No change."

"It's a farthin' for one bunch a' cress, sir—"

"I don't want any cress."

"But sir—" She held the money out to him, her hand trembling.

"Please," Ian said, closing her fingers over the money. "Keep it."

"At least tae' one, sir," she said, thrusting a bunch of cress at him.

"Very well," he said, his hand closing on hers. It was thin and frail as a baby bird, the fingers like icicles beneath the thin woolen gloves. He whipped his scarf from his neck and wound it around hers. "Thank you," he said, giving her hand a squeeze.

They walked on, her shrill voice trailing after them.

"Oh, *thank* ye, sir! God bless ye!"

"Here, Sergeant," Ian said, handing him the cress. "Does your sister like cress?"

"She does—thank you, sir."

They continued in silence, though Ian had a feeling Sergeant Dickerson was bursting to say something. As they neared police chambers, a familiar voice rang out from behind them through the clear wintry air. "Is it true, Detective?"

Ian responded without turning around. "If you've heard it, it's probably not true."

"It's from a reliable source."

Ian continued walking as an out-of-breath Jedidiah Corbin hurried to catch up to him.

"You're a hard man to find," he said, panting as he matched Ian's stride.

"It depends on who's looking. You really should see to your fitness, Corbin—you're quite winded."

"I've run all the way from Cockburn Street."

The High Street sloped uphill steadily from Holyrood Palace to Edinburgh Castle, the grade becoming steeper as it approached the castle.

"That isn't such a great distance," Ian remarked.

Cockburn Street was the location of the offices of the *Scotsman*, Edinburgh's premier newspaper, and Jedidiah Corbin was their star crime reporter. Even shorter than Sergeant Dickerson, he was thin and wiry as a whippet, with close-cut dark hair and small, keen eyes that missed little. Now those eyes darted from Ian's face to the notebook Sergeant Dickerson was carrying.

"I'll reveal what I know and you can tell me if I'm on the right scent," he said. "Agreed?"

"What have you heard?" asked Ian as they approached the station house.

"There's been a murder."

"This is Edinburgh. There's always a murder. You'll have to be more specific."

"A teacher. An attempt was made to make it look like an accident."

Ian stopped walking. "Where did you—?"

Corbin smiled. "Your reaction answers my question. Is Dr. Littlejohn being brought in on the case?"

"If he is, no doubt you'll be the first to know."

"A fine doctor," the reporter said. "Though he does have that odd habit of repeating himself—"

"DCI Crawford will decide what facts are to be released to the public," Ian said, opening the door to 192 High Street. "And now if you will excuse us—"

"I'll be in touch," Corbin called after them as Ian and Dickerson entered the building.

"Y'don' like 'im much, do ye, sir?" said the sergeant as they trudged up the stairs.

"He's just doing his job."

"Are y'gonna tell 'im wha's happenin'?"

"That's entirely up to DCI Crawford," Ian replied, swinging open the double door leading to police chambers.

No sooner had they reached their desks than DCI Crawford charged out of his office, waving a piece of paper.

"The autopsy report is in," he said, thrusting it in front of Ian. "Elizabeth Staley was killed by a heavy blow to the head. Dr. Bell says it was inconsistent with a fall down the stairs—in fact, he's rather convinced the murder weapon was a hammer, or something like it."

Ian studied the report. Under "Manner of Death," it read, *Homicide by Person or Persons Unknown.*

"You were right," said Crawford. "Now you just have to find out who did it."

"The fact that we didn't find the weapon suggests it was planned."

"So the killer may have brought it with him."

"Or her," Ian added.

Crawford frowned and picked at his whiskers. "A woman? Come now, Hamilton."

"May I remind you, sir, of the recent case—"

"Yes, but those were poisonings. Poison is a woman's business, but surely not this."

"We must not rule out anything this early."

"We don' know what may be missin' from the house," Dickerson pointed out. "So the killer could've used sommit 'e found there, an' taken it when 'e left."

"Good point, Sergeant," said Ian.

"That nosy reporter from the *Scotsman* is sniffing around," said the chief. "Trying to get a scoop."

"He already knows some of the facts," said Ian. "I told him you would release information as you deemed appropriate."

Crawford sighed. "I suppose we'll have to make an announcement at some point. Until then, it's all under wraps, eh?"

Out of the corner of his eye, Ian could see Constable Turnbull loitering at the tea service area, watching them. When Ian looked in his direction, he slinked around the corner into the back room. Ian suddenly realized how Jed Corbin probably got his information. He considered telling Crawford, but having no proof, decided that would be a mistake.

"You weren't in this morning when I arrived," he said. "Is your wife all right, sir?"

"Moira's health is continuing to improve, thanks to Dr. Bell. I hear he's attending to the Queen this week," he added with a conspiratorial wink.

"Yes, he canceled his lectures this morning. My brother was quite pleased at being able to sleep in for a change."

"I can imagine," Crawford said agreeably, but seemed distracted. "Would you two step into my office for a moment?" Such politeness was odd—the chief rarely asked when he could command.

Once in the office, he closed the door behind them.

"I've some more specific information regarding that upcoming robbery," he said, lowering his voice.

"Oh?" said Ian.

"It's supposed to take place late next week—Thursday or Friday," Crawford said, lowering himself into his chair slowly, wincing.

"Are you quite all right, sir?" said Ian.

"Yes, yes," Crawford replied, waving him off, and Ian wondered if the chief's own health was the reason for his tardiness this morning. Crawford picked up a piece of string and twisted it between his fingers— his "rosary," the men called it.

"How did you come by this information?" asked Ian.

"Constable Turnbull told me."

Ian glanced at Sergeant Dickerson, whose lips were compressed in a frown.

"Turnbull, sir?" said Ian.

"Why—do you have a problem with him?"

"I can't help wondering where he got it from."

"He didn't care to reveal his source—any more than you did, may I remind you."

Ian saw no rebuttal to that. He took a deep breath. "So he could not be certain whether it would be on Thursday or Friday?"

"No, he couldn't," Crawford replied testily. "But I should think you'd be bloody glad to have it narrowed down."

"We are, sir," Sergeant Dickerson interjected. "It's just—"

"What?"

Dickerson shot Ian a desperate glance.

"We can't be certain if it's reliable, sir," Ian said.

"Why the bloody hell not?" Crawford exploded, tossing his bit of string on the desk.

"We don't know if his source can be trusted."

"And yet *yours* can?"

"Yes, sir. Exactly."

The chief sighed, all the wind going out of him as if from a deflated balloon.

"Very well, Hamilton—you may ask Constable Turnbull if he'll share his source with you."

"Thank you, sir," he said, knowing full well that was a useless venture. "Is that all, sir?"

"Yes. Keep me posted on the Staley investigation, eh?"

"Will do, sir."

When they returned to the main room, Turnbull was nowhere to be seen. Sergeant Dickerson followed Ian to his desk.

"Wha's eatin' the chief, d'you think?"

"I wish I knew. He does seem distracted."

"He seemed t'be in pain."

"Yes, he did."

"I hope it's nothin' serious."

Ian looked out the window. The sun was slowly creeping behind a cloud, as though trying to escape its task of illuminating a city that, it seemed to Ian, was growing darker by the hour.

CHAPTER THIRTEEN

It was a pity, it really was, you think as the lemony light creeps in through the kitchen curtains, turning the glass on the windows opaque. Some revenge was indeed sweet, but it was too bad the teacher had to die, you think as you put the kettle on. She was culpable, of course, but the least guilty of the lot, and you are glad she is out of the way. It was smart to start with her. If you could eliminate her, you could certainly manage to do the rest of them.

Gazing out at the small garden below, you contemplate your next move. You are pleasantly surprised at how easy and natural it all felt; it was quite gratifying, after months of careful planning. Of course, you always were a planner; even as a small child, you thought out your actions carefully before embarking on any course of action, even though other children made fun of you, calling you an old fuddy-duddy. Well, what did they know? you think as a secret smile plays across your lips. They couldn't even contemplate such momentous acts, let alone pull them off.

The kettle whistle rises from a thin, breathy whisper to a shrill, full-bodied scream. You are grateful she made no such sound, you think as you warm the pot, swirling the water around until the porcelain is warm to the touch, ready to receive the delicate tea leaves. You weren't sure what it would actually be like, even with all the planning. She might have howled like a banshee, but she didn't. She made almost no noise at all, just a soft grunt when the blow was struck, the kind of sound you might make stubbing your toe, a startled, muted utterance of pain—but thankfully, there was no screaming.

And then she dropped like a stone, hitting the floor hard, tumbling right down the stairs. That was another surprise—you had thought she might fight back, cry, beg, plead for her life, but luckily that blow was well aimed and so hard it felled her immediately. By the time she hit the bottom step, she was dead.

You hadn't planned to do it on the stairs, but when she headed to the cellar to fetch the jam, it all felt so right. How easy to make it look like she had simply fallen—and you enjoyed adding a few little touches, like the spilled basket of laundry. It all felt so unreal and a little thrilling, like putting together the set for a stage play.

Yes, you think as you inhale the sweet, stringent aroma of the leaves, stirring the golden-brown liquid in the pot, it was thrilling. Unexpectedly, strangely exciting. It wasn't just the accomplishment of revenge—that was gratifying—but it was more than that. It was heady, electrifying, and it took your breath away.

The sun makes a final pass across the window, moist from the steaming kettle, the garden outside embraced in a soft mist, like a scene in a dream. You take a deep breath as you pour your tea, watching the milk cut through the golden brew. You realize now what it was you felt.

It was the feeling of complete, unfettered freedom, and you wanted more.

CHAPTER FOURTEEN

"I'd like to show you something," Ian told Sergeant Dickerson as they shared a midafternoon pot of tea. Neither had eaten since breakfast, but Hamilton barely seemed to notice.

"Yes, sir?" Dickerson said, stuffing another biscuit into his mouth to quell his grumbling stomach. He was always amazed by DI Hamilton's endless obsession with his work. He struggled to keep up, but in truth he often longed to spend more time with his younger sister, to say nothing of his pretty girlfriend, Caroline Tierney. But lately it seemed his whole life revolved around the station house. He wanted to be a good policeman but sometimes resented DI Hamilton's single-minded devotion to duty, wondering why the detective didn't seem to have other interests in his life.

Ian put down his mug of tea and went to the supply closet, where he dug out an artist's easel.

"I have in mind a kind of murder chart," he said, taking up a soft lead pencil. On the left side of the blank paper clipped to the easel, he wrote *Suspects*. "Now then, what does each suspect need in order to be the actual killer?"

Dickerson felt put on the spot. He tried to imagine what answer Hamilton was looking for. He struggled to think, but his mind suddenly felt filled with cotton. He looked at the detective, who was waiting patiently, long arms crossed, his deep-set gray eyes keen.

"Uh . . . a reason t'kill?"

"Excellent!" Hamilton exclaimed. "Well done." He turned and wrote *Impetus* above and to the right of *Suspects*. "What else?"

Feeling emboldened, Dickerson relaxed. "I s'pose they'd need . . . sommit t'do th'deed with. A murder weapon, like?"

"Exactly!" Hamilton crowed, and wrote *Method* on the far side of the board, across from *Impetus*. "A gun, a vial of poison, a fireplace poker—"

"Or a hammer."

"Precisely. That leaves only one more essential element."

Dickerson swallowed his remaining bit of biscuit and scratched his head. Detective Hamilton could be cloudy and close, but now he looked happy as a child with a new toy. The sergeant wanted to extend this good mood, but even more he craved Hamilton's approval. "Uh . . . can y'give me a hint?"

"In order to kill someone, generally you have to come into proximity to them."

"That's a good point, sir." He wasn't entirely sure what "proximity" meant but was not about to admit it.

"So that means the killer needs to have—"

Dickerson squinted at the board, as if the answer lay there.

"Opportunity!" Ian exclaimed, writing the word on the board.

"I see, sir," Dickerson said, disappointed at failing to come up with the answer.

"So we have *Impetus*, *Opportunity*, and *Method*," Hamilton continued, underlining them.

The sergeant gazed longingly at the empty biscuit tin, wishing it would magically transform into a steak and kidney pie.

". . . which means every viable suspect must have all three," Hamilton was saying. Dickerson struggled to absorb what the detective was saying, but thoughts of a meat pie vied for his attention.

"Are you quite all right, Sergeant?" Hamilton said, staring at him.

"Yes, sir. It's just—"

"What?"

"Well, I'm hungry, sir."

"Why didn't you say so!" The detective fished some money from his pocket and handed it to him. "Why don't you get us both a couple of meat pies?"

Dickerson didn't have to be asked twice. "Thank you, sir!" he said, sprinting from the station so fast he neglected to put on his overcoat. Out in the street, he immediately regretted it as the icy December air hit him full in the face. Though it was only midafternoon, the sun was sinking rapidly toward the horizon, and there was already an evening chill in the air. Blowing on his hands, he headed toward the pie seller in front of St. Giles.

"G'day, Sergeant!" the man called out cheerfully upon seeing one of his most loyal customers. "What'll it be t'day? No more steak and kidney left—all I've got at this hour is mutton or bridie pies." He was tall and thin as a scarecrow, with a voice shrill and sharp as a pennywhistle. He always wore the same moth-eaten scarf around his neck in winter, and no matter the weather, was unfailingly cheerful.

"Two—no, three bridies, please," Dickerson said, anxious to fill his empty stomach with as much food as possible. He was especially fond of bridie pies, said to be named after a midcentury pie seller by that name. He would have ordered yet another, but didn't want Hamilton to think him a glutton.

"Three pies it is," the pie man said, handing him a steaming paper bag.

"Ta very much," Dickerson said, handing him the coins. "Keep the change, mate," he added, his mouth filling with saliva as he headed back toward the police station.

As he neared the building, he thought he saw someone in a policeman's uniform duck into the entrance to Parliament Square. The growing darkness made it hard to make out the man's features, but the heavy shoulders and rolling gait resembled Constable McKay's. Quickening his steps, Dickerson turned right at the intersection, walking rapidly until he had passed the Mercat Cross. He peered down the street, but there was no sign of anyone. The street ran alongside the eastern edge of the cathedral before taking a sharp right turn to run directly behind it. There was no one in sight before the turn, so he decided to give up his pursuit, turning his steps back in the direction of the police station.

When he arrived, Hamilton seemed to barely notice he had been gone, ignoring the pie Dickerson placed on his desk. There was something inhuman about the detective, he thought as he munched his pies, savoring the buttery crust and minced beef and onion filling. Studying his board, Hamilton's eyes shone with the familiar gleam the sergeant knew so well. When he was deep in a case, nothing else seemed to matter.

Beneath the word *Suspects*, he had written *Mme. Veselka*, *Gretchen*, and *Major*, drawing a line across the board beneath each name.

"Are they all suspects, then, sir?" Dickerson asked as he gulped down his first pie.

"Until they are eliminated. Of course, her killer may be completely unrelated to the séance group, but it's as good a place to start as any."

"Don' ye need another column fer alibi, then?"

Hamilton stopped what he was doing, and for a moment Dickerson was afraid he was irritated. But he clapped his hands enthusiastically. "Well done, Sergeant!" Dickerson breathed a sigh of relief as Hamilton applied himself writing *Alibi* on the far right side, creating a new row for each suspect.

"That's the stuff," he said, laying down his pencil and admiring his handiwork. "Between us, we'll get the job done—eh, Sergeant?"

"Yes, sir," Dickerson replied, starting in on his second pie.

"Ah," Hamilton said, as if seeing the pies for the first time. "What have we today?"

"Bridie pies, sir," the sergeant mumbled through a mouthful of flaky crust and savory spiced meat. He sighed with contentment—the second pie tasted even better than the first.

"Oh! I nearly forgot," said Ian. "There was a young man at the séance. I believe my aunt said he was the major's son. Can't recall his name—James, Jerry—"

"Jeremy," said a woman's voice behind them. "Jeremy Fitzpatrick."

Dickerson turned and saw Gretchen Mueller standing near the desk sergeant's station. Dressed in a hooded crimson cloak, bright yellow braids wound like thick pretzels around her head, she looked like something out of a fairy tale.

Dickerson leapt from his chair and escorted her past half a dozen policemen, all staring unabashedly. She was not beautiful—her cheeks were chubby, and her eyes too close set—but she was pink cheeked and young and fresh as a loaf of baked bread. It was no wonder the men stared, he thought, scowling at them for good measure, feeling both protective and possessive of her.

Ian smiled as she approached, but when she saw the murder chart, she blanched and sank into the nearest chair. "Y-you believe I kill this poor woman?" she stuttered.

"Not necessarily," Ian said. "We merely haven't eliminated you as a potential suspect."

"B-but I had no reason to vant her dead!" the girl protested, her accent becoming more pronounced. "She gafe money to Madame, vich enables Madame to keep me on as her servant. And I—I barely know poor Miss Staley."

"That may be, Miss Mueller," Ian replied. "But we must consider all people who knew Miss Staley, however casually."

"And Madame? Why vould she kill a perfectly good cli—uh, guest?"

"Please don' worry yerself," Dickerson said, impulsively taking her hand. It was warm and moist—her palms were sweating. He felt a rush of sympathy for her and anger at Hamilton for treating her in such a callous manner. "No one's suggestin' y'killed her," he said soothingly. "Puttin' yer name on t'board is jes formality." Hamilton pursed his lips in a frown, but Dickerson was not dissuaded. "Now then," he said. "Wha' brings y'here?"

She held up a single sheet of paper. "I brought the list you requested."

"Thank you, Miss Mueller," Hamilton said, taking it from her. "Please thank Madame for us as well."

She nodded, but her lower lip trembled. Dickerson took her hand again and squeezed it. "Why don' I get you a nice cuppa, eh?"

"No, thank you—I must be returning to Madame's," she said, rising from her chair. "She needs her supper early—there is a reading tonight."

"At least let me see y'out," he said, taking her gently by the elbow. He looked back at Hamilton, but the detective was immersed in examining the list.

After escorting Gretchen out, he returned to find Hamilton studying the murder chart, the untouched meat pie still on his desk. Dickerson sat moodily, arms crossed, staring at his own half-eaten pie, his appetite vanished. After a few minutes, Hamilton stopped what he was doing and picked up the list Gretchen had brought them.

"This list contains the names of only two persons who were not at last week's séance, Mr. and Mrs. Nielsen." When Dickerson did not reply, Hamilton looked at him. "Are you quite all right?"

"Not really, sir."

"What's the matter?"

"May I speak freely, sir?"

"Certainly."

"I don' like the way y'treated young Gretchen."

"How so?"

"She were truly frightened, and—well, ye didn' seem t'care."

"Oh, but I did care."

"Ye didn' show it."

"I want her to return to Madame Veselka and tell her we mean business."

"Is that any reason t'frighten an innocent young woman?"

"How do you know she's innocent?"

"Well, I—"

"You assume because she's young and pretty that she isn't capable of murder."

"It's not that—"

"It's perfectly all right," Hamilton said with a smile that was too smug for Dickerson's taste. "You're only human, and she is appealing."

The sergeant felt himself redden, and cursed his light complexion. "Might I remin' you I've already got a lady friend, which is more than you—"

"Your gallantry does you credit," Hamilton said, ignoring the slight, which only angered Dickerson more.

"Look, sir," he said. "I jes believe in treatin' people kindly, especially a poor young orphan like her."

"What makes you think she's an orphan?"

"Why else would she leave her homeland an' work fer someone like the madame?"

"I can think of several reasons. One obvious one would be because she's a criminal fleeing prosecution."

That silenced Dickerson at last. He saw the reason in the detective's argument—Hamilton was always so damned logical—but it hardly placated him.

"Wha'ever ye say," he muttered.

"Look, Sergeant," Hamilton said, sitting down across from him. "Crime solving isn't always pretty, and innocent people can get caught up in an investigation. But I will promise you this. If I can clear Gretchen from suspicion, I will, as soon as humanly possible. Very well?"

"As ye wish, sir," Dickerson said, but something in his regard for the detective had snapped. A sour cloud of disillusion settled over him; he felt miserable and restless. He looked out the window, where even the sun had given up on the city of Edinburgh, which lay in a winter darkness as complete as any he had ever seen.

CHAPTER FIFTEEN

By the time Ian left the station house, the evening shift had arrived. Dickerson had left early, ostensibly to go to rehearsal, but was obviously irritated and out of sorts. Ian was sorry the sergeant disapproved of his methods, but that did not dampen his resolve. Throwing his cloak round his shoulders, he headed out into the clear, cold night, stopping to buy another handful of watercress from the poor ragged girl in front of Bell's Wynd.

"Oh, it's you, sir," she said, smiling shyly.

"Hello again," he said, pressing some coins into her hand.

"It's still a farthin' for one bunch, sir," she said, looking at them.

"Please take it. It would make me happy."

"Oh, thank ye, sir." Her pale eyes welled with tears as she handed him her finest bunch of cress. "God bless ye!"

"God bless you, too," he murmured, though he had no belief in such a being.

He turned toward home, past the bravely flickering lamps in front of St. Giles. They were often the first lamps to be lit on the High Street, the leeries climbing the rungs of their tall ladders to give light to Edinburgh's High Kirk, named after the patron saint of cripples.

As he passed the church, Ian's shoulder throbbed, as if to remind him of his own disfigurement. Ignoring it, he lowered his head and bent into the wind. Burned in the fire that killed his parents seven years ago, his shoulder still bothered him. Nerve damage, Donald had said. It was an obvious physical scar, but he had come to think of everyone as damaged in some way. Donald was broken in one way, Ian in another. In what way was Lillian broken, he wondered, that led her to seek the guidance of shady mediums in stuffy sitting rooms, surrounded by other desperate, lonely souls?

And who had deemed it necessary to take the life of one of those wretched souls? What sort of person had so violently ripped poor Elizabeth Staley from the ranks of the living, so intent on her death that they were willing to risk the hangman's noose?

Rounding the corner onto George IV Bridge, Ian caught a glimpse of the castle on its perch high atop the dark rock overlooking the city. The spot was an obvious one for a fortress—indeed, there had been a royal castle there at least since King David's reign in the twelfth century, and a fort of some kind for many millennia prior to that. But though easy to defend, parapets were lonely, removed from the everyday hustle and bustle of humanity—the price of safety was remoteness and isolation. Drawing his cloak closer to his body, Ian contemplated his own impulse for solitude. Had he made a bargain that was no longer viable? Humanity was messy and untrustworthy, but by isolating himself, was he not turning away from life itself?

Crime solving was seldom glamorous. Much of the time, it was merely sad—an overworked husband turning to gambling or stealing, first out of desperation to provide for his family, later just for the thrill of it. The more he got away with, the more invincible he felt, until he made the mistake that landed him in jail. Ian knew it all too well—the shocked looked of recognition, eyes narrowing like a cornered animal's as the detective strode in accompanied by a brace of uniformed constables. That was followed by an unconvincing plea of innocence, which soon gave way to a snarl of defiance as the suspect was placed into custody. Later, in court, there was the defeated sag of the shoulders when the man was sentenced to his fate—invariably leaving behind a family in worse shape than before.

Then there were the career criminals, thoroughly degraded human beings who had lost all sense of honor or shame. Ian was intent on bringing these miscreants to justice. They had no care for others, no sense of moral responsibility. He did not like to think such creatures existed, yet knew better than anyone that they walked largely undetected amid the swarm of humanity that was Edinburgh.

These cheerless thoughts were interrupted by his arrival at his flat on Victoria Terrace, and he opened the door to the friendly smell of beef and cabbage. His brother appeared in the foyer, an apron tied round his bulging middle, hands covered in flour, his face flushed. Bacchus sauntered in behind him, tail swaying languidly.

"I say," said Ian, hanging up his cloak. "You've been busy on your day off."

"Idle hands are the devil's workshop," Donald said, wiping his hands on a tea towel. "I've just put the pie in the oven, so it'll be a while till supper."

"It smells brilliant."

"Beef and cabbage, peas and tatties—good hearty Scottish fare."

"I bought some cress," Ian said, handing it to Donald.

"That will do nicely," his brother said as Ian followed him into the parlor.

Ian looked around for signs of Derek. "Where's—"

"Master McNair decided he'd had enough of my company and set off to poach chickens, pinch apples, pick pockets—whatever young scallywags do."

"You didn't—"

"I was gentle as a lamb. He was just restless—you know how young people can be."

"Still, it's a cold night."

"I'll wager he's endured colder."

"I suppose you're right," Ian said, pouring himself a brandy and sitting by the fire. Bacchus crept onto his lap, purring loudly, turning circles until he was satisfied with his perch. The cat's weight was comforting, the flames mesmerizing, and Ian felt his eyelids grow heavy. The next thing he knew, he awoke with a start, Donald's voice in his ear.

"Dinner is served."

Ian rubbed his eyes. "I'm sorry—I fell asleep."

"And here I thought you were just ignoring me," Donald said, spreading a linen cloth on the mahogany table. "You were out cold."

"'He that sleeps feels not the toothache.'"

"Dear me, have you a toothache?"

"I was quoting—"

"Ah, yes," Donald said, heading for the kitchen, Bacchus trotting after him. "Your penchant for quoting the Bard doesn't annoy me nearly as much as it does DCI Crawford. You really should take pity on the poor fellow," he said, returning with two steaming plates of food. "Now come along, before it gets cold."

The meat pie was mouth-watering, though Ian's hunger certainly played a role in his appreciation. After several minutes, he put down his fork and regarded his brother.

"Where did you learn to cook like this?"

Donald flicked a bit of meat toward the cat, who picked at it delicately. "I spent some time in Glasgow during my rambles. Learned it from an old salty dog who liked his drink as much as I did—fat lot of good it did him."

"What happened to him?"

"His liver finally decided it had had enough. I was with him at the end—not a pretty sight. And yet I kept on, telling myself the lies all drunkards do," he added with a sigh.

"Never mind," Ian said. "You've sorted it now."

"Have I? I often feel I'm a step or two ahead of my demons, and sometimes I can feel them breathing down the back of my neck."

"Conan Doyle's father suffers from the affliction."

"Ah, yes, so Arthur has said."

Ian felt a pang of jealousy knowing his friend had confided the same things to his brother as he had to Ian, then chided himself for such petty thinking.

"Amiable fellow, isn't he?" Donald said, a bit of cress hanging from his lower lip.

"Very. I'm a bit surprised by his interest in crime."

"If there's one thing I've learned in my travels, it's that people are full of surprises."

"Does that include our parents?"

"Especially our parents. Do you know why I eat more than is good for me?"

"I've a feeling I'm about to find out."

Donald shrugged. "Not if you don't want to."

"No, it's important I learn the truth."

His brother stared into the fire's glowing embers. "I don't wish to tarnish our father's memory even further, but . . ." He heaved a sigh that seemed to reach to the bottom of his soul. "You're aware he treated me rather differently than he did you."

"So you've said."

"I believe he found me disappointing."

"I am sorry to hear it."

Donald dismissed him with a wave of his hand.

"It's not your fault, though it was many years before I accepted that. His treatment of me shaped so many things about me, including my attitude toward food."

"I always felt you enjoyed food more if it wasn't yours."

Donald rose and put another log on the fire. "That's because I was forced to steal it when I was a child."

"What do you mean?"

"Father felt I was too plump, so he did his best to deprive me of food."

"Good Lord. Why on earth—"

"He thought my appearance was . . . unmanly."

"Why didn't Mother—"

"She did what she could. But his will usually prevailed."

"Now that you mention it, I do recall one or two incidents, and I remember sometimes thinking I had been served more than you, but . . . I hardly know what to say."

"Start by saying you'd like another helping of beef pie."

"Yes, please," Ian replied, even though his appetite had evaporated when he heard his brother's confession. Donald rose and went out to the kitchen, and Ian gazed into the fire, as if the answer lay in the rapidly flickering flames.

"You know," Donald said as he came back into the room, "I often wondered if you knew. But now I see that you didn't—not really."

"I'm sorry—truly I am."

"You could not have changed anything. He took no one's counsel but his own."

"He was a respected policeman, though, so surely he—" Donald's look stopped him cold. An icicle of dread pierced his heart. "What is it?" he said.

"It's late, and I have morning rounds with Dr. Bell."

"Please—you cannot just leave me wondering."

"This is too delicate a subject to delve into without—"

"Without what?"

"I was going to say without warning, but the truth is . . ." Donald walked over to the sideboard and grasped the bottle of brandy.

Ian's heart jumped into his throat. "Donald—"

"Calm yourself," he said, refilling Ian's glass. "You have more need of it than I."

Ian drained the snifter in one gulp. "I implore you—"

His brother lowered his bulk into the wing chair in front of the fire, and Ian took the matching one opposite. Donald turned to him, his face shiny in the yellow glow of the fire. "Can you recall a single day when our father did not have a drink?"

Ian thought about the many evenings they spent at home as a family, the summertime trips to the coast, the holidays with Aunt Lillian and Uncle Alfred in Glasgow. In every one of them, he could picture his father with a glass in his hand.

"And yet I don't recall seeing him drunk," he said finally.

"Not in front of us, perhaps."

"Are you saying that—"

Donald held up a hand. "I am not suggesting my problem is anyone's fault but my own. However, it is instructive, don't you think?"

Ian looked at his brother, who sat, head cocked to one side, a strand of blond hair falling over one eye. The cat, curled next to him, looked on impassively. "You need a haircut," Ian murmured, unable to focus on what now struck him as a monumental lack of observation on his part. Donald did not reply. Ian stared at the fire, the embers glowing blue beneath the red and yellow flames.

"Well?" said Donald finally.

"What does it mean?"

"In my experience, one often drinks in an attempt to escape unpleasant thoughts and emotions. And if one finds it impossible to go a day without imbibing, it seems logical to infer that one is trying to avoid rather a lot of unpleasantness."

Ian looked longingly at the bottle of brandy on the sideboard.

"Go ahead," said Donald.

"It's not fair to you."

"I'll enjoy it vicariously."

"No. I've had enough."

Donald studied his fingernails, then looked at Ian. "What do you remember of what he was like as a father?"

"Stern, firm, disciplined . . . strong willed."

"A typical Scottish father, then?"

"What are you implying, exactly?"

"Over time, alcohol seeps into your soul. It changes you—what you care about, what you are capable of. It rots you from the inside. It can alienate you from love itself."

"I always had the feeling he loved Mother."

"She was easy to love," Donald said, his voice soft. "But I fear at some point she stopped caring for him."

"When she took a lover, you mean."

"Did you not notice the chill between them?"

"Now that you mention it, they did seem more distant."

"But being a typical Scottish family, of course we did not speak of such things. And now you may be on the trail of their killer," Donald continued. "What do you intend to do?"

"Find this Nate Crippen fellow, for starters."

"And then what?"

"Shake the truth out of him, if need be."

"Have a care, Ian. You always were too impulsive for your own good."

"Time has tempered us both, I think."

"Perhaps." Donald stretched and yawned. "Tempered or not, it's time for this medical student to slip off to bed, or I shall be useless tomorrow."

"It's strange to hear those words," Ian said. "To think of you as a medical student. What I mean is that it's easier to think of you as a physician," he added hastily in response to the look on his brother's face.

"From your lips to God's ears."

"I never heard that."

"A Hebrew friend of mine in Glasgow used to say it. You know," Donald added, "you're still a long way from solving what happened all those years ago. I suggest you be prepared for more unpleasant surprises. Good night."

"Good night."

Donald padded off to his bedroom, Bacchus trotting close behind. Ian sat gazing at the fire for some time, struggling with facts he thought he had made peace with years ago. The world was not a fair place, there was no guarantee of justice, and evil often prevailed over good. He knew these things, yet tonight he could not help feeling oppressed by the stark reality of it all. The thought that he had not seen his father clearly rankled him most of all. He was aware his father was stern, but always felt he was treated fairly. Obviously Donald had an entirely different experience. How was it he had not seen this? His forehead burned with shame at the thought that he had been so involved with his own comfort and happiness that he missed what was right under his nose. What kind of a detective *was* he that he could not even perceive his own brother's misery?

The fire had long died out when at last he rose and retired to his bedroom. Wrapping himself in the comforter Aunt Lillian had given him last Christmas, he fell into a deep and dreamless sleep.

CHAPTER SIXTEEN

Major George Fitzpatrick was uneasy. Pacing in front of the study window in his well-appointed flat on Royal Terrace, he ruminated on his life, the mistakes he had made, and what to do about the situation now facing him. He had fought in Afghanistan with the Gordon Highlanders and seen action in the Bhutan and Second Ashanti Wars, and his shoulder still carried a piece of the bullet that felled him in Kandahar. Yet the disquiet he felt was paralyzing—a threat was apparently headed his way, but he knew not how it would present itself, nor where or when. He wasn't even certain there was any real danger at all. And yet . . . he broke into a cold sweat as he fingered the letter in the pocket of his dressing gown for the hundredth time that day.

He had memorized it by now, the words etched starkly in his brain.

You will pay for your crimes

I'll come for you when you least expect it

Since receiving it earlier in the day, he had languished in a torpor of indecision. He thought of going to the police, but what could they possibly do about such a vaguely worded threat? He could imagine them ridiculing him—and he would be half inclined to agree with them. What on earth *could* they do, indeed?

No, he thought, better to collect his wits and come up with a plan. He was no stranger to battle strategy and resolved to treat this just like another campaign. Analyze the enemy's strengths and weaknesses, and act accordingly. But the letter writer had the advantage of anonymity— how could he create a defense against an unknown enemy? His mind searched vainly for a foothold of some kind, anything to tip the scales in his favor.

The letter had given him one advantage. It had put him on his guard, no small thing for a seasoned military veteran, he thought as he poured himself a glass of whisky from the crystal decanter on the sideboard. Outside, the sky was rapidly losing light, as the sun slunk off to a long December slumber. A shiver slithered down his spine as he contemplated a sleepless night alone in the empty flat. His son had gone back to school, his wife long dead—how he yearned for her company on this cheerless and lonely winter's eve.

Downing the tumbler of whisky in one gulp, he tightened his hand around the pistol in the pocket of his dressing gown. The feel of the metal against his fingers calmed him—the gun was a familiar friend, his only ally in the upcoming struggle with this mysterious foe. He settled in the wing chair at the far end of the study, where he could see through to the parlor and foyer beyond. The dining room and bedroom were invisible to him, not being in his line of sight, but it was the small kitchen in the back of the flat that worried him most. He had double-locked the door leading to the alley behind the building, wedging a chair beneath the door handle, but a determined assassin could surmount that defense. And so he leaned back in his armchair, resolved to spend the night awake, the gun at his side.

The cuckoo clock over the mantel chirped the hour as a thin line of sweat trickled down his forehead. He swallowed hard, his mouth dry from anxiety and whisky. He craved another drink, but needed a clear head. He licked his lips and tried to relax, listening to the hollow sound of his own heart beating against the cage of his chest. The room continued to darken as the last of the evening light slid across the windowpanes, and he rose to light a fire in the grate. The flicker of gaslight did little to lift his spirits or warm the chill in the air as he resumed his solitary watch.

A knock at the front door sent a jolt through his body and triggered an intake of breath so sharp he nearly choked. He crept slowly to the door, his hand on the pistol in his pocket, and peered through the peephole. A warm rush of relief flooded his body as he saw the person standing on his front stoop.

"Oh, it's you," he said, opening the door. "Come in."

His visitor smiled. "Who were you expecting?"

"No one—never mind. Would you care to join me in a wee dram of whisky?"

"I don't see why not."

"Now then," he said, locking the door behind them, "what brings you here on such a cold night?"

CHAPTER SEVENTEEN

The next morning dawned bright and clear, and Ian awoke shortly after sunrise. When he emerged from his bedroom, Donald was already humming away in the kitchen while Bacchus kept watch at his feet, scouring the floor for stray bits of food.

"Poached eggs and ham," Donald said. "Coffee is on the stove."

"Continue to make yourself this useful, and you may become a permanent fixture," Ian said, pouring himself a cup of the aromatic black liquid.

"Is it too strong?" Donald asked, breaking an egg carefully over a pan of boiling water and vinegar.

"Just right," Ian lied. Donald's coffee was always too thick and bitter, but Ian had no desire to dissuade his brother from his domestic inclinations.

Neither of them mentioned last evening's discussion. The pale sunlight streaming through the front windows erased the previous night's dismal mood, and neither of them seemed willing to break the spell of what promised to be a more cheerful day.

"You said last night you have morning rounds at the infirmary today?" Ian said as they sat down to eat.

"Yes," Donald replied, delicately breaking his poached egg, bright yellow yolk spilling across his plate. "Dr. Bell's duty to HRH Victoria seems to be at an end, at least for the time being."

"Mind if I accompany you?"

"Won't you be late to work?"

"DCI Crawford isn't expecting me until later. I told him I would be out investigating Elizabeth Staley's murder."

"Arthur has a taste for that sort of thing. I'm sure he'll be delighted to see you," Donald said, spreading butter liberally on a piece of bread. "And if you're lucky, you might run into Nurse Stuart," he added with a sly smile.

"Is that meant to be clever?"

"I stand by my opinion that there is a mutual attraction."

"Then you will be gratified to know we are having dinner together tonight."

Donald leaned back in his chair. "Well, well. Don't tell me you're taking my advice at long last."

"I wouldn't take too much credit if I were you," Ian said, reaching for the bramble jelly. "She caught me off guard, and I consented."

Donald's mouth hung open. "She caught you—do you mean to say *she* invited *you* to dine?"

"Quick on the uptake, you are," Ian remarked drily.

"Well, goodness me, brother, isn't that just too topsy-turvy for words?" Donald said, tossing a bit of egg to the cat, who lapped it up greedily.

"See here," Ian said, "the more you revel in the situation, the less likely I shall be to continue to see her."

"Blackmail? From my own little brother?"

"Why do you take such keen interest in my private life?"

"I should think that was obvious, as I have none of my own," Donald replied, his face more serious.

"Oh," Ian said after a moment. "I see."

"Vicarious pleasure seems to be all society allows those such as I. So I implore you not to deprive me of that one small consolation." His voice had regained its jaunty, taunting tone, but Ian sensed the pain behind it.

"Very well," Ian said, rising from the table. "You may observe, mock me, play the matchmaker—whatever makes you happy."

"My happiness would involve considerably more than that," Donald said, mopping up the last of his egg from his plate. "But I shall have to console myself with the glacial progression of your love life. Do try to step it up a bit, won't you?"

Ian did not reply. Though he was not without sympathy, he found the subject of his brother's predilections disquieting, and did not know how to respond.

Fifteen minutes later they were seated in the back of a hansom cab as it rattled over George IV Bridge. Congestion was at a minimum at such an early hour, and they soon turned onto Lauriston Place, passing through the infirmary's wrought-iron gate bordered by its twin stone columns.

After Donald went off to morning rounds, Ian found Conan Doyle in his office, studying a medical textbook, a smoldering pipe by his side.

"Ah, Hamilton!" he said, ushering Ian into the cramped interior, the desk piled high with medical textbooks. "Good of you to come by."

"Do you not find that an unhealthy habit?" Ian said, pointing to the pipe.

"We all must have our vices, mustn't we?" Doyle said with a boyish grin. "Surely you have one or two? Or are you all purity and innocence?"

"Innocence, hardly. As to purity, I have been accused of aspiring toward it, but I can assure you I fall far short of it."

"Quite right, too. Purity is for saints and martyrs. And you don't strike me as the martyr type."

"Certainly no one could accuse me of being a saint."

Doyle leaned back in his chair, stretching his athletic form. "To what do I owe the pleasure of this visit?"

"I have a case involving blood evidence and thought it might be instructive to design a series of experiments involving bloodstains."

"Capital idea! Medicine moves forward through experimentation, yet the science of forensics lags far behind."

"I know of only one case in which blood evidence was presented in court."

Doyle leaned forward. "Do tell, dear fellow!"

"It may strike you as rather obvious, but still—"

"I'm all ears."

"In 1514, a London merchant by the name of Richard Hunne was found hanging in his jail cell, and at first it was deemed to be suicide. But the presence of large amounts of blood in the cell indicated something more sinister."

Doyle smiled. "That is the clumsiest attempt at covering up a murder I have ever heard of."

"It was worse than that. The noose was too small to fit over his head, his hands showed signs of having been tied, and there were multiple other clues leading to a verdict of murder."

"Still, the presence of blood is common at so many crime scenes, and yet no one has made a discipline of studying it."

"Precisely. I propose a series of experiments that will begin to throw a scientific light upon the subject."

Doyle puffed thoughtfully on his pipe. "There are some intriguing advances in forensics on the continent. Have you heard of Alphonse Bertillon?"

"The French policeman who pioneered the use of photography to identify criminals?"

"The same! He is working on a system of physical measurements to identify miscreants."

"That is exactly the kind of scientific precision lacking in forensics."

"I should be glad to—" Doyle began, but a commotion in the hall outside interrupted him. They could hear a woman's shrill voice just outside the office.

"He's deid, I tell ye! Deid as a doornail!"

Doyle rose quickly and opened the door. In the corridor stood a short, dark-haired, middle-aged woman. She wore a white apron over a plain black frock and was clearly distraught. Two nurses were attempting to soothe her, which caused her to protest more loudly.

"Calm yourself, now, dearie," said the older nurse.

"I found him this mornin' when I come in t'clean 'is hoose," she wailed. "Lyin' there in 'is study!"

"Found whom?" said Doyle.

"The major!" she cried, clinging to his sleeve. "Saints preserve us— gun still in 'is hand, bluid everywhere!"

"Take me to him," said Ian. She looked at him wildly, terror in her large brown eyes. "Detective Inspector Ian Hamilton, Edinburgh City Police," he explained.

Her body relaxed somewhat, but she clutched his arm with a claw-like grip. "Mary, Mother of God! Will ye come wi' me?"

"I will."

"God bless ye, sir," she said, not releasing her grasp on his arm. "I'm fair puckled!"

"It's no wonder you're short of breath," he said, gently removing her hand. "You've had quite a shock. I'll fetch a cab straightaway."

Her lip trembled and tears spurted from her eyes. "Per'aps we should bring a doctor along," she said, wringing her hands.

"I'll go," Doyle offered.

"But you're—" Ian began.

"I have no classes until this afternoon. And I'm quite capable of assisting in reviving a wounded man, if he is still alive. This hospital can ill spare a proper doctor for such a task."

Ian turned to the charwoman. "Do you think he may still be alive, Mrs.—"

"McMillan," she said. "That's why I come t'hospital straightaway, y'see, in case there was still life in the poor man."

"You did the right thing," said Ian. "Come along—there's no time to waste!"

The Royal Terrace flat was on the ground floor, and Mrs. McMillan let them in with trembling hands, dropping the keys twice before she managed to open the door. Ian sensed a preternatural stillness as they entered the well-furnished rooms, and as they approached the study, he smelled something even more disturbing. It was an odor all too familiar to him—thick, acrid, and unmistakable.

It was the smell of blood.

CHAPTER EIGHTEEN

"I'm afraid he's beyond the surgeon's art," Conan Doyle said, kneeling next to the body sprawled out on the plush blue Oriental carpet. The top of the victim's head was blown off, but the face was mostly intact. He was clad in a crimson dressing gown, and a service revolver lay next to his right hand.

"I know this man," Ian said. "He is—was—in my aunt's séance group."

"Oh, yes," Mrs. McMillan whimpered, wiping her eyes with an embroidered handkerchief. "The major was fond of his séances. Ne'er missed a session. Oh, he was a bonnie lad. I don' know what cause he had t'kill his poor self."

"It appears to be a single gunshot wound to the side of the head," said Doyle.

"That's odd," Ian remarked. "Why aim for the side of his head? Surely the front would be easier?"

"It might have slipped," said Doyle, straightening up and brushing off his trousers. "Sometimes people intent on committing suicide lose their courage at the last minute. I've even heard of people missing altogether."

"But a military man?"

"I'll admit it seems unlikely."

The blood had soaked deeply into the carpet, and was mostly dry. Ian examined the pistol, which had one round missing from an otherwise full chamber. The bullet was lodged in the far wall, at approximately head level for a man the height of the major. Either he had shot himself—albeit clumsily—or the killer had attempted to make it look like suicide. Pulling a pair of tweezers from his pocket, Ian carefully extracted the bullet and tucked it into his waistcoat pocket.

"That's clever," Doyle remarked.

"What?"

"Carrying tweezers with you."

"You never know when they'll come in handy. Has rigor mortis set in yet?"

"Yes," said Doyle. "The limbs are entirely stiff."

"So that means he died—"

"At least four hours ago, possibly earlier."

Ian turned to Mrs. McMillan. "The door was locked when you let yourself in?"

"Indeed, sir. Nothin' seemed out of the ordinary till . . ." She turned away, overcome.

"You've had a terrible shock," Conan Doyle said. "How about a cup of tea?"

"Oh, thank you, sir. I'll make a pot."

"Nonsense. Show me the kitchen and I'll make it."

"Yes, sir—right this way, sir," she said, leading him toward the kitchen.

Left alone, Ian examined the study. The windows were covered by heavy drapes, another indication the crime had taken place the previous evening. Most sunlight-deprived Scots would throw their curtains wide open on such a beautiful day as this. But the drawn drapes suggested that it was night the last time the major drew a breath in this room. Ian thought the curtains could also indicate something more sinister—that he feared for his life and was hiding from a potential threat.

The room appeared to be extremely organized and tidy, as one might expect from a military man. Everything seemed to be in its place, with no sign of a struggle. The desk contained the usual collection of bills and bank statements, correspondence and legal documents. Nothing that suggested the major was in imminent danger—in fact, it was all quite unremarkable.

Conan Doyle entered the room carrying a tea tray, followed by Mrs. McMillan, clucking and fussing over him.

"Really, sir, ye should've let me do that," she said as he set the tray on a handsome mahogany sideboard. Whatever else the major's life may have been, he had money, Ian thought. "I'll pour, sir," the charwoman said, hovering over the tea service.

"Nonsense," said Doyle, leading her over to the wing chair by the fireplace. "You sit down and rest."

"Most kind o'ye, sir," she said, wiping her eyes with her somewhat soggy handkerchief.

Ian accepted a cup of tea and biscuit gratefully—it had been some time since breakfast. Perching on the window seat, he tried to think of what he might have missed. Mrs. McMillan seemed as thirsty as he was, finishing her cup in one long swallow.

"Have some more," Doyle said, reaching for the pot.

"I'll get it, dearie," she said, rising from her chair.

As she did, Ian noticed a slip of white paper poking out from the seat cushion. Carefully extracting it from the chair, he saw that it was a plain white envelope. It was empty, but *Major Fitzpatrick* was printed on the front in block letters.

"What have you there?" asked Doyle.

"I'm not certain," said Ian. "But it does strike me as a curious anomaly in the home of a man who appears to have prized orderliness. Am I right, Mrs. McMillan? Did the major like a tidy home?"

"Goodness me," she said. "So he did. I ne'er did see a man so regular in his habits. Why, a single pen out of place could set him off."

"Do you recognize this envelope?" he asked, handing it to her.

"No, sir," she said. "I don' believe I seen it before."

"Any idea who could have written it?"

She shook her head. "My readin' isn't good as some people's, but I can see it's his name there. Anyone could've writ it, sir."

"Just so," Ian agreed. "Anyone could have. But someone did, and I mean to find out who it is."

"Do you think it's related to his death?" said Doyle.

"I find it curious that it was wedged into the cushion of this arm-chair, when all indications are that neither the major nor this good lady would be likely to leave it there so carelessly."

"His fav'rite chair, that is," Mrs. McMillan said. "He could sit there by the hour, smokin' his pipe or reading."

"Perhaps he was sitting in this chair when he was interrupted by someone or something, leaving the envelope behind."

"But what about the contents of the envelope?" asked Doyle. "Any sign of that?"

"No," said Ian. "Which is also curious."

"Might he have burned it?" Doyle asked, glancing at the ashes in the grate.

"Perhaps. Another possibility is that whoever killed him took it with them."

"Because it was incriminating?"

"Precisely. But they failed to notice the envelope in the cushion of the armchair. Did the major seem anxious or distracted when you saw him last?" Ian asked the charwoman.

"Not so's I noticed, sir."

"When were you last here?"

"Yesterday mornin', sir. I come in most days, as the major likes everything just so, y'see."

"So whatever arrived in this envelope must have come in the past twenty-four hours," said Ian.

"Assuming its contents are related to his death," said Doyle.

Ian held up the envelope. "This is either a coincidence or a clue. Your mentor Dr. Bell claims there are no coincidences in medicine. I believe the same to be true in crime solving. Therefore, I shall regard this as a clue."

An examination of the rest of the flat provided no additional information, and after dropping Mrs. McMillan off at her flat, Ian told the cabbie to take them back to the medical school.

"Are you going to call on Dr. Littlejohn?" asked Doyle as the cab turned onto Lauriston Place.

"It's protocol to report any suspicious death to the police surgeon," Ian said. "But I know he's a busy man."

"You should be able to just catch him in his office," Doyle said as they alighted from the cab.

"Would you care to join me? He may have some medical questions I am ill-equipped to answer."

"I'm afraid I must get back to my duties. Dr. Bell is probably wondering where I am. And I have a chemistry class this afternoon."

"Thank you for your assistance—it was invaluable."

"I'm glad I could be of some use."

"I'll keep you apprised of our progress on the case," Ian called after him as he walked away, then turned in the direction of Dr. Littlejohn's office. He always experienced a sadness in the aftermath of Conan Doyle's leaving. Hardly the most sociable of men, Ian was not used to the feeling, but suspected most people experienced the pull of Doyle's easy charm and good-natured personality.

His friend was right—Littlejohn was indeed in his office nestled in the clock tower overlooking the entrance to Lauriston Place.

"Come in, come in," he called in response to Ian's knock. "Ah, it's you!" he said when Ian entered the room. "Close the door, close it—it's frightfully drafty up here."

Ian complied—like many of the stone buildings in Edinburgh, this one did seem to hold in the cold, even on warm days. The office was as he remembered it—cluttered, somewhat cramped, but with the pleasing atmosphere of a place of study, a retreat from the hustle and bustle of the city. Bookshelves of medical texts lined one wall; on a second bookcase were jars of what appeared to be laboratory specimens. Seated behind his desk, Littlejohn beckoned Ian to sit on the only available spot, a wooden bench half covered with medical texts. "Just move those aside, move them," Littlejohn said with a wave of his hand. "Can't seem to ever put anything away properly," he added. "Too time-consuming, you know. I need a clerk. You know of anyone? Anyone at all?"

"I can't think of anyone at present," Ian said, perching carefully on the bench next to a heavy tome of *Gray's Anatomy*. It was open to an illustration of a skeletal human hand, each bone neatly labeled. He wondered who the hand holding the gun that killed Major Fitzpatrick belonged to. He was fairly certain it did not belong to the major.

"You're one of Toshy Crawford's men," Dr. Littlejohn said, leaning back in his chair. He had grown a rather bushy white mustache since Ian last saw him; this had the effect of softening his face, which could appear quite stern in repose. His broad, high forehead, boarded by soft silver hair, suggested the impressive intellect within. "Let me see, let's see. Detective . . ."

"Hamilton."

"Yes, yes, of course. Neat job you did on that last case—neat job indeed."

"Thank you, sir."

"How is old Toshy?"

"He's well, thank you."

"I hear Joseph Bell sorted out his wife's health."

"Yes, sir."

"Glad to hear it, glad to hear it. Good man, Toshy—no good at cards, but a stout fellow. Now then, what can I do for you?"

Ian told him of the major's puzzling death.

"May I see the bullet?"

Ian pulled it from his pocket and handed it to the doctor.

"And you say it matches the caliber of the service revolver?"

"Yes."

"What was the victim's name again?"

"Major George Fitzpatrick."

"About fifty or so, medium height, athletic build?"

"Yes."

Dr. Littlejohn laid the bullet carefully on his desk. A glint of sunlight from the window behind him illuminated the brass on the projectile, giving it a golden glow. "Which side of the head was the wound?"

"The right side."

The doctor fixed his deep-set eyes on Ian. "Major Fitzpatrick could not possibly have killed himself. Not possible."

"Why not?"

"I treated him for an injury sustained in Afghanistan. Took a bullet to the right shoulder."

"He was your patient?" Ian asked, his heart beating faster.

"As a result of that injury, George Fitzpatrick was unable to raise his right arm that far. He would have been physically incapable of shooting himself in the head."

Ian stared at the doctor, then past him to the city beyond. Somewhere, in those dark and desperate streets, a murderer wandered freely among its unsuspecting citizens.

CHAPTER NINETEEN

"My dear Detective Hamilton, how absolutely divine to see you! Have you come to grace us with your talent again?"

Ian stood in the doorway of the rehearsal hall of the Blackfriars Street Masonic Lodge, home to the Greyfriars Dramatic Society, as Clyde Vincent hurried down the aisle toward him. After spending the afternoon interviewing the major's neighbors, without gleaning much useful information, Ian had come to intercept Sergeant Dickerson at his evening rehearsal.

Clad in a forest-green riding jacket and crimson cravat, the theater director looked dapper as always. Laying a hand on the detective's shoulder, he clasped Ian's hand warmly with the other. "You *do* look well, I must say—put on half a stone or so since last we met, I think?"

"I wouldn't be surprised," Ian replied with a smile. "My aunt is always trying to fatten me up."

"Don't listen to a word he's saying!"

Ian turned to see Lillian charging onto the stage from the wings.

"Aunt Lillian! What are you doing here?"

"I might ask you the same thing," she said, arms crossed. She was unusually well turned out, looking very smart in an attractive blue-and-gold paisley dress with matching jacket.

"Your aunt has graciously agreed to take publicity photographs of our little production," Vincent explained. "And play a small role as an added bonus."

"You didn't tell me about this," Ian said to her.

"Surely I donnae have to tell ye everythin' I do?" she replied, her Glaswegian roots creeping into her voice as usual when she was wrought up.

"It's just as well you're here. I have something very important to impart to you."

"Well? What is it?"

"I'd like to speak in private. Would you please excuse us?" he asked Mr. Vincent.

"By all means, dear boy. There's a little office just inside the front entrance—you won't be disturbed there."

Retracing his steps through the chilly entrance hall, Ian found the office. It was dark inside, but the door was unlocked, opening with a creak when he turned the knob. Lighting the wall sconces, he turned to see his aunt standing in the doorway. Framed by the door, the soft yellow light on her face, she suddenly looked twenty years younger. Perhaps it was the blue dress, or the gaslight—and was she wearing rouge on her cheeks? There was something different about her, a subtle change in spirit that gave her a youthful air.

"What is it you wanted to tell me?" she said, taking a step into the room. It was a cramped little office, with a few filing cabinets, a dusty desk, and several chairs scattered about. It smelled of pine oil and shag tobacco.

"Close the door. This is for your ears alone."

She did as he bade and perched upon one of the chairs, watching him expectantly.

"How well do you know Major Fitzpatrick?"

"I encountered him only at the séances. We have no relationship outside Madame Veselka's. Why do you ask?"

"He was found dead this morning."

Her sharp intake of breath told him the news took her by surprise. "Wh-who found him?"

"His charwoman, a Mrs. McMillan. Do you know her?"

She shook her head, and he noticed that she had curled the edges of her hair in delicate ringlets. "Was it—" she began, then faltered.

"He died of a single gunshot wound. It was made to look like a suicide, but I have evidence suggesting it was in fact murder."

Another intake of breath, this time followed by a long exhale. "Do you have any suspects?" she asked quietly.

"Not yet. It goes without saying that you yourself are in danger."

"Does it indeed?"

"What?"

"Go without saying?"

"Please, Auntie," he said earnestly, pulling a chair up to sit opposite her. "Just this once, listen to me."

"I don't see how it follows that—"

"Two members of your séance group have been murdered! Can you not see what that portends?"

"Who on earth would want to kill an old goose like me?"

"Who would kill a retired army major? Or a middle-aged spinster living alone on a quiet street in New Town? Both of them seem to have led exemplary lives, yet they were targeted for murder. And the only thing uniting them so far is the fact that they both attended the same séances! How can you have no care at all for your own safety?"

Aware that his voice had risen in volume, Ian stood up and paced the room. He was agitated, frustrated at his aunt's stubbornness. "Really," he continued. "I cannot believe that you would even think to contradict me!"

"Your father didn't care for people disagreeing with him, either."

"Why on earth would you bring my father into this?" he exploded. "This has nothing to do with the past! Why must you insist on being so thickheaded and stubborn?"

"Thickheaded, is it?" she replied stiffly, rising from her chair. "I should think you know something about that," she added, sweeping from the room before he could stop her.

His forehead burning with impatience and rage, he kicked the chair she had recently vacated, sending it crashing across the room. "Damn," he muttered. "Bloody stubborn woman!" Although already he could see part of the blame was his, he felt put upon and unfairly treated. He could hardly believe she did not take his warning seriously. What could she be thinking?

He wanted to go home and stew in solitude, but he needed to tell Dickerson of this latest development. Closing the office door behind him, he slipped into the rehearsal hall just in time to see the opening scene between Scrooge and his nephew. He stood in the back watching quietly as the actors recited their lines, scripts in hand, moving about the stage somewhat tentatively as they endeavored to remember their blocking.

The actor playing Scrooge was a rosy-cheeked older gentleman with a fine head of white hair, somewhat stouter than Ian imagined the character to be, but he was a handsome fellow with a strong voice and an amusing way of peering over his old-fashioned spectacles at the fellow playing his nephew. It had always struck Ian as strange that Dickens had failed to give the nephew a name, but the energetic young actor did not seem to care. He played the scene with great vigor, as if he, not Scrooge, were the main protagonist of the story. When his uncle asked why he got married, he uttered his response, "Because I fell in love," with an ironic, humorous swoon that made several of the other actors sitting in the audience laugh. Not to be outdone, the actor playing Scrooge growled out his next line with such utter contempt and disgust that he brought forth an even louder roar of laughter.

"Because you fell in love!"

Ian was impressed with how the actor managed to impart the line with a sense of pathos and loss beneath the contempt, so that it was clear he was covering a chasm of past injury. Yet there was nothing sentimental about it; his anger was so fierce that it nearly compensated for the pain. Almost, but not quite. There was something familiar in the old actor's attitude, he thought. It reminded him of someone . . . At that moment, he caught a glimpse of his aunt watching the scene from the wings. Leaning against a curtain pulley, she wore an expression he had only seen on her face when she spoke of Uncle Alfred. Her eyes were soft, a half smile on her face, and nothing else in the world seemed to exist for her except the scene being played out on the stage. At that moment he knew the reason for her fine dress, the curls in her hair, the rouge on her cheeks. She was in love with the gentleman playing Scrooge!

Perhaps that accounted for her stubborn behavior as well—he knew from experience as a detective that one strong emotion can beget another. His heart beat a pang of envy as he watched her, utterly absorbed in the characters on stage. What a sweet feeling it must be, he thought, being so enamored of another. Suddenly he had a strange nagging feeling he had forgotten something . . . Miss Stuart! It was Thursday, the night they were supposed to meet. It had completely slipped his mind. Fumbling, he pulled out his pocket watch—it was after eight! He had missed their assignation by over an hour.

But he still had not done what he came to do. Scanning the actors sitting in the audience, he spied Sergeant Dickerson. Walking softly to where the sergeant sat, he leaned over and whispered in his ear.

"Wha's that, sir?" Dickerson said.

"Come with me," Ian repeated.

The sergeant sprang from his chair and followed him into the drafty front hall.

"Wha's the matter, sir?"

Ian told him of the major's death.

"I were wonderin' where ye'd got to all day. So he were murdered, then?"

"Undoubtedly."

"Related, y'think, sir?"

"It would be very odd indeed if they are not."

"Does the chief know yet?"

"I left a message at police chambers before coming here."

"Wha' do we do next, sir?"

"Meet me at the station house tomorrow, bright and early."

"Will do, sir," Dickerson said, turning to go.

"And Sergeant?"

"Yes, sir?"

"Tell my aunt she has good taste."

Dickerson cocked his head to one side. "Sir?"

"She'll know what I mean."

"If you say so, sir," Dickerson replied dubiously. He walked away shaking his head.

Wrapping his cloak around him, Ian pulled open the heavy front door. A blast of arctic air hit him square in the face, making his eyes water. Putting his head down, he pushed into the wind.

CHAPTER TWENTY

There was no sign of Fiona Stuart at Le Canard. Ian inhaled the bewitching aroma of fennel-roasted potatoes and duck with cherry sauce while the svelte, haughty maître d' informed him that a young lady had indeed been there, sitting alone for some time, seemingly waiting for someone, though any man who would abandon such a *femme charmante* surely must be a fool or a cad. He wasn't one to judge, of course, but only a man without morals or sense would act with such *orgueil déplacé*. Such a man would naturally deserve whatever he got, though hopefully the *belle femme* had the sense to drop such a careless suitor like the *ordure* he was.

Ian spoke enough French to know *ordure*, loosely translated, meant "piece of filth." Lifting one perfectly groomed eyebrow, the maître d' let it be known that no Frenchman would dream of treating a woman so shabbily, let alone one such as her. Finally he produced a note written on the back of the restaurant's card.

Sorry you were delayed—the next one is on you.

It was unsigned, though the tone and firm handwriting left no doubt as to its author. He slipped the note into his waistcoat pocket under the disapproving eye of the maître d', who shook his head and clicked his tongue dismissively. Ian couldn't quite bring himself to thank the man, so he nodded and winked, which confused the Frenchman completely. The bewildered look on his face was gratifying.

After leaving the restaurant, Ian was approaching West Bow Street when he became aware of someone following him. He turned around to see Derek McNair.

"Miss me, Guv?" Dressed in his usual mismatched, oversized clothing, the boy at least looked warm. He was clad in a navy-blue woolen coat over a green fisherman's jumper that hung down nearly to the tops of his rubber Wellies. With the bright-red scarf wrapped tightly around his scrawny neck, he reminded Ian a little of the young lad playing Tiny Tim in *A Christmas Carol*.

"So, d'ye miss me?" he repeated, scurrying to catch up.

"Indescribably."

"Missed ye, too," he said, chewing on something; Ian did not care to know what.

"I can't tell you how gratified I am to hear it."

They walked in silence, their breath coming in white puffs as they passed beneath the streetlamps.

Finally Derek said, "Don' ye wan' t'know what I got t'tell ye?"

"I assume you'll get to it in good time."

The boy shook his head. "Yer an odd duck, so help me."

"Whereas you are the picture of middle-class propriety."

Derek let out a guffaw. "Ha! Anyways, I got a message from tha' fella Rat Face."

Ian stopped walking. "Yes?"

"He says t'meet 'im tomorrow an' he'll take ye t'this chap Nate."

"Where?"

"Hound an' Hare, five o'clock."

"I assume he gave you something for your service?"

"Contributions are always welcome, mate."

"Here's half a guinea."

"I'd sooner have a whole. Assistants like me are hard t'find."

"You are not my assistant."

"I got a coupla helpers m'self, y'know, an' they need payin' as well."

"Do you now?"

"I'm an enterprisin' lad."

"How many are there in your band of ruffians?"

"We prefer t'think of ourselves as . . ."

"As what, exactly?"

"Sorta like an army, y'know?"

"And you're the general?"

"I guess ye could say that."

"If you were part of the military, you'd definitely be irregulars."

"Right, then, Guv—call us the Irregulars."

"Here's a guinea, then, for you and your 'Irregulars.'"

"Ta very much, Guv!" Derek said, tipping his moth-eaten blue watch cap. Seeing they were nearing Victoria Terrace, he added, "Y'think I might have another bath sometime?"

"If it's all right with my brother."

"Don' think he likes me much."

"He just needs time to get used to you," Ian said, stopping at the staircase to the terrace.

"Well, good evenin' to ye, then," Derek said a little wistfully.

"Come by in a couple of days and we'll get you that bath."

"Right y'are—I'll be off now," he said with another tip of his hat, and disappeared into the darkness.

Ian found Donald in the kitchen, hovering over a pot of soup. Bacchus sat at his feet, tail twitching, eyes fixed on the stove. "Ah," his brother said. "I wondered when you would show up. Hard day, was it?"

"You have no idea. That smells heavenly, by the way."

"Split pea soup," Donald said, stirring the pot. "With ham, carrots, and onion. Would you care for some?"

"I can't think of anything I'd like better."

He was tucking into his third bowl when Donald pulled up a chair and lit a cigarette. "So who failed to appear—you or her?"

"Beg pardon?" Ian said, the spoon halfway to his mouth.

"Obviously your assignation with Miss Stuart did not take place, so I wondered who was the guilty party."

"How do you—"

"You come back earlier than I expected, with a ravenous appetite, making no mention of your meeting. If you had met and quarreled, you would have launched into an indictment of her personality flaws, yet you remain silent on the topic. I therefore concluded there was no meeting."

"Your logic is unassailable, but I can't help sensing Dr. Bell's influence."

"He believes in conclusions based on careful observation. Well?" said Donald. "What happened?"

"I failed to appear at the designated hour."

"I thought so. Your demeanor is rather more sheepish than angry."

"I had a reason, of course, but it was bad form on my part."

"She'll forgive you."

"How do you know?"

"She has motive."

Ian smiled. "Like a criminal?"

"If it's criminal to be smitten with someone."

"Bosh and bunkum, as DCI Crawford would say."

"All you have to do is pick up the bill at the next meeting."

"She's ahead of you there," Ian said, showing him the note.

"Ha!" said Donald, reading it. "Good for her."

"Is there more bread and butter?"

"Lillian's right."

"About what?"

"You do have a hollow leg."

Half an hour later, Ian relaxed in front of the fire while his brother poked at the logs.

"You don't seem quite so jumpy around flames these days," Donald said, lowering his stocky frame into the matching wing chair on the other side of the fireplace. Seizing the opportunity, Bacchus jumped onto him, turning circles on his lap. "Ouch," he said as the cat kneaded his claws into Donald's belly.

Ian smiled. "He does seem to prefer you."

Donald sighed. "The very definition of a mixed blessing."

They sat in silence for a few moments, then Donald said, "Do you think about it much?"

"The fire, you mean?"

"Yes."

"I dream about it quite a bit."

"Do you mind if I ask you something?" said Donald.

"After that soup, I'd say you're entitled."

"We've not really talked about the fire much over the years."

"No." What neither of them said was that it was a nearly unbearable topic, one they only recently had begun circling warily.

"What were you doing in the basement that night?"

"Rex had gone down because of the thunder."

"Yes, I remember how he hated it. Used to shiver uncontrollably."

"I went down to comfort him and found him lying on a mattress in the corner. I curled up next to him and fell asleep."

"If I were a religious man, I'd say it seems like Providence. If you hadn't gone down there . . ."

"Rex and I were the only survivors."

"And me."

"Yes, but you weren't—" Ian stopped. The topic was still sensitive between them.

"I wasn't there," Donald finished for him.

"I didn't mean to suggest—"

"For years I felt it was my fault, and that if I had been there, I might have . . ." He looked away, absently petting Bacchus, who purred loudly, eyes half closed.

"I think I blamed you, too."

"Of course you did. Big brother, supposed to look after you, and all that."

Ian stared into the flames, which leapt greedily to consume the fuel they fed on. "I'm meeting with a man who might lead me to the culprit who set the fire."

"This Nate What's-his-name?"

"Crippen. Nate Crippen."

Donald sighed. "You can't leave this alone, can you?"

"Don't you want to know who killed our parents?"

Donald looked at him with a mixture of apprehension and sadness. "I'm not sure I do."

"Why on earth not?"

"I don't see what good can come of it."

"A criminal can be brought to justice!"

"Don't pursue this, Ian. Leave well enough alone."

"How can you call the murder of our parents 'well enough'? What on earth is the matter with you?"

Extricating the cat from his lap, Donald rose from his chair. "I'm tired, and I have early morning rounds tomorrow."

"What do you know?"

"Leave it, Ian. Take my advice and do not pursue this inquiry."

Donald looked sad and defeated, even more than when he first appeared on Ian's doorstep so many months ago. Ian realized any more attempts at conversation would be futile.

"Good night," said Donald. Wrapping Ian's dressing gown around his body, he padded off to his bedroom.

Ian sat gazing at the fire for some time. Finally, when the flames had burned down to embers, he, too, retired to bed, no closer to having answers to any of his questions.

CHAPTER
TWENTY-ONE

Sitting in the parlor, you study your hands in the lamplight. Turning them over, you gaze with wonder at the finely calibrated bones, tendons, and sinew, all so carefully constructed, capable of so many things. Over the years, your hands have worked, caressed and constructed, mended and molded, most of the time without much thought on your part. Like most people, you took them for granted, pausing to ponder their workings only when something went wrong—a sprained wrist, a banged thumb, a burned forefinger. They were simply an extension of your brain, obeying its commands like a good servant.

But now you regard them with something like awe. Yesterday, these hands fired a gun that killed a man. Even a short time ago, you would not have thought them capable of such an act—would not have believed it lay within your own heart—yet here you sit, a scant day later, contemplating the done deed.

A tingle slides down your spine, burying itself in your groin, as you strive to remember every detail: his nervous manner, the astonished look on his face when he realized he had trusted the wrong person. There was something touching about gazing into someone's eyes when they are looking back at yours and seeing eternity. The sense of power and inevitability took you off guard, though to your credit, you did not let it get in your way. Your will was resolute, and if the finger that pulled the trigger trembled a little, that only made the conclusion more satisfying. His surprised look turned to one of recognition, as though he understood why he had to die. That was especially gratifying—after all, what was the point of vengeance if the offender had no understanding of his punishment? You almost felt sorry for him—almost, but not quite. He was deserving of his fate, and so much the better if he was aware of it as well.

You pour a little tea from the pot—cold now, the milk congealing on top of the cup in an unappetizing swirl. You rise to put some more coal on the grate. The embers pop and glow, sending faint fingers of flame into the air. You can't afford to spend much more time contemplating past deeds. There is so much more to be done.

CHAPTER
TWENTY-TWO

The next morning Ian rose at dawn and left before his brother was awake. The mercury had risen overnight, and the air was radically warmer. The springlike temperature was disorienting, and a sullen sun struggled to break through a low cloud cover as he walked toward the station house. As he turned onto the nearly deserted High Street, the quiet was broken by the slow clip-clop of hooves. Cob the milkman perched upon his gently swaying cart, pulled by Timothy, his big chestnut gelding. The milkman tipped his cap, and Timothy swiveled his ears in Ian's direction as they passed. Returning Cob's gesture, Ian thought about how horses were able to express so much emotion through their ears. Neither of his parents was keen on horses, but Ian remembered Donald teaching him how to read a horse's mood from the position of its ears. He sighed, wishing his brother trusted him enough to reveal whatever secrets he carried so close.

As he approached police chambers at 192 High Street, he was surprised to find Jed Corbin leaning against the front door, chewing on a meat pie.

"Morning, Detective."

"What brings you out so bright and early?"

"I'll grant you it's early. Not very bright, though, is it?" the reporter said, glancing at the overcast sky.

"What can I do for you, Mr. Corbin?"

"I propose an exchange of information."

"You possess knowledge I might find useful?"

Corbin smiled, bits of pie crust clinging to his teeth. "I do."

"What do you require in exchange?"

The reporter spread his hands in a gesture of conciliation. "Merely a tidbit or two on the Elizabeth Staley investigation—exclusive, of course."

"And what have you in exchange?"

"Information on the death of Major Fitzpatrick."

Ian tried not to show his surprise, but it was no use. "Indeed?" he said tightly.

"Don't be alarmed," said Corbin, tossing his leftover crust into the street, where it was seized by a diving seagull that seemed to appear out of nowhere. "Impressive animals," the reporter said, watching it fly away with its prize. "Perfect opportunists, utterly without scruples."

"Like journalists?"

Corbin clutched his heart. "You wound me deeply, Detective."

"What is this information you refer to?"

"The major received a visitor at approximately nine p.m. the night before his charwoman discovered his body."

"Who was this visitor?"

"Alas, that's as much as I know."

"How did you come by this information?"

Corbin smiled. "A journalist never reveals his sources."

"And a policeman never comments on an ongoing investigation," Ian replied curtly. "Good day, Mr. Corbin."

As he turned to leave, the journalist grabbed his sleeve. "We had an agreement!"

"I agreed to nothing," Ian said, extricating himself, "but answer me one question and I shall consider your request."

"That's not good enough. I want an assurance on your part."

"Very well—if you answer truthfully, I shall give you something to put in your paper."

"What is your question?"

"How did you find out about the major's death?"

"I had you followed."

"By whom?"

"A young fellow in my employ. It isn't against the law, you know."

"Interfering with a police investigation is."

"I assure you, it is not my intent to interfere, only to obtain information."

"Here is something for you, then. Elizabeth Staley was undoubtedly murdered."

"How?"

"A blow to the head."

"With what object?"

"I have already given you two details, which is more than I promised."

Corbin sighed. "Beggars can't be choosers, I suppose."

"You are no beggar, Mr. Corbin—you are much more like that seagull you admired so much."

"Any journalist who fails to seize opportunity will never be successful."

"Nor will any policeman who blindly trusts the press."

Corbin smiled. "You strike me as a man whose trust is hard to come by."

"Thank you for the information, Mr. Corbin. Good day," he said, opening the door to enter the building.

"Anytime," the reporter called after him. "I'll be in touch."

The night shift was ending when Ian entered, the officers finishing their last cup of tea, filing papers, writing up case notes. DCI Crawford was a stickler for paperwork, and while Ian disliked it as much as the next man, he approved of the chief's zest for organization.

Pouring a cup of tea, he retreated to his desk while his sleepy colleagues prepared to go home, yawning as they pulled on their scarves and greatcoats. Though Ian did not want to admit it, even to himself, the reporter's words had hit home. Whom, really, did he trust? A while ago he would have said Lillian, but they were on shaky ground. As for Donald . . . putting thoughts of his brother aside, he pulled out his notebook and began studying his case notes on the death of Major Fitzpatrick.

Sergeant Bowers approached Ian's desk.

"I've a note for ye, sir," he said, fishing a crumpled piece of paper from his pocket. "Sorry it's a bit creased—I didn' want tae lose it, so it's been in my pocket."

Ian was about to ask who it was from when he looked at the handwriting. "Thank you, Sergeant," he said, smiling.

"Don' ye want t'know who—"

"Tall young woman, auburn hair, rather cheeky?"

The sergeant's eyes widened. "I don' know 'bout cheeky, sir—"

"Forceful, then."

Bowers grinned. "That she were, sir. Forceful, definitely."

"Thank you, Sergeant."

"You're welcome, sir," he replied, lingering as if he wished to say something else.

"Good day, Sergeant," Ian said amiably. The constable tipped his hat and sputtered a quick farewell before joining his colleagues leaving the building.

Ian looked at the note again. *Eight o'clock tonight at Le Canard. Do endeavor to be punctual this time.* He smiled as he tucked it into his waistcoat pocket. No recriminations, no demand for an explanation; just a simple declaration in the form of a command: be there.

The front door swung open, and a somewhat bedraggled Sergeant Dickerson shuffled in. He looked half asleep. There was beard stubble on his chin, and half-moon shadows beneath his eyes. He clutched a crumpled bakery bag, which he tossed onto his desk before falling into his chair.

"Rough night, was it?" said Ian.

"Rehearsal went long, an' I had trouble sleepin'."

"Any particular reason?"

"It were Scrooge, sir."

"Beg pardon?"

Dickerson pulled out a soggy piece of Selkirk bannock and bit into it absently. "I kept thinkin' 'bout how a man gets to be like that. No friends, no love, carin' only 'bout work."

"He is an extreme character," Ian agreed.

"Sad, really. I can't help feelin' sorry fer him."

"It turns out all right in the end, though."

"On account a' the ghosts, yeah." He shivered. "Wouldn't like t'go through a night like that m'self, mind you. Would ye care fer some, sir?" he said, holding out the bakery bag. "There's another piece."

"You look like you need it more than I do."

"I'll be all right, sir. What's on fer today?" he said, fetching himself a mug of tea.

"I'd like you to interview the rest of the major's neighbors—anyone you can find in the vicinity who might have known him—shopkeepers, bootblacks, newsboys. Find out anything you can about his habits, his history, his family. And do your best to find out who visited him at around nine o'clock the night before he was killed."

"A visitor, sir?"

"Apparently. But that's all I know."

"Yes, sir."

"And mind you, take notes."

"Will do, sir—don' go anywhere wi'out my trusty notebook."

"Good man. That should keep you busy for a while," Ian said, rising and putting on his cloak.

"Where're you off ta, sir, if ye don' mind my askin'?"

"I am going to interview a woman who claims to converse with ghosts."

CHAPTER
TWENTY-THREE

Ian's knock on Madame Veselka's door received no response, and he was about to leave when he heard the sound of meowing from inside. Going around to the front window, he peered in through the French lace curtains. The same fluffy white Persian was perched on the window seat, mewing plaintively. Taking a deep breath, he rapped on the windowpane. Alarmed, the cat darted away. After a moment, he heard a door slam from within the flat. He could make out a person walking through the parlor, and Gretchen's face appeared at the window. Lifting the curtain aside, she beckoned to him to go around to the entrance.

"I'm sorry if I've come round too early," he said as she opened the door. She wore a tartan robe over a long white nightgown, and pulled the robe tighter as she led him into the parlor. There was a lingering odor of gardenia perfume, and the aroma of coffee from the back of the flat.

Seeing the look on Ian's face, Gretchen said, "I have just put on the kettle. You would care for some coffee?" Rather charmingly, she pronounced it "ca-fay."

"Thank you," he said.

Tugging her robe closer, she disappeared into the rear of the flat. The cat sauntered back into the room and perched in the same spot as before. Curling its tail around its body, the Persian regarded him with unblinking blue eyes, as if daring him to transgress. A shiver went up his spine as Ian remembered that cats were often regarded as familiars for witches. Not that he believed in any of that nonsense, of course— still, the animal's sapphire eyes were uncanny, following him around the room as he wandered from the sofa to the front window. He wasn't looking for anything in particular, but keeping an open mind and expecting nothing was often the best investigative approach.

The beaded curtains swayed, a soothing sound like the soft rustle of leaves, and parted to reveal Madame Veselka, dressed in a Japanese kimono. The garment was black silk, with a yellow and crimson floral motif, which set off her black hair admirably. Her hands were devoid of jewelry save for a large ruby on the fourth finger of her right hand.

"Ah, Detective Inspector," she said, "how nice to see you again." Her voice was warm, but her smile did not extend to her eyes, which were black as coal.

"I do apologize if this is an inconvenient time."

"Not at all. My train does not leave for several hours."

"Oh, that's right—you're going to Paris, I believe?"

"Yes, just for a few days."

"Business or pleasure?"

"Please, sit down," she said, waving a hand vaguely in the direction of the burgundy tasseled sofa.

Wondering why she ignored his question, Ian settled onto the couch, which was rather lower than he expected, so that his knees were folded nearly up to his chest.

"I see you have long legs. Perhaps you would be more comfortable in the armchair. Vadoma, away!" she said, waving her hand at the cat, who glared at her before slinking off the chair, tail flicking irritably.

"She likes to keep watch over visitors. But it does her good not to get her own way all the time. Otherwise, she would be in total control of all her humans," she added with a smile.

"What did you call her?" he said. "Va—"

"Vadoma." Ian looked up to see Gretchen standing in the doorway, a tray in her hands. "Her name is Vadoma," she repeated.

He thought he noticed a flicker of irritation flit briefly across Madame Veselka's features, but it was so fleeting he couldn't be sure.

"Gretchen, dear, how thoughtful of you," she said. "You've brought us coffee."

"Yes, Madame," the girl replied, setting the tray down on the sideboard. "You take it with milk and one sugar, like your tea?" she asked Ian.

"Yes, thank you. You have a good memory," he added, wondering what else she might remember.

After passing them each a steaming cup of coffee, Gretchen set a plate of toast, butter, and jam on the marble coffee table in front of them.

"Now then, Detective," said Madame Veselka, sipping her coffee. "What can I do for you?"

"I'm afraid I have bad news. Another of your—guests—has been found dead," he said, watching closely for her reaction.

Even in the dim light filtering in through the lace curtains, Ian could see her blanch a shade paler. Her jaw clenched, and her grip on the saucer tightened. "That's terrible. What happened?"

Ian told her of the major's unfortunate demise, leaving out key details such as the fact that he was shot. He did not say that it was almost certainly murder, to see whether the madame might incriminate herself.

But more surprising was Gretchen's reaction. "No! It's—it's simply not possible," she said. "Major Fitzpatrick—he was a most vital man. He could not just . . . die. It cannot be!"

"You neglected to tell us what killed him," Madame Veselka said calmly, regaining her self-control. "You consider the death suspicious, or you would not be here."

She had him there—her conclusion was sound, if obvious. "It appears he was shot with his own gun."

"What exactly is in doubt—the fact that he was shot, or the weapon itself?"

Ian was taken aback by the calm logic of her response. "You sound like a seasoned investigator."

"In the old country, Madame was—" Gretchen began, but the medium silenced her with a look.

"My father was an investigator of sorts," she said, wiping her mouth delicately with a fine linen napkin.

"What sort would that be?"

"Let us simply say I am no stranger to the questioning process."

This piqued Ian's curiosity—the more time he spent with Madame Veselka, the more the mystery surrounding her deepened.

"How well did you know the major?" he asked.

She shrugged. "He has been coming here for several years, but I have never seen him outside these walls."

Ian glanced at Gretchen, who looked as if she was fairly bursting to say something.

"And you?" he said. "How well did you know the major?"

"The s-same as Madame," she replied, casting her eyes downward, as if afraid to look at either one of them.

"You have never encountered him outside—"

"Never!" she interrupted. Even if it was true—which Ian doubted—the fervency of her response aroused his suspicion.

"What can you tell me about him?"

"Gretchen, dear, would you fetch us more coffee?" said the medium.

"Yes, Madame," the girl said, with a quick curtsy. Taking the empty pot, she headed toward the kitchen with obvious reluctance. Ian longed to question her further, but not in front of her employer.

"I would be appreciative of anything you can tell me about the major," he said.

"He was retired from the military—apparently from a rather illustrious career, though he was quite modest about it."

"How did you know it was illustrious?"

"He was mentioned quite often in the papers."

"His wife is deceased—are there any other family members you know of?"

"Only his son, Jeremy, the young man you met at the séance."

Ian cursed himself for neglecting to speak with him that night. The sullen young fellow had barely said a word to anyone all evening, but still, Ian regretted missing the opportunity. "Do you have any idea where I can find him?"

"I regret I do not."

"Were you aware of anyone who might wish to harm the major?"

She hesitated, and Ian wondered whom she was protecting.

"No," she said finally, making an elaborate show of buttering her toast. "As I said, I knew little about him, other than he lost his wife some years ago."

"And Jeremy?"

"I never had the feeling he cared much for the spirit world."

"Did he always attend séances with his father?"

"No, and when he did, I had the feeling it was so his father could keep an eye on him."

"Why would he need watching?"

"You saw him yourself—would you not say he appears to be a somewhat troubled youth?"

"The list of attendees you provided doesn't include any addresses."

"I do not keep personal information on my guests," she said, dabbing at her face with a flowered handkerchief. The aroma of gardenias floated into Ian's nostrils.

"Miss Davies lives on Gloucester Lane." Ian turned to see Gretchen enter the room with a fresh pot of coffee. "I accompanied her home once when she was feeling unwell."

"Do you happen to know what number?"

"Number thirty-three, I think," she said, pouring the madame more coffee. "I'm not entirely certain."

"Thank you," he said, looking at Madame Veselka, whose face bore the rigid look of someone trying to hide any emotional response.

"Don't you usually meet on Friday nights?" Ian asked.

"Every other week," she said. "We—" She abruptly stopped speaking as her head fell forward, her chin resting on her chest.

Ian leaned forward. "Madame Vesel—"

Her head snapped upright, and she stared straight ahead, face rigid, her eyes wide and unblinking. Her mouth moved, but no sound came out, as if she were a fish gasping for air. Still staring at the opposite wall, she spoke in a low, thrilling voice. "Be careful, Bear. Things are not as they seem. Hidden secrets have yet to come out."

Ian stared at her, panic rising in his throat as he heard a voice that somehow reminded him of his beloved mother. That was replaced by hot anger, fury at the medium for seeking to deceive him in such a shameless and cruel way. He rose from the chair and took a step toward her, bending down to help, when a hand grabbed his wrist. He looked up to see Gretchen, her face stern, grasping his arm in a viselike grip he would not have thought her capable of.

"Madame is in a trance!" she hissed. "Do *not* disturb her!"

He took a step backward and slowly extracted his arm from her hold.

"It is dangerous to interrupt her in the middle of a visitation," she whispered hotly. "You do not want to be responsible for what might happen."

Ian stood, hands at his sides, not because he believed her, but because he did not wish to alienate two people who might prove key to his investigation. Together they watched as the medium passed a hand over her face, then shuddered. Again her head fell to her chest, and she became quiet. She remained that way for so long Ian thought she might have fallen asleep, but then she shivered again and slowly raised her head.

"Are you all right, Madame?" Gretchen said, kneeling at her side.

She stared at the girl as if she were a stranger, blinked several times, then stretched and heaved a great sigh. "Was I out long?"

Ian stifled an impulse to roll his eyes, but Gretchen took the medium's hand in hers.

"Not long, Madame—no more than a few minutes."

Madame Veselka turned to Ian. "My apologies, Detective—I have no real control over the spirit world, and occasionally they visit me at the most inconvenient times."

"Never mind; I was nearly finished. Thank you for your time," he said, throwing on his cloak.

She looked at him curiously. "She told me the earrings were stolen before the fire."

"What?"

"The earrings. They disappeared before the fire."

"Madame Veselka," Ian said coldly, "I don't know what you are playing at, but it won't work. I shall continue my investigation, and if it points to you, I can assure you, you will be brought to justice. And," he continued, "if you continue digging into my personal life, it will not go well for you."

"I only relay messages as they are given to me."

"I am warning you—"

"And I am warning *you*, Detective Hamilton. Do not take these things lightly. The spirits do not always communicate, but when they do, they will not be silenced until they have been heard."

"I will give you the benefit of the doubt and assume you believe in all this folderol," he said, donning his cap. "But do not make the mistake of believing that my patience is endless. Thank you again for the coffee," he said to Gretchen.

Turning on his heel, he strode to the front door, opened it, and did not stop walking until he had gone a quarter of a mile or more. His heart pounded and spots danced before his eyes as he tried to calm himself. He was angry at the medium for working so hard to unbalance him, and angrier at himself for letting her words upset him. For in truth, he was rattled—he needed to be alone and sort out what had transpired.

And so he did what he so often did when his head was muddled, his emotions unsettled, his world suddenly confusing and unmanageable. Wrapping his cloak around his body, he set out to roam the streets of Edinburgh until he calmed down and was able to make sense of a case that threatened to unravel into a thousand disconnected, meaningless threads.

CHAPTER TWENTY-FOUR

Detective Chief Inspector Robert Crawford stood at his office window gazing down on the sweep of humanity trudging along the cobblestones of High Street. One of the city's main thoroughfares, it harbored every type of inhabitant one could imagine, from the wealthiest nobles to the most wretched of beggars. Sooner or later, if you lived in Edinburgh, you would find yourself on High Street, whether riding in a fancy brougham pulled by a pair of fine horses with braided manes, or lugging a turnip cart in worn-out boots and a threadbare coat too thin for Scottish winters. Princes Street housed the fancy shops, where the fashionable shopped and dined, but High Street was the heart of the city. Chimney sweeps rubbed shoulders with rich ladies from the Continent prowling the wool shops that lined the street's western third; counts and earls on their way to Holyrood Palace for a royal audience bumped elbows with beggars and brigands.

Today a light snow dusted the cobblestones, making them slippery and treacherous for people and horses alike as they threaded their way through the thicket of Friday traffic. Crawford watched as a couple of raggedly dressed boys darted in front of a slow-moving omnibus, just missing being trampled by the brace of dapple-grays pulling it.

On this dreary December day, seized by a wistful mood, the chief found himself taking stock of his life. Things at home were looking up, thanks to the ministrations of Dr. Joseph Bell, under whose care his beloved wife, Moira, was improving daily. But the situation at work could not be said to be anything short of dire. The city's criminals were running rampant, emboldened by the recent fiascos in which Crawford and his men failed to stop two major thefts. The criminal underworld seemed organized and unified in a way it never was before.

Turning back to his desk, he sighed at the sight of a half-finished cup of tea that had been there since morning, now cold. He doubted his own ability to set things right—something was indeed rotten in Denmark, as DI Hamilton would say, and he could only hope that with Hamilton's help, he would be able to sort out a vexing and troubling situation.

There was a knock on the door.

"Yes?" he barked, determined to keep up a stiff front of confidence and competence, though he felt neither.

The door opened to admit Sergeant Dickerson, a man Crawford was coming to like more and more. This warm regard was aided by the fact that the little fellow was like a miniature replica of himself, with his red hair and fair, freckled skin, which made Crawford feel fatherly and a little protective. He and Moira had no children of their own, but he imagined that if he had a son, the boy would look somewhat like William Dickerson, who was about the right age—though no doubt shorter than any member of the Crawford clan.

"'Scuse me, sir. I were wonderin' if ye'd seen DI Hamilton?"

"Not since this morning, Sergeant. You have something to tell him?"

"I did th'interviews he requested, and I'd like t'give report, but . . . well, sir—" He hesitated, biting his lip.

"Yes?"

"I've got t'go, y'see."

"Go on, then, if your shift is over."

"I'd like t'stay late, but—"

"What? Come out with it, man."

"I've got rehearsal."

"Doing another Shakespeare play, are you?" Crawford said, strok-ing his whiskers. He wouldn't admit it to Hamilton, but he had quite enjoyed the production of *Hamlet* he and Dickerson had appeared in—that is, until everything imploded.

"No, sir—it's Dickens this time."

"Dickens?"

"Yes, sir—*A Christmas Carol*."

"Well, get on with you, then."

"Yes, sir—thank you, sir," said the sergeant, backing out of the room like a servant not allowed to turn his back on his master.

"You were quite good in the last one," Crawford added, in a rush of warm feeling toward the sergeant.

"Very kind of you t'say so, sir."

"Do you want to leave a message for Hamilton if I see him?"

"Just that I'll be in early tomorrow, if ye don' mind, sir."

"Good man. Before you go, any progress on the investigation you're doing for me?"

"Not so's I'm aware, sir."

"Time is of the essence, Sergeant."

"I understand, sir."

"Now get along with you—mustn't be late."

"Yes, sir. Thank you, sir," the sergeant said, continuing to back up until he had fully cleared the door to Crawford's office.

Afterward, the chief stood watching men come and go as the day shift gave way to night in the station house. They wandered in one by one, shaking snow from their overcoats, greeting their fellow officers on the way out, sitting at their desks, or rummaging around the tea station to see whether there were any biscuits left in the tin. A few of the lads had tried to brighten up the place with sprigs of holly and evergreen boughs, and someone had brought in mistletoe and hung it over the entrance to Crawford's office. He appreciated the joke—Robbie Crawford wasn't entirely without humor, though at times he felt this job had knocked a lot of it out of him. Still, he took it in stride with good humor—anything to lighten the mood in what lately was feeling like a discouraging profession.

Looking at the contented faces of his men, Crawford wondered if he alone understood how dire the situation was in Edinburgh. The signs were all there—the spate of burglaries, the brazen actions of petty thieves and pickpockets, flaunting their crimes under the very noses of the constabulary, the police attempts at criminal apprehension gone spectacularly wrong.

And now these most recent murders—involving some bloody foreign medium in some way no one yet seemed to understand. Beyond it all, there was a *feeling* of disquiet, a sense that all was not well. He could smell it in the air, hear it in the hollow clanging of the clock high atop St. Giles, feel it in the chill wind sweeping in from the Firth of Forth.

Robert Crawford turned back to his office and slung his coat over his shoulders, suddenly aware of the weight of his years. He was weary of it all, and wished he could wash his hands of the whole blasted thing, he thought as he trudged from police chambers down to the street below. He longed to see his Moira, to watch her cooking dinner in their bright kitchen, sitting gracefully in front of the fire, the firelight warm on her face, understanding in her soft brown eyes as she asked him about his day. She alone understood the trials and tribulations of his job, knew the toll it took, and knew how to make everything better with the touch of her soft, cool hands.

From the top floor of a nearby building, a pair of eyes watched closely as he turned the corner onto Old Fleshmarket Close, and toward home.

CHAPTER
TWENTY-FIVE

The sun had long since dipped behind Castle Rock when Ian trudged his way back to police chambers, only to be informed both DCI Crawford and Sergeant Dickerson had left for the day. He had walked longer than he realized, aware of neither fatigue nor hunger, nor the passage of time. He had not yet shaken the feeling that haunted him following his visit to Madame Veselka, though he had managed to locate the residence of Miss Bronwyn Davies, number 33 Gloucester Lane, just as Gretchen had said. She was not home, however, and the landlady with whom he left a message seemed of dubious reliability, judging by the fumes she emitted. The alcohol on her breath was so strong Ian felt tipsy just standing next to her. When she tucked his card into her pocket, he could imagine it emerging days or weeks later on washing day, as she scratched her head, pondering why there was a policeman's card in her skirt.

A copy of the evening edition of the *Scotsman* was on his desk.

SECOND MEMBER OF SÉANCE SOCIETY FOUND MURDERED IN HIS OWN HOME!

GHOSTLY REVENGE OR SOMETHING EVEN MORE SINISTER?

He sighed and tossed the paper aside. This kind of overwrought journalism was standard, calculated to sell papers rather than create panic among readers. However, if the public did react with hysteria, no newspaper editor in the city would take responsibility, insisting that they were simply doing their duty to report the news to Edinburgh's citizens.

Leaving the police station, he wandered in the direction of St. Giles, where he saw a familiar figure huddled near the entrance.

"Keeping watch over the faithful, Brian? John Knox would be proud of you," he said, dropping a coin into the tin cup. John Knox, religious rebel and founder of Scottish Presbyterianism, was probably the most famous minister in the kirk's history.

"The nearer the kirk the farther frae grace," the beggar replied, grinning to reveal teeth the color of cobblestones. "What 'ave I done tae deserve half a guinea?"

Ian smiled at Brian's ability to tell what coin it was by the sound it made as it fell. "You've deserted your usual spot."

"Aye. Time fer a change."

"I thought maybe you'd found religion."

"Not a chance in hell."

"Why did you move from your spot at Waverley Station?"

"Thought it best tae move 'round a bit."

"Are you in danger?"

"Naw. What kinda thug'd hurt a blind beggar?"

"I'm worried about you, Brian."

"I've looked after m'self all these years," he said, tugging his scarf tighter around his neck as a gust of wind swooped down on them, scattering snowflakes in tiny tornadoes. "I reckon I kin take care a'm'self."

"You've been threatened, haven't you?"

"Donnae know why ye'd think that," he said, suddenly seized with a fit of coughing—a deep, liquid sound, like the gurgling of a fountain.

"That's a nasty cough," said Ian.

"Not nearly nasty enough t'take me out, mate."

"You should go to hospital and let someone examine you."

"Don' like doctors much."

"You might have consumption."

"It'll take more than a bit a' catarrh t'kill ol' Blind Brian."

"I know a medical student at the Royal Infirmary. And a nurse as well—"

"That's more like it," he said, grinning. "Nurses are all right. She pretty?"

"I think most people would say so."

"What d'ye say?"

"I suppose she's pretty."

Brian laughed. "You're sweet on her, mate."

Ignoring his comment, Ian scanned the street for any sign of suspicious characters, but the only people nearby were a young couple pushing a child in a pram and an elderly gentleman being pulled by an Airedale. The terrier lunged eagerly on the leash when he saw Ian, nearly tugging the man from his feet.

"Whoa, Digby!" his owner said, attempting to gain control as the two of them careened down the street in the direction of Holyrood Palace.

"Stupid name fer a dog a' that size," Brian muttered when they were out of earshot.

"How do you—"

"He were big enough tae pull a grown man along the street, weren't he? Though from the sound a' his voice, that fellow's a bit past 'is prime."

Ian shook his head. "You—"

"Please don' say I see more than people wi' two good eyes. I don' see nothin', mate. What I do is *listen*. Most people are too busy struttin' aroond tryin' tae make an impression. I got nothin' to prove, so I listen." He coughed and spat into the street. "Ye'd be surprised how no one takes notice of a blind man sittin' quietly in th'corner of a pub. Stupid gits. They figure 'cause I don' see they can say anythin'. So I listen, an' I hear things."

"So what have you heard?" Ian said. He could see the street was clear of eavesdroppers, and yet he couldn't shake the feeling they were being watched. "Have you learned anything about the matter we discussed earlier?"

"'Bout who might be feedin' ye false information?"

"Yes."

"I don' have any specifics yet, but I do know there's a new feelin' among the fellows. One I never quite haerd afore."

"What kind of feeling?"

Brian turned his empty eyes toward Ian, as if he had sight in them, but they looked right past the detective, blank as the night. "Fear," he said in a low voice. "They all sound scared tae death."

"Of what?"

"Can' answer that. I jes hear it in their voices. They're spooked a' somethin'."

"Have you any more knowledge of the jewelry theft, such as when exactly it's to happen?"

Brian shook his head. "Not yet. I'm not sure they've decided on th'exact date."

"Do you know which gang is to pull it off?"

"That's the funny thing, see."

"What is?"

"From what I've haerd, they might be in on it t'gether."

Ian's face darkened. "I don't like the sound of that."

"Bad enough ye've got t'keep tabs on what each of 'em are up to. If they've banded together, it's twice as worse, right?"

"Yes," Ian said, though what he was thinking was that his friend's remark didn't begin to describe the chaos in store for the citizenry of Edinburgh.

CHAPTER
TWENTY-SIX

It was a little past five when Ian arrived at the Hound and Hare. The crowd was just beginning to work itself into the usual Friday night frenzy, as dockworkers mixed with drovers, draymen, and drunkards. Of all the working-class pubs in Edinburgh, the Hound and Hare was the most volatile, and the most unpredictable. Under the influence of alcohol, fast friendships and fistfights sprang up like mushrooms after a spring rain. It was hard to tell what would set a man off—one night he might overlook crude remarks about his sister, only to pound his best mate the next over an offhand comment about his dog. It all depended on how the drink hit him, and how much of it he had.

Into this rough and raucous melee Ian stepped, wary and prepared for anything. The air reeked of cheap tobacco and cheaper whisky, sweat and desperation, aggression and despair. If you weren't ready for a brawl, you didn't drop into the Hound and Hare on a Friday. It was a fighting man's pub, and the barkeeps looked as if they were born of gorillas crossbred with rhinos. Tonight was no exception. Big, beefy, and bullet-headed, the giant behind the bar sported a perfectly bald pate, so shiny it looked as if it had been waxed, and a single gold earring in his left ear. From the tattoos of an anchor on one forearm and a mermaid on the other, Ian surmised he was a seagoing man. Sailors often made good barkeeps, skilled at dealing with drunkards.

Ian ordered a pint of ale, then slipped past a table of dockers engaged in a loud game of rummy. He spied Rat Face sitting at a table in the far corner, sipping nervously from a glass. When he saw Ian, his thin face twitched, and his liver-colored lips spread into what he probably fancied was a smile, but was more like a grimace.

Ian crossed the room in a few strides and slid into a chair opposite him.

Rat Face leaned back and studied the detective. "I wasn't sure you would show."

"Nor I you, and yet here we are," Ian said, taking a long swig of ale.

Rat Face did likewise, wiping his mouth delicately with a monogrammed handkerchief. "I thought this an appropriate meeting place, since this is where we first met. And to think at the time I had no idea how our friendship would blossom."

Ian ignored the remark, thinking that Terrance McNee would be behind bars if he hadn't proved himself so useful to the police. McNee knew this and was just rubbing it in.

"What is that?" Ian asked, pointing to his glass, which smelled of orange peel and ginger.

"Ah, this?" he replied, his face resuming the rather grotesque imitation of a smile. "It's purl—old-fashioned, I know, but I grew fond of it some years back when a lady friend introduced me to it."

Ian tried to imagine Terrance McNee, a.k.a. Rat Face, with a woman, but gave it up as a bad job. He knew purl was a concoction of gin, ale, sugar, and spices that was popular during Dickens' time, but had never seen anyone drink it.

"Where are we meeting this Crippen fellow?" he asked, looking around. He knew a fair number of the men in the room, several with criminal records, but the name Nate Crippen had been new to him when McNee first uttered it.

"First we have a small business matter to attend to," Rat Face replied, licking his lips.

"How much?"

"Would you be able to swing say, half a crown?"

Ian fished a coin from his pocket, wondering why McNee wasn't asking for more.

"Many thanks," his companion said, gazing at the coin fondly. "Would you like to see a trick?"

"I don't—"

"Our assignation won't occur for a few minutes yet."

"Very well, go ahead."

"I—oh, wait, you have something behind your ear," Rat Face said. His right hand shot out and plucked an object from the side of Ian's head—a half crown piece. "I think you forgot this—hang on, there's another," he said, moving his other hand around to behind Ian's left ear. "Ah," he said, pulling forth another half crown, "they look better together, don't you think?"

"You are very gifted at sleight of hand, Mr. McNee. I only hope you are as good at producing people out of thin air."

"Let's find out, shall we?" said his companion, downing the last of his drink.

Ian gulped down the remainder of his pint and followed him back through the crowded pub. The sound level had increased by half, and smoke swirled in thick waves all around them.

"Oiy, Detective!" a voice bellowed from across the room.

Ian turned to see a familiar face.

"Why, hello, Jimmy!" he said, as two muscular arms enveloped him in a crushing hug. Once he was released, he looked up into the smiling face of Jimmy Snead, thief, street fighter, rogue, and Ian's most loyal follower.

"Fancy seein' you here," the big man said. "Hain't seen ye fer ages!"

"What have you been up to, Jimmy? Keeping your hands clean?"

Snead grinned and cracked his knuckles. "Th'only thaing these hands hae done in th'past eight months is good, honest labor. Workin' the docks now—ain't I?" he said, with a nod at Rat Face.

"Yes, indeed." The small man chuckled nervously. "Quite a reformed character these days, heh heh."

The two of them had sustained a formidable crime partnership in the past, stealing and fencing stolen goods, and Ian doubted that Jimmy was as reformed as all that, but kept his thoughts to himself.

"Lemme buy ye a wee dram," Jimmy declared, starting toward the bar.

"First I've some business to attend to," Ian said. "But maybe later?"

"A course, whatever ye say," Snead replied, sounding disappointed. "Police work, is it?"

"In a way," said Ian.

"Well, let me nae stop ye—get on wi'ye," Jimmy said, giving Ian a slap on the back that nearly winded him.

"See you later," said Ian, following Rat Face from the pub.

A blast of wintry air hit them as they emerged into the night, making Ian's eyes water. Flicking away the tears, he followed McNee through the wynd along the side of the pub. The last time he had walked this alley was to fight Jimmy Snead, at their first meeting, earning his affection by—just barely—besting him.

"Brings back memories, doesn't it?" said Rat Face, as though reading his mind. "I have to say, my money was on Snead. To hear him talk, you're the only person to beat him in a fair fight. He never stops talking about the police detective who gave him a good thrashing."

"When is Crippen due to show?" Ian said as they entered the small dirt yard behind the pub. It reeked of onions and rotting vegetables; a bin in the corner overflowed with rubbish.

"Any minute now," Rat Face said, looking around nervously.

They stood for a moment side by side, their breath forming white puffs that quickly dissipated in the frosty air. Ian glanced back at the lighted windows of the pub, smoke pouring from its single chimney. The din inside could be heard from where they stood—bursts of laughter shot into the air like gun blasts.

Rat Face pulled his scarf closer around his scrawny neck. "If he fails to show, I will naturally refund—hang on a minute," he said, taking a step toward the back of the yard.

"What is it?" said Ian.

"There—what's that?"

Peering through the darkness, Ian could just make out a shape on the ground in front of the fence. "Just a pile of rubbish, I should think," he said, already moving toward it. His steps quickened as he got closer, his stomach filling with acid as he realized what he was looking at.

"What is it?" Rat Face said, a few steps behind him. "It's not—"

"I'm afraid it is," Ian said, looking down at the form on the ground.

The man lay face up, his throat slashed, the wound a gaping red cry of outrage at the hand that inflicted it. But it was the injury to his face that made Ian catch his breath. He had been cut ear to ear, from both sides of his mouth upward in a half moon, the effect being to create a grotesque grin.

"A Glasgow smile," McNee uttered softly. The term referred to a punishment often meted out to members of criminal organizations who became police informants, ratting out other gang members being one of the worst crimes one could commit. Once a man had suffered the disfigurement, his resulting scars were a sign that he could not be trusted.

The wound was not fatal, but both men knew it for what it was—torture. And a warning to others who might follow in his footsteps.

"Is it—?" Ian said.

McNee swallowed hard and nodded. "Aye. Nate Crippen. God rest his soul, poor bugger."

Ian bent to examine the body. Crippen's hands were bound behind his back with a strong piece of rope, securely tied with a simple but effective-looking knot. Both wounds were fresh, which meant it was possible that while the two of them were sipping their drinks inside the tavern, Nate Crippen was meeting his murderer.

CHAPTER
TWENTY-SEVEN

An hour later Crippen's body was on the way to the morgue, and, having examined the crime scene as closely as possible with limited light, Ian couldn't wait to wash his hands of the Hound and Hare. He intended to return the following morning to take a closer look in daylight, but for now he was glad to be rid of the place. Rat Face had long since scampered away into the night, the fear of God in him that he would suffer the same fate as Nate Crippen. Ian didn't blame him, but thought of him as the kind of man who managed to slip through hard situations, being far more cunning than the average criminal.

He had one last task to accomplish before leaving. Emerged from that wretched alley, he entered the tavern once more, clutching the rope in one hand. The presence of a dead man behind the pub had barely made an impression on the hard-drinking crowd inside, and the appearance of a detective was only slightly more noteworthy. These were men who stared death in the face every day, either from poverty or violence or both, men who held jobs no one else wanted and worked hours few could survive, in conditions that would horrify the most earnest of social reformers.

Jimmy Snead was nowhere in sight, and Ian received a few hostile looks as he made his way to the bar. Signaling the barkeep with the single gold earring, Ian held out the piece of rope. "Can you tell me what knot this is?"

The giant cocked his head to one side and crossed his arms. "Wha' makes ye think I'd know a rat's ass about knots, matey?"

"Those tattoos, for a start," Ian said, with a glance at his meaty forearms.

"An' if I do?"

"Is it a sailor's knot?"

"What if it is? What's in it fer me?"

"The knowledge that you helped the Edinburgh City Police put away a murderer."

The man burst into laughter. "Half the fellas in here prob'ly kilt a man at some point."

"Well?" said Ian, laying a half guinea on the bar. "Do you recognize this knot?"

"It's a stevedore knot," the barkeep said, pocketing the money. "Mos' sailors'd know it, an' so would any docker."

"So it's used by dockworkers?"

"Aye. Stevedore is wha' them wops call 'em."

"Which is how the knot got its name?"

"Yer a sharp one, aren't ye?" the man said with a wink, filling four pint glasses with one swoop under the tap. "Oiy, Angus—here's yer drinks!" he yelled, sliding them down the bar to a guffawing group of patrons. "Copper here says this one's on him," he added, which brought a cheer from them. "Ye'd better clear out afore ye find yerself buyin' this whole place another round," he said, leaning toward Ian, his powerful forearms resting on the bar.

Ian did not wait for another invitation to leave—he was glad to be rid of the place, pushing the door open so violently he nearly ripped it from its hinges. Out in the street, it was only when he heard the chiming of the St. Giles clock that he realized he had missed a second assignation that night.

He arrived at Le Canard disheveled and breathless, inhaling the aroma of leeks and potatoes emanating from bowls of creamy soup being served at a nearby table. A feathery dusting of finely chopped chives covered the center of the pale white soup, with swirls of green and gold.

The look on the maître d's face said it all. There was simply no redeeming a man who could not be bothered to show up—not once, but *twice*—on an assignation with such a charming young lady. Perhaps the monsieur was married and could not find a suitable excuse to give his wife, or maybe he was ashamed to be seen in public in flagrante—in any case, he was an ungainly and unforgivable *bouffon, un idiot insensé*, because only a man utterly without sense would think of committing such a grave *méfait*, a crime against all that is decent and proper and respectable.

Ian had to admire the man's ability to communicate all this with a twitch of his mustache and a tilt of his sleek head. This time he did not have to ask for the note, which was thrust into his hand before he could utter a word.

I fear the maître d' is of the opinion that you are an irredeemable lourdaud (an oaf). I may very well agree with him, unless you give me a reason not to. The choice is yours.

Once again it felt ridiculous to thank a man who was glaring daggers at him, so Ian simply slipped the note into his pocket, turned, and fled.

CHAPTER
TWENTY-EIGHT

Donald was already in bed by the time Ian arrived home, his rhythmic snoring rippling the air as Ian crept quietly into the flat. There was a note about some soup on the stove, but Ian was too exhausted to eat. Leaving his clothes in a pile on the floor, he slipped into his nightshirt and crawled into bed. Once he was between the covers, though, the moon glared down at him so brightly that he felt it, too, had a message for him. He lay staring at it for some time, wondering why, with so many people anxious to communicate with him, he had so little useful information.

He was unaware of falling asleep, but found himself wandering a foreign landscape, a darkened wood with twisted trees and blackened branches. There was little sign of life as he wended his way down a narrow path leading to an unknown destination. The moon appeared as a glowing yellow eye, glowering coldly at him with neither goodwill nor compassion, as if daring him to solve the pressing questions that consumed him.

A thin sheet of mist covered the ground, and he could not see his feet. He felt as if he was floating rather than walking, gliding through the withered woods lightly as a cloud. As he approached a clearing, he felt inexorably drawn to it but also frightened of what he might find there. He stepped from the line of forest into the scrubby field and heard a long, low whistle. The sound pierced him to the very bones, freezing him where he stood. It was the signal his mother had used to bring him and Donald in for dinner. The sound carried surprisingly well in the glens and hills of the Highlands, and could be heard half a mile or more away. And here it was again, in this barren and lifeless landscape.

He looked wildly around the clearing, nothing stirring save the fog swirling at his feet. Then, across the stretch of abandoned grassland, his eye caught a flicker of movement. The mist seemed to be forming itself into a thin white tornado, spinning and whirling upward in an ever-rising funnel of fog.

Before his astonished eyes, the vapor congealed and transformed. Shadowy as a breath, it became more solid, finally assuming the shape of a hooded human figure. Frozen to the spot, he watched it glide slowly toward him. It, too, seemed to hover just above the surface of the earth, as if riding on the thin blanket of mist still swirling over the ground. Terror gripped him as it approached, but his limbs were as dead as the gnarled trees behind him. Try as he might, he could not move. He could only watch helplessly as the specter floated toward him, arms outstretched.

He tried to see the creature's face, but it was hidden deep within the folds of the robe—he feared worse, that it had no face at all. But the apparition raised a hand to pull back the hood of its garment, and Ian caught his breath as he recognized his mother's face.

She gazed at him sadly, her mouth moving as if in speech, but no sound came from her pale lips. His mother's ghost—for so he knew it must be—stretched a hand toward his face, as if to stroke his cheek tenderly. But instead of a caress, Ian felt a sharp burning sensation, as if its fingers were on fire. He cried out and tried to pull away—and awoke in his own bed with the sound of his voice still ringing in his ears.

Gingerly, he put a hand to his left cheek, which still stung, and felt a thin line of raised flesh, as if a scar had already formed where the specter had touched him. Throwing off his covers, he sprang from his bed and lit the gas lamps with trembling hands. Going to the dresser mirror, he examined his cheek, which did indeed bear a red, throbbing gash. The burn scar on his shoulder began to pulsate as if in response, a constant reminder of the fire that he had so narrowly escaped.

But had he truly escaped? He sank back into bed, perspiration soaking his nightshirt. The familiar objects of his bedroom, usually so comforting, were overshadowed by the memory of the vivid and disturbing dream. His hand went to the raised mark on his face, still burning and twitching. Surely it was impossible for a dream to infect one's waking life—he must have thrashed around in his sleep, somehow scratching his cheek in the process. But he could still feel his mother's fingers upon his skin, a touch he had yearned for these long seven years, only to find it carried not loving tenderness, but fire. And if he had scratched his own cheek, why was it in the exact spot his mother had touched?

The mark of Cain. The words appeared, unbidden, in his mind, as a shiver went through his body. But Ian had taken his brother in, sheltered him, cared for him. If anything, was he not the opposite of the murderous biblical figure? Why, then, did the phrase embed itself in his brain, repeating over and over like the terrible clanging of a death knell?

Pulling the covers up to his chin, he gazed out at the careless moon, with its ridiculous grin, so removed from human striving and suffering, and waited for the dawn.

CHAPTER
TWENTY-NINE

Donald's efforts to coax Ian into eating the next morning met with limited success. Ian's dream of the night before clung like a succubus, leaving him queasy and unsettled. Luckily, his brother was in such a cheerful mood he scarcely noticed Ian's depressed state.

"So you missed her again, I see," Donald said, slathering gooseberry jam onto his toast. "It's getting to be a habit with you."

Ian just nodded, slipping Bacchus one of his kippers. He never fancied smoked fish for breakfast, something Donald had either forgotten or chosen to ignore. The cat dragged the fish under the table and devoured it in three gulps.

"What happened to your cheek?" Donald said, peering at Ian's face. "Did Bacchus do that?"

"No. I must have scratched it in my sleep."

"Tell you what," Donald said, pouring a liberal amount of cream into his coffee. "Why don't you come to the infirmary with me? If she's there, you can apologize. Mind you, she might tell you to bugger off, but might as well give it a go, eh?"

Ian stared at him.

"Am I being too vulgar?" said Donald. "You should hear the way medical students talk among themselves. Absolutely scandalous."

"I don't see what good an apology would do at this point."

"Now you're just sulking."

"Is it my imagination, or is the cat starting to look more like you?" Ian said, pointing to a considerably more bulbous Bacchus, busy cleaning himself. "He certainly seems to have acquired your appetite."

"You should know by now changing the subject is useless with me," Donald said, rising from the table. "Come along—you're going with me, like it or not."

Ian offered little resistance—exhausted, he was relieved to let Donald step in and decide things for him. It was early, and as it was Saturday, he had plenty of time to get to the station house.

Since the weather had turned warmer, they elected to walk. It wasn't far, and the exercise and brisk breeze lifted Ian's spirits. Feeling revived, he took a deep breath, inhaling the scents of the city—meat pies and fish frying in oil, boiled cabbage, and fried onions all mixed with the smell of horse manure. The cries of seagulls hovering overhead blended with screeching children dashing down dank alleys; the calls of street vendors mixed with the cackling of geese being led to market by their owner, a plump, apple-cheeked woman in a snowy bonnet and apron. Edinburgh was not a quiet place, nor a peaceful one, but it was rarely dull.

"Oiy, Guv!"

He turned to see the flushed face of Derek McNair, scrambling to keep up with the brothers' long strides.

"Hiya," Derek said, hopping along beside them, taking two steps for each of theirs.

Donald gave him a dour glance. "To what do we owe the pleasure of your company?"

"What happened to yer face?" Derek asked Ian, ignoring the question.

"A bar brawl," said Donald.

"Last night? What happened?"

"I'm surprised you haven't already heard," said Ian.

"Heard wha', Guv?" said Derek as they swung onto the Cowgate from West Bow Street.

"Nate Crippen was murdered."

"No kiddin'? How?"

"We found him in the alley next to the pub. His throat was slashed."

"Good Lord, Ian," said Donald, his face darkening. "And now you're in danger as well. I told you to give this up, but evidently you didn't listen."

Ian said nothing. He supposed Donald would eventually find out, but he was not going to reveal the detail of the Glasgow smile. It would only support his brother's already entrenched position.

"Any idea who done it?" said Derek as they approached Grassmarket Square.

"None," said Ian.

The Saturday open-air market was in full swing as they passed a juggler entertaining a crowd of onlookers. He was thin and wiry, dressed in a tattered tuxedo complete with top hat, his face sporting a jet-black, elaborately waxed mustache and goatee, which made him look a little like popular images of Satan. He caught Ian's eye as they passed, and gave a little wink. It was like being winked at by the devil.

A sleepy-looking boy in a long white apron was sweeping the front stoop of Edinburgh's oldest pub, the White Hart Inn, which in a few hours would be filled with heavy-drinking drovers, shepherds, and farmers. It was a long day for the men who rose before dawn to bring their wares to the market, and the pubs lining the Grassmarket would do a brisk trade when the day was done.

"Why didn't you tell me?" Donald said as they turned onto Vennel Street.

"Surely that is obvious from your reaction," Ian replied tightly.

"Do you expect me to stand silently by as you put yourself in peril?"

"May I remind you danger is part of my profession?"

"This wild goose chase has nothing to do with your job as a policeman," Donald replied as they passed the Flodden Wall. The wall was one of the city's oldest, erected in 1513 after a disastrous Scottish defeat at the Battle of Flodden, which resulted in the death of the Scottish king, James IV. "In fact, I doubt DCI Crawford would be pleased to hear you are off chasing phantoms on your own."

"Clearly they are not phantoms," Ian said hotly, "as a man is dead."

"Do you intend to be the next victim?"

"Certainly not," Ian replied as they stepped aside to let a wagon piled high with hay pass, the broad wheels wobbling on the uneven cobblestones. He breathed in the sweet, musty smell, and was instantly transported to their neighbor's barn in the Highlands, when he and Donald would sneak over to ride the horses.

"So, Guv," said Derek. "What're ye gonna do now?"

"Find out who killed Nate Crippen and why."

"See here," said Donald. "Why can't you just drop all this nonsense?"

"Why are you so anxious to stop me?"

"I should think that would be obvious. I don't want you to end up in an alley with your throat slashed."

"I can look after myself."

"You have no idea who you're dealing with."

"Do you?"

"Obviously it's someone able to kill a man virtually under your nose and get away with it."

They stood at the corner of Keir Street and Lauriston Place, in the shadow of the infirmary's massive clock tower.

"Guess I'll be on my way, then," Derek said, scuffing his shoe against the paving stones. He looked up at Ian, the sun glinting off the red highlights in his mop of hair. With better clothes and a proper haircut, he would be a decent-looking lad, Ian thought.

"Here," he said, handing the boy some coins. "Buy yourself breakfast."

"Ta very much," Derek said, pocketing the money. "Oh, any chance a' that bath sometime?"

Ian stole a glance at Donald, who exhaled loudly through his nose. "He can come tomorrow night, after Sunday roast at Lillian's," he told Ian.

Derek grinned widely, displaying surprisingly pearly teeth. "I like yer aunt—she's all right by me."

"I can't tell you how gratified I am to hear it," Donald replied drily.

The boy licked his lips. "Sunday roast, eh?"

Donald lifted an eyebrow. "Don't press your luck."

"I'll be off, then," Derek said. "Sorry 'bout yer informant. That's a bad break." He sauntered away, whistling.

Watching his retreat, Donald shook his head. "I still don't trust that boy."

"As I told DCI Crawford, it is only necessary that he be useful."

"How is old Toshy?" Donald said as they walked through the iron gates and up the paved path to the august building.

"That's what Dr. Littlejohn calls him. How did you—"

"I have my ways, brother—you should know that by now."

"You would make a splendid investigator."

"Dr. Bell believes medicine is an investigative science."

"How is the old blowhard?"

"He's a brilliant doctor, you know."

"I've no doubt of that."

"What do you have against him?"

"I just think he fancies himself a bit too much."

183

"You might fancy yourself, too, if you were—speak of the devil," Donald said, as the man himself came striding briskly toward them. His graying hair was as tidy as his trim, athletic figure. Ian put his age as early forties, a man in his vigorous prime.

"Ah, Hamilton—early as usual, I see," he said, rubbing his hands together. They were well shaped, with long, tapering fingers—the hands of a skilled surgeon.

"Good morning, Dr. Bell," said Donald.

His subservient manner in Bell's presence rankled Ian. Feeling his own face redden, he stared down at his feet.

"And good morning to you, Detective Inspector. What brings you to our corner of the city?"

"He's come to see Conan Doyle," Donald lied, to Ian's relief. He had no wish to share his romantic entanglements—or lack thereof—with Dr. Bell.

"I hear you and young Doyle have struck up a bit of a crime-fighting partnership," said Bell. "Mind you don't distract him from his medical duties."

"I wouldn't dream of it," Ian said, unable to hide a certain coldness in his tone. He was aware Donald was glaring at him, but ignored it.

But Bell seemed to have other things on his mind. If he noticed Ian's attitude, he did not remark upon it. "I've an intriguing case I thought you might find interesting," he told Donald. "Like to come have a look?"

"I would be delighted," his brother said. "See you tonight," he told Ian as he followed the great man down the hall. "Good luck," he added with a smile before they turned the corner to the corridor leading to the wards.

"Good luck indeed," Ian muttered under his breath. The morning sun streaming through the tall windows reflected off the polished floors, momentarily blinding him. He blinked, and when he looked up, he saw an angular figure in a crisp white nursing uniform approaching.

"Can I help you, sir?" she said, walking smoothly toward him, her sturdy shoes seeming to glide over the tiled floor. Her snowy white apron and the way she floated down the hall reminded him of the ghostly apparition of his dream.

"I, uh—I was looking for someone."

"I thought perhaps you were seeking treatment for that wound on your cheek," she said, peering at his face.

"No, I . . ."

"Yes?" she said, tilting her head to one side. Nearly as tall as Ian, she was a handsome woman of about forty, with clear gray eyes set over high cheekbones in an austere face with a firm jaw. Something in those steady eyes told him she was not one to be crossed. Or maybe it was the square set of her shoulders, confident attitude, or commanding contralto. He had heard Donald speak of the infirmary's fearsome head nurse, and had no doubt that was the very person now confronting him.

"Are you Nurse Meadows?"

Her eyes narrowed. "And how would you come by that information?" The slight lilt in her voice suggested her origins lay across the Irish Sea.

"I'm a friend of Conan Doyle," he blurted out. Her face relaxed into what was nearly a smile.

"Ah, young Arthur, is it? A fine lad—I know the Doyles from back home."

"Ireland?"

"Aye. They're a respectable family there—prosperous and all, you know. Too bad about that father of his," she said, shaking her head.

"Yes, he's spoken of the troubles with his father."

"Such a pity, so it is. Such a fine fellow, to be saddled with a da like that. So you're after seeing young Arthur? I'll take you to him."

"But first, I was wondering—"

"Well?" she said, crossing her arms. "Go on, then, spit it out."

"Do you happen to know if Nurse Stuart is in today?"

"So that's the reason for your visit," she said with a smug smile. "Thought you were hiding something."

Ian felt himself redden. "Well, I—"

"She's not on shift today. Just as well—she's been distracted lately, and now I know why."

"It's not really—"

"Do you still want to see young Arthur?"

"I do."

At that moment the object of their conversation came striding toward them. "Your brother tells me you're looking for me," he said to Ian.

"Yes," Ian replied, heartily relieved to see him. The air felt clearer when Conan Doyle was around; a sense of calm descended at the sight of his friend's smiling face.

"Hello, Nurse Meadows," Doyle said. "You're looking fresh as a summer breeze."

"Go on with your blather," she said, but her cheeks glowed, and she even giggled—Ian would have thought such a sound was foreign to her very nature. "I'll leave you gentlemen to it—I'll tell Nurse Stuart you stopped in," she added with a nod to Ian, pivoting crisply on her well-leathered heel.

"Fine woman," Doyle said, watching her retreat. "Runs the nursing staff like a general. She's terrifying, of course, but her efficiency is astonishing."

Ian laughed. "How do you do it, Doyle?"

"What?"

"Charm everyone you meet?"

"Don't know what you mean, old boy."

"Nurse Meadows. She nearly ate my head off, but she adores you."

"You exaggerate, dear fellow."

"And you are too modest. But that's part of your appeal."

"Enough of this nonsense," Doyle said, clapping Ian on the back. "By the way, what happened to your face?"

"I scratched myself in my sleep."

"It must have been a beastly dream."

"Care to revisit a crime scene with me?"

"I suppose I could play hooky for an hour or two. What's the plan?"

"I have a theory."

"'Lead on, spirit.'"

They stepped out of the infirmary as a cloud passed over the sun, leaving half the city in shadow.

CHAPTER THIRTY

William "Billy" Dickerson poured his third cup of tea that morning and paced the station. It was gone ten o'clock. He had been waiting for DI Hamilton for over an hour. He didn't know whether to be worried or irritated by the detective's tardiness. He stood before the window, gazing down on the populace of Edinburgh trudging up and down the High Street. Everyone in Edinburgh seemed to be trudging, slogging, or plodding, as if life in the city had so drained the vigor from their limbs that there was barely any left over, certainly not enough to skip, bounce, or prance. Even the horses conserved their energy, the cobblestones ringing with their ponderous steps.

The sergeant watched a pair of massive gray Percherons pull an omnibus in the direction of the Grassmarket. Their muscular necks strained as they lugged the vehicle up the incline, the street rising steadily from its origin at Holyrood Palace to Castle Rock. Dickerson was afraid of horses, but he did admire the powerful but docile French draft horses. His uncle had owned one, and it was the only horse he had ever felt comfortable enough to touch, even creeping into the barn to pet him at night.

"Gazing down on the hoi polloi, Sergeant?"

He turned to see Constable Turnbull, his fleshy mouth pulled into a smile. The sergeant pitied the constable, with his heavily pock-marked face, though Dickerson always felt off balance around him, as if he was expected to say or do something but was never quite sure what. He knew DI Hamilton loathed the man and that the feeling was mutual. But Dickerson was still peeved at the detective over the way he had treated poor Gretchen. Hamilton could be high-handed, a character flaw Dickerson had ample opportunity to observe. He also felt Hamilton ignored him when he pointed it out, and that rankled him most of all.

He smiled at the constable. "How many a' them down there d'you think are criminals?"

Turnbull's smile widened, emphasizing the deep pits in his skin. "Any man is capable of crime under the right circumstances."

"Ye really believe that, do ye?"

"Wouldn't you be capable of killing a man if he were threatening, say, your sister?"

Dickerson frowned. Did the constable know about his sister, or was he just making a lucky guess? "If her life were in danger, a' course."

"Well, there you are—I rest my case."

"But that don' mean—"

"How about a little something to go with that tea? I stopped by Daily Bread on the way here," Turnbull said, walking to his desk in the corner of the room. Dickerson followed him uncertainly. He *was* hungry, having neglected his usual stop at the bakery so he would be on time to meet Hamilton. And now the detective was over an hour late.

"Fancy a bit of Selkirk bannock, Sergeant?" Turnbull asked, pulling out a waxed bakery bag.

"Don' mind if I do," Dickerson said, saliva springing into his mouth as he gazed at the sweet buttery treat.

"Help yourself," Turnbull said, handing it to him. "There's more than enough for two."

"How did you know?" Dickerson asked, biting into the luscious loaf sweetened with raisins and currants.

Turnbull chuckled. "Just a lucky guess. It is one of their specialties."

Chewing contentedly, Dickerson felt his anger at Hamilton drain away. Hunger had put an edge on his temper, but each bite of Selkirk bannock softened his irritation. He would have made a good breakfast for his sister that morning, but she was staying over at a friend's house. He hadn't slept well—he never did when Pauline was out of the house. He felt his obligation to take care of her keenly, but tried not to burden her with it, so when she asked if she could sleep over at Molly's, he said yes, even though everything inside him wanted to say no.

"That went down a treat," he mumbled through a mouthful of bread. "Ta very much."

"My pleasure," said the constable, leaning back in his chair, regarding the sergeant.

There was something unsettling in the way Turnbull looked at him. Technically Dickerson was the constable's superior officer, but somehow he never felt like it. If anything, Turnbull treated him as an inferior, and Dickerson never seemed to have the gumption to object. Now he felt the man's steady gaze upon him, which made him uneasy.

"Speaking of criminals," said Turnbull, "any success in the hunt for the false informant?"

His question caught the sergeant off guard, making him choke on his pastry. Coughing violently, Dickerson reached for his tea just as Detective Hamilton entered the station house. Seeing the sergeant and Constable Turnbull together, he frowned as he whipped off his cape, tossing it onto the rack and striding toward them.

"Good morning, Detective," Turnbull said smoothly as Hamilton approached, a scowl on his handsome face, which was marred by a thin red wound on one cheek.

"Constable," he replied with a curt nod. "Are you quite all right?" he asked Dickerson, who nodded, still unable to speak, the bread still lodged in his windpipe.

Hamilton gave a short, sharp rap with his fist on the sergeant's back, between his shoulder blades, causing the morsel to pop from his mouth onto the floor. Dickerson gave two more coughs, then inhaled deeply.

"Better now?" said Hamilton.

"Yes—thank you, sir," he replied sheepishly. He had meant to give the detective a piece of his mind about being so late, and now here he was, humbled by this embarrassing situation. There would be no reprimand; as usual, Hamilton had the upper hand.

"Where have ye b-been, sir?" he sputtered, giving one final cough to clear his lungs.

"Visiting a crime scene."

"Have ye told DCI Crawford yet 'bout my part in the Dickens play, sir?" he asked, knowing full well Hamilton had not.

"I meant to, but I'm afraid it slipped my mind," the detective said rather more breezily than Dickerson thought appropriate. After all, he had given the sergeant his word, and a promise broken, no matter how small, irked Dickerson, who saw it as further proof of how lightly Hamilton held him in regard.

"Ah, there you are," the detective said as Arthur Conan Doyle entered the station house. Manly and tall, with an athletic, graceful build, Conan Doyle represented everything the sergeant was not.

Dickerson crossed his arms and pursed his lips in displeasure. Bad enough that Hamilton had kept him waiting, but now to show up with Doyle—that really was too much. He knew it was small of him, but he bitterly resented Hamilton's friendship with the medical student. They made jokes he didn't understand, laughing together in ways that, as the detective's subordinate, he wasn't able to. They spoke with the same crisp consonants, whereas Dickerson was keenly aware of his heavy Lancashire accent. Doyle and Hamilton were equals, companions, *friends*. And no matter how much time he spent with Hamilton, how much danger they faced together, he would always be less than that.

He sighed and turned away, catching Turnbull's gaze. The constable made a face, rolling his eyes in a comic way, and Dickerson experienced a rush of relief—he had an ally.

"Sorry," Doyle told Hamilton. "I stopped to put a few coins in a beggar's purse, and we got to chatting a bit. Interesting fellow—former military man. Lost his sight in Afghanistan."

"That'll be Brian. Don't make the mistake of believing everything he tells you."

Doyle threw back his head and guffawed. Even his laugh was athletic, Dickerson thought peevishly.

Constable Turnbull stood and stepped forward. "I don't believe we've been introduced. Constable John Turnbull."

Doyle grasped his hand in a hearty handshake. "Arthur Conan Doyle. I'm a medical student at—"

"Oh, yes—I believe I know your father. He lives at Sciennes Place, I think?" A cloud passed over Doyle's face, and he took a step backward, but Turnbull was undeterred. "Such a pity he's—"

Hamilton stepped forward. "Excuse me, but I have an urgent case to attend to, and—"

"Of course," Turnbull replied evenly. "Pardon me for wasting your time. That's a nasty cut on your face—you really should have it seen to." And with a last look at Doyle, he turned and sauntered away.

There was an awkward silence, which Doyle broke with a good-natured chuckle. "What say you we get on this? I have to return to the infirmary by midafternoon."

Carole Lawrence

"What are ye doin'?" said Dickerson.

"Analyzing this note," Hamilton replied, handing it to him.

Frowning, the sergeant read it.

You will pay for your crimes

I'll come for you when you least expect it

"Where'd ye get this?" he said.

"From the major's flat."

"But y'already searched his place—"

"Ah, but we neglected to look in the coal scuttle."

"Why on earth would it be in th—"

"Detective Hamilton had a theory that the major, thinking himself in danger, would hide the threatening note in a place his assailant would not think to look," Doyle said triumphantly.

"So if the worst did happen, he would leave behind evidence that might help us track down his killer."

"Oh," said Dickerson glumly, wondering why Hamilton hadn't included him in this venture, instead of Doyle, whom he loathed more and more.

"Sergeant, would you be so kind as to fetch the murder chart from the closet?"

"Murder chart—I say, that sounds intriguing," Doyle said, rubbing his hands together expectantly.

Dickerson headed to the supply closet, passing by Turnbull's desk. The constable winked at him, giving a conspiratorial smile that made Dickerson queasy. But he was also flattered—Turnbull had a following among the other officers, a group of cronies of which he was definitely the leader. And now he wanted to enlist Dickerson in his coterie, which was gratifying. DI Hamilton could be terse and demanding; those in Turnbull's crowd were looser and seemed to have fun both during working hours and afterward. With Hamilton, approbation could be hard to come by, which made Turnbull's praise all the more seductive. Who did Hamilton think he was, anyway? He needed to be taught a lesson, taken down a notch or two—it would serve him right.

As he passed Turnbull's desk, William Dickerson nodded and smiled at the constable. It was only a smile, he told himself, but even then, he had a feeling the consequences might be more than he bargained for.

CHAPTER
THIRTY-ONE

Conan Doyle studied the note pinned to the board before him.

You will pay for your crimes
I'll come for you when you least expect it

"No doubt it is an important piece of evidence," he said. "I hope I can be of some use in analyzing the person who wrote it." He looked at Hamilton for his reaction. He appreciated being consulted in the detective's cases, and did not want to appear arrogant. But his friend exhibited keen interest; his gray eyes shone with excitement, and his lean body had the contained energy of a retriever on a scent.

"Doyle has been enlightening me on the study of graphology," Ian told Sergeant Dickerson.

The sergeant frowned. "Graph-whatagee?"

"It's the study of handwriting. Invented by a Frenchman by the name of Jean Michon."

"Actually, the Chinese have known of it for centuries," Doyle pointed out. "They believed a person's handwriting was a key to his character."

"So what does it tell ye 'bout the person what wrote the note? Assumin' they're the killer, a' course."

"Excellent point, Sergeant," Ian said. "We cannot assume the writer of the note was indeed the murderer."

"Agreed," said Doyle. "But how likely is it the major received a threatening letter and was soon after slain by someone else?"

"I'll admit it's improbable," said Ian. "However, Hamilton's Third Rule of Investigation states—"

"Never leap to conclusions," Dickerson finished for him.

"Well done, Sergeant."

Doyle smiled and wiped his brow. He found Hamilton's endless drive to organize and formalize crime-solving procedures admirable, and a tad intimidating. Ian Hamilton was the most intense man he had ever met, and he was drawn to the detective's passion, and, truth be told, a little frightened of it. Like anything powerful, it had a potential dark side, and something about the detective made Doyle want to protect him, mostly from himself. "How many laws are there?" he asked.

"Ten, at present," Hamilton replied. "But it is an evolving list."

"Well, shall we assume for the moment the person who wrote it was the killer, and do our best to analyze the note?"

"By all means."

Doyle turned back to study the document. Hamilton stood beside him, peering at it with a look of intense concentration on his clean-cut features.

"Well?" the detective said after a moment. "What do you make of it?"

"The writing itself is rather flowery and feminine—you see this loop here on the 'Y,' and that flourish on the capital 'I'?"

"Which would indicate the writer is a woman?"

"But you see how firmly the pencil was pressed to the paper?"

"I did observe that. It is quite forceful, which seems at odds with the notion of the writer as female."

"What if the person writin' it were tryin' to disguise their identity?" Dickerson suggested.

"Interesting theory," said Hamilton. "But what are the chances the letter writer is familiar with the relatively new science of graphology?"

"Not much, I s'pose," Dickerson said sulkily, drumming his fingers on the desk.

Doyle was fairly certain the sergeant did not like him, though he wasn't entirely sure why. He resolved to try to make him an ally rather than an enemy. "Still, it's a very good observation," he said cheerfully, but Dickerson slumped in his chair and continued drumming his fingers.

"The language itself strikes me as rather masculine," Hamilton said. "It's very direct."

"And very personal. Do you think it likely the letter writer was someone the major knew?"

"It's certainly someone who knew him. Whether or not that is reciprocal, it is hard to say."

"Why write a note if yer going t'kill a man?" said Dickerson. "Wouldn't it just put him on 'is guard?"

"It would indeed, Sergeant—well said," Hamilton replied. "Which means the intent was to terrorize, to create fear in the victim."

"Major Fitzpatrick was a military man," Doyle said. "He was used to danger."

"Yes, but observe the language of the note. 'You will pay for your crimes. I'll come for you when you least expect it.' Not only is it personal, but it is aimed at striking fear into the victim's heart. 'When you least expect it'—what man alive would not feel trepidation at those words?"

Doyle crossed his arms. "Do you really think it likely a woman could pen such words?"

"I have met some murderous women in my line of work."

Doyle nodded. "Yes, your last homicide case made me reassess my view of the weaker sex."

"Not so weak, if y'ask me," said Dickerson. "Ever seen a woman in labor?"

"Indeed," Hamilton agreed. "I wonder how many men would willingly endure the pain of childbirth?"

"It might cut down vastly on overpopulation," said Doyle.

"What if the firm pressing of the pencil to paper is an indication of the writer's level of anger?" Hamilton suggested.

"Which could also account for the forceful nature of the message," Doyle agreed. "What other clues did you glean from the note?"

"The paper itself is uninstructive," said Ian. "A common type, found at most stationers."

"The fact that it was written in pencil rather than ink could be significant."

"How so?"

"I don't know, but it is worth noting."

The front door to the station house opened to admit a man that Doyle instantly surmised was DCI Crawford. Hamilton had given brief descriptions of him, but it was more his attitude of authority, combined with the effect his entrance had on the men in the station house. There was an electricity in the air, and an aura of general anxiety and alertness. Sleepy constables straightened their uniforms, put down their teacups, took their feet off desks, attempting to look busy doing paperwork or tidying up. He smiled—it mirrored the response of his fellow medical students when Dr. Bell entered a room.

"Good morning, sir," said Hamilton. His attitude toward Crawford was relaxed and more informal than Doyle would have expected; he seemed to fear the chief less than his fellow officers did.

"How's the investigation going? And who the bloody hell is this?" Crawford said, pointing to Doyle.

"This is Arthur Conan Doyle."

"Ah, Doyle!" Crawford said, breaking into a smile. "You're Dr. Bell's right-hand man."

"Well, I would hardly say that," Doyle answered modestly.

"Amazing chap. He saved my wife's life, I'm sure of it. Nobody could seem to figure out what ailed her. Bell took one look at her, asked a few questions, and came up with a diagnosis, just like that!"

"That sounds like him," Doyle said, smiling.

"It's an honor to meet you," Crawford said, shaking his hand warmly. "A true pleasure. What are *you* staring at?" he said to Sergeant Dickerson, who was glowering at them.

"Nothin', sir."

"Then wipe that look off your face. You look as if you're about to murder someone."

"Yes, sir."

"Right. Carry on, men," Crawford said, lumbering into his office. He reminded Doyle of a big, red-haired bear.

Doyle felt waves of enmity from the sergeant. He wished there was something he could do or say, but was beginning to suspect Dickerson regarded him as competition in his relationship with Detective Hamilton. Doyle had no wish to occupy that role but did not know what he could do about it. Ian Hamilton exuded a charisma that not only drew people to him but made them want his approval. Doyle himself was not immune to it, and on more than one occasion caught himself seeking Hamilton's approbation. Even Crawford was slightly deferential to him. Though he tried to maintain his gruff façade, Doyle could see Crawford's admiration and affection for Hamilton.

"The next order of business is to interview more members of the séance group," the detective said, tucking the note away in his desk.

"I must get back to the infirmary, or Bell will have my head," said Doyle. He noticed Sergeant Dickerson visibly brighten at the news of his departure.

"Thank you for your help," said Hamilton.

"It was my pleasure," Doyle said, fetching his coat. "I should like to hear how you are progressing, if you don't mind."

"By all means," the detective replied, seeing him to the door.

As he left the building, Doyle had the unaccountable feeling he was being watched. He looked up and down the High Street but saw nothing suspicious, only the usual parade of people. No one seemed to be paying him any heed, apart from the beggar he had conversed with earlier, who greeted him as he passed.

"G'day, then, Mr. Doyle."

"How did you know it was me?" Doyle asked, dropping a few coins into his cup.

"Your smell."

"I wasn't aware I had one."

"Everyone does. In yer case, it's a combination a' lime shavin' lotion an' rubbin' alcohol. Can't mistake that—and a wee hint a' formaldehyde."

"How do you know what formaldehyde smells like?"

"I used t'work in the morgue. It's not a smell ye ferget."

Doyle laughed. "By Jove, you're a wizard!"

"A dog would know you by yer smell, an' I've jes developed mine, is all."

"You should use that ability to help Detective Hamilton on his cases."

"Oh, I help him, mate, don' ye worry."

"I'm very glad to hear it. Have a round on me," Doyle said, tossing another coin into the cup.

"You're a scholar an' a gentleman," said Brian, grinning to show teeth much in need of dentistry.

"Take care of yourself," said Doyle. "There are bad people about."

"Don' worry 'bout me, mate," the beggar called after him.

Instead of walking west in the direction of the castle—the shortest route to Lauriston Place—Doyle turned his steps in the opposite direction, ducking into Old Fleshmarket Close, heading south. He crept slowly down the narrow passage, smelling straw and mildew, listening for footsteps behind him, but heard nothing. Somewhere a dog barked. It was only after he passed the Advocates Library, where the lane widened, that he finally lost the sensation of being watched. He was fully aware he might be imagining the whole thing, yet a shiver ran down his spine as he contemplated who might be observing him, and why.

CHAPTER
THIRTY-TWO

"Who are we goin' t'see?" Sergeant Dickerson said as he loped down the High Street after Ian.

"Jonas and Catherine Nielsen."

"Where do they live?"

"It's not far—Jeffrey Street."

"How d'ye get their address?"

"Jed Corbin tracked it down for me."

"So I guess y'owe him one?"

"No doubt he'll find a way for us to repay him," he said as they swung onto South Bridge.

"An' these Nielsens are part a' the séance group?"

"Yes, though they weren't there the night I attended with my aunt. She seems to think they're respectable people."

They walked in silence for a while, Ian lost in his thoughts but aware that Dickerson had gone unusually quiet. He knew the sergeant had a bee in his bonnet, but had neither the time nor the energy to ferret out the reason.

The Nielsens lived in a well-kept four-story building near the inter-section of Jeffrey and Market Streets, close enough to the Waverley train yards that Ian could hear the clacking of metal wheels on the tracks and the shouts of railway workers.

The landlady looked alarmed upon seeing Dickerson's uniform, but Ian reassured her—not entirely truthfully—that it was a routine police matter.

The first knock on the door to the flat brought no response, but after the second one, Ian heard voices from inside. After a moment, the door opened to reveal an attractive woman of middle years, clad in a pale-yellow frock that brought out the highlights in her soft brown hair. She had an oval face, clear skin, and large brown eyes with tragic depths. Even had he not been aware she was a member of the séance group, Ian would have known she had suffered a terrible loss, the kind that leaves a permanent imprint. A little brown-and-white spaniel stood at her feet, wagging its tail.

"Good afternoon," she said, her voice a melodic contralto with a faint Nordic accent. "May I help you?"

When Ian explained why they had come, she did not hesitate to invite them in, leading them through to a simply but tastefully fur-nished parlor, its most prominent feature being an ornately carved spinet piano. The wood was a deep mahogany and glistened in the soft afternoon light filtering in through damask curtains. Not a speck of dust marred the perfect ivory keys.

"What a beautiful instrument," Ian said. "Who in your family plays?"

Mrs. Nielsen gazed at it sadly. "Our Lucas loved to play. His teach-ers said he was quite gifted. We couldn't bear to part with it when we lost him."

The cause of her sorrow now clear, Ian said gently, "When did he—?"

"It will be two years this April. And yet it seems a lifetime."

"I am very sorry to hear it."

"How did'e die?" asked Dickerson.

"Fell from de roof of his school," said a man's voice from behind them.

Ian turned to see a man in the doorway. He had not heard footsteps, and it was rather startling to see him there, silhouetted in the hallway light. He was tall and sturdy, with heavy shoulders, and for a brief moment Ian was reminded of the creature in *Frankenstein*, Mary Shelley's popular novel. He took a step into the room, and Ian was able to make out his features. His sparse hair was white blond, and his skin had the ruddy sheen of a Scandinavian native. His deep-set eyes appeared to be light blue, and a faint blond stubble adorned his square-jawed face. He was a handsome man, but his powerful shoulders were stooped, and he bore the same air of inconsolable sorrow as his wife. His voice retained more of the singsong cadences of his Nordic homeland.

"Jonas, these men have come about the terrible deaths of our séance companions," said Mrs. Nielsen. "This is my husband, Jonas," she told them. "Please, gentlemen, won't you sit down?"

"Ta very much," Dickerson replied, settling somewhat gingerly on a delicate-looking rosewood love seat. Ian complied by sitting on a sturdier-looking sofa next to the coal fire.

"Might we have some tea, Jonas?" she said, taking an armchair opposite Ian.

"Of course, my dear," he said, withdrawing silently. In spite of his imposing appearance, Mr. Nielsen was evidently subject to his wife's wishes.

"Now, then, how can I be of assistance?" she said, drawing her shawl around her shoulders.

"Perhaps we can wait until your husband returns," Ian said. "I should like to hear what he has to say as well."

She bent down to pet the spaniel at her feet. "Bandit has been such a comfort—he rarely leaves my side. He misses Lucas, too; sometimes

I catch him staring at the corner of the room at night, and I'm certain it's Lucas."

"Have ye, er, made contact wi' yer son at Madame Veselka's?" Dickerson asked.

A soft smile spread over her face. "Many times. It keeps us coming back—though of course we never know when he will appear. Madame is naturally subject to the whims of those who have passed over."

"Naturally," Ian echoed, hoping he was successfully hiding his disdain for what he regarded as nonsense.

Her husband appeared as silently as before, carrying an enormous silver tray laden with tea and a round cake festooned with almonds. Sergeant Dickerson's eyes widened at the sight of the sweet treat.

"Is that Dundee cake?"

"It is indeed," Mrs. Nielsen replied. "You're in luck—today was baking day. I take it you would like a piece?"

"Yes, please," said Dickerson, his sullen mood apparently forgotten.

"Shall I be mother?" said Mr. Nielsen, setting the tray on the oval, marble-topped table.

"Please," his wife said, moving a knitting basket from the couch onto the floor.

"My aunt knits as well," Ian remarked.

"It helps calm my nerves," she replied. "Thank you, dear," she said as her husband handed her a steaming cup of tea. After pouring everyone else tea, he served himself, lowering his stocky form into the armchair opposite his wife.

"Now, then, Sergeant, would you like a large piece?" she asked.

Dickerson leaned forward eagerly, but, catching Ian's gaze, cleared his throat. "Er, jes a wee bit, thanks."

She drew a knife from an ornately carved leather sheath. The blade was long and thin, with an inscription of some kind. The handle appeared to be made of bone.

"It's made from the horn of an elk," she said, noticing Ian's interest. "A traditional design. It's been in my family for generations."

"Interesting choice for cutting a cake," he replied.

"Nothing else cuts quite like it," she said, deftly slicing off a piece. Ian had to admire the way the knife cut cleanly through the cake—it was indeed a finely made tool.

Once cake was served all around, Ian explained the circumstances of the deaths of Elizabeth Staley and Major Fitzpatrick, leaving out a few salient details in each case. Mrs. Nielsen listened carefully, pausing only to pet the dog lying at her feet.

Mr. Nielsen shook his head sadly. "Rotten business. He was a right square chap, the major. Everyone liked him."

"Can you think of anyone in the group who might have a reason to harm him? A grudge of some kind, perhaps?"

"What makes you think the killer came from within our little group?" asked Mrs. Nielsen.

"Two people are murdered within days of each other, and so far the séance meetings are the only thing they have in common. It would be an odd coincidence if there is *not* some connection to the meetings."

"Ah, but there may be some other factor you are as yet unaware of," she said, slipping a piece of cake to the spaniel. The dog took the morsel delicately, thumping his tail on the carpet as he licked her fingers gratefully. It struck Ian that her attitude toward the dog was not so different from the way she treated her husband—courteously, but with a sense of noblesse oblige, an easy attitude of authority, as if she were the superior being. He could just as easily imagine her husband at her feet, gratefully lapping up proffered treats.

"Did you know either of them well?" asked Ian, as Sergeant Dickerson, having finished his first piece, eyed the cake longingly.

Mr. Nielsen looked to his wife as if awaiting her cue to speak.

"No," she replied firmly. "Did we, dear?"

He nodded in agreement. "Only saw them at the séances."

"We didn't socialize with them or anything like that," his wife continued, as if the very idea was unthinkable. "Right, dear?"

"No," he replied meekly.

"Would you like another piece of cake, Sergeant?" she asked, picking up the slicing knife. For a moment Ian imagined her wielding it overhead, an evil gleam in her eye . . . but neither of the victims had been stabbed.

"Yes, please," Dickerson said, avoiding eye contact with Ian. "Thank ye kindly."

"You are most welcome," she replied, sliding a generous piece onto his plate.

"How did you first come to Madame Veselka's séances?" asked Ian.

"We saw a flyer, didn't we, dear?" she said to her husband.

"Yes—it was posted in the library," he replied.

"That's right—we saw it on the community board."

"And when was that?" asked Ian.

Catherine put a finger to her lips. "Let's see, that would have been just about a year ago." She reached down to pet her dog, who gave a few wags of his tail before stretching out at her feet with a sigh of contentment.

"Was there a reason you did not attend the last séance?"

"Jonas was feeling poorly—weren't you, dear?"

He nodded. "I had catarrh."

"We cured that with a mustard poultice and plenty of nice hot tea, didn't we?"

"We did, aye."

"And what do you do for a living, Mr. Nielsen?" said Ian.

"He's a fisherman," said his wife. "Works on a trawler out of the Leith Docks."

"I come from a long line of seafaring men," he added proudly. "My grand da Olaf was a fisherman—moved here from Norway when my pa was just a lad. The sea is in my blood."

"Is there anything at all you can tell us that might help in our investigation? Anything you saw or heard, something out of the ordinary, perhaps?"

"Not that I can recall," said Mrs. Nielsen.

"What about you, Mr. Nielsen?"

He looked as if he was about to speak, then, catching his wife's eye, was silent. He looked down at his powerful, weather-roughened hands with their cracked nails and strong, thick fingers.

"I can tell you that Madame Veselka is a Gypsy," said Catherine Nielsen, scratching Bandit behind the ears.

"How d'you know that?" asked Dickerson.

"Her name isn't Veselka. It's Raglass. Vadoma Raglass."

"And how do you know this?"

"I saw it on the frontispiece of a book in her parlor. It was lying open," she said in response to his raised eyebrow. "When I confronted her, she confessed, and begged me not to tell anyone."

"So you kept her secret."

"I did not think the less of her because she was a Traveler, as we call them."

"That was good of you."

Gypsies occupied a strange place in British society. Members of the "respectable classes" were fascinated by their exotic looks and outlandish ways, but they were widely discriminated against as being mostly uneducated and illiterate. Many countries still had laws expelling them from their land. It was understandable the medium would wish to hide her Romany roots.

"And Gretchen Mueller?" said Ian. "What do you know of her?"

She exchanged a look with her husband, who cleared his throat. "Madame Veselka rescued her, took her in," he said.

"Rescued her from what?"

He looked at his wife, who gave a slight nod. "From a life of sin."

"She was a prostitute, you mean?"

"On the Continent somewhere, not sure exactly where."

"So it was before they came here?"

"Aye. They came to Edinburgh together."

"How did you learn this?"

"We arrived early one day and heard them talking in the next room. They were arguing over something, and the madame threatened to throw her back into the streets."

"Naturally we were concerned about the girl," said Mrs. Nielsen, "so we had a little chat with her before the others arrived, to make sure she was all right."

"And was she?"

"She didn't seem to take Madame's threats seriously, if that's what you mean."

"Is she afraid of her employer?"

"Not that I can see. They seem to have an almost mother-daughter relationship—wouldn't you agree?" she asked her husband.

He nodded. "I thought they were family when I first met them."

Further questioning did not reveal anything of interest—they claimed to know very little about the other attendees, including Ian's aunt. He carefully avoided mentioning that he was related to Lillian, or that he had attended the séance the week they were absent.

After another pot of tea, and a third piece of cake for Sergeant Dickerson, Ian stood up.

"Thank you for your time," he said, stretching, stiff from sitting so long.

"An' fer tea," Dickerson added. "That cake were brilliant."

"I am delighted you enjoyed it," Mrs. Nielsen replied, escorting them to the door while her husband tidied up, the little dog trotting behind her.

"Oh, just one more thing," said Ian as she opened the door for them.

"Yes?"

"Why isn't Mr. Nielsen at work today?"

"The boat is in dry dock, I believe—isn't that what you said, dear?" she called out to the kitchen.

"Aye," he said, entering the foyer, wiping his hands with a dish towel. "Making repairs this week. It's been a harsh winter, hard on the boats."

"That reminds me—do you know how to tie a stevedore knot?"

The big man laughed. "I learnt every sailing knot there is before I learnt to walk."

"Why do you ask?" said his wife, frowning.

"Just curious. Thank you again," Ian said, pulling on his cap. "Please contact me if you think of anything of interest," he added, handing them his card.

"Like what?" said Mr. Nielsen, scratching his head.

"I have had cases turn on a seemingly insignificant detail."

"That leaves rather a wide field," his wife remarked.

"I leave it to your judgment," said Ian. "Good day."

Out in the street, Sergeant Dickerson seemed bursting to speak as they approached St. Paul's, the church's new building still under construction.

"Out with it, Sergeant," said Ian. "What's on your mind?"

Dickerson kicked at a pebble, sending it skittering into the gutter. "It's naught, sir."

"I don't want you to explode in front of my eyes. Come along, now."

"It's jes . . ."

"What?"

"Well, sir, I jes don' think Gretchen is the type a' girl who'd . . . you know."

"Exactly what kind of girl would you expect her to be?"

"I mean, she's so young an' innocent, like."

"Sort of like your sister?"

Dickerson reddened. "That's not wha' I meant."

"It's a common misconception that women do that kind of thing because they want to, Sergeant."

"Why else would they?"

"Because they must. They have no other options, come from poverty, know no other life, are uneducated, have a family to support, and don't believe they're worthy or capable of anything else. They turn to the world's oldest profession because there will always be men who want 'that sort of woman.' And sadly, that isn't likely to change."

Ian's parents had fairly traditional attitudes, but Aunt Lillian and Uncle Alfie were decidedly more progressive, and Ian had always been attracted to their liberal views and sense of social justice. Lillian was a member of the National Society for Women's Suffrage, and volunteered at various charities. Ian loved his mother, but he admired Lillian, and over the years had absorbed her political and societal philosophies.

Dickerson didn't respond as they turned south on Carrubber's Close.

"Well, Sergeant?" Ian said finally. "What is it?"

"Kin I speak freely, sir?"

"Always."

"Sometimes ye kin be . . ."

"What?"

"Well . . . a bit arrogant, t'be honest, sir."

"I see," Ian said tightly. Dickerson's words stung. Ian wasn't sure what he had expected to hear, but not this.

"Ye said I could—"

"And I meant it. Thank you for letting me know." *Arrogant? Do other people feel that way?* he wondered.

His head spun a little as they walked in silence, the sun glinting off the windows of the buildings on either side of the narrow close. Ian glanced over at Dickerson to see the expression on his face, but the reflected sunlight momentarily blinded him.

CHAPTER
THIRTY-THREE

As he walked, Ian was haunted by the image of Nate Crippen, lying with his throat cut in a back alley. Questions swarmed through his head like a hive of angry bees. What did Crippen know that made someone so anxious to silence him? If he didn't act alone in setting the fire, who else was involved? And who had tipped that person off that Crippen was about to talk to Ian? Other than Rat Face and Derek, Ian knew of no one else who was aware of the meeting, apart from his brother. Rat Face had gone to such extremes to ensure their first meeting was private; surely he was too clever to slip up now. Had Derek succumbed to the temptation to boast to his friends, inadvertently bragging to the wrong person?

Brushing these thoughts aside, he attempted to concentrate on the case at hand. The lack of obvious suspects was compounded by the absence of motive. Nothing seemed to connect the two victims, except the fact that they both attended Madame Veselka's séances. He needed to dig deeper into their pasts, but there was so little time. The clock was ticking, and he feared their killer might be stalking other members of the séance group—even, God forbid, Aunt Lillian. His heart contracted at the thought that her safety might be in his hands.

The sun had long since ducked behind Castle Rock when Ian and Dickerson reached police chambers. The sergeant, who had maintained a moody silence during the walk, went to fetch a cup of tea, just as the door to the station house swung open, and Ian heard a familiar voice. Standing next to the desk sergeant, buoyant energy radiating from him like a spring breeze, was Arthur Conan Doyle.

"Ah, there you are, Hamilton!" he said, striding over to Ian's desk. "I was afraid I might be too late to catch you."

Ian smiled; it was impossible to react in any other way to Doyle's presence. "You're a welcome sight. What brings you here?"

"Mendelssohn," Doyle replied, producing a pair of tickets from his waistcoat pocket. "They are doing his Scottish Symphony and Hebrides Overture, along with some Gypsy airs by Sarasate, with the composer himself as soloist. We've just enough time to get there if we leave now— we shall have to dine afterward, I'm afraid."

"But my work—"

"Surely you are allowed one night off! To be honest, you look as though you could use it."

"Well, I must admit—"

"That's the spirit!" Doyle cried. "Fetch your coat and we'll hail a cab straightaway."

Moments later Ian was seated beside his companion in the back of a hansom cab as it rattled along the High Street, the chestnut gelding trotting at a vigorous pace upon the urging of his master, whom Doyle had promised half a guinea if he made good time.

"I was handed these tickets by Dr. Bell himself just as I was leaving the infirmary," Doyle said. "He had quite forgotten he'd purchased them until he discovered them in his waistcoat pocket. He had another engagement, so he gave them to me."

"It is encouraging to hear that he's human after all," Ian remarked drily.

"You mustn't be too hard on him. After all, the man is a genius, and certain allowances must be made. I know he can be rather full of himself, but one must expect a degree of arrogance in men of talent."

"I was accused of being arrogant myself today," Ian said. "By my sergeant, of all people."

Doyle sighed. "He doesn't much care for me."

"Why on earth not?"

"If I had to hazard a guess, I'd say he regards me as a rival."

"Good Lord. What on earth for?"

Doyle laughed. "You have no idea how much he admires you, do you?"

"I'm afraid you have an exaggerated idea of his regard for me. After all, he just informed me that I am arrogant."

"He is angry at you."

"Whatever for?"

"For allowing me into your confidence on your cases. He sees that as his role alone."

"I shall have to have a chat with him."

"That would only make things worse. I fear the only thing that would satisfy him would be putting an end to our friendship."

"I have no such intention."

"I am glad to hear it. Well, here we are," he said, as the cab jolted to a stop. "I would say our driver has earned his fare," he remarked as they alighted into a light drizzle.

It had been some time since Ian attended a concert, a failing he resolved to address as soon as he heard the opening strains of Mendelssohn's Hebrides Overture, with its moody, lilting melody, the strings crescendoing like waves against the towering rock formations of Fingal's Cave. He had been there with his parents as a boy, captivated by the mysterious majesty of the place just as the young Mendelssohn had been some forty years earlier. The music washed over him like a fountain, a pure sensual pleasure so intense it was startling.

At the interval he and Doyle joined the crowd of people enjoying drinks in the lobby bar. After ordering a glass of whisky, Ian was taken aback to see another familiar face among the crowd. At first he thought he must be mistaken, but there was no mistaking the abundant red locks and green eyes. Dressed in a jade velvet frock with matching hat, Fiona Stuart was hard to miss. Panicked, he tried to duck behind a marble column, but it was too late—she had seen him. He half hoped she would ignore him, but he should have known better. After a quick word to her companion, a slim youth with a cherubic face surrounded by blond curls, she clasped her hat tighter to her head and strode firmly in his direction.

"How surprising to see you here, Detective Hamilton," she said frostily. "I did not take you for a music lover."

"Miss S-Stuart," he stuttered. "Allow me to beg your forgiveness—"

"What on earth happened to your face?" she said, peering at the cut on his cheek, which still smarted as though it was a fresh wound.

"It's nothing, just a slight—"

"Ah, good evening, Mr. Doyle," she interrupted, seeing him approach.

"Why, Nurse Stuart! What a pleasant surprise! May I buy you a drink?"

"That is most kind of you."

"What are you having?" he asked, rubbing his hands together heartily, as if scrubbing for surgery.

"A glass of Madeira would be lovely, thank you," she replied, and he left to fetch it. She turned back to Ian. "Now, then, Detective, you were saying?"

"I fear any attempt at justification for my inexcusable rudeness would only serve to put me in a worse light."

"Not at all. I should be delighted to hear your explanation. At worst, it should prove amusing. If it's convincing enough, I may just give you the chance to make it up to me."

"The fact is, I—"

But they were again interrupted by the arrival of the yellow-haired young man Fiona had been with when she saw Ian.

"Hello, Freddy," she said as he approached, a frown on his attractive features. He was dressed as something of a dandy, in a light-blue frock coat, matching cravat, and striped trousers. His boots gleamed with polish, and his skin had the sheen of untroubled youth.

"I say, old girl, I was wondering if you had been abducted by Bedouins."

"I'm so sorry," Fiona replied, without sounding very contrite. "I saw some friends and got distracted. Allow me to introduce Detective Ian Hamilton, Edinburgh City Police. This is the Honorable Frederick Chillingsworth-Smythe."

"A copper, eh? How jolly!" he said, shaking Ian's hand. He had the soft, delicate hands of a man who had never known manual labor. His accent was posh central London, probably Kensington or Knightsbridge. "I say, do you catch a lot of criminals?"

"Not as many as I'd like, I'm afraid."

"Looks like one of them got you on the cheek with his cutlass," the young man remarked as Doyle arrived with a glass of Madeira for Fiona.

"Thank you," she said. "Arthur Conan Doyle, may I present the Honorable Frederick—"

"Oh, blast it all—just call me Freddy," he said, shaking Doyle's hand warmly.

"That hardly seems appropriate for a man of nobility," Doyle remarked.

"Stuff and nonsense—I'm only a baronet. Bottom of the pecking order, don't you know."

"How are you liking the concert?"

"Oh, it's terribly jolly—don't you agree?"

"Terribly jolly," Doyle agreed, his blue eyes crinkling at the corners. He wasn't exactly making fun of the young man—he was too kind for that—but was obviously amused.

"That Sarasate is quite the pip, even if he is a foreigner."

"The Gypsy melodies are wonderfully evocative," Doyle agreed.

Fiona sipped her Madeira. "This is lovely, thank you—just what the doctor ordered."

"I'm not a doctor yet," he replied with a smile.

"Then let us toast to that eventuality," she said, raising her glass.

As they clinked glasses, Ian noticed a tall, hulking fellow whom he recognized as the young man from the séance, Major Fitzpatrick's son. Ian was surprised to see him at this very concert, but saw an opportunity.

"Would you excuse me for just a moment?" he said. Stepping away from his companions, he trailed the man discreetly, keeping his eye on the fellow as he wove in and out of the crowd. At first Fitzpatrick seemed ignorant of the fact that he was being followed, but he glanced in Ian's direction, and they locked eyes. In one smooth movement, he ducked behind a group of people, and by the time Ian had picked his way through the throng of concertgoers, his quarry had vanished.

The bell announcing the end of the interval rang, and he returned to his seat to find Conan Doyle waiting for him.

"Whom were you following?" asked his friend.

"A young man who is going to some lengths to avoid me," Ian replied as the lights dimmed. He spent the next hour happily lost in the buoyant imagination of Felix Mendelssohn, who could make even Scotland seem like a place of sunshine and promise.

CHAPTER
THIRTY-FOUR

"You really should have that seen to, you know," said Donald, indicating the cut on Ian's cheek.

It was Sunday afternoon, and the brothers were seated before the fire at Aunt Lillian's, while she busied about the kitchen preparing the Sunday roast. In true Scots fashion, neither he nor Lillian mentioned their quarrel several days earlier, though there was an unaccustomed awkwardness between them. Donald's presence helped—his dry wit and sardonic humor was a welcome distraction from the tension.

"It doesn't appear to be healing," his brother added, helping himself to more ginger beer. "Does it hurt?"

"Not really," Ian lied. The truth was the cut stung as if freshly inflicted. Oddly, the pain from the scars on his back had temporarily receded—perhaps the slash on his cheek prevented him from noticing.

"I'll give you some balm to put on. It may aid the healing process, but it will certainly help with the pain."

"I said it didn't—"

"You really should improve your skill at deception, brother. It won't do for a detective to be such a pathetic liar."

Before Ian could respond, Lillian emerged from the kitchen, her face red and sweating, blue eyes gleaming, her cheeks rosier and plumper than usual. There was unquestionably a change in her, which Ian put down to the actor playing Scrooge—but exactly what that meant was far from clear.

"You're looking right bonnie today, Auntie," Donald remarked. "Is that a new frock? The crimson trim brings out the rose in your cheeks."

"Ach, get on wae yer nattering," she said, deliberately exaggerating her Glaswegian accent.

Ian was amazed—Lillian never bought new clothes, insisting that the old ones were perfectly serviceable "for a woman of her age," but now she was displaying the airs of a much younger woman. He was both pleased for her and a little bemused. Change in other people was baffling—especially those you thought you knew well.

Lillian placed bowls of cock-a-leekie soup on the dining room table. "Come along, before it gets cold," she said, taking a seat at the head of the table. When it was just her and Ian on Sundays, they would dine in the parlor, but now the three of them ate in the formal dining room.

"If Alfie were here, he would insist on a prayer," she said, placing her napkin in her lap. "But since we all believe in science rather than *superstition*—" she added, with a glance at Ian.

"I think perhaps we should have a prayer, in honor of Uncle Alfred," said Donald.

Ian looked at him to see if he was being sarcastic, but he appeared entirely sincere.

Lillian rolled her eyes. "Surely you're not—"

"No, I mean it. Let's do one for dear Uncle Alfie."

"If you insist," said Lillian, but Ian thought she looked rather pleased. "Some hae meat and cannae eat. Some nae meat but want it. We hae meat and we can eat and sae the Lord be thankit."

"And God bless Uncle Alfred," Donald added. "Amen."

"Why are you suddenly so concerned with Alfred?" said Lillian. "You weren't that keen on him when he was alive."

"I loved Uncle Alfie—everyone did."

"You did put salt in his sugar bowl," Ian pointed out.

"Only on April Fools' Day."

"You were quite the prankster," Lillian agreed. "But you didn't answer my question."

"This soup is delicious," said Donald. "I don't believe I've ever had better."

"Don't try to distract me. It didn't work when you were a child, and it won't work now."

"All right," he said, putting down his soup spoon. "It sounds as if you have your eye on a fellow who may replace Uncle Alfie, and I'm feeling a bit wistful, is all."

"What has your brother been telling you?"

"Only that there's a certain actor in the Greyfriars Dramatic Society—"

"Idle gossip," Lillian said with a dismissive wave of her hand.

Donald smiled. "So you're not—"

"I'll hae nae mare o'it!"

"When she starts speaking Glaswegian, it's time to move on," said Ian.

"How is your case going?" she asked him.

"I saw a potential suspect at the concert last night, but I let him slip away."

"Who might that be?" asked Donald.

"Jeremy Fitzpatrick. The late major's son."

"Tall fellow, slack-jawed and surly?"

"That sounds like him."

"I was at school with him briefly, though he was some years below me. Quite impressive on the rugby pitch, if it's the same fellow. Bit of a bully. I seem to remember he ended up going to Royal High School."

"Yes, I think the major mentioned that at one point," said Lillian. "Jeremy didn't come to the séances very often, but when he did, his father seemed a bit nervous about it."

"Wasn't the major there trying to contact his wife?" said Ian.

"Aye, and he spoke to her on more than one occasion," Lillian said, collecting the soup bowls. "She seemed like a lovely person. So refined and genteel."

Ian and his brother exchanged looks, but Lillian was already on her way to the kitchen.

"Let us help," Ian offered.

"Pish tosh," she said from the doorway. "I may be no spring chicken, but I'm perfectly capable of serving supper to my favorite nephews."

"You mean your only nephews," said Donald.

"Only and favorite," she replied, disappearing into the kitchen.

"'The lady doth protest too much, methinks,'" said Ian when she was gone.

Donald smeared butter on a piece of thick, crusty bread. "I suppose you think that's proof your theory is correct."

"Just look at her! She's even been curling her hair."

"Do you know the fellow's name?"

"I'll ask Dickerson tomorrow."

Donald took a bite of bread and chewed thoughtfully. "Why don't you stop by rehearsal this week and have a chat with him, see what he's all about?"

"I've other matters to attend to, you know."

"Surely you can spare a few hours for your favorite aunt," Donald replied with a wink.

Ian smiled. "Favorite and only." His hand went to the cut on his face, which had begun to itch.

"Don't scratch it!" Donald commanded. "You'll only make it worse."

Ian sighed and poured himself some more sherry. Lately Lillian had taken to drinking it, and while he preferred single malt whisky, he had brought a bottle of her favorite cream sherry. He wondered if her new preference was also related to the Greyfriars Dramatic Society.

"Are you making any progress on your hunt for your false informant?" Donald asked.

"It's extremely tricky. I don't want to tip off the fact that the department suspects someone."

"Not to mention the possibility of getting your reliable sources in trouble."

"Exactly."

"It's a heavy responsibility to lay on you."

"'Uneasy lies the head that wears a crown,'" Ian murmured as his aunt returned with a steaming platter of lamb surrounded by mint and fresh cress.

"Have one of you recently been elevated to royalty?" she asked, putting it on the table. The aroma of roast lamb and mint set off a spasm of saliva in Ian's mouth.

"I believe my brother was speaking metaphorically," said Donald.

Lillian raised an eyebrow. "'The poet's eye, in a fine frenzy rolling, doth glance from heaven to earth, from earth to heaven.'"

"Well done, Auntie," said Donald, with a wink at his brother.

"Still writing poetry, aren't you?" she asked Ian.

"He is," Donald said. "I catch him at it late at night."

"Speaking of being late," said Ian, "we can't stay too long because I promised Derek he could come over tonight for a bath."

"Why don't you bring him some food as well?" asked Lillian.

"That's very kind, thank you."

"Ach, there's plenty of food." She picked up a long, gleaming knife, its blade shining silver in the gaslight. "Now then, who wants to carve?"

CHAPTER
THIRTY-FIVE

Ian arrived at police chambers to find the morning edition of the *Scotsman* on his desk, its lurid headline splayed across the front page.

MAN FOUND WITH THROAT SLASHED BEHIND POPULAR EDINBURGH PUB!

WHO KILLED NATE CRIPPEN?

COULD IT BE THE WORK OF GLASGOW GANGS?

He looked up to see Jedidiah Corbin standing over him.

"Are you responsible for this literary masterpiece?"

The reporter shrugged. "It sells papers."

"What can I do for you, Mr. Corbin?"

"Please, after all we've been through together, call me Jed."

"I suppose you've come to collect the favor I owe you."

"Maybe I just like your company."

"Maybe I recognize horse shite when I hear it."

Corbin lifted an eyebrow. "I didn't expect such vulgarity from you, Detective."

"I'm rather busy, Corbin—what do you want?"

"A detail or two on the Crippen killing would be nice," he said, taking out a small notebook.

"Such as?"

"Is it true he was found with a Glasgow smile?" When Ian hesitated, Corbin made a note on his pad. "I'll take that as a yes. Do you suspect Glasgow gangs are behind it?"

"That's what your paper says."

"I'd like to know what you think."

"I'm as baffled as you are."

"There's a rumor you were to meet with him the night he died."

"You shouldn't pay too much attention to rumors."

"And you should learn to be a better liar."

"My brother said the same thing."

"What were you meeting Crippen about?"

"Good day, Mr. Corbin," Ian said, turning to the pile of paperwork on his desk.

"Ta very much," the reporter said, slipping on his coat. "I got what I came for."

"I can't tell you how gratified I am to hear that."

"See you around, Detective," Corbin said with a tip of his hat, and sauntered out of the station house.

DCI Crawford stuck his head out of his office. "A word, Hamilton?"

"Yes, sir," Ian said, his heart sinking as he followed the chief into the room.

"What about this Crippen fellow?" said Crawford, sitting heavily behind his desk, the chair groaning beneath his weight. Ian thought he had put on a stone or two—too many lamb dinners, no doubt.

Crawford loved roast lamb with mint jelly, and loved to boast how his wife cooked it with carrots, neeps, and tatties.

"Sir?" Ian said, taking the chair opposite him.

"Bit of a thug, wasn't he?"

"So I hear."

"Any idea who killed him?"

"Not yet, but I'm working on it."

"You have enough on your plate already—the Crippen case should go to someone else."

"I'd like to look into it myself, sir."

Crawford frowned. "You have a personal interest in it?"

"I have some potential leads."

The chief ran a hand through his thinning ginger hair. "I'll give you a week. If you haven't solved it by then, Detective McCaskill takes over."

"He's a good man, but—"

"See here," Crawford said, pulling at his whiskers, "we need to sort this out before this jewelry store business, or we could have a disaster on our hands."

"I understand, sir."

"Do you, Hamilton? Because I'm beginning to wonder."

"I do, sir."

"We can give the séance case to someone else, you know—that would give you more time to concentrate on—"

"Don't do that, sir."

"Constable Turnbull is quite keen on becoming a detective. He and Dickerson could—"

"Please, sir."

"What's the matter?" Crawford said in response to the expression on Ian's face. "He's a bright lad."

"It's not that, sir."

"What, then?"

At that moment there was a knock on the door.

"What is it?" Crawford called.

The door opened to admit Sergeant Bowers, his blue eyes worried. No one liked interrupting the chief in the middle of a meeting.

"Yes, Bowers?" said Crawford.

The sergeant cleared his throat, his pink, round cheeks deepening to scarlet. "I've brought your, uh, poultice, sir."

"Thank you, Bowers. Just leave it there."

"Yes, sir," he said, producing a paper bag, which he deposited on the desk before turning to hurry from the room. The label on the bag read "R. E. Wellington, Chemist," the name of a popular pharmacy on the High Street.

"Are you quite well, sir?" said Ian as the scent of aromatic herbs wafted through the room.

"Quite well, thank you."

"What is the poul—"

Crawford twisted a bit of string round his fingers and sighed. "If you must know, I have a case of piles."

"That sounds painful."

"Never mind—just see that you catch your man, eh? Go on, then— get all this sorted."

"Yes, sir," said Ian, and left the office before Crawford changed his mind.

As he headed for his desk, Ian heard voices coming from the tea station. He turned to see Sergeant Dickerson laughing at something Constable Turnbull had just said. When the sergeant saw Hamilton, he blushed violently, looking confused, but Turnbull laid a hand on his shoulder and whispered something in his ear. Dickerson started to laugh, then stopped himself. He said something to the constable, then broke away and walked toward Ian.

"Good morning, Sergeant," said Ian as Dickerson sat at the desk across from his own.

"Mornin', sir," he mumbled, burying his face in paperwork.

An awkward silence ensued, punctuated by the rustle of papers and the steady tick of the wall clock above them.

Resisting the urge to ask what Turnbull had told Dickerson, Ian leaned back in his chair and stretched. "I thought we would go by Gullan's Close and have a chat with Mr. James McAllister."

"The resetter? Wha' d'ye want from him, sir?"

"I'd like to get a confirmation on what my source told me regarding the upcoming robbery."

"Ye think he'd be likely t'know?"

"I think that as a well-known fencer of stolen goods, he would be on the alert for something like that."

"I'll get my coat, sir."

Ian watched as Dickerson fetched his greatcoat from the rack, carefully avoiding eye contact with Constable Turnbull, who sneered at Ian, as if to say, "I have your man in my pocket."

"Not if I can help it," Ian muttered. Throwing on his cloak, he followed Sergeant Dickerson out of the station house.

The bright skies of the past few days had disintegrated into a thick, wet drizzle that veered uneasily between rain and snow; even the weather couldn't make up its mind what it wanted to do. Dickerson pulled his collar close and stared up at the sky as if the precipitation was a personal punishment meant for him alone. To put him out of his misery, Ian hailed a cab.

By the time they arrived at Gullan's Close, snow had gained the upper hand, and a thin layer of white settled over the cobblestones, muffling the sounds of people and traffic, softening the sharp edges of a city that seemed at times to be all scrapes and bruises. Gullan's Close was damp and dingy, and the screech of an alley cat was followed by the sound of scuttling in a nearby trash bin. Ian did not care to think what the cat was chasing, nor did he want to ponder the fate of the animal after its capture.

They descended the narrow stairs to the basement entryway. The same cracked wooden sign hung by a single nail over the door, but an attempt had been made at sprucing up the lettering.

J. R. McAllister, Pawnbroker

The door was bolted from the inside, and when Ian knocked, they heard sounds very much like the ruckus in the trash bin. Footsteps were punctuated with rattling, crashing, and cursing, as if someone was moving clumsily through a forest of objects. Finally the door opened to reveal the visage of James R. McAllister, pawnshop owner and fencer of stolen goods. A short, powerfully built man, he looked somewhat the worse for wear than the last time Ian had seen him. His face was scratched and bruised, and his small blue eyes were bloodshot. A discolored ring beneath one eye suggested the application of a fist. He sighed when he saw the policemen.

"You, is it? Ach, it's nae my week. I s'pose ye better come in."

"Good morning, Mr. McAllister," Ian said as they followed him into the cluttered interior of the shop. Objects seemed to sprout from the floor, covering every spare inch of space in the cramped room. A carousel pony with one ear missing leaned against a rusting radiator; a chipped credenza was covered in a motley assortment of bric-a-brac, from dusty wooden spoons to tarnished hatpins. A dressmaker's mannequin was draped with an array of faded scarves and torn petticoats, next to which sat a black Scottish terrier. The dog gazed at them with bright little eyes, wagging its stub of a tail furiously.

"I see you've acquired a dog since we were last here," Ian remarked. "What happened to your cat?"

"Deid."

"So you got a dog instead."

"Aye—helps keep away rats."

"The animal or human variety?"

McAllister grinned, showing teeth the color of tar. "Both."

"It looks like you've been in a bit of a scuffle."

The resetter dabbed at a chipped glass vase with a dirty dustcloth. "Don' know wha' ye mean."

"Someone is responsible for the injuries to your face."

"I tripped."

"Was that what caused your face to come in contact with a fist?"

"Ach, it's nae business a' yers, but it wae a pub brawl," he said, swabbing at an overhanging cobweb with his cloth. "So wha' kin I do fer ye?"

"We are in search of corroboration."

"Corrobawha'?" he said, cocking his head to the side. It was small, set on a short, thick neck, muscular as a mastiff's.

"We need some information," Dickerson explained. "'Bout a robbery."

"Wha' makes ye think I'd know anythin' 'bout somethin' like that?"

"Come, Mr. McAllister," said Ian. "Let us dispense with the posturing. I'm sure you don't have time to waste any more than we do."

His small eyes narrowed. "Wha' robbery might that be, then?"

"Murray and Weston."

"On Princes Street?"

"We have information that a major burglary is being planned."

"When?"

"Within the week."

McAllister burst into laughter. "Someone's been pullin' yer leg, mate."

"So you haven't heard of any robbery?"

"No, an' I'll tell ye somethin' else. Only someone wi' a heid full o' mince would try to break in there."

"Why is that?"

"They've an alarm system no one's yet foiled. An' a coupla hounds they let roam at night."

"So you've heard nothing about such a plan?"

"No, an' if I did, I'd tell 'em tae skedaddle aff straightaway."

"Of course you know if there is such a robbery, your shop will be the first place we visit."

"So I've nae reason t'lie to ye, have I?"

"Thank you," Ian said. "You've been very helpful."

"I hope ye'll remember that in't future."

"Oh, one more thing."

"Yes?"

"You haven't by chance had a visit from any of my colleagues recently?"

"Coppers comin' here? That's a laugh."

"Mr. McAllister," Ian said, leaning on the dirty counter, "do you mean to tell me I am the only member of the Edinburgh City Police to drop by your charming establishment?"

The resetter bit his lip, pretending to think. He was not a very good actor, however, and was entirely unconvincing. "Come t'think of it, there was a fella last week. Didnae have a uniform on, but smelt like a copper. He were pretendin' tae shop, but I could tell he were jes snoopin' 'round."

"Did you get his name?"

"No, but I'd know the fella if I saw 'im agin. Skinny, smiles a lot, but slimy, like. Face like spoilt milk."

"Pockmarked, you mean?"

"Aye. Terrible pitted skin. Ye know 'im?"

"Thank you for the information. Good day, Mr. McAllister."

"Always glad to be a' service," the pawnbroker said as Ian and Dickerson left his crowded shop.

Out on the street, Dickerson sneezed.

"Are you coming down with something?" asked Ian.

"Jes allergies. It were dusty as the grave in that place," he said, trotting after Ian. "Where we goin' now?"

"To find my friend Brian McKinney," he replied, flinging his arm in the air to signal a passing hansom.

"That blind beggar fella?" Dickerson said as it slid to a stop on the slippery cobblestones.

"He's the one who told me about the theft, and I've never known him to be wrong yet."

"Wonder wha' happened this time."

"Someone is feeding him false information," he said as Dickerson climbed inside.

"Where to, sir?" asked the cabbie.

"St. Giles, fast as you can. There's an extra shilling in it if you make good time."

The man grinned. "I'll take th' Cowgate. High Street is crowded this time a' day." Ian was barely seated when the cabbie flicked his whip, and the hansom lurched forward with a jerk.

"Afore this is over, ye'll line the pockets a' every cabbie in town," Dickerson remarked as they rattled over the snowy streets. The flakes were flying faster now, thick and heavy, as people scurried along, some holding umbrellas, the rest rushing to reach their destination before getting totally soaked. Some held newspapers over their heads; others pulled up their coat collars and ducked their heads inside like turtles; still others trudged along hunched over, hands in their pockets. The citizens of Edinburgh were no strangers to misery and, like most Scots, took pride in their ability to withstand privation and adversity. A December snowfall was hardly the worst fate, though that was small comfort for the unlucky ones who had gone out ill prepared for Edinburgh's unpredictably moody weather.

"Sounded like he were describin' Constable Turnbull," Dickerson said as they turned south onto St. Mary's Street.

"Indeed. And if I were you I'd mind what you say around him."

Dickerson shifted uneasily in his seat. "He's not tha' bad."

Ian let the remark pass, though he was troubled at the thought of the sergeant falling under the spell of a man he regarded as untrustworthy.

There was no sign of Brian in front of St. Giles, so Ian instructed the cabbie to continue on to Waverley Station. The ride to the train station was short, and the man tipped his hat when Ian paid him.

"Don't get too spoiled," Ian told Dickerson as they alighted from the cab. "Today I'm in a hurry and the weather is bad."

The impressive five-story building was even more imposing shrouded in falling snow, and Ian couldn't help admiring it as they hurried past the line of cabs to get to the main entrance. Each of the building's five stories was different in size and design, breaking the square symmetry of its heavy stonework, culminating in a top floor with a magnificent mansard roof.

Ian looked for Brian in front of the station, but the beggar was nowhere to be seen. Thinking he might have gone inside to escape the inclement weather, Ian passed the throng of passengers waiting for cabs, and stepped into the cathedral-like interior, with its ornate glass ceiling culminating in the central round dome. The quality of sound inside the station was like nowhere else. At once diffused and magnified, it was as if a thousand voices were blending into a massive collective conversation, unintelligible but somehow vastly comforting.

"No sign of 'im, sir?" said Dickerson as they roamed the marbled floors, weaving in and out of groups of people from all walks of life.

"I'm afraid not," Ian said, a sinking feeling worming its way into his consciousness.

"Beg pardon, sir, but isn't it possible he gave ye false information on purpose?"

"But why would he do that now, after being so reliable all these years?"

"Don' know, sir, but isn't it possible?"

Ian had to admit the sergeant was right, but if he couldn't trust Brian, whom could he trust? Ian felt a creeping dread as they stood, immobile and directionless, lost amid the rush of people who knew exactly where they were going.

CHAPTER
THIRTY-SIX

By the time Ian and Dickerson left Waverley, snowflakes were tumbling from the sky as if in a race to reach the ground. There wasn't a cab to be had, so they trudged through the gathering gloom to police chambers. Ian nipped into a shop to buy umbrellas, but by the time they arrived at the station house, their feet were thoroughly soaked. Lounging on the steps beneath a torn umbrella, looking surprisingly dry and comfortable, was Derek McNair. Dressed in his usual assortment of mismatched clothing, he had topped it off with a broad-brimmed oilskin hat.

"Where ye been?" he said as they approached. "I've been waitin' fer ages."

"Strange as it may seem, I don't arrange my schedule to suit your convenience," Ian replied as the boy followed them up the stairs.

"Don' ye wanna know why I'm here?"

"I'm guessing there's a cup of tea and a tin of biscuits involved."

"I won' say no—ta very much."

"You might as well come in," Ian said, holding the door open for him.

The boy entered the station house as if he were walking into a grand ballroom. "Hiya, mate," he said, tipping his cap as he sauntered past the desk sergeant.

"Now then," he said, perching on Ian's desk, "'bout that tea."

"I'll fetch it, sir," said Sergeant Dickerson.

"So what momentous news do you bring me?" asked Ian, as McNair sat swinging his legs back and forth.

The leg swinging stopped. "Momen—what? Wha' ye usin' fancy words fer, mate?"

"Important news."

"He wants t'meet ye again," Derek said, lowering his voice.

"Who does?"

"Who'd ye think? Rat Face."

"He communicated that to you, did he?"

"A' course he did. I'm yer go-between, ain't I?"

"Did he say when and where?"

"Tonight, five o'clock. Same place as the first time."

"The stables?"

"Aye."

"Did he say why?"

"I'm jes the messenger."

"Tell him I'll be there."

"D'ye wan' me t'take ye there?"

"I can find my own way."

"Never know when ye might need a mate."

"Thanks all the same, but I'll be fine."

His answer put a damper on the boy's mood, but that wasn't entirely a bad thing. A few of the other officers looked at him askance as he slurped tea and gobbled down biscuits, finishing nearly half the tin. Luckily, DCI Crawford wasn't around—Ian knew he had little regard for the ragamuffin, and didn't want the chief questioning him about what the boy was doing there. The pursuit of his parents' death was not an official inquiry, and he risked censure—or worse—if Crawford were to learn how he was spending his time.

After devouring the biscuits and tea, Derek grabbed his torn umbrella and pulled on his hat.

"See ye later, Guv."

"Hang on," said Ian, holding out his own umbrella. "Take this one."

The boy hesitated, then took it with a little tip of his hat. "Ta very much. See y'around," he said, ambling from the station with the same cocky swagger. Watching him go, Ian had to admire the steely determination it took to be a boy living by his wits in the streets of a cold and indifferent city.

No sooner had the boy left than the door swung open to admit a tiny, dark-haired woman carrying a large handbag. She wore a light-brown travel suit and a dark-green plaid shawl. Ian recognized her as Bronwyn Davies, the woman from the séance group.

"Miss Davies, thank you for coming in," he said, rising to greet her. "Please, have a seat. Would you care for some tea?"

"Thank you, no. Esodora said you were looking for me," she said in her soft Welsh accent, settling her petite body into the chair and pulling her plaid shawl around her thin shoulders. When she sat all the way back in it, her feet barely touched the ground.

"That's your landlady, is it?" he said.

"Actually, my downstairs neighbor. She's quite the busybody, and overheard you talking with my landlady." She cocked her head to one side, regarding him with big, dark eyes, which appeared even larger in such a small face. Her age was impossible to guess—she could have been thirty or fifty. "I believe she's Egyptian or something—and very nosy."

"And you, Miss Davies—you are Welsh, I believe?"

"I am indeed. I grew up in Cardiff."

"And how long have you lived in Edinburgh?"

"Since my poor sister took ill," she said dolefully. "I came up from Wales to nurse her, and never left. When she died I just stayed on in her flat."

"I believe you told me that you attended Madame Veselka's séances in an attempt to communicate with her?"

Her face brightened. "I am happy to say I have had many conversations with her since she crossed over. It has been a great comfort to me."

"Do you intend to continue attending the meetings?"

"Why on earth would I not?"

"Two of your members—"

"Surely you don't believe their deaths are connected!" she exclaimed, as though the idea was truly scandalous.

"Does it not strike you as odd?"

"Not particularly."

"You are aware they were both murdered?"

"I know that is what the police believe."

"And what do you believe, Miss Davies?"

She leaned in toward him, and he could smell peppermint on her breath. "I believe they were taken by spirits."

He sat back in his chair, quite unprepared for such an outlandish response. He was aware Miss Davies was eccentric, but clearly she possessed very bizarre ideas.

"Think about it," she said. "The major was a military man—no telling how many of his enemies were waiting to avenge their deaths from the beyond."

"And Miss Staley?"

"I don't know enough about her, but I imagine she had a secret buried somewhere in her past—someone she wronged in life, who crossed over just long enough to do her in."

"And you, Miss Davies? Have you no such enemies in your past?"

"I have led a very quiet life, Detective. Some people would say a dull life, and perhaps they are right. But I cannot remember ever harming anyone—at least not consciously."

"Good for you, Miss Davies," he replied, eyeing her enormous bag, still clutched tightly in her arms, as if it was a baby. "That is quite an impressive satchel," he remarked.

"It's my knitting. Goes everywhere with me, in case I have a spare moment. Helps calm my nerves, you know."

"How very commendable," he said, wondering what was wrong with her nerves that they needed calming.

The rest of the interview yielded little of interest. She claimed not to know the major or Elizabeth Staley very well, and could think of no one—living, at least—who might wish to harm them. After another offer of tea, which she again politely refused, he escorted her out of the station.

He turned to see Constable Turnbull staring at him. When he caught Ian's eye, the corner of his mouth lifted in a sneer. He turned to Sergeant Dickerson, who was tidying up the tea station, and whispered something to him. Dickerson let out a guffaw that turned into a cough when he saw Ian looking at him. Clearing his throat, he stumbled over to his desk and sat, pretending to busy himself with paperwork, avoiding looking at Ian.

Ian felt a wave of loathing wash over him. How could Dickerson not see what Turnbull was, how he was playing him? Was the sergeant's judgment so compromised that he was drawn to the constable's insincere flattery and attention? He looked at Dickerson, his ruddy face flushed, burying himself in paperwork.

Ian stood up and threw on his cape. Dickerson looked up with the expression of a puppy who has just soiled an expensive rug.

"I'm going out," Ian said.

"Where to, sir?"

"A funeral," he replied, and before the sergeant could respond, he turned and strode to the front entrance. His anger was mounting to the point that leaving was the only reasonable option. He feared saying anything further to Dickerson would unleash a torrent of recrimination. Apart from embarrassing the sergeant in front of his colleagues, it would give Turnbull the upper hand, if he didn't have it already. But for now, Ian needed to track down Jeremy Fitzpatrick, and he could think of no better place to find him than his father's funeral.

Major Fitzpatrick's funeral was at the Kirk of the Canongate, near the bottom of the Old Town, not far from Holyrood Palace. As Ian approached the church, with its rounded, Dutch-style gable, a line from Robert Fergusson's poem "Leith Races" popped into his head.

An wha are ye my winsome dear,
That takes the gate sae early?

He thought about the young poet, buried within its walls, dead at the age of twenty-four. He gazed up at the tall, thin windows with their many panes, flanking the central round window, peering down at him like a giant eye. The sole festive holiday touch was a large holly wreath on the kirk's front door. The sound of a hundred voices singing "Abide with Me" floated from the building. He tiptoed into the seventeenth-century kirk, laid out in cruciform design, and took a seat at the back of the long central aisle just as the last chords of the hymn lingered in the thin air, echoing through the silent white columns.

As people settled into their pews, he thought of Edinburgh's citizens who had "taken the gate sae early" through no fault of their own. The mother tending to her babies, surprised by a house burglar, delivered a fatal blow by the panicked thief; the young law clerk, strangled before being flung from the parapet of Arthur's Seat; the banker poisoned by his rapacious lover. The list went on, and Ian had determined to seek justice for them all, even if he had to wrench it from the jaws of despair itself.

Suddenly aware of someone moving toward him, he turned to see Madame Veselka, all in black except for a large gold pendant upon her heavy bosom, her face half hidden beneath an ornate black-lace veil. She nodded solemnly and slid into the pew to sit next to him. Her unwelcome presence made him squirm in his seat, as the thick scent of her gardenia perfume surrounded him.

Putting her face close to his ear, she whispered, "It's not over."

Puzzled, he frowned at her. "Aren't you supposed to be in Paris?"

She shrugged. "The trip was canceled. Ghosts ill-treated do not rest easy," she continued, looking at his cheek. "That mark—a reminder of sin and mortality," she murmured, shaking her head. "Restless ghosts will haunt the living. Secrets long buried cry for the air of truth. Look to your dreams—the answers lie there."

And with that, she rose and moved to another section of the church. Her words left him feeling shaky and uncertain. Was she trying to throw him off the scent, keep him from investigating her too closely? She spoke of secrets, but what secrets was *she* hiding? What of the trip to Paris, suddenly canceled at the last minute?

The minister delivered a brief eulogy, after which the audience rose to sing "Nearer My God to Thee." The rest of the service was traditional and concise, and as the mourners left the church, a lone bagpiper playing "The Minstrel Boy" followed the solemn procession of pallbearers. The eight men carried the coffin slowly toward the churchyard, the women standing outside the gates, as was the custom. Madame Veselka was nowhere to be seen. Surprised not to see the major's son among the pallbearers, Ian searched the crowd for any sign of him.

At the far end of the churchyard, slouching next to a tall, ornate monument, was a familiar figure. Half hidden by the headstone, Jeremy Fitzpatrick gazed at the crowd of mourners assembled around the deep hole in the ground, watching as the coffin was lowered down. Weaving between the men in their dark clothing, Ian tried to get closer without being spotted. But as he stepped behind a well-dressed fat man in an expensive waistcoat and top hat, Jeremy spied him and took off at a run.

"Damn your eyes," Ian muttered, sprinting after him across the soggy ground. But the lad had a good head start, ducking through the gate on Old Tolbooth Wynd. Turning right, he ran in the direction of Calton Road. Ian loped after him, but when he reached the intersection, looked on helplessly as Fitzpatrick hopped onto a half-empty tram.

Panting and sweating, Ian watched the horses break away at a brisk trot, the wheels squealing on their metal rails as the tram careened around the corner of Calton Road where it swung north toward Leith Street. He knew the route—the tram ran all the way to Bernard Street in the village of Leith. If the boy disembarked at the port, he could lose himself amid the dockworkers, oystermen, fishmongers, and prostitutes.

Having recovered his breath, Ian wiped the sweat from his brow and turned back in the direction of Old Town.

Jeremy Fitzpatrick had just catapulted to the top of his suspect list.

CHAPTER
THIRTY-SEVEN

The sun had already ducked like a retreating thief behind Castle Rock as Ian set out across the sodden landscape of the city for his rendezvous with Rat Face. Avoiding the squalid swamp of Old Town, he walked up Calton Road to the intersection of Princes Street, joining the throngs of well-heeled gentlemen and elegant ladies trolling the expensive shops lining the broad avenue. The Kirk may have banned Christmas in Scotland, but that didn't stop the merchants of New Town from turning out the shops in their holiday best. Clothiers lined their front windows in red-and-gold trim; bowls of oranges studded with cloves beckoned shoppers to enter festively decorated bakeries and sweets shops; holly wreaths with bright-red bows hung from the front doors of chic haberdasheries.

All the holiday finery made little impression upon Ian as he strode, head down, past the brightly lit shops, the air alive with the smell of fir trees and peppermint. He might as well have been walking through Old Town, with its stench of boiled cabbage and despair, for all the effect his surroundings had upon his churning brain.

Madame Veselka's words swirled through his head, a confusing jumble of thoughts cascading after them. He tried to concentrate on what he knew was his duty—solving the séance murders—yet his attention was divided, as he felt he was drawing ever nearer to his parents' killer. It even struck him that there might be some connection, however faint. As for the search for the corruption within the police force, he felt hopelessly overmatched. He was convinced Turnbull was involved, but proving it was maddeningly elusive.

As he passed Jenners Department Store, a grande dame emerged from the building, and he stepped aside to let her pass. Dressed in white ermine and diamonds, she was trailed by a brace of liveried servants buried in a mass of hatboxes, shopping bags, and—of all things—a gilded birdcage. Her nose was tilted upward, lest she be contaminated by the merest whiff of commoners, her face swathed in a cloud of snowy fur.

One of her servants stumbled on an uneven bit of sidewalk and dropped his packages. The grand lady turned on him, her face scarlet with fury.

"Stupid oaf!" she hissed. "Watch where you're going! Pick all of those up straightaway!"

The lad hurriedly complied, bending over to snatch the precious cargo from the ground. He was hardly more than a boy, slight of build, with a delicate face and a thatch of light-brown hair. Ian put his age at no older than fourteen. No doubt he considered himself lucky to have such a job, while other boys his age toiled in the mills, swept the streets, or loaded cargo on the docks of Leith. And there were unluckier still, boys like Derek McNair, as Ian knew only too well.

Still, as he watched the lad scramble to obey his mistress' commands, Ian felt anger build in his own breast. He longed to give the haughty woman a piece of his mind. He knew it would be of no use, and would certainly do more damage than good to the poor servant, so he held his tongue. The packages were duly gathered, and the procession continued onward.

As Ian stood aside to let her pass, he pondered the nature of greed and want, both so evident in this jewel of the Scottish Enlightenment, luxury tucked amid horrific poverty and deprivation. Would this great lady, like Ebenezer Scrooge, awake one morning to find herself possessed of an unfamiliar humility, and find her place among the teeming mass of humanity? Would this Christmas season bring any Dickensian enlightenment among the rich of Edinburgh?

He feared not. More likely the city's privileged who guarded their wealth would, like Jacob Marley's ghost, wander through eternity dragging a heavy chain fashioned of their own penury and greed. Most people, even when given a chance, did not mend their ways. The criminals he sent down would return to a life of crime straight out of jail. Wife-beaters would continue to beat their wives, repeat offenders would repeat their offenses, and the overprivileged would continue to abuse their servants and hoard their pennies. Only in fiction did enlightenment visit on Christmas Eve in the guise of one's long-dead business partner.

And yet . . . Madame Veselka's prediction burned his ears. Did the answers he sought really lie in his disturbing and vivid dreams?

The air was thick with threat of more snow as Ian turned onto the Mound, passing the National Gallery in all its neoclassical splendor. He loved to roam the halls of the museum, but he did not find its massive columns appealing. Edinburgh might be the "Athens of the North," but he felt Ionic columns belonged in Greece, and looked out of place in Scotland.

A Clarence carriage swooshed past him, headed in the direction of Waverley Station, a steam trunk tied to the roof. As it passed, a young girl poked her head out of the window and smiled at him. She was swiftly pulled back inside by her mother, only to be replaced by her brother, who stuck his tongue out. Ian smiled—the boy was about Derek's age, though considerably more well-nourished. He wondered if Derek had any siblings, and realized he had never inquired about it, resolving to remedy that at some point.

As he wound through the warren of streets beneath the castle, he wondered what news Rat Face had to tell, and what it would cost him. He had come prepared, he thought, fingering the coins in his pockets.

He arrived a few minutes early, walking past the stalls of horses to the booth at the back of the stables. The barn was empty of people save for a young groom mucking out an empty stall. He took a seat at the wooden booth and waited. A gust of wind blew through the barn, and he looked up to see a pair of men standing a few yards away. They were unsavory types, one short and thick, built like a bulldog and twice as ugly. The taller one had a twisted lip and hands the size of dinner plates. It was plain by the look in their eyes they had mischief on their minds. Ian glanced at the rear of the building, remembering that Rat Face had slipped out that way when they had last met.

The taller one took a step toward him, and Ian realized he had little time to make his escape. With one swift movement, he rose and started toward the exit. He did not move quickly enough, though, and felt the blow of a boot on the back of his calf; he stumbled and nearly fell. A hand grabbed him by the collar, pulling him back into the room. Wrenching himself free, he spun around to see Twisted Lip aiming a blow at his head. Ian ducked and drove his shoulder into the man's torso, causing him to fall backward, just as the shorter one came at him, fists flailing. One blow caught him in the ribs, and Ian felt a searing pain as the man's fist connected. Reacting quickly, Ian grabbed the man by the ears and drove his knee into his face, hearing the crunch of cartilage as his assailant cried out. The man staggered backward, blood spurting from his nose, momentarily blinded.

Breathing heavily, Ian saw Twisted Lip rising unsteadily to his feet. He realized if he did not escape now, he might not survive. He could not hold off his attackers for long. Whipping around the corner of the booth, he dashed toward the gap between the rear stalls, toward the door at the back of the building. With a roar, Twisted Lip followed after him. In desperation, Ian seized a heavy rubber feed bucket and hurled it at him. The big man brushed it away as if it were made of parchment, and kept coming. Ian's eye was caught by a gleam of metal on the side of a stall, and he reached for it, his fingers closing around a metal hoof pick. Holding it firmly, he slashed the curved blade at Twisted Lip's face, cutting a deep gash in his cheek.

His attacker fell to his knees, gasping. Ian did not linger to see how much damage he had done. Taking to his heels, he lunged toward the exit, pulling the door open so violently he nearly wrenched his shoulder. Emerging into the alley at the back of the barn, he took off at a dead sprint and did not stop until he could run no longer. Slowing to a steady walk, he turned onto Johnston Terrace and hailed the first hansom cab he saw.

A light dusting of snow had fallen, softening the clatter of wheels against the cobblestones, as the cab whisked him away into the night.

CHAPTER
THIRTY-EIGHT

Bridie Mallon trudged up the stairs of the building on Leith Walk for what felt like the hundredth time. In fact, she had only been working for the tenant in 4F for a few months, but the five flights were wearing even for one as young as she. After slogging through the foot or so of snow that had fallen on the previous day, she was already tired, having cleaned two flats earlier that day. She longed to be carousing with her sweetheart, Bill, who worked in a slaughterhouse, but here it was only Monday evening, and with Saturday so far away.

Her friend Mary, who worked for the same man previously, told her that the money would be left in a carved wooden box on the sideboard every week, and she was not to inquire as to the identity of the tenant, nor discuss the job with any of her friends. She was to come only on Tuesday evenings, after sunset.

Bridie readily agreed, as the wages were twice what she normally commanded, but as time wore on, she became increasingly discomfited at working for someone whose face she had never seen. She didn't even know his name. In all the time she had cleaned the flat, she had never spied so much as a gas bill. It was always empty, and it appeared that the flat immediately below his was unoccupied. She rarely saw any other tenants, and when she did chance to pass a smartly dressed young man last month, he tipped his hat politely and hurried down the stairs.

When she asked Mary why she had given up such a lucrative job, her friend made a vague comment about the stairs, which Bridie saw as a dodge. Mary was about her age, fit as a fiddle, and certainly more than able to navigate the climb. Grateful for the money, Bridie did not pry, swallowing her curiosity for a job she could ill afford to turn down.

This week Bridie had decided to show up a day early. She couldn't see what harm it would do to come on a Monday, and if she ran into him, at least her curiosity would be satisfied. Turning the key in the lock, she opened the door slowly, feeling the same apprehensiveness and unease she always did as she entered the empty flat. Going to the cleaning cupboard in the kitchen, she took out the tools of her trade—feather duster, rags, broom, mop, and bucket. Not every customer let her use their cleaning tools—some insisted she bring her own—but this flat was always well stocked with soap powder, borax, and anything else she might need.

Having gathered her supplies, she began to work. Bridie enjoyed singing to herself to help the time pass. Sometimes she sang good wholesome Catholic hymns she had learned in her native County Donegal, but today one of her favorite murder ballads popped into her head. She supposed it was wicked, but she dearly loved murder ballads, and her favorite was "Henry My Son." The Irish version of the ancient ballad "Lord Randall," it was the story of a young man who, having been poisoned by his lover, has come to his parents' house to die.

Where have you been all day, Henry my son?
Where have you been all day, my beloved one?
Away in the meadow, away in the meadow
Make my bed, I've a pain in my head
And I want to lie down

Bridie had heard the song was based on a real thirteenth-century English earl who was poisoned by his wife, but whether true or not, it seemed to her wonderfully sad and poignant. It was a sweet tune, too, every bit as good as the popular "Barbara Allen." She preferred the tale of the murderous lover to the one of a woman's sweetheart dying merely from her neglect.

Moving on to dust the mantel, she sang with gusto. Her voice was good enough for church solos; ever since she was a wee lass, people had commented on her sweetness of tone.

What did you have to eat, Henry my son?
What did you have to eat, my beloved one?
Poison beans, poison beans,
Make my bed, I've a pain in my head
And I want to lie down

Working swiftly now, Bridie moved on to the small office just off the parlor. There was a desk that was always locked, which Mary had said she was not to ever try to open. It had never occurred to Bridie to try, but for the first time, she saw the key protruding from the middle drawer. Had her mysterious client left it there by accident, or was it a kind of test, to see whether she could resist the temptation to pry? Bridie had never been good at resisting temptation. Not a week went by when she didn't report some small transgression or other to Father Connelly at confession.

As she peered at the key dangling from the lock, so shiny and inviting, her palms began to sweat. She thought of Father Connelly, imagining his disappointed look when she took her place among the other sopranos in the choir, his warm brown eyes mournful, despairing of ever saving her weak and sullied soul. She took a step away from the desk, busying herself with dusting the bookshelves along the far wall, humming "Holy Innocents," a sober hymn that Father Connelly liked, hoping it would mend her wicked thoughts.

> Lovely flowers of martyrs, hail!
> Smitten by the tyrant foe,
> On life's threshold, as the gale
> Strews the roses ere they blow

But the more she tried to divert her attention from the desk, the more of her consciousness it occupied, until her entire brain was consumed with the image of a giant, gleaming key. Finally, unable to stand the torment any longer, she flung down her feather duster and lurched across the room to the desk. With trembling hand, she grasped the key and turned it. The sound of the bolt clicking softly into place sent shivers of terror through her, yet she continued, gently sliding the drawer forward on its well-oiled hinges.

The drawer contained a single manila folder. Licking her lips, she lifted it carefully, set it on the desktop, and opened it. Inside was a thin stack of yellowing newspaper articles cut out of various publications—the *Scotsman*, the *Edinburgh Evening Courant*, and others. There were over a dozen articles all told, but the subject matter was the same. They were about the mysterious fire that had claimed the lives of an Edinburgh detective and his wife seven years ago.

Bridie remembered it well—tongues wagged around town for weeks afterward. Many theories were advanced, from an accidental blaze to arson. As one of the victims was a policeman, it was thought the fire might have been set by a criminal he had sent down. Even more outrageous claims were made by more superstitious folks—some claimed it was the ghost of Deacon Brodie, come to exact revenge for his hanging a century ago.

No one was ever arrested or charged, and the tragedy slipped slowly into the background of a city that was no stranger to violence. But the mysterious client on Leith Walk had carefully saved these clippings, though to what end Bridie could not fathom. Was he hoping to some-day solve the case? Was he a member of the police force himself, perhaps a friend of the dead man, bent on avenging his death?

With a sigh, Bridie placed the articles carefully back in the enve-lope. She could tell no one about this—certainly not Mary, who would see it as a betrayal. And Bill, bless him, was like a mewing babe when he got the drink in him. Anything was likely to spill out of his mouth when he was in his cups, and like as not, he'd have no memory of it the next day.

No, this would remain her secret, though its significance was lost on her. Even Father Connelly would not hear of it. She had plenty of other sins to confess, and felt no compunction about keeping this one to herself.

As she reached down to return the envelope to the drawer, Bridie heard the sound of someone ascending the stairs with light, quick steps. A bolt of panic shot through her as she heard the front lock slide quietly in its chamber, and she dropped the envelope to the floor. She barely had time to turn her head as the door to the flat opened. She did not hear the harsh caw of the raven perched on the windowsill, as it watched the scene inside the flat with sharp, beady eyes, hard and black as coal dust.

CHAPTER
THIRTY-NINE

"You should probably avoid strenuous activity for a while," Donald remarked, looking at Ian's ribs. "In fact, you might take some time off."

"Impossible," Ian said, wincing. Donald was seated on the sofa, examining his brother's injuries. When Ian stumbled in after disembarking from the hansom cab, Donald had immediately ordered him to seek medical treatment. When Ian refused to go to the infirmary, his brother had fetched his medical kit.

"There is considerable bruising, and while I don't think you have a cracked rib, I can't guarantee it," Donald said, winding a bandage around Ian's torso. "You should avoid exacerbating the injury."

"Thank you for your advice," Ian said, pulling on his shirt. The effort was painful, and he turned away to avoid his brother's gaze.

"I pity any doctor who has you as a patient," Donald said, returning the roll of gauze to his medical kit. "As Lillian would say, you're a thrawn puggy."

"Isn't that a case of the pot calling the kettle—"

"Very well; we're both stubborn monkeys. But that does not excuse your cavalier attitude toward your injuries. Now then, let's have a look at that leg. Turn up the gaslight a bit, would you?"

Ian complied, standing patiently while his brother completed his examination. Bacchus was curled on the sofa next to Donald, eyes half closed, purring. The cat did indeed seem to prefer Donald, sleeping on his bed most nights, though Ian suspected it was because his brother fed him at table, a practice Ian did not approve of, though admittedly he was occasionally guilty of it himself.

"Bacchus is putting on weight," Ian said. "You shouldn't slip him so many scraps during meals."

"Nonsense. He's perfectly healthy. If I left it up to you, he would be a Skinny Malinky, just like you."

"You seem to have acquired Lillian's love of Scottish slang."

"Stand still," Donald said, dabbing iodine onto Ian's leg. "I don't want to spill this on the carpet. I saw Fiona Stuart today, by the way. She asked after you."

"Ouch," said Ian as the liquid stung the cut on his leg.

"Stand still!" Donald commanded. "There—finished," he said, putting the cap back on the bottle. "I don't understand what she sees in you."

"Perhaps nothing."

"Rubbish. It's obvious she fancies you. You should do something before it's too late."

"I have more pressing matters on my mind," Ian said, pouring himself a tumbler of whisky.

"Cheers," said Donald.

Ian hesitated, glass halfway to his lips.

"I have my ginger beer," said Donald. "Carry on."

"Right," Ian said, lifting the glass. "Cheers."

Donald leaned back on the couch, idly stroking Bacchus, whose purrs increased in volume. "Any idea who sent these thugs, or what they were after?"

"I have some theories."

"Is it possible they were ordinary thieves?"

"Their sole intent seemed to be to give me a thrashing."

"And you've never seen them before."

"No."

"Is it a warning, do you think?"

"Either that or an attempt to put me out of commission for a while."

"Or worse."

"If they had intended to kill me, they would have brought weapons."

"Such as?"

"Guns, knives—cudgels at the very least."

Donald stood up and poked the fire. "I don't like it. You should ask DCI Crawford to be taken off the case."

"I don't think the attack is related to the séance murders."

"What, then?"

"The meeting with Rat Face was about our parents' death."

His brother stared at him. "Give it up, Ian. For God's sake, I implore you."

"What do you know that you're not telling me?"

Donald turned away. "I don't *know* anything—but obviously your life is in danger."

"I already told you they weren't there to kill me."

"But next time they might! And what of Rat Face? Perhaps they have done away with him already."

Ian downed the rest of his whisky. "He can take care of himself," he muttered, but he didn't entirely believe it. The truth was, he was worried about his informant.

"Did they strike you in the face?" Donald asked, peering at him.

"No. Why?"

"It's bleeding."

Ian put a hand to his left cheek. It felt wet. He looked at his fingers, smudged with blood.

"Does it hurt?" said Donald.

"Not at the moment."

"It's in the same place as that other nasty cut."

"Maybe I did get hit there during the fight and didn't notice. There was quite a lot going on."

"The mark of Cain," Donald remarked. "I'll put some salve on it."

"Why did you say that?" Ian asked as his brother opened a tin of liniment.

"What?"

"About the mark of Cain."

"I was just nattering. Hold still."

Ian complied, inhaling the aroma of mint and cloves as his brother smeared the medicine on his cheek.

"There," said Donald. "That should help." He stretched and yawned. "I'm all in. Early day tomorrow. I'm going to turn in. I suggest you do the same."

"I will."

"There's a joint and some boiled potatoes in the kitchen if you're hungry."

"Thanks."

"Good night, then," Donald said. Picking up his medical bag, he headed toward his bedroom.

"Thank you for the medical care."

"I'll send you my bill in the morning."

"Donald?"

"Yes?"

"Do you think our father was murdered because he was about to expose corruption within the force?"

His brother sighed. "Good night, Ian."

Bacchus twitched his tail and sniffed the air, then followed Donald into his bedroom.

Left alone, Ian sat staring into the flames of the fire in the grate before retiring to his bedroom. He lay awake for some time, Madame Veselka's words running through his head. *Ghosts ill-treated do not rest easy. Secrets long buried cry for the air of truth. Look to your dreams . . .*

He found himself standing in front of Waverley Station. It was nighttime, and he was looking for someone. He turned to see a tall man approaching, dressed in a long green robe, wearing a holly wreath on his head. In his hand was a flaming torch. Ian recoiled when he saw the torch, but as the man drew nearer, he realized it was Brian the blind beggar. Ian took a step forward, but as he did, his friend began to dissolve into a mist in front of his eyes. Within moments, there was nothing left of him but a thin wisp of white smoke.

Ian awoke with a start, surprised to find himself in his own darkened bedroom. He lay for a while pondering the meaning of the dream, until finally sleep claimed him once more.

CHAPTER FORTY

Early the next morning, Ian stopped at the office of the *Scotsman*. When he asked to see Jed Corbin, he was directed to a cubicle by the window. Walking through a cloud of cigarette smoke, past men in shirtsleeves hunched over their work, Ian spied Corbin scribbling away furiously at his desk, buried in piles of reference books, periodicals, loose paper, and broadsheets. At his elbow was an ashtray full of cigarette butts.

"This is a pleasant surprise," the reporter said, removing a stack of magazines from a nearby chair. "Have a seat. Just give me two seconds to finish this sentence, if you don't mind," he said, turning back to the notebook in front of him.

Ian perched on the chair, surveying the controlled chaos of the newsroom.

"There—all finished," Corbin said, laying down his pencil. "Can't keep inspiration waiting, you know. Now then, what can I do for you?"

"A friend of mine is missing."

Corbin leaned back in his chair and lit a cigarette. "Oh?"

"A blind beggar by the name of Brian McKinney."

"Usually sits in front of Waverley Station—erudite chap, on the witty side? Has an amazing sense of smell?"

"That's him."

"I know him well."

"I thought you might."

"How long has he been missing?"

"I haven't seen him since Friday, in front of St. Giles. I thought you might have heard something."

Corbin rested his cigarette on the already overflowing ashtray. Seeing Ian stare at it, he smiled. "Filthy habit, I know. I imagine newsmen smoke even more than coppers. Oiy, Jack!" he called, snapping his fingers at a passing boy. "Tell Cooper I've gone out on a story if he asks, eh?"

The boy nodded. "Aye, sir. Anythin' else?"

"Fetch me a candle, would you?"

The lad disappeared round the corner, returning with a long white taper, which he handed to the reporter.

"Well done," said Corbin, flipping him a coin. "Buy yourself a bag of sweets."

The boy caught it deftly and slipped it into his pocket. "Yes, *sir!*"

"What's the candle for?" asked Ian.

The reporter winked at him. "I'll just grab my coat. I have an idea or two of some people who might know something."

Minutes later, they were striding along Cockburn Street toward Waverley Station.

"Useful fellow, young Jack," Corbin said as a wagon piled high with winter wheat passed them, pulled by a muscular dapple-gray. The farmer tipped his hat and flipped his whip, which the horse ignored. Not increasing its pace in the least, it plodded on as if bored with the whole affair.

"I believe Jack knows that urchin friend of yours," Corbin added.

"Derek McNair?"

"Yes. It seems McNair organized a bunch of boys into a club of some kind, a group of—"

"Irregulars."

"Is that what they call themselves?"

"Actually, I suggested the name when he told me about them."

"I suppose they're up to no good."

"I suspect you could get them to do just about anything if you paid them enough."

The reporter gave him a sideways glance. "You don't think I—"

"I know Derek's sold you information. I don't suppose you'd balk at using his services for other things."

"Surely you don't believe I work outside the law?"

"I think you'd do whatever it takes to pursue a story."

Corbin shook his head. "How dreary it must be, always suspecting the worst of people."

"It's better than being consistently disappointed by them."

It was a short distance to Waverley, and Ian followed the reporter through the front entrance, past throngs of travelers scurrying in every direction. The steady clatter of leather heels on the polished floors reverberated through the high central dome, softening as it echoed back in a soothing symphony of sound, each footfall blending into the next.

"This way," Corbin said, leading Ian through a narrow door at the rear of the station. Ignoring the "No Entry" sign, he continued down a series of stairs into an underground corridor.

"Where are you taking me?"

"You'll see," Corbin replied, pushing open a heavy steel door with a broken lock. A whiff of stale air hit Ian's nostrils, followed by an even more unpleasant smell—the odor of unwashed human bodies. He followed the reporter into a dark, dank chamber that appeared to be part of an abandoned rail line. Several dilapidated passenger cars sat on rusting rails, some with broken windows, others missing wheels. It was evident they had not been in use for some time.

They were also clearly inhabited. Some sported makeshift curtains; others had laundry lines strung from them; the smell of cooking arose from several others. Ian thought he detected the creamy aroma of col-cannon from the rearmost car.

"How do you know about this place?"

"I'm a reporter. It's my job to know things."

"How long has this been here?" Ian said, as several pairs of eyes peered at him from lifted curtains.

"The railways abandoned this area approximately a year ago. Some of these cars have been there longer than that, obviously. But for the most part, the community is less than a year old."

A large man of about fifty with a scruff of gray hair stepped from one of the cars. He was dressed in a green sou'wester, thick woolen scarf, and rubber boots, the type a fisherman might wear. "Who're ye lookin' for, mister?" he asked as two younger men came up behind him, both very fit looking. Ian thought they might be the man's sons.

"Detective Hamilton, Edinburgh City Police," Ian replied.

"Well, then, Detective Hamilton, Edinburgh City Police," the man echoed in a heavy Irish brogue, "what can we do fer ye?"

Jed Corbin stepped forward and held out some coins. "We're look-ing for Brian McKinney."

The man looked at the money and licked his lips. "Blind Brian, is it?"

"The same."

The man seized the coins and smiled, revealing a mouth with as many gaps as teeth. "Why didn' ye say so?" he said, waving off his com-panions, who took a step backward. "Ye'll find ol' Brian's digs jes over yonder." He pointed to a passenger car still sporting most of its green paint. "Be sure t'knock, now—he don' much care fer bein' disturbed sudden like."

"Thank you," said Corbin, heading toward the green car.

Ian followed, keenly aware they were being watched not only by the three men but by other eyes peering from behind curtains as they passed.

They knocked on the dented door of the green car, but were met with silence. Ian peered inside and saw only darkness.

"Can't see a thing in there," said Corbin.

"What need has a blind man of an oil lamp?" said Ian.

"Maybe he's not in."

They knocked a second time, with the same result. Calling his name produced no response. Ian tried the door, which was unlocked. Pushing it open slowly, they stepped inside. Corbin produced the candle from his pocket and lit it, holding it aloft as the two men made their way through the interior of the car.

"I see why you thought to bring the candle," said Ian.

The moment they stepped into the rear of the chamber and saw the crumpled form upon the makeshift bed, it was clear something was amiss. The air was heavy with the smell of death. Kneeling beside his friend, Ian discovered rigor had not yet left his limbs. He detected no smell of putrefaction, and there were no flies, so the body could not have lain there for long. There were no obvious signs of violence. Nothing in the room appeared to be disturbed, and there was no blood visible on the body. Ian stood up and looked at Corbin, whose face was grim. Neither man spoke for a time.

Then Corbin said gently, "Good Lord. Do you suspect—"

"May I use your candle?"

"Of course."

With only the flame of a single candle, Ian did his best to investigate the tidy but cramped dwelling. There was a portable gas stove, and his search produced a box of matches but no candles. He supposed visitors—if there were any—brought their own. He found nothing of obvious interest. There were a few changes of clothes, toiletry items, cans of food, a few tins of nuts, some fruit, and half a loaf of bread. A shelf held a dozen books or so in braille, including works by Robert Burns and Robert Louis Stevenson. It was the simple existence of a man whose life Ian had seldom contemplated. Yet confronted with it here, he felt a deep sense of sadness. It was uncomfortable peering into his friend's life, doubly so now that he was past explaining or defending it. Ian felt like an intruder. He had encountered death before, but he seldom knew the victim. This was different—more personal, a strange and unwelcome intimacy.

Returning to the bed, he examined the scene more closely. A feather pillow lay next to McKinney, but there was none beneath his head. Holding the candle close to the dead man's face, Ian looked closely at it, and found what he was looking for. A single down feather clung to his lips. Ian lifted it carefully and slipped it into the pocket of his waistcoat.

"What is it?" asked the reporter.

"Very possibly evidence."

"So you think it was—"

"It seems a strange coincidence, does it not?"

"But who—"

"I believe an autopsy is in order. Could you lend me a hand?"

They lifted the body, made easier by the stiffness of his limbs, and carried him gently from his makeshift home. The effort hurt Ian's injured shoulder, as well as his sore ribs, and he suppressed a groan as they carried their burden from the railcar. He was somewhat taken aback to see a crowd had gathered, as motley an assortment of ragged and forlorn individuals as he had ever seen. There must have been a dozen or more—young mothers with babes in their thin arms, children clad in ill-fitting garments that looked as if they had been purchased from a rag picker, even a few elderly people who hardly looked strong enough to survive the winter. The haunted look in their eyes was all too familiar to him.

But he had a job to do. He and Corbin carried poor Brian past the throng of his neighbors. The big man who had greeted them stepped forward from their ranks—he was evidently the closest thing they had to a leader.

"Poor ol' Brian," he said, shaking his head. "Was it the drink that got him, then?"

"I see no evidence to suggest that," Ian replied. Looking over the assembled company, he said, "Did any of you see anyone visit Mr. McKinney in the past day or so?"

There were murmurs and head shaking among the onlookers. Ian was about to move on when a small girl stepped forward.

"I heard voices," she said shyly. "It sounded like he were arguin' with someone."

"A man or a woman?" asked Ian.

"It sounded like another man."

"When was this?"

"'Bout six hours ago. We live next door an' I couldn' sleep so I got up tae play wi' my dolly," she said, holding up a tattered doll in a stained blue dress, with buttons for eyes. "That's when I heard it."

"Could you make out what they were saying?"

"Not really. Somethin' 'bout somethin' breakin'? Don' know wha' they meant, sir."

"A break-in, perhaps?"

"Could be, sir."

"You've been most helpful," said Ian. "What's your name?"

"Suzie McGovern."

"Thank you, Miss McGovern."

"If he kilt Brian, I hope ye find him," said a tired-looking woman who appeared to be her mother. "Brian were a nice fella, so he was."

"I'll do my best."

The large man stepped forward again. In his hand was a lantern. "Ye don' have t'go out through the station. There's another way out."

"There is?" said Ian.

"It leads to an alley. We use it mostly to come an' go. Attracts less attention that way."

271

Ian and Corbin exchanged a glance. They both knew attracting attention was not helpful to their mission.

"Lead on," said the reporter.

They followed the man down the deserted rail platform, past a few more deserted cars, to where the tracks ended. The wall appeared solid, and there was no door leading to the outside, but their host beckoned them forward. Holding his lantern aloft, he pointed toward a narrow opening where the bricks had been knocked away. A few of them still lay scattered on the ground, chipped and broken. Ian peered at the break in the wall, which was just wide enough to accommodate an average-sized man.

"Think we can make it?" Corbin asked. In the gaslight, Ian could make out prickles of sweat on his forehead. Corbin was not a big man, and even for Ian, Brian's body was beginning to feel like a deadweight. His shoulder throbbed more insistently, and his ribs felt as though they might give way. Taking a deep breath, he forced his mind away from the pain.

"Steady on," he said. "We'll find a cab once we're outside."

The reporter nodded. "Let's carry on, then."

Ian turned to their guide. "Thank you, Mr.—"

"O'Connor. Niall O'Connor."

"Thank you, Mr. O'Connor."

"If someone kilt Brian, ye'll get 'em, won' ye?"

"I will do everything in my power."

The two men lifted their dead comrade and stepped through the narrow opening and into the hazy light of a late December morning.

CHAPTER
FORTY-ONE

DCI Crawford leaned back in his chair and tugged at his whiskers. "An autopsy on a blind beggar? I don't think so, Hamilton."

"But sir," Ian said, "I believe he was killed to stop him from talking."

"And you're basing this on something overheard by a child? Who wasn't even certain what she heard? Let alone whether it had anything to do with his death."

Ian gazed out the window of Crawford's office. A light drizzle dotted the panes, in the ever-changing moods of December in Edinburgh. His spirits were sinking along with the weather, and he wished he could just burrow beneath a pile of blankets and hibernate until spring.

"Where is he now?" said the chief.

"At the morgue."

Crawford sighed. "See here, Hamilton, Dr. Littlejohn is a busy man. I can't just demand he drop everything to investigate the death of a beggar."

"I wish you would reconsider, sir."

Crawford reached for his "rosary" and twisted the string absently around his fingers. "This has been a hard winter, and he's trying to contain a measles outbreak. Not to mention countless cases of catarrh, whooping cough, and tuberculosis. I'm sorry, Hamilton."

"But I'm quite certain—"

"'There is no such uncertainty as a sure thing.'"

Ian realized his efforts were useless. When Crawford started quoting Burns, it was time to concede defeat.

"As you like, sir," he said, and slipped out of the room. Without a word he walked through the main room, through the double doors, and out of the station house. Once on the street, he thrust his arm into the air, ignoring the stab of pain in his shoulder. A hansom cab slid to a stop in front of him.

"Where to, sir?" said the driver.

"Royal Infirmary, quick as you can."

"Yes, sir," he replied, snapping his whip lightly in the air. The sleek chestnut gelding didn't need any more urging, and started off at a smart trot, polished hooves clicking on the slick cobblestones.

When they arrived, Ian tipped the driver generously and entered the majestic building, heading straight for the tiny office at the end of the main corridor. When he knocked, the door opened to reveal a familiar face.

"Hamilton!" said Conan Doyle. Dressed in a belted tweed jacket, he looked hale and hearty as ever. His face was ruddy, as if he had just come from a hike on the moors. "You're a sight for sore eyes."

"You may change your mind when you hear why I've come."

"Nonsense! You're welcome here anytime—come in, won't you?"

It didn't take long for Ian to explain the situation. Doyle listened intently, puffing on an ornately carved meerschaum pipe.

"So you want me to perform the autopsy?" he said, laying down the pipe.

"Is that an utterly outlandish request?"

"Well, I have assisted in a number of autopsies, and performed a few in my early days as a medical student. I don't have the same expertise as Dr. Littlejohn or Dr. Bell, but—I'm game if you are. What exactly are you looking for?"

Ian told him, and Doyle nodded solemnly. "I'm terribly sorry about your friend. It's a bad business, finding him like that."

"Then you can understand why I'm keen to find the person responsible for his death."

"Let me just finish up some paperwork for Dr. Bell, and I'll accompany you to the morgue."

"I don't know how I can ever repay you."

"I rather think a glass of decent port should do the trick."

"Perhaps you would dine with me afterward, at the place of your choosing."

Doyle's blue eyes crinkled at the edges. "I can't refuse such a handsome offer. The life of a medical student is not terribly flush. If you don't mind cooling your heels in the waiting room for a bit, I shall join you shortly."

As he reached to open the door, a groan escaped Ian as his injured shoulder shot a bolt of pain through his body.

"Are you quite all right?" said Doyle.

"I had a bit of a kerfuffle with a pair of gentlemen yesterday evening."

"I'd say they were hardly gentlemen if they caused you such injuries. It would appear you are in need of medical attention."

"My brother patched me up last night."

"Still, why don't you let me—"

"Thank you, but you've done enough for me already," Ian said, and left the office before his friend could protest further.

Lost in thought, he walked down the long corridor toward the front of the building. Turning the corner toward the waiting room, he came face-to-face with none other than Fiona Stuart.

"Good afternoon, Detective Hamilton," she said evenly. "It would seem your efforts to avoid me have failed at last."

He stared at her as if she were an apparition. Clad in a snowy-white nursing uniform, her head framed in a cloud of auburn curls, she was indeed a vision. The hazy afternoon light streaming in through the tall windows created a kind of halo around her, softening the edges of her corporeal form, so she did appear to be almost floating. It took him several moments to find his tongue. Meanwhile, she stood, arms crossed, gazing at him as coolly as if he were a laboratory specimen.

"P-please accept my abject apology," he stammered finally. "You must think me an utter cad and a bounder."

"On the contrary, I think of you as neither. I do, however, think of you as someone who is overmatched—though by what, I cannot say."

"I am indeed over my head at the moment," he said, relief spurting like sweat from his brow. "But that does not excuse my unforgivable behavior toward you."

"Nothing is unforgivable—certainly not lapses in social decorum."

"You are kind to say so."

"If one were to keep score of every slight in life, one's friends would be few indeed."

He stared at her again, momentarily speechless.

"What is it?" she said.

"Forgive me. I am unaccustomed to such wisdom from one so young."

She cocked her head to one side. "There must be a way of saying that without appearing condescending."

"Your presence makes a fool out of me," Ian said, astonished at the words that shot out of his mouth. It was as if he had no control over them.

"You speak of me as 'so young,' but I can't help but think we are much the same age."

"Perhaps, though I surely lack your wisdom."

"A fault you can remedy by taking me to Le Canard this evening. My shift ends in two hours."

"The maître d' there loathes me."

"Then this is an opportunity to correct his erroneous impression. It is now three o'clock. I shall be waiting for you there at five o'clock." And with that, she turned and swept away, the skirts of her uniform skimming across the polished floor with a swooshing sound.

Ian stood watching her, dazed and distracted, nearly jumping out of his skin when he felt a hand on his shoulder. He spun around to see Conan Doyle, wearing a topcoat and hat.

"It's only me," his friend said, smiling. "Were you talking to Nurse Stuart just now?"

"Yes," said Ian. "I'm afraid I owed her an apology."

"Which no doubt you remedied."

"I hope so. Oh, blast!" Ian said. "Would you mind terribly postponing our dinner engagement?"

"Not at all. I'm not nearly as pretty as Nurse Stuart."

"It's not that. I—"

Doyle laughed. "She only looks intimidating. She's only flesh and blood, after all."

Watching the retreating figure of Fiona Stuart, Ian wasn't entirely sure his friend was right.

CHAPTER
FORTY-TWO

Half an hour later, morgue attendant Jack Cerridwen having been duly placated with a bottle of whisky, Ian and Doyle stood over the prostrate form of Brian McKinney as he lay in the cold and dank chamber where the recently deceased awaited the next stage of their journey. The room was eerily silent, save for the steady drip of a leaky pipe overhead. Ian held a lantern for better visibility, while Doyle selected a pair of tweezers from his medical kit.

Carefully lifting the dead man's eyelid, Doyle peered at his eye. "There is our first clue as to the manner of death," he said. "Have a look for yourself."

Holding the lantern closer, Ian bent over to see what Doyle was looking at. The clouded eyes were unevenly dotted with spots of blood.

"Petechial hemorrhage," Ian murmured.

"So you know what that points to, then?"

"Strangulation. Could it also indicate smothering?"

"It could. Why do you ask?"

"I found a feather on his face, and a pillow next to his body, yet there was none under his head."

"Since your friend was blind, there was already some pathology to the eyes, so I'm going to check one more thing."

"What are you looking for?" Ian asked as his friend made a shallow incision in the dead man's neck.

"Fracture of the hyoid bone, which would be an indicator of strangulation."

"There are no marks upon the neck."

"True enough, though that is not conclusive. Aha," he said after a moment. "The hyoid is intact, but look what I found lodged in the windpipe." Carefully lifting them with his tweezers, Doyle held up two goose feathers. "I think your initial suspicion was correct. If I am not mistaken, the murder weapon was indeed a pillow."

An hour later, Ian and Doyle were in a hansom cab on the way to Le Canard. Taking no chances, he was a full ten minutes early. Doyle had suggested dropping Ian off before continuing on to his rooms near the university.

"I'll wait here just in case," his friend said as the driver pulled up in front of the restaurant.

"In case of what?"

"In case Nurse Stuart decides to teach you a lesson."

"What do you mean?" Ian said, alighting from the cab.

"Just come back out and tell me if she's there."

"We're early."

"All the same," said Doyle. "Go on, and close the door, would you? It's bloody freezing out there."

The maître d' favored Ian with one raised eyebrow when he entered, but managed to convey a remarkable range of emotions in that single gesture. Flashing a broad smile, Ian breezed past him into the dining room. A survey of the room failed to locate any sign of Fiona, and he was about to return to the lobby when he felt a tap on his shoulder. Turning, he saw the maître d' holding a folded piece of paper.

"Mademoiselle left you a note," he said, his French accent even thicker than before, and Ian wondered if it was fake. He waited until the man returned to his post before opening it. The familiar handwriting was firm as ever.

Emergency at hospital. My apologies—another time, perhaps? (No, I am not trying to teach you a lesson, no matter what Mr. Doyle may say.)

Ignoring the maître d's inquisitive stare, Ian strode out of the restaurant and into the street, where the cab was waiting, the driver huddled against the cold, his breath visible in white wisps in the frigid air. Ian couldn't help thinking what a thankless job it was, especially in such weather, resolving to give him a generous tip.

"I was hoping I was mistaken," Doyle said after Ian explained the note. "But how the devil did she know what I was going to say?"

"Evidently she knows you better than you think," Ian replied, slipping the note into his waistcoat pocket.

"It's easy enough to confirm her story about the emergency, so I imagine she is telling the truth. Even so—"

"We'll speak nae mere on it," Ian said, imitating his aunt's Glaswegian dialect. "Are you thirsty?"

"I thought you'd never ask."

Opening the roof hatch, Ian called out to the driver.

The man's face appeared in the opening. "Where to, sir?"

"The White Hart, please."

"Right you are, sir," he said, and the cab rattled off into the night.

Edinburgh taverns were hardly temples of propriety, but the White Hart was one of the more respectable ones, popular with university students and professors alike. It also catered to a somewhat rougher crowd, and late-night carousing was not uncommon. The evening was young when Ian and Doyle arrived, and the rowdier elements had not yet arrived. They selected a table in the back, and as they walked toward it, Ian caught a flash of movement out of the corner of his eye. He turned just in time to catch Terrance McNee, a.k.a. Rat Face, slipping out the back door.

"Excuse me a moment," he said to Doyle, darting back through the front entrance and down the narrow close along the side of the building. Short of climbing the fence behind the pub, his quarry was trapped. As McNee turned the corner into the alley in his attempt to escape, he could not hide his expression of astonishment at seeing Ian.

"Fancy meeting you here," he said with an unconvincing smile.

"Would you like to explain yourself?" Ian said, barring his way.

McNee cleared his throat and looked around nervously. "Ah, yes, sorry about that. I found myself with a second engagement the other night, and no time to contact you."

"Why don't you save us both time and tell me what really happened."

The little man swallowed nervously. "Perhaps another time. I really must—"

"I'm afraid I must insist," Ian said, grasping him by the collar. "The two gentlemen who did show up gave me a beating, and might have done worse had I not escaped."

"Oh, dear," said Rat Face. "That is most unfortunate."

"Why did you not show up for our meeting?"

"As I said, I was overbooked—"

"It was your idea in the first place."

"Alas, something pressing came up at the last minute."

"Did you know I was to be attacked?"

"I swear I didn't."

"What, then? What frightened you so much that you decided not to come?"

"Please," Rat Face said. "You don't know what you're asking."

"Tell me, then."

He looked around furtively.

"No one is watching us," said Ian.

"The walls have ears," Rat Face said weakly.

"What is it, Mr. McNee? What has happened?"

He licked his thin lips. "There is . . . how can I say it? A *change* in the criminal community, a new . . . presence, I suppose you would call it, that no one seems to be able to identify, and yet its effect is felt everywhere."

"Is it a person?"

"No one knows. It seems to be a unifying force of some kind that knows all, sees all, and is bent on controlling what happens in the criminal world."

"Is there a new gang in town? One of the Glasgow crews, perhaps?"

"I think not. It would be impossible to hide an entire group of people."

"A man, then?"

"It could hardly be a woman, but as I said, no one seems to have actually *seen* him. And yet his effect is felt everywhere—he gives orders, instructions, warnings."

"He must have lieutenants."

"They all claim never to have actually seen him."

"They are lying. Someone has seen him."

"If they have, they are not admitting it."

"So why did you not come to our meeting?"

"I received a warning not to show."

"How did you know it was from him?"

"I knew."

"Do you have the warning note?"

Rat Face shook his head. "There was no note. The message was whispered to me as I walked along a narrow close such as this one, but when I turned to look, there was no one in sight."

"Do you believe he was responsible for the attack on me?"

Rat Face squirmed uncomfortably. "Please don't ask me anything further. I could be in danger just from speaking with you."

"You have Jimmy Snead to protect you."

"He's no match for—"

"For what, McNee?"

"A Glasgow smile wouldn't be very becoming on me, I'm afraid," he said with a nervous little laugh. Ian could smell fear oozing like sweat from his pores.

"So he's behind Nate Crippen's death?"

"What do you think?"

"What about Brian McKinney?" said Ian.

"What about him?"

"He's dead."

McNee's eyes widened. "*What?* How?"

"Smothered in his own bed."

He gave a rodent-like squeak. "I know nothing of that, I swear."

"Why did you want to meet me yesterday? What did you intend to tell me?"

"I really must be off," Rat Face said, wrenching himself from Ian's grasp.

Realizing the man would tell him nothing further, Ian stepped aside to let him pass. As he watched him scurry down the street, he pondered what or who could terrify an entire community of thieves, blackguards, and rogues.

CHAPTER
FORTY-THREE

The girl was a mistake. He knew it moments after it happened. He had lost control, which was something he had vowed never to do. He had succumbed to anger, his privacy violated by her nosiness. Ordinary human emotions were his enemy, something he had foolishly forgotten in the heat of the moment. He would not make that mistake again. He did not enjoy killing—or so he told himself—but he had an overwhelming need to maintain control, a drive so deep he could not separate it from other, more basic needs like eating or sleeping. Years ago, he would have included women in that list, but he had weaned himself from them, training himself away from the pull of sexual attraction. Not because he was without desire, or even because it had proved disastrous in his life, but because it was another step away from total control. To desire a woman was to become vulnerable, to put oneself in her power, and that was a step into chaos.

He would have weaned himself from food and drink, if he could, but as that was impossible, he ate sparely and drank only occasionally.

As for sleep, he had never needed much of it, fortunately, and had conditioned himself to function with even less. Tobacco was the one pleasure he allowed—it sharpened his mind and senses. He was as close to a purely cerebral being as was humanly possible, he thought as he closed the heavy drapes just far enough so he could peer out of the flat's tall windows, but no one could see in.

He gazed down at her, lying on the floor, so tranquil and peaceful looking, save for the imprints his fingers had left on her tender white neck. He sighed. He must rid himself of her body as soon as possible. He knew how to dispose of a body, best done under the cover of darkness. He would wait until the wee hours of the morning, when the leeries had finished prowling the city with their long ladders and tapers tucked under their arms.

Night had fallen over the city, and the great unwashed masses had sequestered themselves behind closed doors, locked and bolted against the criminal element always lurking in the darkened alleys and winding wynds of the city. But there was no bolt sturdy enough to keep the citizens of Edinburgh safe from him, no door so thick that he could not penetrate it sooner or later, if he wished. As the unsuspecting inhabitants slept, thinking themselves safe and sound in their beds, he would sit throughout the night and scheme how to consolidate his already growing riches and power.

The séance murders had been pathetically easy to set in motion. It was all a matter of timing—his stooge had motivation; all he had to do was provide the opportunity and watch the dominoes fall. And Ian Hamilton would be too preoccupied to concentrate on what was really going on, who was really behind the slaughter. Like a master magician, he had provided a convincing distraction while consolidating his power in the criminal underworld. Hamilton had gotten too close to solving the one crime that could bring him down in an instant—he had managed to arrange Nate Crippen's death just in time, but it was a close call, one he did not care to repeat.

The people he preyed on were mere sheep—docile, domesticated, and dull. They had become weak and complacent, unable to see past their own immediate needs. He was an entirely different creature altogether.

He was the Watcher.

CHAPTER
FORTY-FOUR

The next morning Ian rose before the sun, venturing into the predawn stillness as the city paused to catch its breath before the start of another workday. He arrived at police chambers, well before his shift was due to start, to find Jed Corbin leaning against the building, smoking a cigarette.

"You're up bright and early," said the reporter, tossing his cigarette stub into the gutter.

"I could say the same of you," Ian replied, opening the door to the station house.

Corbin followed him inside. "Any autopsy results yet?"

"Yes."

"What was the cause of death?" he asked as Ian started up the stairs. When Ian didn't respond, Corbin followed him.

"If you spend much more time here, we'll have to start charging you rent," said Ian.

"I helped you out yesterday," Corbin said as they reached the landing. "I would say you owe me, wouldn't you?"

Ian turned to face him. "But it's up to me how to repay you."

"Why won't you tell me?"

"Because I haven't yet told my superior officer. It's his decision what to release to the press."

Corbin snorted. "If I waited for permission from my editor to pursue a story, I'd be sitting on my hands all day."

"As soon as I inform DCI Crawford, your paper will have an exclusive on any information he cares to release."

The reporter brightened. "An exclusive? Have I your word on that?"

"You have."

"Do you believe his death is related to the fire that killed your parents?"

"What makes you say that?"

"You are investigating those events, are you not?"

"There is no official police inquiry into the death of my parents."

"That's not what I asked."

"What I do in my free time is no one's business but my own."

"Then you *are* looking into it."

"Don't press your luck, Mr. Corbin."

"But isn't it true—"

"Good day," Ian said. Entering police chambers, he left the reporter alone on the landing.

It was quiet inside the spacious room, with its high ceilings and tall windows overlooking the High Street. Sleepy constables were finishing their usual routines before heading home. No time of day in Edinburgh was quite like early morning. The rambunctious, bustling city had not yet discarded the blanket of night that muffled the hurly-burly of the workday.

Ian busied himself with paperwork until a faint glow seeped into the room, as the pale light of dawn crept across the windowsills. Yawning, he stretched his stiffening muscles and got up to fetch a cup of tea. He heard voices coming from the small room just the other side of the tea service. The room functioned as a storage area, as well as the place for an occasional furtive nap when the chief wasn't looking. Recognizing one of the voices as Constable Turnbull's, Ian paused to listen.

"He's hardly the one to look for false informants."

"Why's that, then?" The voice belonged to Constable McKay, a well-meaning but simple-minded fellow Turnbull had twisted round his little finger.

"What, do you not know?"

"Know what?"

Ian listened, his heart dropping like a stone in his chest. He could take it no longer, and burst into the room, with no idea what he was going to do or say. Both men looked at him in surprise, but Turnbull's pockmarked face soon assumed its usual superior sneer.

"Do you need something, Detective Hamilton?" he inquired coolly.

Ian's eyes narrowed dangerously, and it took great effort not to plant a fist in that smug face. The consequences were not worth it, he reasoned—he wouldn't let a man like Turnbull force him into acting rashly.

"We're out of biscuits," he said tersely, opening the cupboard containing tea supplies. Grabbing a tin, he strode from the room. He heard Turnbull snicker softly, but moments later both constables emerged from the room—for now, at least, the spell was broken.

Taking his tea back to his desk, Ian pondered what he had heard. The constable obviously knew Crawford had charged Ian with finding the false informant. But how had he found out? He certainly matched the description James McAllister gave of the man who visited his pawnshop. It was not proof, but it came perilously close.

Just then, Sergeant Dickerson entered the station, shaking snow from his overcoat. Was it Ian's imagination, or did Dickerson avoid looking at him as he hung his coat on the rack? Was there something guilty about the slope of his shoulders as he shuffled toward his desk? An unwelcome thought burrowed into Ian's brain: Was it possible that Dickerson was Turnbull's source of information? After all, who else knew about the assignment?

No, he told himself—Dickerson would not do such a thing, no matter how irritated he was with Ian. It was unthinkable, surely. Ian chided himself for entertaining such a supposition. But as Dickerson took his seat, their gazes met, and Ian did not like what he saw in the sergeant's eyes. Instead of admiration and deference, he saw resentment and wariness. He was about to say something when the door to Crawford's office opened and the chief himself appeared.

"Could you come in here a minute, Hamilton?"

Rising too quickly from his chair, Ian felt a stab of pain from his injured ribs, and could not suppress a groan.

Crawford frowned. "Are you quite all right?"

"Yes, sir," he replied, and followed the chief, trying not to wince as he passed Turnbull, who gave him a smug smile and muttered something under his breath.

"What's that, Constable?" said Ian.

"Nothing," said Turnbull.

"Nothing—what?"

"Nothing, *sir*," he muttered sulkily.

Ian experienced a moment of victory for which he knew he might pay a price later. But he had no idea how high that price might be.

CHAPTER
FORTY-FIVE

"Close the door," Crawford said as Ian entered the office. "So what have you done to yourself this time?"

"It's nothing, sir—just a touch of muscle strain." Telling the chief about his injuries would mean revealing the reason for his trip to King's Stables Road, and he didn't think Crawford would take kindly to it.

The chief looked unconvinced. He grunted and lowered himself gingerly into the chair behind his desk.

"How are your piles, sir?"

"My piles aren't the issue," he said, shifting his weight in the chair. He did not look comfortable. "What's this I hear about you collecting information about the jewelry store theft from—a *resetter?*"

"James McAllister of Gullan's Close, to be exact."

"What on earth of value could he tell you?"

"I asked him if he had heard anything, and he had not, which leads me to suspect the report we received is false."

"McAllister is one of the most notorious resetters in Edinburgh!"

"Which is precisely why he is valuable. If any large robbery such as that were in the works, he would be in the forefront of people who knew about it."

"Why would you trust him to tell the truth?"

"I gave him a very convincing incentive."

"I see what you're getting at," said Crawford, stroking his mutton-chops. "The thieves would look to him to fence the stolen property—"

"Precisely. He would certainly be among the first to hear of such a plan, so that he could prepare for such a haul."

"Damn," said Crawford, shifting his weight in the chair again. "We're right back where we started."

"Not entirely, sir. The information we received may be partly correct."

Crawford pointed to a cushion on the chair next to Ian. "Hand me that, would you? What do you mean, 'partly correct'?"

"Perhaps there is to be a robbery, but somewhere else," Ian said, giving him the cushion.

"I fail to see how that could be helpful," Crawford said, slipping it underneath his backside. "What good is it if we don't know the location?"

There was a timid knock on the office door.

"What is it?" Crawford bellowed.

The door opened a crack. Sergeant Bowers stuck his head in, his pale cheeks pink, his light-blue eyes apprehensive. The chief rather liked Bowers, so the task of interrupting Crawford often fell to him.

"Yes, Sergeant?" said Crawford. "What's so important that it can't wait?"

"Sorry sir, but she's insisting on speaking to Detective Hamilton."

"Who?"

"The young lady, sir."

"Very well, Bowers," Crawford said, and the sergeant slipped out of the office.

Crawford sighed. "Off you go, then, Hamilton. And try to stay out of trouble, will you? Can't afford to have you knocked about like that."

"I'll do my best, sir," Ian said, and left the office.

Returning to his desk, he saw a young woman standing near the entrance, looking around nervously. Clad in a forest-green cloak over a simple woolen skirt and bodice, she was plump and robustly built, with delicate features and dark, wavy hair that looked as if it had been hastily pinned up. A few loose strands dangled around her face, which was pink and damp. It appeared she had come in a great hurry.

"Can I help you, miss?" he asked, approaching.

"Detective Hamilton, is it?" she said shyly.

"At your service. What can I do for you?"

"I want tae report a missin' person." Her accent was unmistakably Irish, possibly from Donegal.

"And who might that be?"

"It's me mate, Bridie."

"Does she have a last name?"

"Mallon. Bridie Mallon."

"And your name?"

"Mary Sullivan."

"And why do you believe your friend is missing, Miss Sullivan?"

"I haven' seen her since Monday."

"Is that unusual?"

"We share rooms, y'see, an' she always comes home after work. She don' show up Monday night, nor last night neither."

"Is it possible she has a beau?"

"She has a fella she sees, but she's not that kind o' girl," Mary said, reddening. "Always comes home at night, so she does."

"When did you last see her?"

"Monday, afore she left fer work."

"And her occupation?"

"She's a charwoman—we both are. We work fer diff'rent folks."

"Who was she working for on Monday?"

"It's funny, because it's a client she's supposed to clean for on Tuesday, y'see."

"So why did she go on Monday?"

"She got it into her head t'go on a diff'rent day, so she did."

"And who is this client?"

Mary averted her gaze. "I don' know."

"Is there anyone who might know?"

"I know where he lives, I jes don' know him personal-like. He's very . . . mysterious, ye might say."

"How so?"

"He doesn't seem to want us to lay eyes on him."

"Why not?"

She shrugged. "I couldn't say. It's very odd, so it is."

"Can you give me the address, then?"

"Forty-one Greenside Row. Four F, flat on the top floor."

"Where can you be reached?"

"Leith Wynd, across from Happy Land, if ye know where that is—"

"Only too well," Ian said. Happy Land was one of two notoriously run-down tenement buildings on Leith Wynd, the other being Holy Land. The residents who weren't members of the criminal class were poor souls who could afford nothing better.

"We've been savin' money tae be able t'afford a better place," she said, seeing his expression.

"Please let me know if your friend returns. Meanwhile, have a care for your own safety. If something happened to her, you may be in danger as well."

Her eyes widened. "Do ye really think so?"

"Just promise me you'll be careful."

"So I will, sir—thank you, sir."

She turned to leave.

"Just a moment," said Ian. "Why did you ask for me?"

She blushed. "Your aunt—Lillian, isn't it?"

"You know my aunt?"

"She sometimes teaches paintin' classes at the church. One time she mentioned her nephew was a policeman."

"I see."

"She said ye were the best detective in Scotland."

"Did she indeed?"

"She said ye had a gift for seein' things others might miss."

"I hope I can live up to my aunt's flattering report. Good day, Miss Sullivan."

"Good day, sir, and thank you, sir."

After she left, Ian looked around for Sergeant Dickerson. Not seeing him, he set off in the direction of Greenside Row. He was about to hail a cab when he heard a voice behind him.

"You're not angry wi' me, are ye, Guv?"

He turned to see Derek McNair, hands in his pockets, a look of contrition on his grimy face. He appeared sincere, but with Derek, honesty was a matter of convenience rather than policy.

"Why should I be angry with you?"

"I haerd the meetin' didn' go so well."

"Just exactly what did you hear?"

"Ye were ambushed."

"Then you heard right."

"I didn' know nothin' 'bout that, I swear on me mother's grave."

"Last I heard, your mother is still alive."

"Then I swear on—"

"I don't blame you for what happened."

"Are y'all right, Guv? Rat Face tol' me it were two blokes wha' attacked ye."

"I'll live," Ian said, raising his hand to signal a passing hansom cab.

"Where y' off to now?"

"I'm going to investigate a disappearance."

"Kin I come?"

"I think not. It might be dangerous," Ian said as the cab pulled up in front of them.

"Derek's my name, danger's my game," the boy said eagerly.

"It's official police business," Ian said, getting in.

"When has that ever stopped me?"

"It's about time that it does," Ian said, and closed the door. The cab rattled off down the High Street, leaving a very disappointed Derek McNair watching as it swerved to avoid a couple of inebriated toffs staggering out of Old Fleshmarket Close.

Ian looked out the window at the pair of young men weaving heedlessly down the High Street. He guessed from their clothing that they were law clerks, on their way from the Advocates Library just around the corner, though he didn't know why they were so obviously in their cups at this time of day.

As the cab turned onto North Bridge, he thought about Derek McNair. He was genuinely fond of the boy, but hardship had molded him into someone for whom morality, as defined by polite Victorian society, was a luxury. What mattered was to survive, and if that meant lying, stealing, and cheating, then so be it. He didn't blame the boy for this any more than he blamed a fox for stealing chickens. He sometimes worried that allowing Derek to help him in his cases put the boy in danger, though he knew only too well that life on the street had its own perils.

Ian gazed out the window as the cab turned onto New Street, leaving the squalor of Old Town behind as it headed toward the steep rise of volcanic rock known as Calton Hill. High atop the hill, Ian could see the Nelson Monument, listing tipsily to the side. Built to honor the vice admiral who lost his life defeating the combined French and Spanish fleets at the Battle of Trafalgar, it was designed to resemble an inverted telescope, an appropriate design for an admiral. While Edinburgh had its share of military statues, it boasted an equal number of memorials to literary luminaries like Walter Scott and Robert Burns.

Poets and generals, Ian thought as he watched the pale sun glinting off the tower's windows, opposites in life's journey, just as he was the reverse counterpart of the criminals he pursued. What accident of fate had led them down the path of crime, he wondered, while he was consigned to pursuing them? Did the same flick of time's arrow create their inevitable destinies, or were they free to choose their lot in life? The more he saw of Edinburgh, privilege living cheek by jowl to the most abject poverty, the less he believed men were captains of their own destiny.

Such thoughts swirled like the gathering mist in the streets as the cab rumbled toward its destination. High atop Calton Hill, the tepid December sun still poked feebly through the clouds, but on the cobblestones below, a haar fog was rolling in from the Firth of Forth, blanketing the ground in thickening white wisps. Still the horse trotted briskly onward, urged by his master, no stranger to the changeability of Scottish weather.

Greenside Row ran along the northwestern border of Calton Hill, and after the long stretch on Calton Road, they turned onto the narrow lane. Number 41 wasn't far, and after paying the driver, Ian stood facing the five-story building, its stone façade gray from years of soot and smoke, like so many of its kind in Edinburgh. Behind him was parkland, the increasingly steep cliffs cutting off the buildings from view. The trees were bare, though a few gnarled gorse bushes along the edge clung stubbornly to their leaves.

Looking up at the darkened windows, Ian felt a shiver slither down his spine. Though just like its neighbor on either side, there was something uninviting about the building, an air of invincibility, as if it was a fortress rather than a perfectly respectable New Town tenement housing with no doubt rather expensive flats.

Shaking off his feeling of foreboding, Ian rapped the lion's head knocker smartly against its black iron base. He was met with silence. A dove cooed softly from the gorse bushes across the street. He knocked again, with no response. Just as he was turning to leave, he heard footsteps from inside, then the sound of several locks clicking in their tumblers. The door was cracked open, and Ian saw a sleepy-faced young man peering at him.

"Can I help you?" he asked in a plummy voice. His accent was educated, probably central London, and Ian noticed the fingers holding the door open were well cared for. His manner and grooming suggested money and privilege. Judging by his expensive silk dressing gown and patrician air, he had no plans to alter that status in the near future.

"Detective Inspector Hamilton, Edinburgh City Police," Ian said, doing his best to peer at the hallway behind, but the man's body blocked his view.

"What's this all about?" the fellow asked, scratching his head. He had a long, pink-cheeked face, high forehead, and very light-blue eyes. He would have been handsome except for his fleshy lips, which gave him a rather fishlike appearance. From the disheveled look of his hair and beard stubble on his chin, it was evident he had just awakened from a deep sleep.

"I'm investigating a case," said Ian. "And who might you be?"

The question did wonders to jolt him into a more alert state of consciousness.

"Nigel Metcalf," he said, his pale-blue eyes wide. "I say, I haven't done anything wrong, you know."

Shaking off an impulse to reassure him, Ian decided it was better to keep Mr. Metcalf a little off balance. "Is this your place of residence, sir?" he asked sternly.

"Yes—I live in the ground-floor flat," Nigel Metcalf said, opening the door so that Ian had a good view of the foyer.

"Would you mind answering a few questions?"

"Not at all—come in, please."

The flat had the look of university student digs—a football jersey tossed over a chair, textbooks open on the table, exam books on the sideboard.

"Are you a student, Mr. Metcalf?"

"Yes, I'm preparing to enter the medical school next autumn."

Had this been a casual conversation, Ian might have mentioned his brother, but he merely nodded.

"I was up all night studying for an exam," he added.

"I won't keep you much longer," Ian said, looking around the flat. A pair of women's kid gloves lay on the mantelpiece.

Seeing Ian's gaze on the gloves, Metcalf took a step forward. "Those belong to my girlfriend. She left them here two days ago."

"I see," Ian replied, sounding as if he didn't. In fact, he thought the gloves far too expensive to be the property of a poor charwoman, but wished to keep pressure on Metcalf as long as possible. People said things they didn't mean to when they were on edge, betraying themselves in all sorts of little ways.

"I say, would you care for some tea? I could do with a cup," Metcalf said, nervously rubbing his hands together.

"Thank you," Ian said, realizing that he was a bit faint from hunger, having had nothing to eat or drink since before dawn.

He was glad when Metcalf reappeared with raisin scones and plenty of fresh butter. The student listened carefully to his questions about the upstairs tenant, then shook his head.

"I can't say I've ever met him. I do hear the front door opening sometimes, in the middle of the night."

"And you hear him go upstairs?"

"I'm usually too sleepy to notice."

"What about last night, when you were up studying?"

He shook his head. "I heard nothing all night—mind you, I was fairly engrossed in my anatomy textbook."

"And you have lived here how long?"

"It'll be just over a year this month. I had rooms nearer the university, but saw this advertised for an even lower price, so I took it."

"And no one moved in or out during that time?"

"Not that I'm aware."

"What about the flat below the top floor? Who lives there?"

"Used to be a nice old lady, but she moved out a few months ago, and no one's come to take her place."

"And your landlord?"

"Away on the Continent somewhere. I send my check in every month to a law office in Lyons. I can give you that address if you like."

Further questioning brought no useful information, and when Ian knocked on the door of the top-floor flat, there was no response. As he turned away from the door to the flat, Ian felt a sudden bone-chilling cold, but there was no source of drafts that he could see. He headed back down the stairs, anxious to leave, though he could not say why.

"Thank you for your time, Mr. Metcalf," Ian said, putting on his cloak.

"I wish I could have been more helpful," he replied. "Hang on a minute. There was one thing. I don't know if it will be of use, but—"

"Yes?"

"Once as I arrived home from studying, I saw a policeman leaving the building."

"When was this?"

"Perhaps a month ago."

"Had you ever seen him before?"

"It was late at night, and I didn't get a good look at him, but he wore a uniform."

"Is there anything you can tell me about him?"

"He was slim—like you, only not so tall."

"Anything else, such as facial hair or hair color?"

Metcalf bit his lip. "I'm not certain, but I think he may have had bad skin."

"How so?"

"Pitted—you know, pockmarked."

"Thank you, Mr. Metcalf," Ian said. "You have been very helpful." Wrapping himself in his cloak, he left the building.

From a perch high atop Calton Hill, unseen, a pair of eyes watched as he turned onto Greenside Row and toward the city below.

CHAPTER
FORTY-SIX

After a bite to eat at a public house near the base of Calton Hill, Ian headed toward his next destination, the Royal High School. The building was hard to miss, rising from its stone terrace on Regent Road, with its heavy Doric columns and neoclassical architecture. Modeled after a temple in Athens, it was a much-praised structure, but Ian had never cared for it. The sun was fleeing a darkening sky, and fog wrapped itself around his ankles as he trudged up Regent Road.

Upon informing the hall monitor of his arrival, he was escorted into the office of the rector, James Donaldson. A tall, long-faced man with a receding chin and keen, gentle eyes, Donaldson was a prominent citizen—a Fellow of the Royal Society of Edinburgh, classical scholar, and theologian. When Ian entered, the great man rose from behind his desk and came around to shake his hand. He did not appear pleased to see Ian.

"Please, Detective Inspector," he said, "do sit down." His voice was educated, but with remnants of the twisting, narrow vowels of the northeast—Aberdeen, perhaps.

Ian complied, taking a chair opposite his desk, while Donaldson remained standing, leaning against the front of his wide oak desk. "Now, then," he said, "what can I do for you?"

"I've come about a former student of yours, Jeremy—"

"Fitzpatrick?"

"Yes, as a matter of fact."

"What's he done now?" Donaldson asked with a sigh.

"I take it he has a history of problems, then?"

"He's a bully, a real ne'er-do-well. Surly fellow. If it weren't for his father, I would have expelled him, quite frankly."

"Major Fitzpatrick?"

"The fellow's a decorated war hero. Took a bullet in Afghanistan. We made . . . allowances, you might say. Terrible business about his death. Have you caught the culprit yet?"

"That's why I'm here, sir. Do you think his son is capable of—"

"Killing his own father? Good Lord, I hope not. He's an unpleasant boy, but—good Lord," he repeated. "That's just unthinkable. Why, it's inhuman."

"I see a lot of things in my line of work you might find inhuman, yet all of them are committed by people."

Donaldson shook his head. "Your faith in the human race must be stretched rather thin at times." He returned to sit behind his desk, and Ian noticed an ornately carved cuckoo clock hanging on the wall over him. At that moment the doors to the clock swung open and a wooden bird duly appeared, chirping the hour in its eerie mechanical voice.

"Ah," said the rector. "Four o'clock. Time for my constitutional. Will you join me in a wee glass, Detective?"

Ian hesitated. He rarely drank while on duty, but the bottle Donaldson pulled from his desk drawer was Glenkinchie, a single malt he was especially fond of.

"Thank you, sir," he said, licking his lips.

"It's a bit of an oddity, that clock," Donaldson said with a smile. "It was a present from an especially devout Jesuit monk who found something of value in my writings. Made it himself at his monastery in Switzerland."

"I understand you are quite a renowned theologian."

"I dabble in theology," Donaldson replied, handing him a tumbler of whisky. "Education is my true calling."

The whisky burned Ian's throat before releasing its subtle aroma of peat and smoke and good, clean earth. He felt his shoulders relax as he savored the faint floral bouquet, soft and sweet as a Highland summer.

"Good, isn't it?" Donaldson said.

Ian nodded, taking another sip. He wanted to finish his glass and have another, to drink until the images in his head softened and faded like the swirling mist outside the window.

Donaldson leaned back in his chair. "'A now-and-then tribute to Bacchus is like the cold bath, bracing and invigorating.'"

"Robert Burns?"

"A sensible man as well as a great poet."

"My commanding officer would be delighted. He is a particular admirer of Burns."

"DCI Robert Crawford, isn't it?"

"You know him, sir?"

"Our paths have crossed. His wife is a fine woman."

"He is devoted to her."

"Quite rightly." Donaldson took a sip of whisky and sighed. "I suppose young Fitzpatrick's problems started when his mother died. A boy needs his mother. Miss Staley did what she could, but—"

"Is that Elizabeth Staley, by any chance?"

"Yes. She was Jeremy's teacher at the time."

"I knew Miss Staley was a teacher, but did not realize he was her pupil."

"Good Lord, do you think her death and the major's are related?"

"It is entirely possible."

"Miss Staley was an excellent teacher. Poor woman. She did what she could with young Jeremy . . . and then there was the Nielsen child's suicide."

"Lucas Nielsen?"

"Why, yes. Jeremy bullied him ruthlessly, and he eventually killed himself."

"His parents told me—"

"That it was an accident?"

"Yes."

"They were deeply ashamed—insisted on calling it an accident."

"I believe there was an investigation."

"Certainly. The manner of death was labeled Undetermined, but we all knew Lucas Nielsen had taken his own life by climbing up to the roof and jumping off."

"Boys can do dangerous things to show off. Perhaps he was—"

"Lucas Nielsen was no daredevil. He was a timid boy."

"Is there any chance he was pushed?"

"He left a note. But his parents didn't tell anyone about it until the investigation was over. They claimed he told them he was going to do it 'on a dare.' The police didn't know any different, and certainly nothing could be proved, so that was that."

"It wasn't featured prominently in the papers."

"The Nielsens did what they could to bury the story. I believe it cost them some money. I would have expelled Jeremy Fitzpatrick then and there, but his father pleaded with me, and he only had another year remaining, so . . . I told him he had no more chances left, and that seemed to put him straight, at least until he left school."

"You were quite convinced Lucas was a suicide?"

"Mr. Nielsen showed me his note later, and it was quite sad. I don't believe his wife knew he told me about it."

"Could it have been forged?"

"Miss Staley claimed it was his handwriting."

"She was his teacher as well?"

"He and Jeremy were in the same class together."

Ian sat back in his chair, his head spinning. Lucas Nielsen, Elizabeth Staley, Major Fitzpatrick . . . What were the chances their deaths were *not* related?

"Is something wrong, Detective?"

"No, sir. I was just . . . thinking."

"Care for another wee dram?"

"Thank you, but I—"

"I won't tell if you won't," Donaldson said with a wink.

"Is there anything more you can tell me about Miss Staley? Or Lucas Nielsen and Jeremy Fitzpatrick?"

Donaldson leaned back, stroking his chin in a gesture than reminded Ian of DCI Crawford. "Miss Staley was a gifted teacher, devoted to her students, especially the troubled ones. If she couldn't get through to the Fitzpatrick boy, I suppose no one could."

"Would you say they had a special connection?"

"I do know that she was one of the few people he confided in after his mother's death."

"How did his mother die?"

"Terrible thing, really. She fell down the stairs."

Ian felt as if a bolt of lightning had shot through his body. If there was one thing he knew about criminals, it was that they tended to repeat their behaviors, especially the ones that worked. Elizabeth Staley had died the same way as Jeremy's mother. But why would Jeremy kill his own mother?

"Did Jeremy get on with his mother?"

"As far as I know. I only ever met her once. Nice woman, very pretty. Quite elegant, you know. The major was devastated by her death."

"And Lucas Nielsen? Was he close to Miss Staley?"

"She tried to help him, to stop the bullies from picking on him. He was a sensitive child, you know, an artistic nature and all that. Played the piano rather well. Once Jeremy set his sights on Lucas . . . well, he was sneaky. Bullied him when no one was looking. As I said, an unpleasant sort of boy."

"Thank you, Mr. Donaldson," Ian said, rising. "You have been more helpful than you know."

"Are you sure you wouldn't care for another glass?"

"Thank you, but I really must be going."

Out in the street, Ian flagged down a hansom cab. The driver was a lively fellow of middle years he recognized, having been his passenger a number of times.

"Evenin', sir," the fellow said, tipping his hat. "Where to?"

"The Hound and Hare, if you please. How have you been, George?"

"I'll nae complain, sir. Whit's fur ye'll no go by ye."

"I suppose you're right—what's meant to happen will indeed happen," Ian said as he climbed in. George was fond of colorful Scottish slang, but there seemed something eerily prophetic in his words on this still, misty night. Whatever was meant to happen, Ian feared, might be something he was entirely unprepared for.

CHAPTER
FORTY-SEVEN

The carousing at the Hound and Hare was just picking up steam when Ian arrived. He could hear drunken hoots and hollers from the pub as he climbed out of the cab.

"Ta very much," said George when Ian tipped him generously. "Good luck, sir."

"Thank you, George—I may need it."

"Failing means yer playin', sir."

"Failure isn't really an option, but thanks just the same."

He entered the pub, the reek of cheap tobacco assaulting his nostrils.

Stray bits of conversation trailed after him as Ian shouldered his way through the crowd.

"Aye, he's shot tae fuck!"

"Dinnae teach yer Granny tae suck eggs, laddie."

"I'll gie ye a skelpit lug, so I will!"

Ian looked at the hulking fellow offering to cuff his friend's ears.

"Hello, Jimmy," he said.

A grin broke out on Jimmy Snead's face. "Hello, mate!" he cried, embracing Ian in a bear hug. "Wha' brings ye tae this hellhole?"

"Same thing as you. I need a drink."

Jimmy let out a guffaw like the braying of a mule. "There's better places tae buy a drink."

"Seems like you've had a few already."

"Aye. I'm mad wi' it," Jimmy said with a grin. "Totally bladdered."

"Hammered, eh?"

"Aye. I'm wrecked, mate. Oiy, Alan, buy us a drink, won' ye?" he yelled at a massive bald fellow with a build like a Percheron.

"Yer already oot yer face, Jimmy!" he called back.

"Awa' an bile yer heid!" Jimmy shouted, and the bald man laughed and moved on.

"His head looks like he's already boiled it," Ian remarked.

Jimmy brayed again, wrapping a long arm around Ian's shoulders. "Come along, boyo, let's get ye a wee drink."

As Ian followed his friend through the press of bodies, he noticed a muscular, compact man with sun-bleached hair and a weathered face watching him intently from the far corner of the room. His striped trousers and loose-fitting blouse marked him as a sailor. Years of wind and sun had dug deep grooves in his cheeks, and even in December his face had a sunburnt glow. Ian took a step toward him, and the man bolted like a rabbit, slipping through the crowd toward the back door as smoothly as if he was greased.

Ian took chase, but the bodies seemed to close in around him, and by the time he reached the back alley, his quarry was gone. He looked up and down the narrow wynd leading to the street, but the clatter of wooden wheels and voices obscured any sound of retreating footsteps. Disappointed, he returned to the pub, where Jimmy was waiting for him with a dripping pint of ale.

"Whair hae ye been?" he said, handing Ian the drink.

"Do you know the sailor who was sitting over there?" Ian said, pointing to the recently vacated chair.

"Small but well built, wi' hair like straw?"

"Aye, that's him."

"Mos' likely that would be Sammy. Always stops in 'ere when his ship's in at Leith docks."

"Does he have a last name?"

"I never haerd it."

"What do you know about him?"

"Nasty piece a' work. I once had tae gae 'im a beatin' fer skelpin' 'is lady friend."

"Why was he slapping her?"

Jimmy gulped some ale and wiped his mouth with his sleeve. "Don' know an' don' care. No proper man does that tae a woman."

"You're a prince, Jimmy."

"I'm a rascal an' a rogue, but I'd sooner cut off my hand than raise it tae a female. Why are y'interested in the likes a him?"

"He may have murdered a man I was looking for."

"Oh, aye, Nate Crippen."

"His hands were tied with a sailor's knot."

"Plenty a' them come through this place," he said, his fingers tracing the grooves in the table where someone had carved a rude word. His fingernails were tobacco stained, the nails dirty and ragged.

"What have you heard about his death?" said Ian.

"Ah dinnae ken who done it, but Sammy's as likely as anyone. He'd a needed help tae do a Glasgow smile, though."

"So you know about that?"

Jimmy shrugged. "Somethin' like that gets around."

"If you hear anything, will you let me know?"

"Ye kin count on Jimmy," the big man said, giving Ian a friendly slap on the back. "But ye didn' come here tae see me. Who are y'after?"

"Your . . . colleague. Have you seen him?"

"Rat Face? He's made 'isself scarce lately."

"He's frightened, I suppose."

"Pure bloody terrified is more like it."

"Do you know how to reach him?"

Jimmy shook his head. "When Terry McNee don' wannae be seen, there's nae findin' him."

"Oiy, Jimmy!" shouted a tall, thin lad with shaggy brown hair. "Are ye blootered yet?"

"I'm steamin'," Jimmy yelled back. "Ma heid's mince!"

"Wannae fight?"

"Ach, maybe later," Jimmy said, and the man moved on.

"Can we talk somewhere quieter?" said Ian, as the din in the pub had reached a deafening volume.

"Aye," said Jimmy. "Out back."

Ian followed his friend through the rear exit, once again stepping into the dim alley behind the pub. The ground was covered in mist, which swirled and twisted around their feet before twirling upward into the unseasonably warm air. The tinny sound of a concertina came from the pub, accompanied by drunken singing.

"Haar fog in December," Jimmy remarked. "It's a bad omen."

His words sent a shiver through Ian. The last time he stood in this godforsaken alley, he was looking at the mutilated body of Nate Crippen.

Jimmy lit a cigarette, the smoke joining the wisps of mist curling around his head. "What did ye wan' tae talk about, then?"

"Rat Face spoke of a new 'presence' among you—a kind of unifying force, uninvited but powerful."

"Aye," Jimmy said, blowing a smoke ring.

"What can you tell me?"

"Not much. Some a' the lads are receivin' instructions if they do this or that, they'll get paid a large sum fer it."

"And do they get the money?"

"Aye. Every time."

"Where does it come from?"

"No one knows. One morning there's a note slipped under yer door with instructions, or ye find it in yer coat pocket. Or yer mate says he's heard from so and so tae do this an' that."

"And the money?"

"Same thing. It jes—appears."

"No one's ever seen leaving it?"

Jimmy shook his head. "Nope. It's like he knows everythin' goin' on in this bloody town."

"What sort of things does he ask you to do?"

Jimmy flicked his cigarette into the gutter, where it glowed briefly and died. "Bad things."

"Have you taken money from him?"

Jimmy hung his head. "Aye. Once."

"What did you do for him?"

"Don' ask me that, mate," he said quietly.

"You wouldn't know anything about a missing girl, by any chance?"

"No. God, no."

"Her name is Bridie—"

"I tol' ye no!" Jimmy said tightly, his face red, big fists clenched, and Ian caught a glimpse of the criminal behind the friendly demeanor.

"All right," he said. "One more question. What about the big break-in later this week?"

The question took Jimmy by surprise. He gulped like a fish gasping for air, his Adam's apple jumping up and down in his neck.

"Don' know what ye mean," he said lamely.

"Rumor has it the target is Murray and Weston."

Jimmy's body relaxed, which told Ian the jeweler was not the intended victim.

"All right," Ian said evenly. "If it's not the jewelry store, what is it?"

"Don' know," Jimmy muttered as a rat skittered across the muddy ground, headed for the garbage bins behind the pub. There was a rustling sound as the animal burrowed in between the containers.

"Don't know or won't say?"

"I really don' know. He won' tell anyone till the day of."

"How will he notify people?"

"It's different every time. Random, like. Could be a note in the post, or a telegram—anythin'."

"I can't ask you to betray your mates, but this is important."

"I might not find out—'specially now that I've been seen talkin' tae you."

"Is your life in danger?"

Jimmy shrugged. "I kin take care a' m'self."

"Thank you, Jimmy—you've been very helpful."

"Are ye lookin' tae bring him in?"

"It is my intent."

"Be careful. Some say he's the devil himself."

CHAPTER
FORTY-EIGHT

Ian arrived at the Blackfriars Street Masonic Lodge just as the evening rehearsal of the Greyfriars Dramatic Society was getting underway. He had come not so much to watch as to check in on his aunt. He also knew Dickerson was likely to be there, and he did not like the way things had been left between them.

A feeling of anticipation hung in the air as Ian entered the building. The Freemasons seemed to be ignoring the ban on celebrating Christmas—the front vestibule was festooned with fragrant boughs of evergreen, and a holly wreath hung on the door leading to the main hall. The aroma of apples, cinnamon, and cloves greeted him as he opened it.

No sooner did he enter the hall than Clyde Vincent came loping up the aisle, a tin cup in his hand. "You're just in time for a bit of grog," the director said, thrusting it at him. "Come along," he said when Ian hesitated. "The actors aren't allowed any until after rehearsal. Don't want people going up on their lines, you know."

Ian accepted it gratefully, taking a sip as Vincent watched, beaming. "What do you think?" he said. "It's a family recipe."

"It's very good," Ian replied. He was very thirsty, and the hot spiced drink was comforting.

"My mother always added cinnamon and cloves. The bits of apple are my invention. All right, everyone," he said, turning toward the stage, where a few actors stood studying their scripts. "We start in five minutes." There was no sign of Sergeant Dickerson, though Lillian stood near the wings, chatting with the actor playing Scrooge. Her cheeks were flushed, and she wore a smart blue frock Ian had never seen.

Seeing him, she waved. "Ian—come meet our lead actor."

He complied, following Clyde Vincent down the aisle toward the stage. The director disappeared into the wings, dispensing instructions to a couple of stagehands.

"Ian, this is Alistair McPherson. Alistair, this is my nephew, *Detective* Inspector Ian Hamilton," she told McPherson, emphasizing Ian's title.

"Your aunt speaks glowingly of you," McPherson said, shaking his hand warmly. "To hear her talk, you are defeating crime in the city single-handedly."

"My aunt is given to exaggeration," Ian remarked, sizing him up. His hand was strong and muscular, but with few calluses. He was broad shouldered, but the lack of lines on his face suggested he did not work outdoors.

"I am *not*," Lillian protested. "Ian is the most gifted detective in the force. His superior officer told me so himself."

"Crawford said that?" Ian asked dubiously.

"He did indeed. I sometimes work as a police photographer," she told McPherson proudly. "I received an inquiry from DCI Crawford to do a sketch of a missing girl."

"Absolutely out of the question," said Ian.

"It's really not for you to say," she replied, frowning.

"I already explained that you might be in danger. I don't want to expose you to any more peril than necessary."

Lillian rolled her eyes. "You see it's my nephew who exaggerates," she told McPherson.

"Perhaps it runs in the family," he suggested with a smile.

"Now that you know my profession, would it be rude of me to inquire as to yours?" Ian asked.

"Not at all," he replied.

"Alistair—Mr. McPherson—is a jeweler," said Lillian.

"Indeed?"

"Speaking of things running in the family, my father designed and made jewelry, as did his before him. You might say it's in my blood."

"He's very good," said Lillian. "He made me this necklace," she added, pointing to a thin pendant around her neck in the design of a flower. The petals were made of gold, with tiny inlaid pearls at the center.

"It's a lily of the valley," McPherson said. "Because her name is Lillian, you see."

"Yes," said Ian. He suddenly felt a twinge on his left cheek, and put a hand to his face.

"That's a nasty cut," said McPherson. "Shaving accident?"

"He scratched himself in his sleep," said Lillian.

"The mark of Cain," McPherson murmured.

"Why do you say that?" asked Ian.

"Sorry—it just popped into my head. I didn't mean to offend you."

"He's not offended—are you, Ian?" said Lillian.

"All right, everyone," said Clyde Vincent, entering from the wings. "Places for Act One. Would you care to stay and watch?" he asked Ian. "By the way, where's that sergeant of yours? I haven't seen hide nor hair of him tonight."

As if in response, the door swung open and a flushed Dickerson hurried in. "Sorry t'be late," he told the director. "I were finishin' up a bit of police business."

"Hello, Sergeant," said Ian, stepping out from behind Vincent.

Upon seeing him, Dickerson's face flashed surprise and annoyance, but he quickly recovered. "Hello, sir. What are you doin' here, if ye don' mind my askin'?"

"Apart from seeing my aunt, I wished to speak with you."

"Oh?"

"Do you have a minute?"

Dickerson looked toward the stage, where Vincent was assembling the company. "I think they're about t'start—"

"This is more important. Where did you go off to today?"

"I were tryin' t'find more out about the major's son. I tracked down one of the major's mates from the military, and he tol' me the lad is troubled. Got into some sort a' scrape in school."

"You're a bit late in delivering that news," said Ian. "I already know about all that."

Dickerson frowned. "I were jes tryin' t'take initiative, sir."

"Next time why don't you ask me before you go off chasing a lead on your own?"

"Yes, sir," the sergeant replied tightly.

"Look," said Ian. "I need to know I can trust you."

"How could y'ever doubt that?" Dickerson said, his blue eyes tragic.

"Well, you've been spending a lot of time with Constable Turnbull lately, and I—"

"He likes me! Treats me like an equal. Makes me feel important, like."

"But he's not to be trusted—"

"How would *you* know? You're so busy tellin' me wha' I done wrong, puttin' me in my place."

Ian felt his face redden. "I never—"

"Lecturin' me on this an' that, so's I don' forget who's in charge. Well, I don' forget, but I don' always have t'like it, either!"

"Sergeant Dickerson, are you ready?" Clyde Vincent called to him from the stage.

"I were jes comin'," Dickerson replied. Turning back to Ian, he said, "Oh, and Gretchen tol' me that Mr. and Mrs. Nielsen haven't been comin' t'seances near as long as they claimed. She said they've only been there fer two, maybe three months at most."

"That's odd—why would they lie about it?" Ian mused.

"Sergeant!" called Clyde Vincent.

With one last glare at Ian, Dickerson turned and stalked toward the stage.

Watching him go, Ian felt a stab of pain in his cheek. When he put his hand to it, there was blood on his fingers. Cain's words from the Old Testament popped into his head. *I am not my brother's keeper.*

If he was not his brother's keeper, Ian wondered, whose keeper was he?

CHAPTER
FORTY-NINE

Donald settled into his armchair and took a swallow of ginger beer. "No doubt you are right about this Constable Torn—Tern—"

"Turnbull," said Ian.

They sat before the fire in the parlor, Bacchus curled up on the sofa next to them. The logs crackled merrily in the grate, casting a warm glow around the room, but Ian's mind was far from the serene setting on Victoria Terrace.

"You must let the sergeant make his own mistakes," said Donald. "He will discover his error soon enough."

"But what if he realizes it too late?"

"What are you afraid will happen?"

"It could be ruinous."

"For Dickerson?"

"And the force. I don't know what Turnbull is up to, but I don't trust him."

"It sounds as if your sergeant has fallen under his spell."

"He must know he is playing with fire, and yet—"

"From what you say, it sounds as though he is doing it to spite you."

"I cannot understand how he could avoid realizing what Turnbull is," Ian said, taking a drink of whisky, deep and bitter and comforting. "So many ills in life are the result of a refusal to face the truth."

His brother rose and plucked a clay pipe from the rack over the fireplace. "Do you imagine you have a monopoly on the truth?"

"Certainly not, but at least I—"

Donald pulled a pouch of tobacco from his pocket and began stuffing the pipe. "Forgive the tautology, but people are only human, after all."

"But—"

"The truth is often hard and frequently bruising. Can you really blame them for not having the stomach to face it?"

"It's not going to go away, and any attempt to circumvent or deny it can lead to disaster."

"And yet so many men spend their lives dancing around the inevitable, trying to avoid what's plainly in front of their face."

"Precisely my point! Building one's life on a bedrock of lies is insupportable and disastrous, and yet—"

"It is common," Donald said, taking a box of matches from the desk drawer.

"Unfortunately, yes."

"Except for you, the heroic truth-seeker."

"I didn't say that."

Donald lit his pipe, wisps of blue smoke curling around his head. "It certainly informed your choice of a profession."

"As a medical man, you seek truth as much as I do."

"Ah, but my field is nature, not human behavior."

"You deal with diseases just as ugly as murder—cancer, consumption, typhoid."

"Without having to gaze into the souls of my fellow man."

"But—"

Donald sat back in the chair and puffed at his pipe. "Has it ever occurred to you that some truths are better left unspoken?"

"I don't see why—"

"Because people aren't ready for them, Ian. Take my own situation, for example—"

"You have overcome your weakness for drink admirably."

"That is not what I was referring to."

"Oh," said Ian, looking away. "I see."

"Do you, brother? Do you really see? Most people regard me as a pervert, an aberration. A monster. Is that what you see when you look at me—a monster?"

"Certainly not—don't be absurd."

"But are you ready to face the truth about me—about who or what I am?"

Ian held his head in his hands. He did not care to think of his brother's private life. He knew what Donald did with other men, but could not pretend to understand it. It was a chasm between them, perhaps unbreachable, and it filled him with misery. "I don't know. It's so difficult to—"

"I rest my case. People turn away from the truth because it is too difficult—too painful—to even think about."

There was an uncomfortable silence between them. Then Ian said, "Do you think I'm pompous?"

His brother gave a short laugh. "Of course you are. So am I. It runs in the family."

"Odd—that's the second time tonight I've heard that phrase."

"Don't make anything of it," Donald said. "It's just coincidence. Aunt Lillian has enough superstition for the lot of us."

"I see you put some evergreen over the mantel. And a bit of mistletoe on the windowsill."

"That's not superstition—it's just holiday spirit."

There was another silence, as they listened to logs crackling and hissing in the fire.

"Are you going to see Lillian in the play?" said Ian.

"We'd jolly well better, or we'll never hear the end of it. Besides, I'm fond of Dickens. Always have been."

"Do you think . . ."

"What?"

"Do you think people really get a second chance?"

"If they don't, then I'm bloody well done for."

"What I mean is—"

"Do angels and ghosts interfere to change the course of a life? I think not—but I wager Aunt Lillian might take issue with that."

"What I meant to say is, are some mistakes too dire to recover from?"

"Some, I suppose. But surely not all."

"Do people ever really change, though? Is Scrooge's redemption wishful thinking?"

Donald pulled at his pipe thoughtfully, exhaling a cloud of tobacco vapor. "No, I don't think so. Optimistic, perhaps, but . . . surely a change of heart is always possible, at any age." He regarded his brother with one eyebrow raised. Ian knew the look. "Have you someone in particular in mind?"

Ian looked down at his empty whisky glass. "I've been having disturbing dreams lately."

"Oh?"

Ian told his brother about the three strange dreams, and their odd, vision-like quality.

"Dickens would approve," Donald remarked when he had finished.

"Good Lord, you're right," Ian said, suddenly aware of the connection he had not seen before. "The creature with the candle on his head is much like—"

"The Ghost of Christmas Past," Donald finished for him. "And the apparition of our mother bears a strong resemblance to—"

"The Ghost of Christmas Yet to Come!"

"And in the third dream your friend the beggar appears much as the Ghost of Christmas Present."

"I suppose you're right."

"You said Madame Veselka told you to pay heed to your dreams. Didn't your third dream presage your friend's death?"

Ian frowned. "Yes, but one could argue I was simply worried about him."

"I know what Lillian would argue," Donald said mischievously. Yawning, he rose from the chair and stretched. "I'm all in. Mind if I retire?" The cat opened one eye and regarded him languorously before closing it again.

"Go on, then," Ian replied moodily, staring at the leaping yellow flames of the fire.

"That wound on your cheek doesn't seem to be healing. Would you like me to put some salve on it?"

"No—go onto bed. I'm sure you're tired."

"Want a word of advice?"

"Can I stop you from giving it?"

"Don't take everything so seriously, brother," he said, laying a hand on Ian's shoulder. "Good night."

"Good night."

Later, Ian lay in bed gazing at the starless sky, until his lids were so heavy he could no longer fight it, and sleep claimed him.

CHAPTER FIFTY

You arrive home late, breathless with victory. The flat is quiet except for the sound of gentle snoring from the back of the building. You pull off your gloves, flinging them onto the table in the foyer. A light drizzle has speckled your overcoat, and you brush it off impatiently before hanging the coat on the wall rack, along with your hat.

Blowing on your hands to warm them, you head for the sideboard. This calls for something stronger than tea—a celebration is in order. Uncorking the bottle of brandy, you pour a stiff shot or two into the snifter, swirling it for a moment to release the liquor's heady aroma. Savoring the burn as it slides down your throat, you sit by the fireplace to relive the events of the past few hours.

Your planning was impeccable, your preparation perfect. Of course there was luck involved—there always is, in any momentous encounter—but you could not have timed it better. In fact, it all went so smoothly you wonder if perhaps you missed something. You take another swallow of brandy, eager for the sweet release of the spirit—not so much that you dull the quaver of excitement simmering in your breast, but just enough to slow the tremulous beating of your heart, so you can enjoy the triumph so dearly won.

The hand holding the glass trembles a little, not from fear but rather exhilaration. In all your years on this earth, you did not realize anything could be so entrancing, so fully engaging, as hunting another human. What began as a mission of vengeance has become a rarified pleasure, a secret pastime of such excitement that your only wish is that you could share it with someone.

But of course you can't. No one can be trusted to keep your secret; you will have to keep your own counsel as you continue. Luckily, your mission is not over yet, you think as you drink eagerly from the nearly empty glass. There is more work to be done.

CHAPTER
FIFTY-ONE

The next morning dawned so insistently bright and cheerful that Ian turned his steps in the direction of the Royal Infirmary before heading to police chambers. He half hoped Nurse Stuart would not be in, so he could leave a message and be on his way. But when he inquired after her, the same stern-faced matron he had met earlier informed him she would be out shortly, then disappeared with a disapproving glance into the bowels of the hospital. He did not know where Nurse Stuart lived, and did not care to know; looking for her at her place of employment struck him as a less intimate and therefore much safer option.

When she appeared, he had the impulse to flee—the sight of her auburn curls and freshly scrubbed face set off a panic he was scarcely prepared for. He had become accustomed to thinking of her as clear, firm handwriting upon a page, forgetting the flesh-and-blood person behind it. The reality of her physical presence was almost too much for his senses, and he took a step back as she approached, the heels of her boots clicking smartly on the polished floors.

Everything about her was too intense—her cheeks too red, her green eyes too deep a color of jade, her auburn hair too lustrous and shimmering. Even her scent was distracting—a combination of rose water and Brown Windsor spice soap.

"Why, Detective Hamilton," she said in her brisk, matter-of-fact way. "What a surprise to see you."

"Not an unpleasant one, I hope," he mumbled, feeling the heat rise to his face, but also noticing with some satisfaction that the color on her cheeks also deepened.

"Not at all." She smiled, displaying unreasonably white teeth. "After all, I believe you still owe me a dinner."

"Ah, yes, so I do."

"You really should have that cut attended to," she said, peering at his face. "Would you like me—"

"No, thank you—I'm quite all right."

There was an awkward pause, and then she said, "You must not think I have been languishing, waiting anxiously for you to pay attention to me."

"I would not dream of it."

"Because my life is quite full without you or any man."

"I have no doubt of that."

"I merely wanted to make it up to you for my beastly behavior earlier."

"Understood."

"Good. As long as that is perfectly clear."

"Perfectly."

She crossed her arms over her starched white uniform. "What do you propose?"

"Since we have had such ill luck at meeting for dinner, I thought perhaps you might accompany me to a play. My aunt is in a performance of *A Christmas Carol* at the Greyfriars—"

"Oh, yes, I had been meaning to see that. When shall we go?"

"I was thinking perhaps the Sunday matinee?" By then, he knew, the supposed jewelry store theft should be resolved, for better or for worse.

"Splendid."

"And if we are not ill met by luck again, we might venture out for a bite afterward."

"Agreed. Perhaps we may lift the curse by meeting at the theater first."

"Precisely what I was thinking."

"Very well—I shall meet you there."

He felt he should offer to pick her up, but reticence overcame him, and he merely nodded.

"Until Sunday, then," she said. Turning crisply, she marched back down the hall from whence she came.

Ian felt his own steps lighten as he left the infirmary, walking with an unaccustomed buoyancy. Colors seemed more vivid; passing cloud formations suddenly captured his attention—he became caught up in the loveliness of their shifting abstract beauty. Dull gray cobblestones shimmered in the morning light; the clop of horses' hooves summoned his racing heart to match their steady beat. He suspected what he was feeling was infatuation but regarded the timing to be utterly insane, given all that he was facing. He had not sought it out; he had avoided it as long as possible, and still the arrow had found his heart. And yet he could not but think of how the crimson in her cheeks matched his own, the gleam in her jade eyes as they met his. For half a mile he floated in a swoon of happiness; everything seemed possible, and the world opened to him like a flower.

But as he neared police chambers, his mood darkened. So much weighed upon his mind. The supposed threat to Murray and Weston's jewelry store seemed unimportant in comparison, though he knew DCI Crawford did not see it that way.

He entered police chambers to find Sergeant Dickerson and Constable Turnbull hobnobbing at the tea station. Dickerson barely acknowledged Ian when he came over to pour himself a cup, and Turnbull turned away, his mouth set in its accustomed sneer.

"Good morning, Sergeant," Ian said in as friendly a tone as he could manage.

"Mornin', sir," Dickerson mumbled without looking at him.

As Ian headed back to his desk, he heard the constable mutter something about "a blind beggar," adding, "Beggars can't be choosers," which caused Dickerson to snicker.

Ian spun around so fast the tea flew from his cup. Letting it fall to the floor, he grabbed Turnbull by the collar and threw him against the wall.

"What's that you said?" he hissed, his face close to Turnbull's. He could smell the oil oozing from his pockmarked skin, and the greasy hair tonic smeared over his cheap toupee.

"I was merely pointing out your little friend had it coming," the constable replied smoothly. He seemed utterly unintimidated, which only increased Ian's rage.

Tightening his grip on Turnbull's collar, Ian pushed him harder against the wall, cutting off his air. "What would you know about it?"

"No—more—than—you do," the constable gasped. Ian released his hold a bit, and the sneer returned to Turnbull's face. "From what I hear, your father had it coming as well."

That was it. Ian's vision narrowed to a thin, dark tunnel, and before he knew what he was doing, he aimed a blow at Turnbull's jaw, knocking him halfway across the room. Ian tensed, setting himself up for a return attack, but the constable picked himself up from the floor, smiling as he wiped a thin smear of blood from the side of his mouth.

"You'll have to watch that temper of yours," he said, wiping the dust from his uniform. "It'll get you in trouble one of these days. Just like your dear old da."

Ian was about to launch himself at Turnbull again but was suddenly aware the room had gone utterly silent. He turned to see everyone staring at him. Some of the men looked up from their desks, papers still clutched in their hands, while others gaped at him from the entryway, just arriving for the morning shift. Sergeant Dickerson stood, jaw slack, staring at him. The sound of Crawford's door opening drew all eyes in that direction.

"In my office, now!" the chief thundered. "Close the door behind you!" he said as Ian entered.

Crawford heaved himself into his chair and tugged at his whiskers, as if he wanted to pull them out by the roots. "Blast it, Hamilton," he muttered. "What the hell's got into you?"

Ian stared at the floor, fists clenched, still trembling with rage.

"I asked you a question, Detective!"

"I lost my temper—sir."

Crawford rose and paced the office. "Good God, Hamilton—what were you *thinking*?"

Ian bit his lip. "He insulted my friend."

"Just *words*, man—hardly worth taking to fisticuffs over!"

"And my father."

Crawford ran a hand through his thinning ginger hair, making it stand straight up in startled-looking wisps.

"Your father?"

"Yes, sir. He insulted the memory of my father."

Crawford looked as if he were about to say something, then changed his mind. He took a deep breath and exhaled a gust of air. "I won't have my men attacking one another. Do you understand?"

Ian chewed on his lower lip.

"Do you *understand*?"

"Yes, sir."

"If you were anyone else in the force—*anyone*—I swear to God I'd suspend you!" Crawford grabbed the piece of string from his desk and twisted it so hard it looked as if it might break.

"Turnbull is dirty—I *know* he is."

"Look," said Crawford. "I think it's best you take it easy for a while. I shouldn't have asked so much of you. You've enough on your plate as it is."

"What about the upcoming burglary? Surely it's—"

"I've stationed men at Murray and Weston round the clock. They've instructions to call for assistance if they see anything slightly suspicious."

"But my intelligence suggests the break-in will be elsewhere—"

Crawford sighed and tossed his bit of string onto the desk. "So you've said."

"Where did you get your information?"

Crawford hesitated. "Now, see here—"

"It was Turnbull, wasn't it?"

"I have several sources—"

"You can't trust him, I tell you!" Ian insisted. "Why can't you get that through your thick skull?"

Crawford took a step back, as if he had been struck. There was a deadly silence as Ian realized what he had done. Neither of them spoke for some time, then Crawford said, "I think it's best you go home. You're obviously unfit for duty."

"I'm sorry, sir. I don't know what came over me. It's just that—"

"You are officially suspended until further notice."

"But sir—"

Crawford turned and gazed out the window. "That will be all, Detective."

"Please, sir—"

"I said that will be *all.*"

Ian knew the chief well enough to realize that retreat was the only option at the moment. There was a chance he might be malleable later, but now there was no point in arguing. Ian left the office, closing the door behind him.

Most of the men turned away when he entered the main room. There was no sign of Sergeant Dickerson or Constable Turnbull. He couldn't help wondering if the constable had taken Dickerson aside to poison his thoughts further, but could not stop to worry about that now.

Throwing on his cloak, he headed for the exit, but heard his name being called as he was about to open the door.

"Beg pardon, Detective Hamilton?"

Turning, he saw Sergeant Bowers looking at him sheepishly.

"Yes, Sergeant?"

"A gentleman come in early this mornin' an' asked tae see ye."

"Did he give his name?"

"I asked 'im, but he said he'd come back later."

"Can you describe him?"

"Tall, powerful lookin', with strong hands. Broad shoulders, like an ox. Oh, an' he had an accent."

"What kind of accent?"

"Foreign—Dutch, maybe."

"Could it have been Norwegian?"

"Might be—I'm not so good with accents an' all."

"Thank you, Constable," said Ian, and was out the door before Bowers could utter another word.

CHAPTER
FIFTY-TWO

Ian was not entirely pleased to see the familiar figure of Jed Corbin striding toward him as he descended the steps from the station house. The reporter's face was red from exertion, and he appeared to be out of breath.

"Good morning," he began, but Corbin cut him off.

"I'm afraid it's bad news," he said, breathing heavily.

"What is?"

"It's the Fitzpatrick boy."

"Jeremy—the major's son?"

"Yes. He's dead."

A bolt of shock and disappointment shot through Ian. His chief suspect—dead. "What? H-how?" he stammered.

"Apparently he was run over by some swell in a speeding carriage near the Grassmarket."

"When?"

"Late last night."

"Why am I hearing of this only now?"

"I only just found out, and came to you straightaway."

"Why did no one file a police report?"

"It seems to have been an accident."

"Were there witnesses?"

"Everything I know is secondhand. I'm heading down there now if you would like to come."

Without answering, Ian shot his hand into the air and flagged down the very next passing cab.

"The Grassmarket," he said as Corbin scrambled in after him, "quick as you can."

When they alighted from the cab, the scene at the Grassmarket appeared to be that of a typical Thursday morning. Residents shuffled sleepily down the streets, yawning, tired from the festivities of the previous day. A low, flat hollow beneath the rising granite of Castle Rock, the Grassmarket had been a marketplace since the Middle Ages. It was still littered with remnants of yesterday's midweek open-air market, animal droppings, straw fallen from drovers' carts, bits of twine and string, discarded sweets wrappers. As Ian gazed across the wide expanse, his eye caught a cloth bag of marbles fallen from some lad's pocket. As he bent to pick it up, another hand snatched it away. He straightened up to see the grimy, soot-streaked face of Derek McNair.

"I'll tae' that, if ye don' mind," the lad said, pocketing the marbles. "Finders keepers, an' all that."

"Have you been following me?"

"Nope. Jes so happens I've a meetin' wi' me lads nearby, an' I saw ye drive up in a hurry. What're ye investigatin'?"

Ian exchanged a glance with Corbin. The reporter knew Derek—the *Scotsman* had paid him for information on more than one occasion—but didn't trust him to keep a secret any more than Ian did.

The boy seemed undeterred by their reticence. "Is it 'bout the fella what fell under the carriage yesterday?"

"What do you know about that?" said Ian.

He shrugged. "Me mate saw it all. Tol' me 'bout it this mornin'."

"Which mate is that?"

"Danny."

"Does he have a last name?"

"Danny O'Leary. Lives wi' his mum over yonder," he said, pointing to a small, two-story house with dormer windows. "She works fer the family what lives there. He's one a th'lucky ones—got a proper home, even if it is servant quarters." He said this with no hint of self-pity; it was a simple statement of fact.

"Can you fetch him?" asked Corbin.

"A' course. I'm seein' 'im anyhow."

"He's one of your 'Irregulars'?"

"Yep. Today's our weekly meetin'."

"The lad shows real initiative, doesn't he?" Corbin asked Ian.

"If that's what you call a group of miscreants to assist him in his somewhat shady endeavors."

"We ain't miscreaints," the boy said, frowning.

"Street urchins, then."

Derek crossed his arms. "Look, Guv, do ye wanna talk wi' Danny or not?"

"I do indeed, and I'm willing to reward him for his time."

Derek grinned. "My cut is ten percent—no, make that twenty."

"I see your lack of education has not prevented you from acquiring the necessary maths skills."

"Always been good wi' numbers, Guv. Be right back," he said, scampering off across the flat, wide expanse of land.

The Grassmarket had a long and bloody history. In addition to being an ancient marketplace, it was the site of public executions for many years. Sir Walter Scott wrote of the terror he experienced as a child, waking on an execution day to see the wooden gallows towering over the square "like the product of some foul demon." The gibbet was always erected before dawn on the day a prisoner was to die, and was taken away after nightfall. The sight struck fear into the hearts of young

Scott and his friends, at a time when a fifteen-year-old boy could be executed for stealing a loaf of bread.

But now Ian watched the people of Edinburgh going about their daily lives—lugging groceries, hawking wares, hanging laundry, exchanging news and gossip, seemingly oblivious of the area's violent past. A couple of plump housewives in long white aprons stood in front of their homes chatting, elbows resting on their front gates. A pair of smudged toddlers played in the mud at their feet, smearing it on their faces and laughing as they plunged their fat little hands into the muck. Their mothers didn't seem to notice or care about their offspring's she-nanigans; they seemed grateful the tykes were occupying themselves for the time being.

Derek came loping across the wide expanse of ground, followed by a tall, freckled boy with sandy hair and a long, homely face.

"This here is Danny," Derek said. "He saw wha' happened yesterday."

"What did you see?" asked Ian, as Jed Corbin licked his lips. Normally Ian would not allow the reporter to eavesdrop during an investigation, but as Corbin had brought him the news, it seemed only fair to let him hear what the boy said. Besides, there was still no firm evidence pointing to a crime.

Danny looked down at his feet and kicked at the ground. "I was playin' gird and cleek wi' me mates, an' this load a' swells comes outta the White Hart, totally blootered."

"So they were drunk," said Ian. "Hardly surprising, coming from a pub. What time was this?"

"Round 'bout five."

"So it was dark already."

"Yeah, it was like pitch las' night."

"Go on."

The boy looked up at him with bright blue eyes. "Derek said ye'll pay fer my time, yeah?"

"If you tell the truth. How old were these men?"

"Younger than you. Early twenties, mebbe. They were bein' loud, an' swearin' like the devil. There's a crowd a folks round, ladies and children, an' they didn' like the language these toffs were usin', tol' 'em tae cut it out."

"And did they?"

"Most of 'em, yeah. They just wandered off bletherin' among themselves. But this one yellow-haired toff jes stands there wi' a stupid grin on 'is face. Fitzpatrick, his name is—I'd seen 'im plenty a times afore. Eyes red as radishes—totally hammered, he was." He stopped and looked at Derek.

"Tell them wha' happened next," Derek urged.

"Well, I don' know if he lost 'is balance or wha', but suddenly there's a carriage tearin' 'round the corner, an' he jes falls forward into its path. Gets trampled 'neath the horses, an' run over by the wheels—it were an awful mess, wi' the ladies screamin' and cryin'."

"Was it possible he was pushed?" said Ian.

Danny shrugged. "Yeah. It were market Wednesday, an' there was a big crowd."

"But you didn't see anyone push him?"

"Nope."

"So it could have been an accident?" said Corbin.

The boy nodded. "Like my mum says, whit's fur ye'll no go past ye."

"Let's assume for a moment it wasn't an act of fate," said Ian. "Did you see anything else out of the ordinary?"

"Naw . . . hang on a minute, there was a lady left the crowd right after, seemed tae be in a hurry. Din' make much of it at the time, but she was walkin' pretty fast, as if she wanted tae get away."

"Can you describe her?"

"Like I said, it was dark, an' one or two streetlamps don' work."

"Any details at all you can remember?"

"Medium height, not fat nor skinny."

"Hair color?"

343

"Light brown, mebbe?"

"Manner of dress?"

"Not a fine lady, but not poor, either."

"Thank you, Danny," Ian said, fishing some coins from his pocket. "You've been most helpful."

"Ta very much, mister!" the boy said, staring at the money as if it were a mirage that might suddenly vanish.

"Ain't ye forgettin' sommit, Guv?" Derek said.

"Here's your fee," said Ian, handing him some change. "Just one more question, if you don't mind."

"Sure," Derek said, pushing his cap up on his head. His thick brown hair was shaggy and in need of a trim.

"Either of you know anything about this Jeremy Fitzpatrick?"

"Oh, sure," Danny volunteered. "He's skilamalink."

"In what way is he shady?" said Ian.

"He were a pickpocket," said Derek. "Sleekit one, too."

"But not as talented as you, I'm sure," Ian remarked.

"Don' know wha' ye mean, Guv," Derek said with a smirk.

"Never mind. Thank you for the information."

"At yer service," the boy said, tipping his moth-eaten cap. "Come on, now, Danny, we've a meetin' tae get to."

They scampered off, leaving the two men to ponder what they had just heard.

"Well," said Ian finally, "if young Fitzpatrick was pursuing a life of crime, that accounts for his reluctance to speak with me."

"Could he not still be the murderer?" said Corbin.

"He could indeed," Ian replied grimly. "Time alone will tell."

As he gazed at the hustle and bustle of the Grassmarket, Ian felt time was the one precious commodity they could not afford to squander.

CHAPTER
FIFTY-THREE

"What do you hope to find from examining his body?" Conan Doyle asked Ian as they thundered toward the city morgue in a hansom cab, the horse's hooves kicking up sprays of water from puddles of melted snow. The mercury had continued to climb throughout the day, and the late-afternoon sun bathed the city in a soft, unreal glow. Ian had managed to shake Jed Corbin by promising to send word of further developments in the case, after which he headed straight to the Royal Infirmary to procure the services of his friend.

"I don't know," he replied, "but I hope I recognize it when I see it."

"Would it not be likely he died from his injuries?"

"Possibly. But I should like to see for myself."

They arrived just as the last rays of the setting sun settled across the city, illuminating the evaporating rainwater in a milky haze. Even the stern exterior of the morgue lost its ominous air in the gentle light.

The moment he saw Ian, Jack Cerridwen's face broke into a broad grin. Over the years, Ian had purchased enough whisky for the morgue attendant to earn the Welshman's undying loyalty. Ian considered it money well spent.

"I'll bet yer here for th' fella who came in last night," Cerridwen said with a knowing wink. "Mr. Fitzpatrick," he added, consulting his log.

"We are indeed," Ian replied.

Pushing a strand of stringy dark hair from his eyes, Cerridwen rose and grabbed a lantern. "Right this way, gentlemen," he said, leading them through the maze of corridors to the room housing the recently deceased.

"It's rather like the Labyrinth, isn't it?" Doyle said as he and Ian followed Cerridwen through the dank, poorly lit hallways.

"Let's hope the Minotaur is not awaiting our arrival," Ian said as they emerged into the large central chamber, with its tall, thin windows, the walls lined with marble slabs draped with white sheets. Beneath each sheet was a body, and behind each body was a story, Ian knew, though they were only there to investigate one specific story.

"Here he is, our most recent arrival," Cerridwen said, leading them to a metal gurney beneath one of the windows. The light outside had already faded, leaving only a faint gray glow. "You're the first to come— no family members yet."

"His father is recently deceased," said Ian. "And his mother died some years ago."

"Pity," the Welshman said, shaking his head. "I hate it when there's no one t'claim them. Well, I'll leave ye to it, then," he added, licking his chops hopefully.

"We were in a bit of a hurry today," Ian said, "but I'll find a way to show my gratitude in the near future."

"No problem," Cerridwen said with forced cheer, obviously disappointed. "Take as long as ye like."

When he was gone, the two of them turned to the dead man on the gurney. Ian experienced the same solemnity he always did in the presence of death, but there was no time to be wasted. Lifting the sheet, he gazed at the young man before them.

In death, Jeremy Fitzpatrick's face showed none of the surliness it had in life. In fact, he looked rather angelic, with his flaxen hair and pale skin, now gone rather ashen.

"Too young to die like this," Doyle murmured as he examined the body.

To Ian's surprise, there were few signs of injury—a bruise here and there, but no obviously broken bones or deep wounds.

"It's curious," Doyle said. "It doesn't appear he was—oh, hello," he added as he turned the body over.

"What is it?" said Ian, his heart beating faster.

"Take a look," said Doyle. "There, at the base of the skull."

Ian looked at the place Doyle pointed to, and saw a small but deep wound, bits of dried blood clinging to the edges.

"What is it?" he asked.

"Hang on a minute," Doyle said, looking through his medical bag. "Ah, this should do," he said, grasping a long, thin instrument with a wooden handle. "A surgical probe," he said, and proceeded to slide it into the wound. It went in nearly six inches before meeting resistance.

"I think we may have the cause of death," he said, carefully extracting it. "And it would have been nearly instantaneous."

"What did—?"

"Inserted at this angle, the weapon would have penetrated the brain, causing a massive, fatal hemorrhage."

"So that means—"

"Jeremy Fitzpatrick was already dead when he fell in front of the carriage."

"What could have inflicted a wound like this?" Ian said, struggling to comprehend this new information.

"Something long and thin and nearly perfectly round," Doyle said, studying the wound. "And with a pointed end, I should think."

"A metal knitting needle," Ian said abruptly.

"That would do it."

Ian slapped his forehead. "I've been a fool! It was there, right in front of my nose, all the time."

"What was?" said Doyle.

"There's no time to waste!" Ian cried. "We must hurry. Are you with me, Doyle?"

"Where are we going?"

"To intercept a murderer."

CHAPTER
FIFTY-FOUR

"You said something was in front of your nose the whole time," Doyle said as they rumbled across town in the back of a hansom. He imagined Ian Hamilton spent a small fortune on cabs. He wondered if the Edinburgh City Police reimbursed him. "What were you referring to?"

"Motive," said the detective. "I was so fixated on evidence I forgot to consider the importance of motive. It might have led me to the solution more quickly."

"What exactly was the motive?" said Doyle, intrigued.

"Revenge. The source of so much evil. Unfortunately, it is too often sneaky, like a thief in the night."

Doyle took a deep breath and rubbed his hands together. His palms were sweating. His heart beat faster when he was accompanying Hamilton on a case. Everything took on more importance, urgency, meaning—he felt so *alive* when he joined the detective in pursuit of a criminal. Medical school was hard, demanding work, but crime solving—he felt useful, like he was really doing something in the service of humanity. He couldn't help wondering if he would feel the same about medicine once he got his degree, or whether . . . He looked at Hamilton's sharply etched profile as he stared intently out the window of the cab, as if willing it to go faster. Doyle sighed. He couldn't imagine being a doctor would be nearly as satisfying as this.

"'Oft have I heard that grief softens the mind, and makes it fearful and degenerate; think therefore on revenge and cease to weep,'" Hamilton murmured.

"Shakespeare?"

"It is as if he was writing about this killer, who used revenge to soothe grief," he said as they pulled up in front of their destination on Jeffrey Street. Doyle wanted desperately to ask what he meant, but Hamilton handed the driver some coins and, without waiting for change, sprang from the cab and dashed up the walk to the well-maintained building near the intersection of Market Street.

Doyle caught a whiff of smoke from the train engines at Waverley Station as he followed the detective up to the front door. A woman who appeared to be the landlady answered his knock, and before he knew it, Hamilton had talked his way past her, conveying a sense of urgency that made the good lady back away as he climbed to the first-floor landing, taking the stairs two at a time.

This time his knocking produced a faint reply from within—a man's voice, sounding very weak.

"Help . . . please help."

"Please open the door!" Hamilton told the landlady, who obeyed, her hands trembling as she turned the key in the lock.

No sooner had the bolt clicked open than Hamilton dashed into the flat, with Doyle close behind. They followed the sound of the voice to a comfortable sitting room, where a middle-aged man lay upon the sofa, groaning and writhing in pain.

"Thank heaven you've . . . come," he groaned upon seeing them.

Doyle knelt beside the stricken man and took his pulse, which was racing and irregular. He was sweating profusely and clutched at his stomach.

"What did she give you, Nielsen?" said Hamilton.

"Not sure . . . could have . . . been rat poison."

Hamilton turned to his friend, his face taut. "Doyle?"

"That would fit his symptoms," Doyle agreed. He turned to the landlady, who stood nearby, wringing her hands. "Have you any oil of castor?"

She stared back with wide, frightened eyes.

"There is no time to waste!" said Hamilton.

"And a large basin as well," Doyle added.

"Now!" Hamilton commanded, and she fled the room.

Conan Doyle turned back to the ailing man, who was doubled over in pain, his breath coming in gasps. "Easy," he said. "Try to breathe as deeply as you can."

Nielsen gazed up at the medical student, his eyes glazed with pain, and Doyle's knees went a little weak at the sight of such torment. He wondered how he could face such suffering day after day as a physician. Luckily, the landlady soon returned with a bottle of castor oil, which she thrust at him with trembling hands. He wasted no time in uncorking it and forcing a large swallow down the patient's throat. Nielsen gurgled and retched before vomiting an immense amount of fluid, most of which Doyle was able to catch in the basin.

The landlady went pale and turned away, and even Hamilton appeared taken aback by the violence of his reaction. But almost immediately there were signs of relief in the patient. His breath slowed, his face relaxed, and he loosened his grip on his stomach. After a few moments, Doyle gave him another dose, with the same response. It was not pretty, but he hoped he had administered the remedy in time to save Mr. Nielsen.

"Where did she go?" Hamilton asked Nielsen.

"Madame . . . she went to Madame's," he replied weakly.

"Can you stay with him, Doyle?"

"Of course."

"I must go—thank you, dear fellow," he said, and with three long strides, was gone.

Doyle turned to the landlady, who was still shaking.

"W-will he be all right, sir?" she asked.

"I believe he will recover. We arrived just in time."

She burst into tears, and Conan Doyle knew just how she felt.

CHAPTER
FIFTY-FIVE

When Ian Hamilton emerged onto Jeffrey Street, Derek McNair was perched on the low brick wall lining the street. When he saw the detective, the boy jumped lightly from his spot.

"You owe me fer a cab," he said, brushing dust from his pants.

"How did you find me?" Ian said, striding in the direction of High Street.

"I got my ways, Guv," Derek said, scrambling to keep up. "I got some information fer ye."

"From what source?"

"Billy Striebel—he's one a' me lads—overheard somethin'."

"Overheard where?"

"His da were talkin' t'a mate."

Ian stopped walking. "Is his father William Striebel, the safecracker?"

"Tha's him, yeah."

"What did Billy hear?"

"His da was knockin' back a few wi' his mate, an' Billy was s'posed t'be in bed, only he wasn't."

"What did he *hear*?"

"Well, his da asked if everythin' was on, an' someone said somethin' 'bout minding the construction in the back."

"Did he mention where?"

"No, jes that there was construction in the back. An' someone said somethin' 'bout how the coppers would never think they'd try somethin' so bold, like."

"Are you certain? They said all this?"

"That's what Billy said. Think it might be useful?"

"It could very well prove vital. Can you do something for me?"

Derek's face brightened. "Yep!"

"Fetch Sergeant Dickerson and tell him to meet me at Madame Veselka's straightaway. He knows where it is."

"Right, Guv!"

"Tell him to bring along a couple of constables," Ian added, tossing him a coin. "Quick as you can!"

"Right-o!" Derek said, scampering off toward the police station.

Ian took to his heels in the opposite direction. It wasn't far to Blackfriars Street, and as it was near the end of the workday, cabs would be in short supply.

In less than ten minutes he was at the ramshackle tenement where Madame Veselka lived. He thought he heard voices coming from inside, but his knock on the front door brought no response, so he went around to peer in the front window. The French lace curtains were drawn, and a heavy drape had been pulled over them, preventing him from seeing inside.

Returning to the front door, he knocked loudly and announced himself.

"Edinburgh City Police! Open this door!"

When no response was forthcoming, he threw himself against the door, splintering the termite-ridden wood, sending spears of pain through his injured shoulder and ribs. Tumbling into the foyer, he got to his feet and hurried to the parlor, where he found Madame Veselka cowering in a corner, Catherine Nielsen holding a knife to her throat. He recognized it as the long knife she had used to cut the Dundee cake, and it looked even more lethal now.

"Not one step farther!" she hissed as Ian entered the room. "Stay where you are!"

"Put the knife down, Mrs. Nielsen," he said calmly.

"Just as soon as I slit the throat of this liar."

Madame Veselka sobbed, tears running down her face, leaving salty streaks on her plump cheeks. "G-Gretchen—she killed p-poor Gretchen!"

"She deserved it," Catherine Nielsen muttered through gritted teeth. "Stupid girl."

"Where is she?" said Ian.

"I-in the b-bedroom—she was trying to protect me," the medium whimpered.

Ian made a move, but was stopped by Catherine Nielsen's voice, sharp as the steel blade in her hand.

"I said *stay* where you *are!*"

"Are you unhurt?" he asked the medium.

"I'm all right," she replied. "Poor G-Gretchen . . ."

"What did they do to you that deserves death?" he asked Catherine Nielsen.

"Madame was going to rat me out—said she saw it all in a 'vision,' and knew I was guilty! She tried to convince me to turn myself in—ha! That's a laugh—turn myself in! Why on earth would I do that?" she said, her eyes wild. Ian wondered if she had ingested something—she seemed positively demented. She brandished the knife, flailing it in the air.

Afraid she was about to kill Madame Veselka, he took a step toward her. In an instant, she sprang at him, slashing him across the face with the knife. He reeled backward and fell to the ground, looking up just in time to see Sergeant Dickerson barrel into the room and launch himself at Catherine Nielsen. She was ready for him, and plunged the knife into his side. He grunted with pain but tackled her to the ground, the knife still in his body.

Ian got up, blood spurting from his face, and wrestled Catherine away from the injured sergeant. She shrieked and fought like a lioness, with such fierce strength that he could barely contain her, scratching at his injured cheek with her nails. He finally managed to get her under control, wrapping her hands behind her back.

"Handcuffs, Sergeant!"

Groaning, Dickerson rolled onto his side and extracted a pair of cuffs from his uniform. Ian took them and fastened them round Mrs. Nielsen's wrists. Wiping the blood from his face with his free hand, he pulled her down onto the couch. "If you so much as move a muscle, I'll tie your feet as well," he told her. "Can you keep an eye on her?" he asked Madame Veselka, helping her to her feet.

"I'll kick her bloody teeth in," she muttered, staggering toward the couch.

"No! Just watch her," Ian commanded. "She'll face punishment later." He knelt beside Sergeant Dickerson, who was breathing heavily, sweat beading on his forehead. "Steady on, Sergeant. Let's have a look at that wound, shall we?" he said, gently examining where the knife protruded from the sergeant's side. There wasn't as much blood as he expected, but he knew if he pulled out the knife Dickerson might bleed to death. "We'd best get you to hospital. Where are those constables I asked you to bring along?"

"Chief put . . . ev'ry spare man . . . on watch at jewelry store," Dickerson said through clenched teeth. "Tonight's s'posed t'be . . . big break-in."

"No more talking—save your strength," Ian said, trying to figure out what to do next. It was imperative to get Dickerson medical attention, yet he couldn't leave the madame alone with a killer. The medium hovered over Mrs. Nielsen, swaying a little, looking rather murderous herself. There seemed to be no way out of this predicament.

Then he heard the most welcome sound of his entire life.

"Hamilton! You in there?" It was Conan Doyle.

"In here!" he called.

Doyle appeared at the door, medical bag in his hand. "Good Lord," he said, kneeling beside Dickerson.

"He needs to go to hospital straightaway," said Ian. "Can you manage that?"

"You're bleeding," Doyle said.

"There's a girl in the back room. Can you see if she's still alive?"

Doyle disappeared through the beaded curtain, emerging a few moments later.

"Well?" said Ian.

"I'm afraid we arrived too late to save her."

Madame Veselka let out a wail like a wounded animal, and lunged toward Mrs. Nielsen.

"No!" Ian commanded, grabbing her arm. "If you can't do as I say, I'll have you in cuffs, too!" He turned to Doyle. "Can you get Sergeant Dickerson to the infirmary?"

"Help me get him into a cab. I left one waiting outside."

"Can we leave you alone for just a moment?" Ian asked Madame Veselka.

"Oh, yes," she replied, her hands clenched into fists.

"Don't do anything, or I swear I'll have you thrown in prison along with her," he warned. "Just watch her."

The medium turned back to her captive. "If she so much as twitches, she'll regret it."

Mrs. Nielsen looked up with a worried expression, as if she believed the medium's threat.

"Quickly," Ian told Doyle. "We haven't much time."

"Steady on," said Doyle, as they lifted the injured sergeant to his feet. Dickerson looked pale and shaken, but remained conscious.

"I don't know what I'd have done without you," Ian told his friend as they settled the sergeant into the back of the hansom. "What about Jonas Nielsen?"

"He's going to make a full recovery," Doyle said, sitting gingerly next to Dickerson. "The crisis was past, so I thought you could use my help."

"Thank you, Doyle. Your timing—"

"Get that wound looked after," his friend said, closing the door behind him.

Ian turned and charged back into the building. A few tenants had gathered in the hallway outside the flat, come to see the source of all the commotion. "Step back—Edinburgh City Police," he said, brushing past them.

Madame Veselka was true to her word and had not harmed Mrs. Nielsen, however much she wanted to. Promising to return as soon as he could, he left the grieving medium in her flat, escorting Mrs. Nielsen out, a gathering crowd of curious onlookers watching as he walked her from the building. The commotion had also finally attracted the attention of a couple of beat constables, and he handed her over to them, glad to be rid of her.

"Get her to jail quick as you can. Mind—she's violent," he said.

Their expressions indicated they didn't believe his depiction of the respectably dressed middle-aged woman. "I mean it," he repeated. "Mind you keep an eye on her."

"Yes, sir," said the older of the two. "Come along, now," he said, taking her arm. "We don't want no trouble, now."

Watching them disappear into the night as a light rain began to fall, Ian thought it was far too late for that. Trouble had found its way into the winding streets of the city, and showed no sign of letting up before the night was over.

CHAPTER
FIFTY-SIX

Detective Chief Inspector Robert Crawford looked up from his desk to see the bedraggled form of Ian Hamilton appear before him like an apparition.

"Good Lord, man, you look like Hamlet's ghost," he said, startled at the sight of the detective, his face smeared with dried blood.

"Never mind about that," Hamilton said, breathing heavily.

"Have a seat—you look like hell."

"There's no time."

"You're not even supposed to be here. I suspended you indefinitely, remember?"

"I've information about the theft—"

"What sort of information?"

"It's not to be at the jewelers—"

"Where, then?"

"The Bank of Scotland."

"That's absurd! No one would dare try to—"

"I tell you, it *is*!" Hamilton said, holding onto the front of the desk to steady himself.

"For God's sake, sit down before you collapse," said Crawford. "You look like a drowned rat." Hamilton really did look terrible. His hair was matted, his clothes were half soaked, and there were streaks of blood from the cut on his face.

"We need to move the men you have stationed at Murray and Weston's over to the bank building on North Bank Street!"

"Where did you get this 'information'?"

"From someone involved in the burglary—or rather, his son."

Crawford's eyes narrowed. "It's that wretched street urchin of yours, isn't it?"

"It's from a friend of his."

"What makes you think you can trust this intelligence?"

"They spoke of robbing a place with construction in the back of the building. There's no construction going on at Murray and Weston—"

"But there is at the Bank of Scotland," Crawford finished for him. "I saw it myself the other day—in the back of the building." He sighed and tugged nervously at his whiskers. "I don't know, Hamilton, it's not much to go on."

"They also joked about no one believing they would have the gall to take on such a target."

"If they're even thinking about it, there must be someone on the inside."

"Very likely, but we don't have time to ponder the details—we must act before it's too late!"

"It's awfully thin evidence. What if you're wrong?"

"Then leave a few men at the jeweler's. But it's imperative—"

"I hope to God you're right, Hamilton," he said, getting to his feet and lumbering to the door.

"I hope so, too, sir."

"Well, there's only one way to find out. Bowers!" he bellowed.

The sergeant appeared, looking a bit like a scared rabbit, with his pink skin and light eyes. "Yes, sir?"

"Assemble every available man you can—"

"A lot of 'em are over at—"

"Yes, yes, I know—pull them off the watch at Murray and Weston, and—"

"Sir?"

"You can leave a few on guard, just in case."

"Yes, sir."

"Send them over to the Bank of Scotland on North Bank Street."

"Sir?" the sergeant said, his eyes wide.

"I'll explain later. Hamilton and I will meet you there."

"Yes, sir," Bowers replied, hurrying off.

"Now," Crawford said, pulling his coat and hat from the rack. "Let's go foil a bank robbery, shall we?"

CHAPTER
FIFTY-SEVEN

The rain had increased to a steady drizzle by the time Ian and DCI Crawford headed out into the night.

"You'd better be right about this one," the chief said as they settled into the back of a cab.

Ian stared out the window as they turned onto Bank Street. It was a very short distance to their destination, and they were likely to arrive before reinforcements. The ringing of the bells at St. Giles jolted Ian into a realization that tomorrow was Christmas Eve.

"Are you quite sure it's a good idea for you to come along, sir?"

"And why not?"

"Well, sir, it's just that—"

"Are you suggesting I'm past it, Hamilton?"

"No, sir; I was just thinking about your, uh, piles—"

"Blast my piles! I'll have you know I'm as fit as I ever was!"

"I'm sure you are, sir."

"Let them try to outrun me—I'll be all over them!"

"Of course, sir."

"Hmm," Crawford grunted, as if not convinced Hamilton believed him. "What's all that blood on your face, then?"

"We've arrived," Ian said as the cab pulled up in front of the massive building, with its ornate Roman baroque façade, and its statue of Victory perched high atop its gold dome. Ian couldn't help wondering who she would favor tonight.

They promised the driver extra pay if he waited, but there was no sign of Bowers and his reinforcements as they crept around to the back, the hiss of rain shadowing their steps.

"Perhaps we should wait, sir," Ian suggested as they stood outside the wooden scaffolding surrounding the rear of the building.

"Nonsense," said Crawford. "I don't see anything amiss. Best to carry on and find out if we're on a wild goose chase."

"But sir—"

"Come along—it's bloody wet out here," Crawford said, striding up the wooden ramp leading to the rear entrance. "That's odd—this door is unlocked," he said, pushing open the small door, which functioned as a service entrance.

"Sir, I think perhaps we should wait," Ian said, lowering his voice to a whisper as he followed the chief inside. They were met with a series of corridors leading in all directions. Ian turned at the sound of footsteps echoing down the hall.

"What's that—" Crawford said, his words cut short by the sharp report of a pistol.

He fell heavily, blood spurting from his left side.

Ian threw himself on top of his superior officer, shielding him with his own body, but the footsteps retreated at a run, followed by silence. The rear door creaked open again, and he looked up to see a familiar figure enter.

"Corbin! What on earth—"

"I saw you leaving the police station and followed you here," said the reporter.

"It's not safe—"

"You once saved my life, remember? Pulled me out of that wretched house before I was poisoned to death."

"That—"

"You may have forgotten, but I assure you, I have not," he said, kneeling beside Crawford. "Let's see what we have here. It's not too bad," he said. "The bullet seems to have caught his shoulder."

"You need to leave before you get hurt."

"If you help me get him into that cab, I'll take him to hospital."

"Very well," Ian agreed. The chief was a large man, probably weighing nearly the same as Corbin and Hamilton put together.

Crawford began to regain consciousness. "Hamilton . . ." he said groggily.

"It's all right, sir—we're getting you to hospital," Ian said as they lifted him.

"No . . . must stay and help catch . . ." he said, and passed out again.

"It's a good job you showed up when you did," Ian told Corbin as they carried him outside and loaded him into the back of the hansom, the worried driver looking on.

"Mind you don't get blood all over the seats," he instructed them.

"We'll pay for any damage," Ian said. "Thank you," he told Corbin.

"Glad to be of service. Mind how you go," the reporter said, and they drove off, leaving Ian alone in the rain.

There was still no sign of Bowers. Ian took a deep breath, willing himself to remain where he was. But he was drawn back into the building as if by magnetic force, and before he knew it, was striding back up the ramp and into the arms of danger.

The hallway was once again silent, but the fresh blood droplets on the floor reminded him how deceptive that quiet was. Someone had shot at them, and that person was still somewhere in the building. Ian crept down the hallway in the direction the shot had come from.

Carole Lawrence

Reaching the end of the corridor, he took another deep breath and turned right.

Something came down hard on the back of his head. His first impression was that the ceiling had collapsed, but in the brief moment of consciousness as he dropped to the floor, he realized he had been attacked and hit by a heavy object—a police truncheon, perhaps.

And then he felt nothing at all.

CHAPTER FIFTY-EIGHT

He awoke to the smell of smoke. Panic gripped him, transported instantly to his parents' basement seven years ago, trapped beneath burning timbers as the house above him erupted in flames. He tried to scream, but found himself bound and gagged, tied to a water pipe. Looking around, he realized he was in the boiler room—just as in the fire that killed his parents, he was trapped in a basement. He looked around the room for something to cut his bonds with, and spied a nail at the base of the opposite wall. Stretching his leg out, he tried to reach it with his toe, but it was too far away. Sweat stung his face, running into the raw wound on his cheek, as the burning smell grew stronger.

He peered desperately at the small window set in the wall above him, as thunder ripped the skies, followed by jagged streaks of white lightning. He strained against his bonds, but they were fastened tightly. Though he was panting and exhausted, hope surged through his breast at the sound of approaching footsteps. Twisting around as much as he could, he looked in the direction of the entrance, as the metal door swung slowly open to reveal a tall, thin figure wreathed in swirling smoke.

"So we meet at last, Detective," the man said in a hollow, raspy voice.

Ian struggled to speak, but the gag in his mouth prevented him from making any sound other than a muffled groan.

"Don't try to talk," the man said. "It will only wear you out." Nearly as tall as Ian, he wore a long black coat. In spite of the heat from the fire, a thick wool scarf was wrapped around his throat. Ian blinked, trying to make out the man's features through the swirling smoke, but a wide-brimmed hat was pulled over his eyes, and Ian's vision was blurry. He fought against the panic gathering in his stomach.

"Brings back memories, does it?" said the man, giving a short, sharp cough. His voice sounded damaged, as if someone had drawn a wicker broom over his vocal cords. "We haven't much time, so I'll be brief," he continued. "You have inconvenienced me greatly, you know. You must stop, you really must."

Again Ian struggled to speak, and the man chuckled softly. "Why not just kill you now, you are thinking? I have my reasons. But even my patience is not eternal. Take care, Detective—get in my way once too often, and even you will not be safe from my wrath. Do not go down the path you so foolishly seek, or you may end up like Nate Crippen. It should be clear now that you cannot trust your sources as you once did.

"Oh, by the way, congratulations on solving my little distraction. It was a pretty puzzle, wasn't it? And who knew a woman could be so murderous? Your poor sergeant must be quite disillusioned, with his chivalrous notions of femininity. And now I must be going. Pleasant dreams," he said, and slipped out the door.

Ian fought to remain conscious as the sound of falling timber mingled with the reports of pistol shots, but overcome by smoke and exhaustion, he sank into semiconsciousness. Then he heard the wild, gleeful cries of young boys. Ian wondered if he was hallucinating, but a flash of lightning revealed the source of the sound. Running through the rain toward the building, followed by a band of wild-looking urchins, was Derek McNair. Ian could hardly believe his eyes, but the sound of pattering feet overhead confirmed that Derek had indeed turned up, with his ragged band of Irregulars.

Ian struggled harder to free himself—a gaggle of boys was no match for a gang of bank robbers. Where were Bowers and his men? What could be holding them up? But his vision began to dim—he felt groggy and dizzy, and consciousness became harder to hold onto. He tried to keep his eyes open, but to no avail, and once again, darkness claimed him.

"Sir! Wake up, sir—it's time to leave!"

He opened his eyes to see the worried face of Sergeant Bowers, his blue eyes crinkled in concern.

"That's quite a lump on the back of your head, sir."

"What happened?" Ian said, blinking to clear his vision. His head was indeed throbbing.

"We caught 'em in the act, sir—a few got away, but you were right. The bank was the target, not the jewelry store."

"What about the fire?"

"Fire department's come, sir—it's all in hand."

"And the boys? Are they all right?"

"What boys, sir?"

"The Irregulars—they were here. I saw them."

"There weren't no boys here t'night, sir."

"But I heard them—I tell you, I *saw* them!"

"You've a nasty blow to your head, sir. Let's get you outta those ropes, shall we?"

CHAPTER
FIFTY-NINE

"Looks t'me like ye've had a bit of a rough time as well, sir," said Sergeant Dickerson.

Ian was seated beside Dickerson's hospital bed the next morning, his face heavily bandaged, after convincing the medical staff he was ambulatory. Having slept like the dead the night before, he rose late and went straight to the Royal Infirmary to check on Dickerson and Crawford, who had both been admitted.

"What you did was very foolish, Sergeant," said Ian.

"Yes, sir."

"And very brave."

"I figured t'take her by surprise, sir."

"I hope you weren't trying to prove yourself to me."

"Course not."

"Because it wasn't necessary. I know you're a stalwart fellow. I hear you've already made yourself a great favorite of the nurses," Ian said as a pretty young brunette slipped into the room, a thermometer in hand.

"Time to check your temperature," she told Dickerson, who pretended to be bored by the idea, though he clearly enjoyed the attention. When she had finished, she winked at him and left the room.

"I see the reports are not unfounded," Ian remarked.

"Has Mrs. Nielsen confessed, sir?"

"To everything. Once she started talking, she couldn't stop. I interviewed her last night at police chambers."

Dickerson grinned. "After ye foiled the bank robbery."

"After *we* did, Sergeant."

"But I weren't—"

"You were invaluable in every step of this investigation."

"So what'd Mrs. Nielsen say, sir? Why'd she do it?"

"After her son took his own life, she blamed it on anyone she considered culpable—Jeremy Fitzpatrick for bullying him, and Major Fitzpatrick for using his influence to shield his son from repercussions. You were right about the timeline—she did lie about when they joined the séance group. And that lie helped put me onto her. Well done, Sergeant."

"Thank you, sir. What 'bout Miss Staley? What'd she ever do?"

"Catherine Nielsen felt that as the boys' teacher, Miss Staley should have done something to stop the bullying."

"An' poor Gretchen?" he said, his lower lip trembling.

"She died trying to protect Madame Veselka."

Dickerson nodded. "She were a good 'un, she were."

"Yes," Ian agreed. "She died a heroic death. Once she started, Catherine Nielsen didn't seem to be able to stop killing. She even tried to poison her own husband."

"Why?"

"He suspected her. That's why he came by the station house to see me. She realized he was onto her and tried to kill him."

"That's cold, that is," Dickerson said, shaking his head. "Don' like t'think women kin do that kinda thing."

"How are you feeling?"

"I'll be all right, sir. Can't do my part in t'play t'night, though."

"I'm sorry to hear that."

"Mr. Vincent says he'll do my role. I'm sure he'll be better than me."

"You were excellent as the Second Gravedigger in *Hamlet*."

Dickerson brightened. "Ye really think so, sir?"

"Indeed I do. Everyone said so."

"Quite right, too."

They turned to see DCI Crawford standing at the door, his left arm in a sling.

"How are you, sir?" said Ian. "I was afraid we'd lost you there for a moment."

Crawford grunted. "Giddy Fortune's furious fickle wheel hasn't done me in yet."

"Well done, sir."

"*Henry V*," Crawford said, smiling broadly. "Are you sure you're quite all right, Hamilton?"

"Never better, sir."

"Bowers tells me you were hallucinating a bit at the end. Thought you saw a gang of street urchins or something."

"Apparently I wasn't as conscious as I thought."

"Have you seen this?" Crawford asked, handing him the morning edition of the *Scotsman*.

CLEVER POLICE RAID FOILS OUTRAGEOUS BANK ROBBERY

CRIMINAL GANG MEMBERS CAPTURED IN LATE NIGHT SKIRMISH

The article gave a detailed report of the evening's events, with a byline attributing it to Jed Corbin.

"I guess he came back to the bank after taking you to hospital," said Ian. "It's not far."

"Bowers gave me a report this morning. There were over half a dozen captured at the scene, but some escaped. The odd thing is there were members of different known gangs, and a few new faces as well."

"Wish I'd a been there," Dickerson said wistfully.

"Was Constable Turnbull on the scene?" asked Ian.

"Apparently he never turned up," said Crawford. "But he wasn't on duty at the time."

"Some of the lads put in an extra shift that night," Ian pointed out, glancing at Sergeant Dickerson, who looked away. "Sergeant Dickerson, for example—"

"Well, they couldn't have done it without you," said the chief.

"Or the tip from Derek McNair and his friends."

Crawford looked around, then lowered his voice. "Still no idea where the false leads are coming from?"

"Not as yet, sir." Ian had an impulse to tell him about his strange visitor in the boiler room, but had not yet had time to ponder who he was, and did not want to share the information with Crawford here in public, where anyone could be listening. He wasn't entirely sure the whole thing wasn't a hallucination induced from the blow to his head. Catherine Nielsen had disavowed any knowledge of the man, and, given her willingness to divulge everything in her confession, Ian believed her. There was so much he didn't yet understand.

"In the meantime, sir, might I suggest a play to take your mind off everything?" he said.

The chief tugged at his whiskers and glanced out at the hallway. "If they let me out of here. What about you, Sergeant? I suppose they'll put on your understudy, eh?"

"Mr. Vincent, the director, will do it, sir."

"It's no fun being on the sidelines, is it? Much better to be in the heat of the action, eh?"

"I expect they'll manage without me, sir."

"I suppose they always do," the chief said with a sigh. "Manage without one, I mean . . . no one's really irreplaceable, are they?"

"I think some people are, sir," said Ian. "Maybe in some way, everybody is."

Crawford stared at him. "Too deep for me, Hamilton—what I really want right now is a glass of whisky and a decent lamb chop. Have you had the food here? It's dreadful."

"I don' think it's so bad," Dickerson remarked.

"You're welcome to it, then," Crawford muttered, shuffling out of the room. "I'm going to see if I can't get someone to spring me from this place."

"Good luck, sir," said Ian, as Fiona Stuart appeared in the doorway.

"Hello there," she said.

"Hello," Ian replied. "What are you doing tonight?"

"What did you have in mind?"

CHAPTER SIXTY

A few hours later, Ian and Fiona were seated next to each other at the Greyfriars Dramatic Society's production of *A Christmas Carol*. Fiona was in an unexpectedly chatty mood.

"This is much more fun than seeing a matinee," she said as the lights went down on the stage. Later, she whispered, "He's very good, isn't he?" as they watched Alistair McPherson as Scrooge display great terror in his scene with Jacob Marley's ghost, cowering at the sight of his rattling chains. The actor playing the ghost was beautifully costumed, all in gray, so in the dim lighting he was only half visible.

The production spared no expense, with wonderfully convincing stage effects—the audience gasped at the entrance of the Ghost of Christmas Yet to Come. He was well over eight feet tall, dressed in a tattered shroud hiding his face, with long, pointed fingers. Ian realized the effect had been created by putting the actor on stilts and fastening extensions to his fingers, so they appeared to have long, knifelike nails.

When the children playing Ignorance and Want appeared, Ian was reminded of the little cress girl at the intersection of Bell's Wynd, and the cruelties of a society that allowed children to huddle on cold street corners without proper food or a warm fire to come home to. At the end, when Tiny Tim cried, "God bless us, everyone!" Ian was surprised to find his eyes welling up at the sight of the poor Cratchit family celebrating Christmas with the newly reformed Ebenezer Scrooge.

The curtain was lowered to tremendous applause, and the actors took three curtain calls each.

"I say, that was rather well done, don't you think?" said Conan Doyle, coming up to Ian and Fiona as the house lights went on.

"Yes, excellent," Ian agreed.

"You're looking especially well, Miss Stuart," he added, tipping his hat to Fiona. "And your aunt, Hamilton—hope you don't mind my saying so, but she looks ten years younger," he said, rubbing his hands together in his hearty way. "How's that slash on your cheek?"

"Not too bad," Ian replied, though it throbbed constantly. "Have you seen DCI Crawford?"

"He's still in hospital. He claims he's chafing to be released, but I suspect he stayed in to keep Sergeant Dickerson company."

That seemed uncharacteristic, Ian thought, but maybe Ebenezer Scrooge wasn't the only one having a spiritual reformation this Christmas season.

"Well, I'm due at surgery, I'm afraid," said Doyle. "I just got word Dr. Bell is doing an emergency appendectomy and I'm to assist. No rest for the wicked."

"Good luck with the surgery," Ian said as his friend hurried from the room. He turned to see Donald coming toward him.

"They acquitted themselves especially well, don't you think?" his brother said. "Good evening, Nurse Stuart—you are looking particularly resplendent, if I may say so."

"In my nurse's uniform?"

"It suits you."

"I shall take that as a compliment."

"That performance was far better than I expected, truly," said Donald.

"Yes, it was very good," Ian agreed.

"Lillian just told me there's to be a celebration at her house, and we're invited."

"I'll have to beg off. I'm afraid I'm all in."

"You'll have to tell her yourself," Donald said. "I'd sooner disappoint the Queen than Aunt Lillian. It seems you got quite sliced up," he added, peering at Ian's bandaged cheek.

Ian shrugged. "It could have been worse."

"At least it's on the same side as your earlier cut. That's probably going to scar, you know."

"You can pretend it's from a duel," said Fiona.

"A bragging scar," Donald added, referring to their popularity among German fencing students, who proudly sported facial wounds as examples of manly courage. He turned to Fiona and gave a small bow. "Good to see you, Miss Stuart."

"And you," she said. "I like your brother," she told Ian when Donald was safely out of earshot.

"I do, too—most of the time. What do you say we have that dinner together at last?"

"I thought you were tired."

"There are different kinds of fatigue. What do you say?"

"I just have to pop home to change. I had to come straight from hospital tonight—can't very well turn up at Le Canard dressed like this, can I?"

"I suppose not."

"Can I meet you there in, say, forty minutes?"

"You're not thinking of standing me up, are you?" he asked with a sly smile.

She rolled her eyes. "Hopefully we're past that."

As Fiona made her way from the room, Aunt Lillian approached from the stage.

"What's this I hear about you not coming to our party?"

"I'm just—"

"Ach, I *see*," she said, pointing to the retreating figure of Fiona Stuart. "'Let me not to the marriage of true minds admit impediments.'"

"Since when did you take to quoting—"

She patted his arm. "It's quite all right. If anyone understands, I do." She turned toward the stage, where Alistair McPherson stood smiling at her, holding a single red rose. "He was good as Scrooge, wasn't he?"

"Very. You have excellent taste."

She gave him a quick peck on the cheek and bustled away, quick as a schoolgirl. Apparently being in love conquered the stiffness of arthritis, at least for a time. He was happy for her.

In fact, he thought as he left the building, he was rather happy with everyone. As he walked, with the city spread out before him like a flower, Ian realized that just as Ebenezer Scrooge had begrudged others his money, he had withheld his feelings. He was as stingy with his emotions as Scrooge was with his pennies; could it be that he was having the same kind of change of heart as Dickens' famous miser? If a fictional character could have a spiritual awakening, surely he could as well. It was simply a matter of perspective, of seeing things differently. The circumstances of his life had not changed, but perhaps he had. Like Scrooge, surely he could let go of the memories that haunted him. Perhaps choosing to live differently was even more courageous than facing bullets.

The sound of Christmas carols floated across the darkened landscape, and Ian was suddenly filled with a warm regard for his fellow man; the unexpected surfeit of emotion made his throat swell and his eyes burn.

He had not gone far when he saw the familiar figure of Derek McNair approaching. There was something different in his stride—his usual bounce was gone, and though his expression under the streetlamp was difficult to read, Ian thought he looked chastened.

"Hello, Master McNair."

"Evenin', Guv."

"What brings you out tonight?"

"Got sommit fer ye," he said, digging a piece of paper from his pocket.

"Who gave you this?"

"Fella I never seen afore. Ugly, like, wi' a face that looks like it's been knocked around."

"You weren't by any chance near the Bank of Scotland last night?"

"What, durin' the robbery an' all? I wish I had, Guv—heard ye took 'em by surprise. Well, ain't ye gonna read that?"

"You haven't by chance read it first, have you?"

"Me? Naw—I can't read, Guv."

"Yes, you can."

"Well, only a bit. An' why would I read a note meant fer you?"

"You don't seriously expect an answer to that."

"Read it, would ye?"

"Why, are you expecting a reply?"

"Jes *read* it, mate!"

Standing beneath the light of the streetlamp, Ian complied, and the words chilled his heart.

Did you ever stop to think how the Nielsens found out about the séances? Have fun with that.

PS You'll never find the girl. And if you know what's good for you, you'll take care to stay out of my way from now on.

There was no signature, but Ian knew who had written it.

He looked at Derek. "Thank you," he said.

"Don' like it, mate. Not at all."

"I thought you said you hadn't read it."

"Come off it," the boy said, kicking at a pebble. "Y'all right, then?"

"Yes," said Ian. "You take care, though, will you?"

"Ye know me, Guv—I kin look after meself."

"See that you do. Good night."

"Night, Guv," the boy said, and with a final searching look, drifted off into the night.

Ian scanned the note once again, and as he did, a drop of blood fell onto the page. His hand went to his face, and his fingers came away damp. His wound was bleeding through the bandages on his face. Stuffing the note in his pocket, Ian continued toward his rendezvous. Several things were suddenly clear. His boiler room encounter was not a hallucination after all. After reading this, he would much rather it had been. And, as this man brazenly implicated himself in Bridie Mallon's death, Ian knew where he lived. Most disturbingly, Turnbull did, too, if Greenside Row resident Nigel Metcalf's description of the constable's face was accurate—though what he was doing there was as yet unclear. This was bad, maybe very bad, but he refused to let it spoil his night. He would deal with it tomorrow.

Fiona arrived at Le Canard just a few moments after Ian, and they entered the restaurant together. The maître d' could not hide his amazement—and disappointment—at seeing the two of them. Ian made no attempt to disguise his enjoyment of the man's confusion.

"Bonsoir, monsieur," he said with a wide smile, tipping his hat.

The maître d' looked as if he had just tasted a particularly sour lemon. His attempt to twist his mouth into a convincing smile was heroic but doomed to failure. He showed them to a cozy table in the corner, seating them with the stiff smirk of a martyr facing certain death.

"So," she said when he had gone. "Here we are at last."

"Yes," he agreed. "Here we are." The candlelight was soft, the air gentle, and a dozen delicious aromas beckoned. Ian was determined to put all thoughts of Edinburgh's criminals aside for one brief evening.

"Well, then," she said, running her finger over the lip of her wine goblet. "What now?"

"Tell me all about yourself."

She laughed. "What do you want to know?"

He leaned forward.

"Everything," he said. "I want to know everything."

ACKNOWLEDGMENTS

Thanks to my awesome agent, Paige Wheeler, as always. Much gratitude to Thomas & Mercer—Jessica Tribble, for her cheerful and steady presence, and Matthew Patin, for his excellent editorial advice and eagle eye.

Deepest thanks to Alan Macquarrie, scholar, musician, and historian, for his invaluable input, and for being such a gracious host in his glorious Glasgow flat, and to Anne Clackson, for being such a boon (and bonnie) companion. Special thanks to my dear friend Rachel Fallon for her generosity and loyal spirit, and for another wonderful stay at Villa Fallon. Much gratitude to my dear and accomplished cousin Jacques Houis—scholar, teacher, writer, translator—for his help and advice on French words and phrases. Thanks also to Anthony Moore for his sense of adventure, and for joining me on our many wonderful walkabouts in Edinburgh and beyond.

Thanks to Hawthornden Castle for awarding me a fellowship—my time there was unforgettable—and to Byrdcliffe Colony in Woodstock, where I enjoyed many happy years of residency, as well as Animal Care Sanctuary in East Smithfield, Pennsylvania, and Craig Lukatch and the fabulous Lacawac Sanctuary.

Deepest gratitude to my dear friend and colleague Marvin Kaye for his continued support, and for all the many wonderful dinners of mutton chops at Keens. Thanks to my assistant, Frank Goad, for his intelligence and expertise. Thanks, too, to my good friend Ahmad Ali, whose support and good energy has always lifted my spirits, and to the Stone Ridge Library, my upstate writing home away from home.

Finally, special thanks to my mother, whose patience in reading to us night after night was matched only by her talent at portraying so many characters, and who taught me the power of a good story.

ABOUT THE AUTHOR

Carole Lawrence is an award-winning novelist, poet, composer, playwright, and author of *Edinburgh Twilight* and *Edinburgh Dusk* in the Detective Inspector Ian Hamilton series, as well as six novellas and dozens of short stories, articles, and poems—many of which appear in translation internationally. She is a two-time Pushcart Prize nominee for poetry and winner of the Euphoria Poetry Prize, the Eve of St. Agnes Poetry Award, the Maxim Mazumdar playwriting prize, the *Jerry Jazz Musician* award for short fiction, and the Chronogram Literary Fiction Award. Her plays and musicals have been produced in several countries, as well as on NPR; her physics play, *Strings*, nominated for an Innovative Theatre Award, was produced at the Kennedy Center. A Hawthornden Fellow, she is on the faculty of NYU and Gotham Writers, as well as the Cape Cod Writers Center and San Miguel Writers' Conferences. She enjoys hiking, biking, horseback riding, and hunting for wild mushrooms. For more information, visit www.celawrence.com.